Stolen

REBECCA VOSS

Contents

Chapter 1

"Bring 'em back! Bring 'em back!"

Calvin Edwards awoke to his wife crying out in her sleep. He was unsure which hurt worse, the situation or his wife's pain. Either way it had been a long, painful six months since their two daughters had been stolen. The word "kidnapped" just didn't fit this situation, he thought to himself.

"Wake up sweetheart." Cal gently touched Amanda's arm. When Amanda realized what she'd been doing, tears replaced the words. Calvin pulled her close to him. "I'm here, sweetheart. Go ahead and cry," he lovingly assured her.

A short time later Amanda had cried herself back to sleep wrapped safely in Calvin's arms. Cal lay awake, allowing his thoughts to painfully retrace the past six months. Surely there must be something they were missing. It seemed their daughters had disappeared off the face of the earth, he thought as he drifted back to sleep himself.

Calvin awoke a short time later to the sound of his alarm clock. The music was a blur until the strong sound of Rich Mullins' voice made its way to his ear. "Our God is an awesome God. He reigns from heaven above with wisdom, power, and love. Our God is an awesome God." An awesome God indeed, Cal thought, as he turned off the alarm. He didn't blame God for his daughter's disappearance, but neither did he understand why God had allowed them to be stolen. He promised not to give us more than we could handle,

1

Calvin reminded himself. Admittedly, some days that was hard to remember.

Calvin pulled his six-foot frame from the bed, trying not to disturb Amanda. He stretched as he stood up, then knelt beside the bed to start his day. His morning prayer always ended the same, "If You choose not to bring the girls back to us, please give us the strength to endure. Remind us daily of Your care for both us and them." After closing in his Savior's name, Calvin rose and ran a calloused hand through his sandy blond hair.

Once in the bathroom, Calvin stared at his reflection, reminded once again he needed a haircut. He thought about leaving Amanda a note asking her to schedule an appointment for the next day. Since their children were stolen he knew she no longer felt needed in spite of his best efforts to show her otherwise. I wish I could have her back at work, he thought. He recalled how they had already discussed her return but they both felt they could not ask their current bookkeeper and good friend to leave. Calvin ran his fingers through his scruffy hair.

Amanda had taken on the responsibility of his scheduling and to his pleasure, sometimes accompanied him to his appointments. Today would not be one of those days however, he noted as he climbed into the steaming-hot shower. For a moment he felt a twinge of regret at the thought of her being at home all day without him. Well, he thought, maybe her mother will keep her busy somehow. He smiled to himself, knowing more than he could tell.

Calvin mentally checked his time, then hurried through the remainder of his shower. His left brain thinking took over and his day was off and running. He shaved then dressed quickly and quietly, then brushed the long brown hair away from Amanda's face, kissed her, then headed to the kitchen. Breakfast would be some of whatever he picked up for the crew. This morning he thought bagels would be better than donuts. He wanted everyone to be bright and ready to tackle the day. It was starting out to be a sunny, unseasonably warm day for February and he wanted to take advantage of it.

He reached into the refrigerator to retrieve the lunch he knew Amanda had packed for him, then turned to fill the extra-large thermos with the coffee she'd prepared the night before to be ready at just the right time. I'm married to the most thoughtful woman in the world, he thought as he headed out the door. After pushing the garage door opener, he walked over to his well-used pickup. As he turned his head to back out, he noticed the curtain on the door window leading to the kitchen move. He knew Amanda was awake and he didn't want to miss the chance to remind her that he loved her.

Amanda stood just inside the doorway in her old housecoat. Cal smiled as he thought of the many times he had offered to replace it with something newer. Her response was always the same so he stopped offering. As he stepped through the doorway he caught his five foot eight inch wife up in his arms.

"Thought you'd get away without saying good-bye, did ya?"

"Of course not, I was coming back in to wake you up as soon as I started the truck." They both knew better. In the almost six years of their marriage he'd rarely wakened her. "I came back for something," he said as he leaned her away from him. "What it was, though, is beyond me," he teased.

Her beautiful smile soothed his aching heart. "Now I remember. I was going to ask if you'd schedule a haircut for me for early tomorrow afternoon."

"Sure, I can do that, but early afternoon? Are you planning ahead to miss the appointment?"

"Not fair," he protested. "I didn't plan to miss the last one."

"Plan to or not, you did! And Judy wasn't happy about it either," she playfully scolded him.

"I thought we might do something special. Don't tell me, Miss Right-Brain, oh sentimental one, that you forgot tomorrow is Valentine's Day? A man would have to be deaf, dumb, and blind not to notice the hints you've been dropping. It would serve you right if you forgot after all the hints you've left me." Amanda blushed, aware of the many hints she'd used, so her over logical sometimes less than romantic husband wouldn't forget. "You be thinkin' about what you'd like to do tomorrow with this good-lookin' guy of yours."

He paused, as if thinking of something. "What else did I come back for?" He scratched his still damp head and looked lovingly into her eyes. "I came back to tell you I'm the luckiest man alive to have such a beautiful wife." He no longer added the part about being even more beautiful since the girls were born. Though he thought it, he spared her the pain. "And," he kissed her again, "to remind you that I love you very much and that there isn't anything that will happen to you today that you and God can't handle together."

"I love you too. You better be on your way with breakfast before you have a hungry pack of wolf dogs for employees when you get there. Bagels or donuts today?"

"How bout you join me and find out?"

"Are you out of your mind? I can't go anywhere looking like this!"

He stepped back to admire his wife. He saw nothing lacking in her appearance. Her hair was suffering from serious bed head and her beautiful dark-brown eyes told of her early morning cry, but she still shone just as bright as ever when she smiled. "Well, I can't wait for you, or what you say will be true." He kissed her again and then turned to the door. "You know how to reach me if you need me," he called over his shoulder.

"I do," she called after him and then closed the door. Through the window in the door she saw him wave. She lost sight of him as the garage door closed with him on the other side. She was tempted to run to the front window and wave good-bye like she'd taught the girls to do. The memory of the girls made her realize that she'd been up for almost ten minutes without thinking about them. She wondered if that was a good or bad thing. She didn't want to forget them, but she loathed the pain thinking about them caused.

At the thought of pain she became aware that she had not taken the time to pray before leaving the bedroom. She returned to remedy that. She knelt beside the bed to restart her day. Her prayer always ended the same, "If You choose not to bring the girls back to us, please give us the strength to endure. Remind us daily of Your care for both us and them." She thought of just how much during the past six months she'd been given the strength to endure their children being stolen.

So far she'd thought of only a few things she really needed to do, and none of them would take very long. Her shower would be a long one, just as it had been every day since the girls were stolen. She stepped into the shower, and even though she'd been in the girls' bathtub the day they were stolen, she shuddered.

As she adjusted the water to the right temperature and tilted her head to wet her hair, the memory of that day was so clear. It was a Monday. She'd spent all morning cleaning the house and working on laundry. Both girls had been particularly fussy at lunch so she decided to put them both down for an early nap. It was a humid day in August, but she still longed for a hot bath. With the girls safely tucked into their beds, she rechecked the screen door to be sure it was locked, then took a radio into their bathroom for a nice long soak. The radio hadn't been very loud, but she hadn't heard anything outside the bathroom. That's when it happened.

She lathered her head and tried to rinse away the memory with the shampoo. Try as she might to forget, the memory haunted her. She'd gotten out of the tub and left the bathroom almost an hour later feeling refreshed. She'd hoped to read a few pages from the latest issue of *Christian Parenting Today* before Jessica woke up. To her surprise she'd started and finished the magazine before her four-year-old came out of her room. In fact, Jessica never disturbed her at all. By three thirty Amanda decided to wake her up. She didn't think anything of it when she found Jessi's room empty. Jessi often went into her sister's room and slept on the floor. Amanda remembered feeling a bit uneasy when she gently pushed Katrina's door open and didn't see Jessi on the floor. She couldn't see into Kat's bed but she was sure Jessi had climbed in with her. Uneasiness turned to horror as she looked in the bed and found it empty.

Amanda finished her shower and prayed the pain had gone down the drain with the last of the soap. After dressing, she started her daily chores. She emptied the clean dishes from the dishwasher, ate breakfast then cleaned up the mess. Well, my day's work is almost done. Only two things remain, make an appointment for Calvin and dinner. How different one's life is without children under foot, she thought. She didn't allow herself to go there. Instead, she decided to vacuum the floors. She got the sweeper, then mundanely went about pushing and pulling the machine around the room. It was hard to tell when she was done since the floors hadn't really needed to be swept in the first place. It was just "busy work" for her.

As she put away the sweeper, the phone rang. "Hello" was the only word she spoke before her mother took over completely.

"Oh Manny, you are never going to believe what your father's done!"

There was excitement in her voice so Amanda ignored being called by the nickname her baby sister had given her. Doreen was unable to say Amanda as a baby so she called her big sister Manny. It'd stuck with her ever since.

Amanda started to say "What," but was quickly cut off by her excited mother.

"He has made arrangements…oh, I can hardly believe this. We are going on a cruise."

"Where?" Amanda managed to interject.

"He hasn't told me yet. He said I need to be prepared for warmer weather. We leave in the morning." Sandy Steinman took a quick breath. "I don't know what to pack. I don't have time to buy anything. I'm so excited I can barely stand it. Honey, I was going to come over today, but with so much to do, I can't."

"That's all right," Amanda said with excitement now in her voice too. Sandy's enthusiasm for life had helped Amanda get through the past six months. Amanda's offer to help was greeted with more excitement. "I'll get the rest of the details when I get there. See you in fifteen." Amanda said good-bye and hung up, eager to help.

Amanda opened the garage door with the push of a button, then started the van. As she looked back to maneuver from the garage, her gaze rested on the two empty car seats. As she drove mindlessly toward her childhood home, her mind drifted back to the last time the girls sat in the seats. It was the Sunday before they were stolen. Her dad had suggested they all stop for breakfast on the way home from church. Amanda remembered putting Kat into the car seat first, much to Kat's displeasure. She never did like to ride, or maybe it was that she didn't like to be still, Amanda thought. Cal had spent a few more minutes with Frank before returning with Jessi to strap her in. During the short ride home, both girls had fallen asleep. Amanda felt a mix of happiness and sadness with the memory.

She brushed away tears as she pulled into her parents' drive. The livingroom was just as Amanda expected it, suitcases and clothing strewn from "here to next week" as her father would say. Amanda helped with some laundry and made lunch. She was glad to be busy. So often her days were empty with nothing to do but remember.

Frank joined the women for lunch, but still wouldn't say where he was taking his wife of thirty-two years. He assured them that she would fully enjoy the trip. He asked where Calvin was for the day and if he'd gotten the bid on the gas station remodeling job.

"Yes, he got the job," Amanda told him. "It's very seldom Edwards Construction doesn't get the jobs they bid on." A sense of pride welled up inside Amanda as she thought of her husband's dedication to his business. She thought of how long ago it started. Even in middle school he was determined to own his own construction company someday. What the seed of determination can do for a man, Amanda thought. She regretted that determination wasn't all it had taken to find their daughters. There was no doubt that they'd been determined. It reminded her of what Jesus said about the spirit being willing, but the flesh being weak. Calvin and Amanda had both been willing to do whatever it took to find their daughters and, in fact, had done all they could. But, Amanda thought, everything we've done is still not enough.

When it seemed nearly everything her mother owned was packed into three suitcases, Amanda asked, "What's Daddy taking?"

"Oh, you know him. He'll pack some clean underwear and his toothbrush." The two women laughed, knowing how Frank hated to pack. Sandy motioned toward the last empty suitcase. "That's his. He'll pack in the morning to be sure he doesn't forget anything." The women laughed, knowing Frank would pack ten to fifteen minutes before it was time to leave for the airport.

Amanda kissed her parents good-bye and promised to return the next day to drive them to the airport. She insisted they let her do that much for them. They'd done so much for her in the past six months when she needed them.

She drove home still brimming with excitement left over from her mother, and some of her own. She would have a full day tomorrow and that thought alone was enough to excite her. She had a surprise for Cal. She'd scheduled to have Judy do her hair an hour before Cal's so she would be back home, looking beautiful, when he arrived at their friend's house.

Over pizza, chips, and pop that night, Amanda told Calvin about her day. He didn't seem surprised, so she questioned him about it.

"Last week Frank asked if I would stop by during the week and check on things around the house. I suggested that the job would be better suited for you."

"Thank you. I'm thrilled with having something to do this week."

After dinner and two highly competitive games of backgammon, Calvin and Amanda settled in with their favorite pastimes. Amanda made her way to the beautifully handmade built-in bookshelves and chose to read Janette Oke's book *Love Comes Softly*. In the kitchen she poured herself a tall glass of refrigerated water, then one for Calvin. She placed the glass of water out of his way, but not his reach, on the table where he looked over the latest requests for bids. Calvin's favorite pastime was not the paperwork, but rather anything that had to do with his business.

By ten thirty, Calvin had finished going over the bids and his eyes had become heavy during the process. He rubbed them without even realizing it.

"Ready to call it a night?" Amanda asked.

Calvin responded, "It never ceases to amaze me that no matter what you're doing, you always know what I'm doing, too." He'd been impressed and grateful for her ability to do the same with the girls, but he chose not to mention that fact for fear she'd be sad again. Instead, he teased her. "You're like the captain of a ship knowing what's happening everywhere at any given time."

"Off to bed with ye, ye scallywag," she teased back.

After they readied themselves for bed, they knelt together, to hold hands and pray. Calvin began, "Father God, we give You glory for Your provisions this day, for the strength that helped us through yet another day without our daughters. We know our daughters were gifts to us and that You were free to take them back at any time, in any way. We also know it will take nothing less than Your strength to help us deal with what has happened in our lives. We pray for the safety of our little girls." Amanda had come to expect this part of his prayer every night since the girls had been stolen, but it didn't make it any easier to hear.

Calvin prayed for a safe journey for his in-laws, and that He would use this time away to refresh them both. He thanked Him for the wife He provided for him and the love that grew between them. Closing the prayer in his Savior's name, Calvin squeezed the smaller hand that he had been holding and then helped her up.

"Sweet dreams," he told her as he kissed the back of her head and pulled her close to his chest. Within minutes the sound of her steady breathing told Calvin she was asleep. He took a moment more with his Maker. "Lord, please do give her sweet dreams tonight." Praying in faith, he knew it would happen.

Chapter 2

Saturday morning Calvin awakened to the song "Deep Enough to Dream" rather than the cries of his wife. For this and his wife, he thanked God before his knees bent to pray.

"Thank You God, for giving Amanda something to look forward to this week while her parents are gone. I ask for Your guidance this day, especially where our new guy, Ronnie, is concerned. I pray You'll watch over our daughters. If You choose not to bring the girls back to us, please give us the strength to endure. Remind us daily of Your care for both us and them. In Jesus' name, amen."

He looked lovingly at his sleeping wife, then headed for the shower. Aware that this morning he would need to wake her before he left, he hurried through his routine.

To his surprise, he found an empty bed when he returned. When the smell from the kitchen finally made its way to his senses, he knew where she was. He dressed, then quietly made his way to the kitchen where he found Amanda just the way he'd hoped he would, with her back to him. He snuck up close behind her and wrapped his arms around her waist.

"Did I scare you?"

"You never do," she said as she turned to face him. "Keep practicing, my little Indian." She'd told Jessi the same thing when she tried to sneak up on her. The memory brought tears to her eyes.

He gestured toward the oven. "Those smell wonderful." He loved her sweet rolls.

11

"It's my Saturday morning treat for you and the guys. They should be done in about ten minutes. I hope you can wait."

He smiled at the thought of his wife's generous spirit. He'd seen and experienced it many times, and it always brought a smile to his face.

"Why don't you take a few minutes to yourself while I grab a quick shower?" She picked up the timer and headed for the bathroom. Before the timer went off, she was completely ready for the day.

When she returned to the kitchen, she found Calvin with his head bent over his Bible and the Sunday school lesson from Kay Arthur's book *Lord, I Need Grace To Make It* on the table. As she returned to the kitchen the timer rang. He'd been so engrossed in his study that he didn't hear her walk back into the room. He looked up at her and smiled. "You always were a better Indian than me."

"You're too much of a beaver," she teased back, knowing his impeccably organized personality so well.

She'd been quick to pick up on the study of personalities from the book *The Two Sides of Love* their Sunday school class had studied.

He smiled as she carefully packaged the rolls for his drive to work. "Well, the beaver in me wants to tell it like it is," he stated.

"And how is *it*?" she asked.

He stood up and quickly closed the distance between them, turned her to face him and placed a gentle kiss on her mouth. "I think you are beautiful with an inner spirit to match. I thank God that He brought us together and I'm looking forward to spending the rest of my life with you, but for now I have to get to work or the guys will never forgive me for bringing them cold cinnamon rolls." He longed to stay. Just wait until I get home from Judy's, he thought. "Happy Valentine's Day," he said aloud as he took the thermos, his lunch, and the steaming package she offered him.

"Happy Valentine's Day to you," she said as she reached for her coat and followed him out the door.

As she looked in the mirror to maneuver the van from the garage, she looked at the empty seats with sadness. Maybe I should consider Calvin's suggestion that we buy a different vehicle. Looking into the backseat of a different vehicle might be a little easier on me, she thought to herself. Just then she realized she hadn't felt the usual pain while in the shower. "From now on, I'll hurry through my shower. Being busy keeps my mind from painful things," she said to her reflection in the mirror.

Unfortunately, driving to her parents' was not busy enough. Even the excitement of their trip couldn't keep her from thinking about the girls. She often wondered if they were still together, what they were doing, how much they'd grown, if they missed or even remembered her and Calvin, and if the people who had them were taking care of them.

She took some comfort in knowing they had not been killed as they first feared. It seemed as though they had vanished without a trace, so everyone feared the worst. Six weeks into the investigation, police uncovered a child-selling market. They had a tip from a source that told them about a house in downtown Lansing. They found drug paraphernalia and maps of the surrounding small towns, as well as pictures of their children and another child that had been reported missing. The police told them from the looks of the house, whoever had been living there left in a hurry.

There were signs that the children had been in the house. The officers fingerprinted everything and eventually identified three suspects—two young men and an older woman. The men had prior drug convictions, and the woman had been arrested in Alabama for trying to sell her daughter's illegitimate child. She'd gone free on a technicality that Amanda didn't understand. Amanda struggled, but she prayed for the woman who had stolen not only her children, but also the joy they brought into her life, though it was never easy.

Amanda backed the van into the drive and popped the back hatch. Her mother was waiting at the front door. Before Amanda put the van in park, Sandy was on her way out the door.

"I was so excited I almost couldn't sleep," she told Amanda. Even with little sleep, Sandy had more energy than most women half her age. Amanda welcomed the opportunity to push aside the thoughts she'd had on the way over. "Your Dad's still packing. I'm still so excited I don't know if I'll be able to eat anything," she said as the two of them placed her three suitcases in the back of the van.

As they turned to go inside, Frank appeared at the door with his suitcase in hand. "You weren't thinking of leaving without me, were you?"

"Never!" his wife replied. "Besides, other than knowing where to go for breakfast and that we need to be at the airport, we'd be lost without you darling," she teased, knowing full well she'd be lost without him in so many other ways as well. "Do you have everything?" she asked.

"Anything I don't have…" he began.

"I can buy when I get there." Sandy and Amanda laughed as they both finished his sentence, accustomed to his standard answer.

"Are you ready?" Amanda asked them.

As they all made their way to the van, her father replied, "Never been more ready to leave a place than I am right now. The house is locked and the cat's been put out." Sandy got into the back seat while Amanda got into the driver's seat. When her father settled himself in the passenger's seat, Amanda rolled her eyes at him. Her parents didn't have a cat.

Breakfast was not a rushed affair or one of great leisure. It was just right for eating and trying, unsuccessfully, to get Frank to tell them where they were going.

The drive to the airport was one of mixed emotions for the two women. Both were filled with excitement for the upcoming event, but sad they would be apart for a week. Sandy spent the drive time praying for Amanda, asking their Heavenly Father to give her extra strength this week.

Finally at the airport, the ladies stood in front of the departure board with no less than twenty outgoing flights to choose from. They discussed how most of them would be a great winter destination.

Frank let them speculate for a while, then asked, "How does Orlando sound? Would you like a little fun in the sun?"

Sandy replied, "I would *definitely* like a little fun in the sun right now."

"But what if we got on a boat when we got there? Would *that* be okay?" he asked playfully.

"A boat? What kind of boat?"

Frank removed a travel brochure from his inside coat pocket and handed it to Sandy. She and Amanda looked over the brochure for just a second before they realized the *boat* wasn't a boat at all, but rather a cruise ship that would take them to the Bahamas. Then they would travel to New Orleans and fly home from there. Sandy's excitement could hardly be contained. She let out a little scream of excitement and flung her arms around her husband's neck.

Frank hugged her back and winked at Amanda, who was smiling from ear to ear for her parents.

"You know I've wanted to go on a cruise since we got married. How long have you been planning this?"

"Since we got married." He smiled. "It's taken me this long to pay it off," he joked.

After the luggage was checked and the boarding check made, the trio hugged one last time. As they hugged, Frank led them in prayer. "Father God, I pray You give us a safe journey and that You watch over our children while we're away. We thank You for all You've done for us and continue to do for us. In Jesus' name, amen."

Both women said amen.

"Don't forget to feed the cat," Frank said to make Amanda laugh. She waved good-bye as they left to board the plane. Two and a half hours later, Amanda returned home.

With three hours to wait for her hair appointment with Judy, Amanda changed into comfortable clothes, then settled down on the couch to read the book she'd started the night before. Time inched by as the story unfolded. Without noticing the time, she fixed herself a sandwich and returned to the couch. Before she realized it, she was in danger of being late for her appointment. She quickly slipped into her boots and grabbed her jacket before rushing out the door.

Amanda recognized the car already parked in Judy's driveway as that of their company's bookkeeper, Laurinda Bowman. I hope Laurinda isn't in a hurry to leave, Amanda thought as she got out of the van.

"I beg your pardon for being late," Amanda said to her lifelong friend as she walked in the salon door. "Why didn't you tell me Laurinda was going to be here?"

"Guess it's just a day for surprises," Judy said with a knowing smile. "I'm running late, too."

"I hope I won't be here by the time your next appointment arrives," Amanda teased.

"I won't let you down," she said as she positioned the last rod in Laurinda's hair. The strong smell of permanent wave solution ended their conversation. "Amanda, wet your hair for me, would ya?"

"Yes, ma'am," Amanda replied.

Amanda finished as Judy secured the plastic bag around Laurinda's hair. Laurinda moved to the vacant chair to wait for twenty minutes. Amanda took her spot under the professional hands of her best friend. Normally twenty minutes would have flown by for all of them, but with the strong smell of the permanent solution, the twenty minutes seemed to drag. By the time Judy had removed all the snarls from Amanda's long hair and cut the allowed one inch, it was time for the two women to trade places again so the neutralizer could be applied to Laurinda's hair.

After the neutralizer was applied, the two women traded places again so Judy could rewet and then braid Amanda's hair. After Amanda was reseated in the chair, she asked Judy if she'd had any more trouble with her eyes.

"Yes, I had one on Tuesday. It's a wonder that I can even keep my business running with these annoying things. I never know from day to day if I'll feel good enough to get out of bed. Then I'll go a week or two without one and I just think, okay, they're gone, but that's obviously not the case. I have an appointment with my doctor next week."

"I *know* you'll let me know what she says."

"Yes, mother," Judy replied.

Amanda turned her attention to Laurinda. "Tell me about the new guy Calvin hired. All I've gotten from Cal is that the man, not much more than a boy, is a little rough around the edges. He asked me to pray for him. Calvin's pretty sure he's unsaved."

Laurinda's head jerked up from the magazine she had been thumbing through but not really looking at. "Unsaved?" she questioned Amanda as if she had not already considered it herself.

"It's just what Cal thinks, it doesn't make it so. Tell me about him from a female perspective."

"Amanda, Ronnie's gorgeous. I'm certain God threw away the mold after making him. He's six foot if not more. His arms are as big around as my thighs."

Both of the other women looked at Laurinda's thighs and decided that they weren't so big. They looked at each other, but made no comment. Instead, they let her go on about this handsome man.

After the full physical description, both women were sure they must see this fine specimen of a man for themselves.

"Any plans to make him yours?" Judy asked candidly. Laurinda blushed. "Now I understand the sudden desire for a perm. You don't think he's the type that likes straight hair, huh?"

Laurinda blushed again. "No, it's nothing like that. I was just ready for a change," the younger woman protested. "For me!" she added matter-of-factly. "Besides," her gaze returned to the magazine on her lap, "if he isn't saved, it wouldn't be worth my time to get to know him better." She paused, then added, "Would it?" Outwardly she appeared to be speaking the truth, but inwardly she was heartbroken to discover that Cal shared her thoughts about Ronnie's standing with God. She wondered if she'd ever find a godly man to share her life. Amanda's next question brought Laurinda's head back up from the magazine with a sudden jerk.

"Have you prayed about it?" she asked as if she'd read Laurinda's thoughts.

"Prayed about what?"

"About the man God has selected for you, of course," Amanda said.

"Not really," Laurinda admitted.

"I think that should be your first course of action," Amanda suggested. "And if you hope it might be Ronnie, I'll remind you that beauty is only skin deep. It's what's inside the heart of the man that matters more to God." She lovingly added, "It should be what matters most to you as well."

"Oh, it does. I was only thinking that maybe..." Her words were left hanging, but Laurinda's thoughts continued. What am I thinking, she asked herself.

Amanda was sensitive to her struggle. She'd wanted more than anything to be Calvin's wife from the time she began thinking about marriage. As she matured in Christ, she became aware that just because she wanted it, didn't mean God wanted it. She'd spent countless hours praying for direction. She'd finally been sure it was all right to go out with him after she accidentally found out that he'd been financially supporting a missionary from their church. She took this knowledge to God and asked Him to help her know the truth where this man was concerned. Her prayer was answered. This particular time it had been more obvious than other times, so she felt confident with the decision to date him if he asked.

After spending a great deal of time together at church youth functions, they began to spend time with each other's families. When Amanda confided in her mother about her feelings for Calvin, her mother gave her approval. Amanda took this as confirmation from God about the rightness of their relationship. To keep their relationship pure, they were seldom alone.

At the junior-senior prom he had more than one opportunity to kiss her, but didn't. She asked him if there was something wrong.

"No," he replied.

"I don't want to kiss you because I'm afraid I wouldn't stop there." He said that some of his guy friends talked about who they'd slept with and he knew all too well how it had started for them. "I respect you too much to bring that kind of sin into our lives," he explained. After he explained his feeling about kissing, she wholeheartedly agreed with him.

They left the prom early and went to an all-night diner. "I've been praying a lot about the future. I'd like to own my own construction company someday. I'm seeking God's will in every area of my life," he told her as he placed a gentle kiss on the back of her hand that he'd been holding. Because he put God's will first, Amanda had been even more confident this man was for her.

"Remember, sweetie," Amanda said as she brought herself back to the present and broke into Laurinda's thoughts, "it needs to be God's will first."

"I say go for it if you want him," Judy interjected.

Amanda looked in the mirror at her friend and gave her a sour look. "Don't give this Christian girl worldly advice."

Judy knew not to argue with Amanda about God, so she dropped it. Amanda said a prayer for her friend. Oh, how many times she had hoped Judy would return to the church, but she knew not to push.

"Thanks for the advice, you two. I'll keep you posted," Laurinda told them.

"All done," Judy proclaimed as she gave Amanda a handheld mirror and turned the chair around for her to see the results of her hard work.

"Beautiful," Amanda heard from beside her.

Wow, was her own thought. "I had no idea you could do so much with so little," she told Judy. "I look great if I do say so myself. You've never created a heart out of the two braids in the back before. I love it!" Amanda exclaimed.

"Don't mess this up when you change your clothes for your big date."

"I won't," Amanda assured her.

"Now get out of here so I can finish with Laurinda and you don't get caught by your hubby."

Amanda retrieved cash from her wallet, but Judy refused. "Think of it as my contribution to your date."

Amanda gave each woman a quick hug, wished them a Happy Valentine's Day, and left.

Chapter 3

Calvin told Amanda their date would be a casual one so she'd know how to dress. The first outfit was too casual, she decided, so she stripped and tossed everything on the bed. The next outfit seemed to go to the other extreme, joining the first. She decided the third outfit, a pair of off-white dress pants and jacket, with a satin sleeveless brown top with delicate lace in the shape of a V at the neck, fit the bill perfectly.

She began returning the unwanted clothes to the closet, then decided she had enough time to sort through some of her old clothes before Cal would be home. She made a pile of things to give away.

When Calvin came in he asked, "What happened? Couldn't figure out what to wear so you decided to wear it all?"

"No, I did a little early spring cleaning," she stated matter-of-factly. "So, where are you taking me tonight?"

"Tonight?" he said with a question in his voice. "You thought this was just an evening date? Then I have a surprise for you. I have the afternoon, evening, and night planned out for us. And by the time you wake up in the morning, you won't even be in your own bed."

"What!" she exclaimed.

"I'm just full of surprises. When you've finished ransacking your closet, please pack an overnight bag."

"We will be at church in the morning, right?"

"Yes. So take along a dress and whatever you need to go with it. Our first stop is in one hour and we still have to eat lunch here, so don't dawdle. I have everything worked out," he explained to her.

"Except I left one thing for you to decide. Should we take the van or the truck?" He winked at her and then headed to the bathroom.

After a light lunch, they were in the van and on their way. This had already been an exciting day, and they were on their way to more excitement. Amanda wanted to bottle it and save it for a day that was boring.

"First stop," he said, interrupting her thoughts, "will be the movie theater."

He dropped her off at the door, then went to park. Joining her a few minutes later at the door, he wrapped one arm around her waist and guided her directly to the ticket taker. By the time the movie ended it was too early to go for dinner, so they walked around the mall with no particular place to go.

At one store she showed particular interest in the Thomas Kinkade print *Teacup Cottage*. Calvin asked her if she wanted it.

"We can't afford it right now." She paused. "But maybe for my birthday or Christmas," she said, showing her heartwarming smile.

He kissed her on the cheek, then allowed her to wander to the back of the store without him. He spoke to a sales clerk, then found Amanda a few minutes later and suggested that they make their way to dinner before it got too crowded.

"Since the van is halfway between here and the restaurant, do you want to drive over or just walk?" Calvin asked as they stepped outside the mall.

"It's unseasonably warm for a February in Michigan, and I'm not wearing high heels so, let's walk."

Calvin gave his name to the host. "Yes, Mr. Edwards. I'll have your table ready in just a moment," the young man said, then hurried away.

"What's that all about?" Amanda asked.

"Have I told you yet today how beautiful you look?"

"You've only told me about three times an hour."

"Only three times an hour? I'll have to do something about that."
He paused, pretending to be deep in thought. Finally, he said, "You
look beautiful, Mrs…"

The host interrupted him. "Your table is ready, Mr. Edwards,
please follow me."

Amanda looked at Cal with a raised eyebrow that said, "What
have you done?"

He shrugged his shoulders.

When she turned from looking at him, she saw a beautiful
bouquet of flowers on the table with a card in front of them with her
name on it. Once they were seated, he handed her the card. Carefully
opening it, her eyes took in the sweetest card she'd ever read. Afraid
her voice would quiver, she silently read the front. *Whenever I need
someone who's strong and true, to support me in the things I do, I'm
thankful there is you.* She read the inside with tears in her eyes.
*Whenever I'm busy, quiet or sad, excited, discouraged, or just feeling
glad, I'm thankful there is you. Whenever I need kindness, tenderness
or care, someone I know will always be there…for always caring…for
being the wonderful person that you are. With love always.* He added,
I thank God for you daily. All my love, Calvin. The card brought more
tears.

"If I'd known you were going to cry all night, I'd have left you at
home." His light, playful mood caused her to laugh.

Amanda reached across the table and placed her hand over his.
"You are so thoughtful. I'm grateful God brought us together."

Calvin lifted both of her hands to his lips, gently kissing one, then
the other. "Me, too."

Their waiter stood back until the two released hands and eyes.
Looking embarrassed for having observed the exchange, he stepped
forward to take their order.

After Calvin placed their order, they began to discuss their
Sunday school lesson for the next day. Studying their lesson together

had been their long-standing practice, beginning the Saturday after they were married. The addition of each child had brought about new challenges, but somehow they had managed to juggle everything.

The waiter brought their dinner, and after a prayer of thanksgiving for the food, they resumed their discussion.

"I sometimes feel like Paul did in his letter to the Romans," Calvin said between bites. "I find myself doing the things I know I shouldn't."

Amanda nodded in agreement because she had felt that way, too, though she couldn't think of anything Calvin had ever done that he shouldn't have. She wondered for a moment about the man she'd married. She was sure he wasn't perfect, but at the moment she couldn't think of any of his flaws. She felt blessed to be his wife. She was certain that if there'd been a Proverb's husband, hers would have been a perfect match. As Calvin moved forward in the lesson, she was lost in her thoughts.

"Romans 3:20 shows clearly how we aren't obeying God's laws," he was saying.

She agreed, and returned to the conversation and her meal. "Did you notice how Galatians 3:19 strongly supported Romans 3:20?"

"Yes," he said as he set his wine glass back on the table. "Doesn't Kay have a wonderful way of helping us see our need for a savior?"

"Anyone could lead you to these passages, but I think Kay's questions and comments help so much to understand them." Amanda's mood and head lowered. "I did have some trouble with the part where she talked about teaching your children the Ten Commandments. Jessi was just beginning to learn them. Not that she understood all of them, but she could tell you the gist of each of them." Amanda wiped tears from her eyes. "Oh, Cal, I pray that whoever has them is teaching them His laws."

They both feared that anyone who would accept stolen children were probably not Christian. That fear didn't stop them from hoping that whoever had the girls didn't know they had been stolen, and that they were Christians.

Calvin had been afraid this would happen when he'd read the same section of the lesson. He placed a hand over hers. He wanted very much to hold her in his arms. He squeezed her hand to assure her he understood and agreed. He often prayed that his daughters would come to know the Lord, even if it wasn't he and Amanda who got to introduce them.

"How did you do on writing out the Ten Commandments?" he asked, hoping to redirect her attention.

"I got them all, but not in the right order," she said as she wiped away a tear. "How 'bout you?" she asked.

"Same."

Their meal and lesson progressed until both were finished. Calvin led them in a simple prayer. "Father God, we thank You for Your grace. As You have promised, 'For by grace we have been saved through faith; and that not of yourselves, it is the gift from you, not as a result of works, that no one should boast.' Thank You that we need not try to work our way to heaven. Thank You for giving us grace, making us worthy of Your love. In Jesus' name, amen."

"Amen," Amanda repeated.

They emptied their wine glasses, then left the restaurant, content in knowing they were constantly under God's care and grace. Hand in hand they returned to their van, Amanda carrying the card and Calvin carrying the flowers.

"Is this how you felt while carrying your flowers on our wedding day? All giddy, I mean?"

"You feel giddy because you're carrying flowers?"

"Not because of the flowers, but maybe because of what I know, or at least hope, will happen later."

Amanda smiled at him and shook her head. "You're incorrigible!"

After helping Amanda into her seat, Calvin placed the flowers in a box he'd placed in the back of the van earlier, closed the hatch, and took his place in the driver's seat.

"Where to now?" she asked excitedly.

"It's a surprise. So you can wait patiently and without question or you will have your eyes covered."

"I'll wait."

Within twenty minutes he pulled the van to a stop in front of a bed and breakfast. Amanda broke into a broad smile. He knew she had wanted to visit this place from the many times they'd discussed it.

"You look pleased," he said, "but not surprised."

"Does that mean we don't get to stay?"

"No. I'll get the bags. You go in."

Amanda waited only a few minutes before Calvin returned with their bags. An older woman welcomed them.

"Your room is ready, follow me." At the top of the stairs and just to the right the woman unlocked a door and handed the key to Calvin. "If you need anything, let me know. I'll be downstairs in my room. I'll be up for a while yet."

"Thank you," they said in unison.

Amanda admired everything in the tastefully decorated room. A large oak canopy bed stood in the middle of the room. When Amanda looked at the bedspread, she noticed a package on it.

Calvin stood quietly as he watched his wife take in the room, then make her way to the bed and the package. There was no tag and no indication of where it came from, but Amanda knew immediately, based on its shape, that it was a picture. She was uncharacteristically oblivious to Calvin watching her, so she didn't hear him close the door or walk up behind her as she stood next to the bed.

"It won't bite." His voice startled her.

"Is it for me?"

"Of course it's for you, beautiful."

She sat down on the bed and pulled the package onto her lap. She didn't answer because her full attention was on the package.

"Will you open it already?"

She turned it over and found where it'd been taped. She tugged at the paper, trying not to rip it. She finally removed the paper and was looking, speechlessly, down at the picture.

"This has to be a first," he teased her. "You seem to be at a loss for words." He reached down and gently lifted her chin, not at all surprised to discover tears in her eyes.

"You shouldn't have," she managed to whisper before the tears rolled down her cheeks and splashed onto the glass.

"Hey, don't ruin the picture before we can get it home," he said as he wiped the tears from her face, then took the picture from her and laid it on the bed beside her.

"Thank you," she whispered as he pulled her into his arms.

"You're so welcome," he whispered. They stood embraced in each other's arms for a while before Calvin leaned back and asked if she was tired. "That bed, minus the picture, looks awfully inviting to a tired man."

"Yes, it does," she answered. "But I doubt that sleep is all you have in mind." She smiled at him, removed the picture from the bed, laid it near their bags, and then took her bag into the bathroom. To her surprise there was another gift. This gift was hanging from a satin hanger on the shower curtain rod. She thought about saying something, but decided that not saying anything would bother Calvin for a few minutes, or at least until she could come back out with it on. Amanda undressed, then slipped the negligee over her head. The satin, hunter green negligee was a perfect fit. She folded her clothes and placed them inside the bag next to the negligee she'd brought for the evening, and then brushed her teeth. She called to Calvin through the door, "Close your eyes."

"What?"

"Close your eyes. I'll get into bed, then you can use the bathroom to finish getting ready for bed."

The exchange took place without her being seen.

When he returned, there was a soft glow in the room. Amanda had lit the candles on each of the nightstands.

"Now may I see?" he asked with a sheepish grin.

Amanda pulled the covers off herself, then quickly back again. With an equally sheepish grin she asked, "Long enough?"

"I don't think so," he said as he reached for the covers and gently pulled them back. He extended his hand to her and pulled her from the bed so that she stood directly in front of him. "You are such a beautiful woman," he breathed the words into her ear, silently thanking God for such a wonderful wife.

He placed a few gentle kisses on her shoulders before she remembered his card. She tried to explain that she wanted to give it to him on Valentine's Day, but his kisses quieted her lips.

"Forget the card," he told her. And forget the card she did.

Chapter 4

They slept longer than they planned and were running late. With little time for breakfast, they thanked the hostess for a wonderful night's rest and politely declined breakfast.

On the way through a drive-thru, Calvin told Amanda, "Jimmy helped me with his surprise for you."

"Oh no!" Amanda exclaimed. "Jimmy saw my negligee?"

"He delivered the picture and had no need to go into the bathroom," Calvin assured her.

"It was a perfect fit," she said. "At least for the short time I wore it." Amanda smiled. Calvin smiled too as he parked the van in the church parking lot.

They slipped into their class a couple minutes late. Jimmy nodded his head to acknowledge them.

With twenty group-discussion questions available to them, the class could have spent much more than an hour in discussion. With limited time, they focused on how God's law had pointed to the need for God's grace. After some lively discussion and a closing prayer, the class ended and everyone went to listen to God's word brought to them by the associate pastor.

Amanda had joyfully sung praises to God and watched quietly as Calvin had slipped their tithe into the offering. She remained quiet as the service continued, watching with mixed emotions as the children were dismissed for their service downstairs.

Her thoughts began to wander until Dave spoke one word, "Forgiveness." Pastor Dave gave great emphasis to the word as he began his sermon.

Amanda wanted to be anywhere but right there. She knew what was coming. God would be speaking directly to her heart and she knew it.

Calvin tightened his grip on her shoulder then, as if he'd read her thought. He leaned close to her and whispered in her ear, "Remember, His grace is sufficient in all things."

Dave began again. "Forgiveness is something we often talk about, but do we really understand it? By definition, forgiveness means to conceal or send away. Think for a moment about what God has sent away or concealed in your life. I don't usually ask you to think about your sins, but in this case I'd like you to." He stood silently as the congregation considered his request.

Amanda searched her heart. Feelings of humiliation and shame swept over her as she remembered times in her life she had failed to obey God in various ways. Before she could slip into condemnation, Dave spoke again. "Open your Bibles to Luke 23:34. Brother St. Johns, please read the verse to us."

An elderly deacon rose to speak. In a loud, clear voice he read the passage. "Jesus said, 'Father, forgive them, for they do not know what they are doing.' And they divided up his clothes by casting lots."

"Thank you, Tom. Was Jesus asking God, our Father, to forgive the soldiers for gambling for His clothes? No, Jesus was asking God to forgive them for crucifying Him. Obviously, none of us were present when this event took place. Please compare the sins you just called to mind with the one Jesus asked His Father to forgive. I usually don't like to compare one thing or person to another, but in this case I will so you can see for yourself what true forgiveness is. If God can forgive the ones who murdered His Son, I know, brothers and sisters, that He can, and will, forgive us for anything and everything we've ever done wrong."

Many amens came from the congregation.

"We all know and understand God's forgiveness. Indeed, many of us have accepted that forgiveness and asked the Savior into our hearts, and even followed in the believer's baptism. But I must ask you: Do you forgive others as you were forgiven?" He paused, allowing the question to sink in. "Who can forget Peter's question to the Lord? Turn with me to Matthew 18:21. Brother Edwards, please read this verse."

Amanda froze as Calvin stood and read aloud. "Then Peter came to Jesus and asked 'Lord, how many times then shall I forgive my brother when he sins against me? Up to seven times.'"

"Thank you, Brother Edwards. Now please tell us Jesus' answer."

Calvin read with a clear voice without revealing the pain he felt inside. "Jesus answered, 'I tell you, not seven times, but seventy times seven.'"

Calvin sat back down next to Amanda and nearly cried. She reached for his hand and gave it an understanding squeeze. Forgiveness was the toughest aspect that they had to deal with since the girls were stolen. At first they found it impossible to do. But, by the grace of God, they strived to do so every day. They no longer harbored ill feelings for the family that had their daughters, nor did they seek to punish the ones who'd taken them. They knew in their hearts that no punishment on earth could bring their children back to them. They understood that to harbor bitterness and anger in their hearts would serve no purpose except to separate them from God. Someone once told them that unforgiveness in a person's soul was like swallowing poison and waiting for the other person to die.

Pastor Dave hadn't been insensitive in asking Calvin to read the passage. He'd felt the Lord leading him to ask Calvin to read it.

31

"My brothers and sisters," Dave resumed, "we've all heard the passage before. We all know how to say 'I forgive you' to our brothers and sisters. But do we know that we must let go of the anger that can accompany the need to forgive? We can say that we forgive this person or that one. But if we seek justice or revenge, we have not given complete forgiveness. To have disappointment in our lives and refuse to return it, or pass it on, is an act that requires an extraordinary amount of generosity. Science says that for every action there is an equal and opposite reaction. God's word teaches us differently. We are to absorb the effect of an unjust act against us, but we are not to pass it on. In Matthew 5:39, Jesus tells us to turn to him the other cheek."

Pastor Dave closed his Bible and stood silently for a moment before continuing. "Before I close I want to share a story with you. Once a little boy was visiting his grandparents and was given a slingshot to play with. The boy practiced for hours in the woods near the family's home, never hitting his target. Upon his return to the yard, he spotted Grandma's goose. He took careful aim, and low and behold, hit his mark, killing the defenseless animal. Fear gripped the boy, so he hid the goose behind the woodpile. Looking up, he discovered his sister, Jane, had seen everything. Being a smart girl, she took full advantage of the situation. Her brother became her personal slave by taking over doing all her chores. After many days of this, the boy tired of his sister's punishment, so he confessed to his grandma. Grandma calmly stated that she had seen the whole thing from the kitchen window. She explained to him that she loved him and she'd forgiven him. She went on to say, however, that she wondered how long he was going to let Jane make a slave out of him.

"Folks, this little boy had been a slave to his sister, or his sin as it were. He was a slave until he sought forgiveness from Grandma. Once forgiveness was granted, the boy was free, no longer enslaved by his sister or his sin. Every person in this room can experience that kind of forgiveness in their lives, and they can give it in return.

"My friends, forgiveness does not come naturally to any of us. It takes the grace of God, and much prayer, to not seek justice when we've been wronged. As Christians we are called to do this uncommon task. When we do, we are a shining example to the world of God's forgiveness of our sins and of His love for all His children."

The organist began to softly play a melody that Amanda quickly recognized as "Amazing Grace" as Pastor Dave left the podium to stand in front of it and continued to speak. "If you know the words to this song, sing softly. If not, just enjoy the tune. It's not enough for us to say that we forgive someone who has wronged us. We must mean it in our hearts."

Many voices softly sang as the pastor continued. "If there is anyone here who's in need of God's forgiveness, or if there's anyone you need to forgive, please come down front and we'll pray. Please don't leave here today with anger in your heart or revenge on your mind. God has given us the commandment that we are to forgive each other no less than four hundred and ninety times."

As Pastor Dave spoke, the Spirit of the Lord came upon many in the congregation. As the music played and people sang, Pastor Dave prayed with three different people. Several more, including Calvin and Amanda, went to the altar to pray. As people began to return to their seats, Calvin stopped and spoke to Pastor Dave.

"If you'll all have a seat for just a few more minutes, Calvin Edwards has something to share," Pastor Dave said.

"As most of you know, the past six months have been very trying for my wife and me." He squeezed Amanda's hand that he continued to hold after praying. "By the world's standards, we have every reason to seek revenge and harbor anger in our hearts toward the people responsible for stealing our daughters. I'm not going to stand here and tell you we forgave them right away. We didn't. But, folks, our anger with them didn't hurt them, it only hurt us. At times we even turned our anger on one another. I was even angry with God. I knew God never promised us an easy road. It wasn't until I remembered that He promised to always be with us on whatever road we had to take that I was able to forgive Him and the thieves. Through my lovely wife, He showed me Philippians 4:6-7 and I haven't been the same since. I still long to hold our daughters, but I no longer hurt their mother, myself, or my relationship with God because of my anger. God has given me a peace that truly does surpass all understanding."

Calvin paused to look at Amanda to be sure she was all right before he continued. "Some of you may have thought it cruel of Pastor Dave to have asked me to read those verses this morning. It wasn't. It was exactly the reminder I needed. He'd told me before the service that the Lord had laid it on his heart to ask me. I wasn't about to say no. The Lord has blessed my life so richly that if what we're suffering can in some way help someone else, then I won't stand in God's way. Friends, what I'm trying to say is this: If any of you need to forgive someone, or even seek forgiveness from someone, don't wait. Do it today. God will give you His peace and there is nothing to compare to it. God bless each and every one of you."

Pastor Dave shook Calvin's hand and publicly thanked him for sharing with them what God had laid upon his heart. Pastor Dave asked Deacon Earls to close the service with a word of prayer as the Edwardses made their way back to their seats.

Deacon Earls spoke the words on many people's hearts as he prayed, "Father God, thank You for this time we've had to come and worship in Your house. Thank You for Your word and how it is always true. Thank You for teaching us how to forgive by forgiving us. We pray that You will be with each of us as we go our separate ways today and bring us back into Your house to worship You again this evening. We pray a special blessing for the Edwardses that You'll continue to provide Your grace for them to endure their situation until You bring their children back. We know it's Your will that families be restored, so we pray this in Jesus' name, amen."

Then all of God's people said amen. Many of the Edwardses' friends came to hug them and remind them that they were in their prayers. Jimmy was the last to make his way over to his longtime friend. "Man, I just don't know how you keep going."

"I just explained it," Calvin told his friend.

"You are a better man than me. I'd want…"

Calvin cut off his sentence. "I wanted to, too, until I let go and let God. Believe me, sometimes I have to give it to Him daily." Calvin paused to make sure Amanda couldn't hear him before saying, "Especially the days I wake up to my wife crying out in her sleep. But it works. There is nothing like this peace."

"I'm proud to call you my friend, Calvin Edwards."

"And I, you. By the way, thanks again for making that delivery last night."

"Was she surprised?"

"Yes, but I almost got into trouble."

Jimmy gave him an inquisitive look.

"I had stopped by before my haircut and placed a personal gift in the bathroom. When I told Mandy that you'd helped me with the surprise, she thought you'd seen the other gift as well. She was either about to die of embarrassment the next time she saw you, or she was gonna kill me. I didn't know which. I had to do some fast explaining."

"You're funny." Jimmy winked at Amanda over Calvin's shoulder when she turned toward him. "Beth wanted me to ask if you two wanted to join us for some steaks on the grill this afternoon. She stayed home with the baby this morning. We were ready to leave and the little guy decided to give her back his breakfast all down the front of her dress. She didn't want me to be late so she told me to go ahead without her."

"I know you with your weak stomach. You were out of there the minute you heard the first sound!"

Jimmy laughed. His friend's comment had not been far from the truth. He'd been very nervous about becoming a father. Calvin assured him that his love would teach him what he needed to know to be a great dad. "Just follow your heart," Calvin had told the nervous father-to-be.

Amanda finished talking with Mrs. Earls and turned her attention to Calvin and Jimmy just in time to hear about Jimmy Jr. throwing up on his mom. She didn't miss being thrown up on, but she wouldn't trade the memories for anything.

"Jimmy and Beth want us to join them for steaks this afternoon," Calvin informed Amanda as she slipped her hand into his.

"That would be great," she said as she smiled at him. "I'll leave it up to you. I don't know what you have planned for the day, if anything."

"Oh, I'd planned to lay around in the backyard in the hammock and take in a few rays of sun." Calvin smiled as he teased his wife.

She simply shook her head at him and directed her attention to Jimmy. "We'd love to come. What time and what can I bring?" She paused. "Besides Calvin, that is."

"You know better than to ask me questions I can't answer. Call Beth when you get home, please. I was just supposed to deliver the invitation." Jimmy threw his hands up in mock frustration. "I can't believe you women would expect anything more from me than that!" He winked at Calvin.

Now Amanda was shaking her head at Jimmy. "You're right. I beg your pardon. You left-brain thinkers drive me nuts."

Amanda pulled at Calvin by their joined hands, telling her own left-brain thinker it was time to move on. "I'll call the one in her right mind as soon as we get home. Good-bye, Jimmy," she called over her shoulder. Calvin threw up his free arm as if to protest being dragged away. Jimmy headed for a different door.

*   *   *

At one o'clock, with a fresh leafy salad in hand, Calvin and Amanda arrived at the Steward's home. Jimmy already had the steaks going and Beth had the table set with all the trimmings, except the salad. She made room for the bowl, then she and Amanda went into little Jimmy's room. He was sleeping so they only peaked in at him. Amanda missed the smell of a baby and her heart ached for hers. At the same time it was filled with joy for her friends. At first it was very difficult for Amanda to see any child without crying. Then she'd been able to only *want* to cry, but didn't. She'd finally reached a point where she was able to feel joy for other mothers. Sadness was not her favorite place to be, so she learned to be happy whenever she could.

The women returned to the kitchen just as Jimmy and Calvin came in through the sliding glass door with steaming hot steaks.

"Who's ready to eat?" Jimmy asked in a booming voice.

"Not so loud," Beth scolded him. "I worked hard to get your son to sleep after his upset stomach this morning and I don't need you waking him up."

"Sorry," Jimmy said sheepishly. "You know I haven't gotten used to having him around yet."

"He hasn't gotten the hang of changing diapers yet, either," Beth told their friends.

"If I know Jimmy," Calvin started, "he hasn't even tried."

"Thanks, man, get me in trouble." Jimmy stepped in front of his wife and said, "Let's eat before it gets cold."

When everyone was seated, Jimmy gave thanks for the meal and friends. Their conversation turned from Edwards Construction's latest project to the next project, back to diaper changing abilities, to summer vacation plans. On it went from one subject to another until the food was gone.

After the kitchen was cleaned, the two women and a five-week-old infant joined the men in the rec room in the basement. Calvin felt very much at home in Jimmy's basement since the two men had worked side by side to finish it off the year before. The two men bantered back and forth as they played pool. The two women sat on the couch nearby and enjoyed little Jimmy before he decided he had been awake long enough without eating.

Amanda stayed close by but was respectful of their time together. A pang of sadness swept over her as she remembered sharing this special time with each of her daughters. Katrina had only been weaned for about five months when they were stolen. Amanda had been grateful she'd already weaned Katrina. She couldn't imagine how horrible it would have been if she had still been nursing her. There would have been physical ache on top of the heartache.

Amanda wondered if Katrina had begun potty training since she'd be two in a month. Amanda remembered how quickly Jessica had caught on to using the "big girl potty." Katrina began showing interest before they were stolen. Amanda smiled as she remembered the times Jessi had gone into the bathroom with Katrina right behind her. They'd teased her, calling her a nosey Kat. Amanda was almost to the point of tears from the memories when Calvin called her name.

Amanda joined Calvin and Jimmy beside the pool table. They were good-naturally arguing over something Amanda considered trivial. She settled the argument, kissed Calvin, and returned to her place beside Beth, who had just finished nursing little Jimmy.

"Would you hold him while I run upstairs and put myself back together?" Beth asked.

"As long as he doesn't throw up on me like he did you this morning."

"JJ, don't throw up on Auntie Amanda," Beth said as she passed her son to her friend.

Amanda cuddled JJ. Don't remember, she told herself. Don't remember. Just think about the little bundle of joy in your arms. Amanda cooed, snuggled, and kissed her small charge until his mother returned. Beth didn't ask Amanda to return JJ, but Amanda felt compelled to do so, lest she cry again over the loss of her own bundles of joy.

Beth and Amanda chatted as JJ slept in his mother's arms and the men played pool. Finally, Calvin mentioned wanting to go home before the evening services. Everyone wrapped up their socializing and the Edwardses bid their hosts good-bye.

Once in their van, Calvin asked Amanda what it was that almost made her cry while Beth was feeding Jimmy Jr.

"I was thinking about the feeling of relief that Kat had been weaned before she was stolen and if their new parents had begun potty training her yet." Calvin reached between them and found her hand, giving it an understanding squeeze.

"Was it that obvious I was about to cry?"

"No. I just know you that well."

"I thought I'd lose it when Beth handed JJ to me. My arms ache so bad to hold our babies." Tears filled Amanda's eyes and sadness swept over her.

"I know how that feels." He squeezed her hand again. "Maybe we shouldn't talk about that for now. I can see it's upsetting you and I can't hold you right this minute like I want to. Let's talk about something else."

Amanda withdrew her hand to wipe her eyes. His hand was waiting for her when she finished. As his hand found hers again, he asked, "Where do you want to put your new picture?"

"I was thinking in the living room on the west wall if you don't mind."

"That's exactly where I pictured it when I first saw it. I think it belongs there. That's probably why we haven't put anything up there since we moved in," he said. "And I think," he lifted their hands to his mouth, gently kissing hers, "you belong with me."

"You have always been such a sweet talker and romantic. Even the weather works for you."

"Huh?"

Amanda indicated out the window as a light snow began falling.

"I hadn't noticed. But if it works to my advantage, I'll take all the help I can get."

Amanda smiled as he pushed the button to the garage door.

"Wait right there," Calvin told her as he pulled the van to a complete stop. He killed the engine, then quickly made his way out of and around the van to open her door.

"Aren't you just the perfect gentleman?" Amanda eyed him suspiciously as he opened the door and extended his hand to her. "You wouldn't be looking for something, would you?"

"No, ma'am. I'm just part of a dying breed of," he changed his voice to mimic hers, "perfect gentlemen." They entered the house laughing.

They changed clothes for the second time and returned to the van for the trip back to church.

* * *

"Do you want a piece of pie?" Amanda asked Calvin when they returned an hour and a half later.

"Sure, but let's get this picture up first so we can enjoy looking at it while we eat."

"Good idea. But will we get to bed before midnight?" Amanda teased him.

"As it happens, I already have the level and stud finder in the living room. I just need to get the hammer and nails out of my truck."

"When did you find time to put that stuff in the living room?"

Calvin lovingly wrapped his arms around his wife and tilted her chin up so he could look into her eyes. "Lady, you are so beautiful. I found the time while you were still changing before church tonight." He ran his hand over her backside and squeezed. "You have to slow down for the curves."

Amanda wiggled out of his arms. "Do you mind?"

He reached for her. "Don't you think I'll complete my appointed task if I'm distracted?"

"I do think that," she said matter-of-factly.

"All right then, you fix the pie and I'll find a stud."

"I already found my stud," she said as she gave his backside a swat when he walked away.

"Hey!"

"What's good for the gander is good for the goose." She smiled.

Later, after the picture was hung and the plates empty, the Edwardses readied themselves for bed.

As they knelt beside their bed, Calvin asked, "Do you have any prayer requests?"

"Laurinda and Ronnie are on my mind. She was at Judy's yesterday when I got there. The way she described him told me she didn't just think of him as just another employee. I'm concerned she'll rush into something without thinking about the consequences."

They joined hands as Calvin began, "Dear Heavenly Father, please forgive us of our sins and help us to always serve and please You.

"You know our concern for our friend Laurinda and new employee, Ronnie. Father, they are showing a great deal of interest in each other. We know Laurinda loves You dearly but we don't know about Ronnie. We know Your word says we are not to be unequally yoked, so, Father, I pray if Ronnie doesn't know and love You, that You will use me to led him to You. If You intend for them to be together, I pray You will give them the peace You gave me before I asked this beautiful lady to marry me. If there's any way we can help along the way, please show us.

"I'm amazed that the Creator of the universe would take time to listen to us, but am so grateful You do. I'm grateful that what concerns us, concerns You. So I ask these things in confidence knowing that if we seek Your will, things will be done here on Earth as they are in Heaven. In Jesus' name, amen."

Calvin gently squeezed Amanda's hand, then opened his eyes and helped her up from the floor. They climbed into bed and he pulled her close to his chest, wrapping his strong arms around her. "Sweet dreams," he told her as he kissed the back of her head. Within minutes the sound of her steady breathing told Calvin she was asleep. He took a moment more with his Maker. "Lord, please do give her sweet dreams tonight." Praying in faith, he knew it would happen.

Chapter 5

Calvin's prayer from the night before had been answered. Amanda hadn't been tormented by bad dreams. Instead, he was awakened by the radio playing a song he didn't recognize, but took a moment to enjoy before turning it off. He kissed Amanda lightly on the forehead before climbing out of bed to kneel beside it.

When he finished his prayers and opened his eyes, he noticed Amanda beginning to stretch. "Good morning, beautiful."

She rolled over to face him with a smile across her face. "Good morning, yourself."

Calvin wanted very much to climb back into bed and stay with her all day, but knew he had responsibilities he could not put off. Instead, he leaned over the bed and gave her another kiss. Her response made him want to stay all the more. "That bed looks as inviting as do you, Mrs. Edwards."

"Really?"

"I know. You stay right there 'til I come home and we'll pick up from here."

"Yeah, right!" she laughed. "You know I have a full day ahead of me. For a change," she added as an afterthought.

"So you do, and so do I. But if I don't get out of here, I won't get any of it done." With that, he turned and headed for the bathroom.

Amanda took his place beside the bed to start her day. She'd read something a year before about not having time to pray and how the whole day was messed up because of it. By the end of the story

43

the author had decided he didn't have time *not* to pray. Ever since then, she'd started her day in prayer. It helped that Calvin shared her feelings, but she would have done it either way.

Amanda considered joining Calvin in the shower, but decided against it based on his earlier comments. Instead, she went to the kitchen to make breakfast for them both, a rare occurrence on a weekday but something they both loved.

After Amanda stopped by the bathroom to tell Calvin she was fixing breakfast for them, he hurried through his morning routine to have extra time with his wife. After breakfast, he accepted the full thermos and his lunch from Amanda, then reluctantly left after kissing her good-bye.

Mechanically, Amanda went through the motions of starting the shower. Though she tried to concentrate on what needed to be done today, her thoughts returned to that day, as they so often did, when she was in the shower. Horror had taken over after she realized that neither of the girls were in Katrina's room. She'd checked the back door screen, then the front. Panic gripped her as she realized the screen door was not only unlocked, but cut as well. Amanda searched outside for them but in her heart she knew they were gone. She called Calvin. He told her to call the police when they hung up and that he was on his way home.

Amanda had thought waiting for both Calvin and the police had been the hardest waiting she'd ever done. Over the days and weeks and then months that followed she realized she'd been wrong.

Amanda turned off the shower, dried off, and then curled up on the bed, still unable to pull herself from the memory.

The police had arrived just moments ahead of Calvin. Amanda was already answering their questions when she saw Calvin. She ran out to meet him and he wrapped his strong, loving arms around her. Many questions raced through his mind, but he knew Amanda needed to be talking to the police, not him, so he gently guided her back into the house.

She recalled sitting on the couch next to Calvin, answering every question the best she could. No, the girls were not likely to have just left the house. No, she couldn't think of anyone who would want to take or hurt them. No, she hadn't heard anything. No one had been following them that she knew of. So many "no" answers finally lead to one "yes." She took the pictures of the girls from her wallet and gave them to the officer.

After the police had fingerprinted nearly everything in the house, they left with a pad full of information, a picture of both girls, but no answers. Calvin had remained quiet through most of the questioning since Amanda had been the one there when it happened. After Calvin escorted the police to the door, he turned on Amanda.

"How could you let this happen? Why weren't you watching them? What if we never see them again?" Calvin had never spoken to her like that and she was shocked. The look of horror on her face made him stop and think.

"Amanda, I'm sorry. I shouldn't have said all that. I'm just scared. I didn't mean to accuse you. I know you're a great mom and you would never knowingly let anything happen to either one of them." His apology came as quickly as his tears afterward. He closed the distance between them in two large strides, then encircled his wife in his arms. "Baby, I am so sorry," he kept saying softly to her as she finally began to cry.

Both Calvin's and Amanda's parents had been called and together all six people watched the six o'clock news report that told of the girls' disappearance and showed their pictures. Howard and Delilah Edwards had thought to order pizza, but it sat untouched as they prayed for the recovery of their grandchildren. By the eleven o'clock news, the pizza was gone and so were the grandparents. Calvin and

Amanda stayed up long enough to see their daughters' story once more.

Amanda tried to sleep, but couldn't. She wandered from bedroom to bedroom, lying first in Jessica's bed, then on Katrina's floor. She held their pajamas close to her nose trying to breathe them back to her somehow, back home into her aching arms. More tears fell as Amanda hurt, knowing she couldn't bring them back and not knowing if she'd ever see them again. She'd cried herself to sleep on Katrina's floor, sleeping fitfully.

Calvin slept fitfully, too. He'd checked on Amanda each time he heard her cry out. She'd been asleep so he left her alone. He wanted her with him, but he understood her need to be in the baby's room.

Morning came before either of them were ready. They met in the hall looking like zombies. Calvin suggested that they go back to bed and Amanda agreed. Calvin called the work site the day before explaining what had happened. He told them not to expect him the next day or two. He knew they would be all right without him.

They slept for a couple of hours before the phone rang. The eleven o'clock news report had produced a call from an airline attendant from the Capital City Airport. She'd seen both girls and a little boy with an older woman whom the attendant presumed was their grandmother. All the children appeared to be fine, so there was no cause for suspicion at the time. The woman purchased tickets to Chicago, telling the attendant that they were meeting the children's parents to travel on from there. The attendant said the oldest child had been especially quiet, as if someone had threatened her to do so. The little girl wouldn't even answer the attendant's casual questions.

The attendant was scheduled to give a description to a sketch artist at one o'clock that afternoon. Amanda and Calvin had readily agreed to go to the station, eager to meet the woman who'd last seen their children.

Presently Amanda rolled over on the bed so she could see the pictures of the girls that hung on their bedroom wall. She remembered looking at the completed sketch but was unable to identify the woman. At the time she was sure she'd never seen the woman before. Amanda stared at the pictures of her babies until her eyes filled again with tears. Finally, emotionally exhausted, Amanda fell asleep in the middle of the bed.

Forty minutes later she awoke to the phone ringing. "Hello," she said in a groggy voice.

"I'm sorry, did I wake you?" Judy asked. "I can call back later. I just wanted to know if Calvin liked your hair and if you two had a good time on Saturday."

Amanda focused on the clock. "It's okay. I should be up and around anyway. I cried myself to sleep because I was remembering the girls this morning."

'Oh, I'm so sorry, Amanda. Do you want to come over so we can talk?"

"No, thank you. I've got laundry and a few other chores to do around here. Besides, you don't need me over there all red eyed and sad. I might scare away your customers."

"Any customer of mine who didn't understand wouldn't be a customer for long."

"Thanks, but I'll just stay here."

"You know where I am if you need me."

"You always take such good care of me."

"Speaking of taking care of you, how did it go Saturday? Did he like the braid?"

"Yes, of course. I don't know how many times he told me I was beautiful or called me beautiful. It was almost embarrassing. Did you know about the surprises?"

"When you were here I only knew he was taking you out to dinner and a movie. By the time he left I knew about the negligee.

You know I can get my customers to tell me just about anything when I have a pair of scissors in their hair."

Both women laughed.

"So he told you about the negligee?"

"Yes, and how he had to have help picking it out. He was so embarrassed. Nothing was gonna stand in that man's way of treating you to a night you'd never forget." Judy paused. "Sooooo, was it a night to remember?"

"Judy!" Amanda exclaimed. "You know that I never kiss and tell. So he had to have help with the negligee?"

"Don't ever tell him I told you. He might not ever forgive me. Or worse, he might not ever tell me another secret."

"And how, exactly, would that affect me?" Amanda jokingly inquired. Before her friend could answer, she asked, "Did you know about the picture?"

"What picture? You guys took pictures? Manny, I never figured you two for that type of couple. Do tell."

"Get serious." Amanda told her about the picture and how Jimmy had taken it to the bed and breakfast. "Judy, it's the most beautiful picture. It's number three in his Sweetheart Hideaways Collection. It's called *Teacup Cottage*. There's a little church and cottage in the background on the left. The road leading by the main cottage in the foreground is muddy and rutted. There is a third cottage between the main one and the church. The details in this picture are fabulous. The main cottage looks so real and inviting that you want to knock on the door and go in for a cup of tea with whomever you find inside."

"Sounds wonderful."

"I doubt there's a real cottage like this anywhere. God gave Thomas Kinkade a wonderful talent. That he is a Christian as well makes the painting all the more valuable to me." Amanda paused and thought for a moment. "Because it came from my husband and the way he did it makes it totally priceless."

"I never knew Calvin was a romantic. You are so lucky to have him. It's not fair. You get it right the first time and I have to go through two bums before I realize I'm better off without the male species around."

"I am blessed to have him. Luck had nothing to do with it and you know it. You just needed Divine help on the search committee."

"Yeah, yeah, whatever. So where's the picture now?"

"He hung it in the living room last night."

"How long did it take the perfectionist this time? Half hour or was it more?"

"This time he had the level ready and found the stud he wanted to use right off. It only took him ten minutes. He didn't yell at me this time. I was so proud of him."

Amanda recalled the first time they'd tried to hang a picture together and he'd gotten upset with her because she thought it looked level but it was not. He refused to put the picture up until the nail holes he'd created had been repaired and painted. That had been early in their marriage "before many of the kinks had been worked out" as Amanda liked to say. Calvin told people she had finally trained him to do whatever she wanted. Anyone who knew them knew the truth. They had learned early on to put the other person first. When they began doing that, everything fell into place for them, just as the Bible had said it would.

"I still say you married Prince Charming and I got the frogs."

"I am blessed," Amanda said. "So did you talk to your doctor today or do I have the wrong day?"

"I went this morning and she said that the trouble with my eyes are probably stressed related. She wants me to slow down at work. I laughed at her and said if I slowed down at work, I wouldn't be able to pay her bill. I also said I wasn't coming back unless I was dead."

"Don't talk like that. You aren't going to die. She is right, though, you know. I know that you could use some help paying your bills.

Have you ever considered getting a roommate to help with the mortgage?"

"I doubt I'd find anyone who would put up with the smell and the crazy hours I sometimes keep."

"Just think about it. I'll be praying for you," Amanda said as her friend was saying good-bye because she had a customer walking in. They made plans to have lunch together on Wednesday.

* * *

Amanda decided to wait until after lunch to start laundry. Right after the girls were stolen laundry became her hardest task. Standing over the pile of clothes needing to be sorted, she remembered the last time she'd washed the girls' clothes. It'd been difficult to wash their clothes for the last time, but it'd been even more difficult for her to do the first few loads of clothes without the presence of any of the girls' things. Tears swelled in her eyes as she threw clothes into different piles on the basement floor. Before she knew it, she was once again drowning in her sorrows. Mondays were so difficult for her that she wished she could eliminate the day entirely.

There's no going to sleep this time, Amanda thought as she pulled herself together and went on with her painful task. She considered getting some of the girls' clothes to wash and then dismissed the idea as foolish, just as she had done many times before. She wiped her eyes and loaded the washer.

With the machine started and the tears stopped, Amanda decided to read the Janette Oke book she'd chosen a few nights before. With a tall glass of water beside her, she settled herself on the couch to wait for the washer to stop. Thankful for the distraction from her painful memories, she dove into the book and stayed until the end. The washer finished before she did, but she didn't care. She put the clothes in the dryer and started the second load, then returned the book to the bookshelf. The second book in the series, *Love's Enduring Promise,* would serve as her next distraction.

Only a few minutes into the book the phone rang. A lady from church called to ask for help in sorting the clothes they'd received for their clothing bank. Amanda agreed to stop by on Thursday afternoon. It would be a welcome interruption to the jobs she had planned at her parents' and could easily fit into her plan of having the drapes cleaned. She was sure she'd be able to pick them up on Thursday afternoon if she got them dropped off tomorrow morning, she reasoned.

She returned to her book and the laundry, alternating between the two until the laundry was completely done and ready to be ironed. She unwillingly laid the book aside to go about the unpleasant task of ironing. By the time she finished it, it was time to start dinner. She replayed the day over in her mind, trying to decide whether or not to tell Calvin about her bouts of crying. She decided to, since she never kept anything from him, except for the occasional surprise.

As she set the table her memories returned. This easy task had become Jessica's first chore after she turned three. Jessi was so proud the first night she set the table that she had insisted on resetting it just to show Daddy how she'd done it.

By the time Calvin came through the door, Amanda was once again in tears. He closed the distance between them in seconds after realizing she was crying. He helped her up from the chair and held her close, trying to comfort her. Without even knowing for sure why she was crying, he had said all the right things to help her stop.

Once she was breathing calmly, he reseated her, took off his coat, tossed it over the closest chair, and knelt down in front of her. "Rough day?"

"Monday" was all she managed to say before the tears sprang up again in her eyes.

"I know," he said sympathetically, rubbing her back with his callused hand. "Next week why don't you plan to spend Monday with me?"

"Doing what?" she asked as she dried her eyes on her sleeve.

"Well, I could use an extra roofer." His lighthearted mood helped her to laugh at his suggestion. "Seriously, I'm sure I can find something for you to do besides laundry." Calvin was pretty sure that's why she was crying. It had been happening since the first Monday after the girls were stolen. He'd suggested that she do laundry a different day or that they send their laundry out. She had adamantly refused to send it out, saying he worked hard for his money and that is would be a foolish way to spend it. He didn't argue with her logic, but he would have gladly spent the money to spare her the pain.

"I'm not crying because of the laundry right now, but I was earlier. I'm crying now because I remembered the first time Jessi set the table."

"Amanda, we need to remember those things with gladness, not sadness. Think of all the wonderful smiles our daughters gave us while God allowed us have them."

Amanda knew he was right because they had discussed this before. But knowing it and doing it were two different things. Her heart ached so bad it was almost impossible to remember the girls without the pain.

As though he'd read her thoughts, he said, "Remember, with God all things are possible."

"Yes, I know." She looked directly at him. "I wish I had your faith."

"I'd be lost without it," he said as he continued to lighten her mood.

She joined his playful mood this time. "Yes, you would be lost without your faith in more ways than one." She put her hands on his chest and playfully, before the master of the house gets upset with me, "tried to push him over.

He backed away but caught her as she stood up. Pulling her close to him, his kiss reminded her of the morning and promises for the evening before releasing her to finish dinner. He reached for his coat and playfully stated, "The master of the house would return," after he'd hung up his coat and washed his hands. He growled as he left the room. He had often sent both girls running for their mother when he'd done that in the past. He smiled at the memory, then asked God to help his wife have *pleasant* memories as well.

After dinner, Calvin sent Amanda out of the kitchen, insisting he could handle the clean up. He suggested that she read until he was done, and that she should be prepared to lose at cribbage when he was finished.

"I'm not sure you got up early enough," she said as she left for the living room.

"I don't have to get up early to beat you," he called after her as he cleared the table. As he wiped the table off, he stopped to watch her. Sensing his stare, she told him to get back to work.

With the kitchen in order, he retrieved the cribbage board and cards from the dresser drawer. Amanda sat waiting at the table when he returned. In spite of many hands, which were not in his favor, Calvin came from behind to win the first game. Amanda pleaded with him to give her one more chance, which he strongly considered rejecting, but didn't. To his dismay she won the second game. Not like he'd won the first, but rather by a big gap between them. The competitive side of him wanted to play a tiebreaker, but the husband in him had another idea.

After bedtime tasks were completed, Calvin and Amanda took their usual place beside the bed to pray. He gently took hold of her hands and began speaking to her instead of the Lord. He used their joined hands to turn her to face him before he spoke. "Honey, I want to warn you about what I'm going to be praying about tonight."

She gave him a questioning, but trusting, look.

"I don't want you to be surprised or hurt by what I feel led to say."

"I trust you," she said. "God made you my spiritual leader and neither of you have let me down so far."

"Thank you. I'm just afraid that what I say may cause you to cry," he said with a great deal of compassion in his voice.

"Well, Jesus promised never to leave me and I'm fairly sure you won't either after prayers, so I'll be all right." Amanda squeezed his hand. "Go ahead."

They turned back toward the bed. After asking for forgiveness of their sins, Calvin took his petition to his Savior. "Dearest Father, I come humbly before You tonight claiming Your word over the helpmate that You've given me. Father, she is suffering from the effects of the evil one's work. I know that Your Spirit dwells in her and because of that You have promised her peace. The evil one has stolen her peace by stealing our children, Lord. You know that our hearts are heavy and laden with this pain. But we, I, ask that You restore Your peace to her heart, Lord. Help her to cast all her cares on You. Make her shine like the sun, and hold her in the palm of Your hand. I pray You will help her to be anxious for nothing and thankful in everything so that she may have Your peace, which surpasses all understanding. She needs Your strength every day to help her make it through. I know that she trusts in You, so I claim Your word from Isaiah that promises to keep in perfect peace those who do. I pray You will give her Your peace for all the days which You have preappointed for her."

He prayed for the safety of their little girls and that God would continue to watch over them. "Thank You for all You've given us and for all You do for us. If You choose not to bring the girls back to us, please give us the strength to endure. Remind us daily of Your care for both us and them. In Jesus' name, amen."

"Amen," Amanda repeated after him.

This morning, Calvin's desire had been to share with Amanda in a physical way tonight. After seeing her pain, his desire changed to wanting to comfort her. He knew the best way to do that was to lay her hurt at their Master's wounded feet.

He helped her up from her knees and handed her a tissue. His tender act seemed to bring a new flood of tears. Through the tears she managed to say, "Thank you. Thank you for filling in for me and asking the Lord for what I knew I needed but didn't know how to ask for. I'm grateful He put us together."

"You're welcome, my love. There isn't anything I wouldn't do for you. Now let's get some sleep."

Amanda wiped her eyes, blew her nose, climbed onto the bed, and took her spot wrapped safely in the arms of the man she loved.

Chapter 6

Tuesday morning brought a new day and new feelings for Amanda. She sensed a peace inside her that she hadn't known since before the girls were stolen. To her disappointment, Calvin was already gone by the time she woke up, but even that didn't bother her as much.

After her morning prayer, she breezed through her shower, and was out and ready for breakfast without the usual flood of painful memories. During breakfast Amanda looked over the list of things she'd wanted to do for her parents. Some things she had gotten approval for, others she decided to keep as a surprise. She was looking forward to cleaning the garage apartment, one of her surprises. Since she and Judy had lunch plans for Wednesday, she decided to start the apartment today. She decided to make the curtains her first priority, hoping she would get them back by Thursday. With her own kitchen in order, Amanda left for her childhood home with a spring in her step despite the less than spring-like weather conditions.

A short time later she removed all the curtains from the house and the apartment and was back in the van headed to the cleaners.

"Would you like us to rehang them for you?" the sales clerk asked Amanda.

"I'd better not spend the extra money. I'm doing this for my parents. But thanks for the offer."

"Ma'am, there is no extra charge. We would have stopped out and taken them down for free as well."

"In that case, yes. I would like someone else to rehang them. It was a chore for me to take them down alone. I wasn't looking forward to putting them back up." Amanda gave the clerk the additional information needed to complete the job, and then scheduled a time early Friday morning for it to be done. Amanda paid, then left, feeling very satisfied with that job out of the way and glad to have more time available to help sort clothes at church later in the week.

Amanda returned to the house and gathered her mother's cleaning caddy and a new roll of paper towels, then headed for the apartment that had once been hers and Calvin's home. She and Calvin had turned the space above her parents' garage into an apartment before they had married so they could live there until they could build a home of their own. Over the years since they had left, Frank and Sandy rented it from time to time. A new couple from the church found themselves in need of a place to stay short-term so the Steinmans decided to rent it again. Sandy told Amanda that she was planning to clean it until Frank whisked her away on vacation. Amanda decided to surprise her by having it done when she got back.

Amanda climbed the stairs, then turned the key with her free hand and pushed the door open for the second time today. It didn't smell bad, but Amanda decided it didn't smell good, either. The new tenants wouldn't want to find it this way. Amanda began cleaning and scrubbing everything. As she did, pleasant memories of the days she and Calvin had spent making it into an apartment flooded her memory.

The apartment had been Frank's idea in the beginning, but soon the whole family warmed up to the idea and wanted to get involved. After the initial excitement wore off, Amanda's sisters saw how much work it would be and only Amanda and Calvin had been left to work on the project. Wedding plans were in the works at the same time, but Sandy and Amanda worked on those during the day while Calvin worked on building his business. At night he would come over and together he and Amanda would work until ten or eleven. Amanda was concerned that Calvin was going to make her a very young widow even before they were married. His enthusiasm and youth, combined with his love for her, gave him more than enough energy to complete all his tasks. This project, he told her, was a labor of love. Besides, he had reasoned with her, he always took Sunday off.

As Amanda ran a damp cloth along the walls, she remembered the first night they began installing drywall. She had listened closely as Calvin explained how the drywall was to be hung, then plastered. Waiting to paint it seemed like a very long week. When they finally did get to paint, Doreen offered to help Amanda during the day to surprise Calvin. That surprise was the first of many between them. The Thomas Kinkade picture had been the most recent. Amanda's mind switched from remembering the past to thinking of a surprise for Calvin. It wasn't that she was trying to outdo him, she just loved the look on his face when he discovered the surprise. She thought of the surprise that had taken her parents away for the week. A little more than I can swing, she thought as she moved from the living room to the bedroom to wash those walls.

The little room brought back a flood of memories, including their first night here after returning from their week-long honeymoon. The long hours they spent discussing the future, including their home and children. They both wanted two children, but had decided to wait until they started their house.

Ten months later they began construction on their home on the land that Calvin's grandparents had left him. Calvin worked harder on their house than he had on the apartment. Amanda spent as much time as she could helping him. One month after construction began she became pregnant with Jessica. She was less helpful until the morning sickness had passed.

She continued to work days as the bookkeeper for Edwards Construction and nights on the house when she could. Before she could step down as the bookkeeper, she had to hire her replacement and train them on how Calvin liked things done.

The first question she asked the candidate, Laurinda Bowman, was about her name. Laurinda explained that it was the feminine version of Lawrence. When she told Amanda her suggested life scripture verse was 1 Corinthians 15:57, Amanda knew she was the girl for the job. Amanda tried finishing the remaining interviews with an open mind, but her heart was set on Laurinda as long as Calvin agreed. That evening Amanda told him about Laurinda and her own desire to hire her on the spot. After they discussed it, they prayed for wisdom. The following day Amanda called Laurinda and asked her to come back for another interview with her husband. After meeting her and feeling the Lord's guidance, Calvin gave his approval. It was a decision none of them had ever regretted.

After training Laurinda and feeling comfortable that she knew the job well, Amanda stopped working five months into the pregnancy. With only three months to the completion of the house, Amanda devoted her time to putting the finishing touches on their home.

Awaiting the arrival of their first child took only a month longer than waiting to move in. On moving day, Amanda was only allowed to direct people on where to put things. Her time for hard labor came on July 11 when Jessica Marie Edwards decided to make her appearance a few days early.

Amanda remembered waking early in her new bedroom feeling a little uncomfortable but not in pain. She went to the bathroom and knew from the classes they'd taken that the baby was coming soon. She slept restlessly until Calvin's alarm went off a short time later. Then, as if Jessi thought the alarm was for her, Amanda was gripped with a tight contraction. Amanda was actually out of the bed before

Calvin. She began pacing until the contractions became too much to take standing up. Calvin took the fastest shower of his life, then dressed and called the doctor's answering service. The doctor was delivering a baby so the nurse returned Calvin's call. After Calvin explained what was happening, the nurse told Calvin to come in right away.

They went through the emergency room because of the early hour. Calvin dropped Amanda off to a waiting intern, then parked the car and ran back to check her in. Amanda had been taken to the labor and delivery floor without stopping. She was already on the bed by the time Calvin had changed into scrubs and found her. The doctor walked into the room just behind Calvin. Calvin took his place beside Amanda's head and the doctor checked her progress.

Being a woman of few words, the doctor told Amanda, "On the next contraction, I want you to push."

Within minutes, Amanda and Calvin were looking into the beautiful blue eyes of their first child. Calvin voiced a prayer from both of their hearts. "Thank You, God, for this healthy daughter that You've given us. Help us to raise her in Your ways."

Presently, Amanda cleaned the room with a new sense of joy and peace. Remembering Jessi's birth the day before might have brought pain and tears. After Calvin petitioned the Lord on her behalf, pain had been replaced with peace. Amanda thanked Him for His peace and for Calvin.

Amanda went into the bathroom to empty the dirty water. The water was shut off to the apartment, so Amanda returned to the house for fresh water. She fixed the water and a sandwich for herself before returning to the apartment. She sat on the floor by the kitchen sink and recalled more pleasant memories while she ate. She recalled when Jessi found out that she and Calvin had lived above Grandpa and Grandma's garage. Jessi wouldn't rest until she had been shown the efficiency apartment that they'd created. Amanda told her about how it had once been a playroom for herself and her sisters. Then Jessi insisted they turn it back into a playroom. They explained that Grandpa and Grandma were going to let someone else live there. Jessi accepted this after she was reminded of the playroom in her own home and the one inside this house.

Amanda finished her lunch, then cleaned the bathroom. Behind the toilet she discovered some of the flooring was coming up. She made a mental note to ask Calvin to have someone come over on Friday to fix it. She made short work of the small room, then gathered her cleaning supplies and returned to the house to the get the vacuum cleaner. After the apartment was completely vacuumed, she relocked the door, then returned to the house where she quickly swept there as well.

By three the mail had been delivered. After depositing it on the table with the previous day's mail, she locked up and headed for the grocery store.

By six thirty when Calvin got home, dinner was ready and waiting. Amanda told him about everything she'd done, then remembered the bathroom floor.

"What do you think it needs?" Calvin asked.

"Probably just a little glue, but I'm not the carpenter in the family."

"You've lived with one long enough, haven't you?"

"Not unless my life is over, I haven't." Unlike many couples she knew, they had both truly meant the "death do us part" section of their wedding vows.

"You said Friday is the next time you'll be there?"

"Yes. I made arrangements to have the curtains rehung in the morning and I'm planning on repotting the plant mother keeps putting off."

"I'll have someone over there around ten if that works for you."

"I'll be elbow deep in dirt, but I can stop to let them in."

Calvin had seen his wife elbow deep in dirt, mud, bread dough, and a few other things as well. He decided right then who he'd send to fix the floor.

"I meant to ask you about Laurinda and Ronnie."

Calvin's change in subject didn't surprise Amanda, but his comment did. "Has something happened?"

"Not that I know of, but it might. Laurinda has been asking me about him ever since I hired him. I forgot to tell you that on Monday morning she asked me if I thought he was a Christian. I guess your concern in our prayer Sunday night was answered."

"What did you tell her?"

"That I didn't know for sure, but I didn't think so. Why?"

"Remember I told you Sunday night that she was at Judy's house on Saturday?" Calvin nodded in acknowledgment. "When I mentioned that I had the impression that you didn't think he was saved, her head jerked up so quickly I thought it would snap off. The look of disappointment was obvious. I think she'd like to get to know him better, but she won't if he isn't saved. I'd like to meet him. Maybe he could do the floor for me on Friday."

"Maybe," Calvin said, deep in thought.

"What's going on? I know that deep thinking look of yours. What are you up to?"

"Maybe we could have both of them over for dinner some night."

"She doesn't want anything to do with him if he's not saved. I just said that."

"You did say that. And you are right. Two people are not to be unequally yoked." He finished dinner and rose to begin clearing the table. "Maybe I'll just ask a few questions if the timing's right. You know, find out a little more about him. They would make a nice couple if…" Calvin let his thoughts trail off as he continued cleaning the kitchen.

Amanda asked what he wanted to do for the evening as she helped clean up.

"Maybe a video?"

"Sounds good to me."

* * *

"Smoking or nonsmoking?" the hostess asked Amanda after she requested a table for two.

"Nonsmoking, please. I'd like a booth by the window if you have one available."

"I'll check."

"Thank you." While Amanda waited, Judy came in. "She's getting us a booth by the window. Is that okay with you?"

"You know it is." Judy and Amanda hugged. "How are you today? I've been thinking about you since our conversation on Monday. I tried to call yesterday but got the machine."

"I am much better than I was on Monday. In fact, I'm feeling great. I cleaned the apartment yesterday so Mom wouldn't have to rush through it when she gets back."

"Ladies, if you will follow me, I will take you to your table."

"Thank you," Judy and Amanda both said after they were seated.

"Have you heard from them?"

"Not yet. I expect to get my first postcard today. I'm sure Mom's sent one every day. I'll keep getting them even after they get home." Both women laughed.

"Your mom has always been that way. So…what did you do with yourself this morning?" Judy asked as they looked over the menus the hostess had left them.

"Worked on my Sunday school lesson, took a shower, straightened the house. You know, the usual stuff."

"Still studying the Bible, are you? How can you keep doing that and going to church after all God has put you through?"

"God hasn't put me through anything. He may have allowed it to happen, but He didn't do this to me. He can take things or loved ones away from us. Our lives are mirroring the life of Job from the Bible. I'm trusting that God is still in control and that one day I will see my daughters again. If it weren't for God's strength, I wouldn't be able to go on without them. I get His strength from the Bible, church, and Calvin. So, yes, I'm still studying the Bible and I will continue to study it until the day I die or Jesus comes back. It wasn't so long ago that you believed in God and His word, too, you know. I remember praying the believer's prayer with you in tenth grade. What happened, Judy?"

"I guess I just thought His way was too narrow. It didn't look like as much fun as some of our other friends were having. Beside, you know what happened."

"You mean the…" Amanda began.

"Yes, the abortion. I know you don't even like to say the word. I know you didn't really want to be there because you thought what I was doing was wrong." Judy leaned across the table. "I thank you most for not acting all high and mighty. You know, for not condemning me or making me feel worse about what I did."

"It's not my place to condemn you. Only God can do that."

"And I'm sure He did. I know what I did was wrong. I bet I fell from grace that day, maybe even out of reach."

The waitress interrupted their conversation briefly to take their order. Amanda placed her order, then, as Judy placed hers, Amanda said a prayer that God would speak to Judy through her.

He didn't let her down. When the waitress left, Amanda held Judy's hand before speaking. "We've known each other for a very long time, right?"

"Right."

"Have I ever lied to you?"

"No."

"Judy, God will forgive you if you ask. He promised in His word that He will forgive us of *all* our sins and even cover them with the blood of Jesus so that He will remember them no more."

Tears filled Judy's eyes as Amanda spoke of the abortion as sin. She knew it was, but if she didn't acknowledge it, she didn't feel so guilty. God had been knocking at the door of Judy's heart since that time, and through Amanda, Judy was beginning to understand the feelings she'd been experiencing.

"Do you remember the prayer you prayed in tenth grade? First you acknowledged that you were a sinner, then you asked for forgiveness from that sin and asked Him to come into your life."

Judy nodded with tears in her eyes and a heavy heart.

"He loves you so much, He sent His Son to live among us, then die for us. He loves you so much that He gave up His only Son. He knows what it's like to give up a child. Your baby is in the arms of the most loving Father there's ever been." Amanda moved to sit beside her in the booth. Amanda gently placed her arm around Judy and together they prayed.

Judy spoke with a broken and humbled heart. "Dear God," she began, trying to remember prayers she had heard Amanda pray, "I know that I don't deserve to be forgiven for taking my unborn baby's life…" Judy sniffled. "Amanda says You love me no matter what. I want You to love me and I…" Judy sniffled again, rubbing her nose on the back of her hand. "I want You to forgive me. I need You to forgive me. I beg You to forgive me."

Amanda squeezed her shoulder for reassurance, encouraging her to go on. Amanda waited. Judy cried. No one spoke. Finally, Amanda began to pray. "Father, I lift Judy up to You. I pray that You'll touch her heart and heal her. Remind her daily of Your love and the forgiveness You've given her. Help her to know that You do care for her and that You're caring for her baby." Judy's shoulders shook. "Touch her life, Lord, make it whole. I pray that You'll give her a hunger for You and Your word because I know from personal experience, Lord, that she'll find comfort there." Amanda remained silent as Judy's sobs lessened. Judy swiped her nose again and gently nudged Amanda with her shoulder indicating she was done.

"We ask these things in Jesus' name, amen."

"Amen." Judy hugged her friend. "Thank you. I thought I was coming to cheer you up and look what happened."

"You did. Why don't you come to church with us on Sunday? Get to know the One who's just forgiven you."

The waitress approached the table carrying their meals, uncertain of where to place Amanda's plate.

"Just set it over there."

The waitress asked if everything was okay. Judy sniffled, then said, "Yep! I was just forgiven."

Amanda listened as Judy shared her testimony of what had just happened and some of the past. Amanda saw tears roll down the waitress's cheek. She prayed for the interaction.

Judy gave the waitress a business card and suggested she call sometime to talk. The waitress took the card and agreed to call.

After their meal the two friends hugged good-bye in the parking lot. Judy promised to be at church on Sunday.

Amanda stopped at her parents to take in the mail and water the plants before returning home. She could hardly wait to see Calvin to share her day with him.

* * *

Calvin arrived shortly after her. Amanda was thrilled to have him home early and shared with him her day of great enthusiasm.

After dinner was on the table and a blessing had been said, Calvin shared his day. "I spent some time with Ronnie today," he began. "I found out a lot about him, including his interest in Laurinda. He was raised Catholic but no longer attends church anywhere. He believes in God, but feels he'll never be 'good enough' to get into heaven."

"He believes the works mind set?"

"I'm afraid he does. He told me he'd been raised to believe you get to heaven by leading a good life, being honest with people, and by doing what the church tells you to do, including being baptized as a baby, which his parents did for him before his father left them. They taught him he had to go to classes, communion, and confession to get to heaven, and entrance into heaven is a merited reward. He said he had to be in church every weekend and holy day. After a while he became discontented with just being there and not *feeling* anything. He said he hoped the good things he'd done on earth would sit well with the Big Guy. He figured he'd never be good enough to get into heaven, so he stopped trying. Eventually, he stopped going to church and joined a gang."

"Oh, my gosh!" Amanda exclaimed. "Now I know that I don't want Laurinda to have anything to do with him."

"Hang on, wait 'til you hear the rest of the story. I invited him to Sunday school this weekend and he agreed to come."

"I guess the Edwardses will have two guests. Praise God! I hope and pray they both become permanent parts of our church family."

"Me, too. I would have just invited him to church, but since this week's lesson is on faith versus works, I thought it would be good for him."

"Isn't he going to think you're singling him out?"

"I don't think so. I explained the lesson and offered him the use of my book to look over the lesson before Sunday. I explained to him that he doesn't have to say anything in class unless he wants to.

I assured him no one will call on him. Besides, you know Romans 8:28."

"I do know that. You wanna know what else I know?"

"What?"

"I know I'm proud of you and glad God put us together. I know I love you more today than the day I married you." Amanda leaned closer to Calvin and joined him in an intimate kiss.

After the kiss, Calvin held his wife's chin between his thumb and forefinger and said, "Don't be proud of me. I didn't do anything. It was all God."

"I know that, but you didn't have to witness to Ronnie."

"Like you could've not witnessed to Judy?"

Neither of them knew it, but at that very moment God smiled because of them.

*   *   *

On Thursday Amanda didn't wake up until after Calvin had left. Again she showered without the pain she'd become accustomed to in the past six months. After breakfast, Amanda got her slippers from the bedroom and her boots and jacket from the front hall closet.

Amanda recognized the vehicles in the parking lot when she pulled in. She killed the engine, then popped the back hatch so she could get the clothing bags she'd brought from home. She picked up the bag of infant girls clothing and breathed in the smell of fresh fabric softener. Amanda shifted the small bag from her right hand to her left so she could remove the larger plastic bag that held her and Calvin's clothes. After setting that bag on the ground, she closed the hatch, retrieved the bag, and went inside.

Four elderly ladies greeted her. She was hugged by everyone before getting her bags set down. They all talked at once as they welcomed her and told her how they appreciated her help. They all knew about her heartbreaking experience and went on about how brave she'd been to bring the baby clothes.

"Calvin recently prayed for me to have peace. When that man talks, God really listens because I've had peace ever since. I no longer wake up crying. I still have tough moments, like last night sorting their clothes. Calvin reminded me of the good times we had with them," Amanda explained.

Once her bags were on the empty table, she addressed the oldest member of the group.

"Miss Margaret, it's wonderful to see you today. I know it's tough on you to get out. I've missed you the past two Sundays. I'm glad you're feeling better." Amanda gave her another hug. "Miss Ruby, you're a blessing to bring her and see after her. You should be careful, you know. No good deed ever goes unpunished," Amanda teased her. "Some wonderful blessing might just happen to you."

As the ladies went back to sorting clothes, Miss Ruby suggested a blessing that Amanda herself could provide. "Please get on the schedule to sing again real soon. You have a beautiful voice. I love to hear you sing. Sometimes I've wondered how you make it through a song without crying when I'm in my seat just bawling."

"You know, it has been a while."

"Too long," Miss Ruby said. Everyone agreed.

"I'll talk to Brother Jim on Sunday to let him know I'm available."

"And I'll tell him to do it soon!"

Amanda laughed with her. She knew Miss Ruby was a woman to be reckoned with, so she didn't argue. She did mention she'd need a little time to pick out a song and practice.

"All right then, I won't tell him to put you on next Sunday."

Amanda patted her on the back as she walked by her. "Thank you. To return the favor I promise to look for a song while I'm at the Family Christian Store today. I'm getting a book for one of Calvin's employees. By the way," Amanda directed her request to everyone, "would you all pray for Ronnie and my best friend Judy? They're both coming to church this Sunday. Ronnie was raised Catholic, while Judy was raised in a family of nonbelievers. She accepted the Lord into her life when we were younger, but after high school she stopped coming to church. Maybe you'll remember her."

"No trouble, dear," Miss Ruby spoke for all of them, "we'll pray for them."

The ladies completed their task in short time, leaving Amanda most of the afternoon for shopping.

Chapter 7

On Friday Amanda was giddy as she drove to her parents', partly because they'd be home the next day, and partly because she and Calvin had guests coming to church Sunday.

When the installers arrived, Amanda sent them to the apartment, then started separating and repotting the overgrown plant. She was pleasantly surprised to discover the man Calvin sent to fix the floor was himself. He smiled at her with a twinkle in his eye. He still loved to surprise her.

When the plant was done, Amanda cleaned up, signed the curtain hangers' release form, and then went to join Calvin.

"Ronnie asked me to thank you for the book you dropped off."

"Please tell him it was my pleasure," she said as she stood watching her husband work.

Calvin looked at her and said, "You're my pleasure." He stood up, his chore forgotten, and took her into his arms. "Remember?"

Amanda nodded.

"I'm glad we waited for that night. Our first time together right there." He pointed past her toward the first bedroom they shared. "If those installers weren't here, I'd…" He whispered in her ear, making her blush.

When he finished speaking, Amanda lifted her eyes to meet his. "They left just before I came up."

*   *   *

Saturday morning dawned bright and beautiful looking from inside the Edwards house. Outside was another story. Bitter cold set in during the night as light rain fell. By morning everything was covered with ice.

The weather kept Calvin home from work so the pair enjoyed a leisurely morning together. Over breakfast their conversation turned to the girls. They laughed about the time Jessi came to the kitchen where Calvin was looking over project specs, held up her right index finger, and said, "Noisy you, Dad," in her most grown up voice. She'd been so serious Calvin had to fight not to laugh. Calvin tucked her back in bed and promised to be quieter. The next morning she didn't remember anything.

They laughed about Jessi taking it upon herself to change six-month-old Kat's diaper. Amanda'd been grateful the diaper was empty. They recalled many times when Jessi had joined Kat in her baby bed. Sometimes the two were inseparable. Other times Amanda had to send, or take, each of them to their own rooms to separate them. The memories and laughter continued until they were in danger of being late to the airport.

They showered, then dressed quickly, not wanting to rush on the slick roads. They were grateful Jimmy had salted their drive and their road leading to the main road, which the county trucks had already salted.

"It's a blessing to have a friend in the landscaping business who does plowing and salting during the winter," Calvin said. "Remind me to call and thank him when we get back home."

A short time later, Calvin parked as close as possible to the main door. The flight board indicated the flight was delayed thirty minutes.

The minute Sandy and Amanda saw one another they squealed with delight. Bystanders would have thought they hadn't seen each other in seven years, not seven days.

With the luggage stowed in the back of the van, the foursome set off for the Steinman's home. Frank rode up front with Calvin. Amanda tried to direct her mother's attention to giving details about the trip, but Sandy said that could wait, she wanted to hear about Amanda's week. Amanda told her about Ronnie and Judy, and then described the rest of her week, excluding certain parts.

"Thanks so much for repotting that plant and getting the drapes done. Maybe when I get another coupon I will have the apartment curtains cleaned. I know I asked a lot of you last week, but do you think you'd have time to help me get the apartment ready for the renters? I'll have lots of laundry Monday and won't be able to get to it 'til Tuesday."

Amanda smiled and agreed to help. She told her mother about Calvin praying for her and how much better she felt. Sandy was thrilled that Amanda had finally found peace. She was also excited that Miss Ruby had talked her into getting back onto the music schedule.

When they arrived at the Steinman's home, Amanda could no longer keep her secret and took her mother upstairs to see the apartment. She opened the door with the key she'd put in her jacket on Friday. Sandy squealed with delight and thanked Amanda profusely. While Sandy admired the apartment, the men unloaded the van.

There wasn't much food in the house, so the foursome ordered pizza and settled in for a night of stories and pictures. Amanda couldn't get over the many amenities that were available to them on the ship.

Maria called to be sure everyone had gotten there safely. She said they would have to see them later when the roads were clear. Later, Doreen called from college to check on them, too.

Hours later the Edwardses said good-bye and returned home to discuss the next day's lesson.

"I thought of Ronnie when Kay talked about people who think God weighs a person's good works against their bad and admits people into heaven if the good outweighs the bad. I certainly hope that part doesn't offend him."

"Let's do more than hope."

They joined hands to pray. "Father God, we pray that Ronnie will come tomorrow with a searching heart. Don't let him take offense to Your word. Help him to understand we're saved by grace through faith and not through our works. Open his eyes to Your truth and help him to come to know You as his personal Lord and Savior.

"We give You thanks for the healing in Judy, and for Frank and Sandy's safe return. I thank You for this one You've given me. She is truly a blessing. I pray You'll help me to be the husband You'd have me to be for her. Thank You for the many blessings You've given on us. In Jesus' name, amen."

Calvin opened his eyes to find Amanda crying. "You're sweet to say I'm a blessing."

He squeezed her hand, then kissed her nose. "Lady, next to the Lord Jesus Christ, you are *the* most important person in the world to me. I'd lay down my life for you."

"Then you're every bit the husband God would have you to be."

Calvin kissed her again; then they continued their discussion.

"I wonder if Ronnie's even looked at the book."

"He asked a few questions on Friday so I'm sure he has. I told him we're on chapter 4 this week. I didn't suggest that he start at the beginning or there."

"I'm sure he did the right thing, whichever he chose. Besides, think about what Kay said on day six." Amanda flipped through her book until she found the right page. "'It's impossible ever to do or fail to do anything that can't be covered by the grace of God.'"

"I thought of Judy when I read that. I know it might be a crazy idea, but do you think she'd do this study with us?"

"I doubt she'd be comfortable coming in right now, but she might be willing to start with me from the beginning. I've learned so much from this book already, I'm sure a second time through it I'd learn even more. I'll suggest it to her tomorrow."

Calvin looked at his watch. "We need to wrap this up, it's time for bed."

*   *   *

The Edwardses arrived early the next morning anticipating Ronnie's arrival to Sunday school. To their surprise, he was waiting for them on the front steps.

The two men shook hands and then Calvin introduced Ronnie to Amanda. As Ronnie thanked Amanda in person for the book, the party made their way to their classroom where Calvin introduced Ronnie to the group leader.

After handshakes and some small talk, Ronnie told Calvin he'd read to chapter 4 yesterday. "I guess that ice storm was a blessing for me."

"God works in mysterious ways."

As the classroom filled up, Laurinda stuck her head in the door to say good morning to her friends. She was going to ask if that was Ronnie's car she'd seen in the parking lot, but her eyes answered that for her. Amanda excused herself to speak to her.

"What's he doing here?" Laurinda asked once they were out of earshot.

"It is a public place. Maybe he just wandered in off the street," Amanda teased her.

"Come on. Really, tell me."

"Calvin talked to him this week, then invited him to class, so I bought him the book on Thursday. He caught up to us yesterday since they didn't work."

"Now I'm really sorry I didn't sign up for this class."

"You don't sign up for a class because of who is in it…"

"I didn't mean…well, you know what I mean," she said, blushing.

"Yes, I do," Amanda said with a knowing smile.

"So, is he saved?"

"He's Catholic."

"Oh," Laurinda looked at the floor.

"Why don't you pray that God will speak to his heart today?"

"I will," Laurinda said, then left for her own class.

Amanda sat down next to Calvin. Their concern from the night before about Ronnie being offended by the topic disappeared as he joined the class discussion.

Calvin shared a commentary from his Bible about James 2:14-24. "It asks the questions, 'Is faith enough?' and 'Are we saved by grace through faith alone as Ephesians 2:8-9 suggests or do we also need works?'" Calvin read the lengthy answer, then concluded, "So then, we don't need anything but faith—the right kind of faith—to be saved. Our behavior shows what our faith is made of, whether or not it's legitimate."

Someone else joined the conversation adding what the "right kind of faith" meant. Discussion continued around faith versus works for the entrance into heaven until the timekeeper indicated it was time to stop. Calvin was asked to close the class in prayer. He prayed that if anyone had any uncertainty regarding their entrance into heaven, that they would make it right with God this very day.

Amanda excused herself after class to wait for Judy. Calvin stayed behind to introduce Ronnie to some of their classmates. Ronnie asked Calvin if they could stay behind because he had some questions. Calvin agreed.

Once alone, Ronnie began, "I've already told you what I was taught as a child. Everything I've read in this book," Ronnie held up the study book, "and everything I've heard here today says the opposite." He took a deep breath and continued, "Is communion necessary? What is the priest saying and doing up there? Do we have to offer a sacrifice every week? What *does* it take to get to heaven? Was Mary always a virgin like the creed says? Did she ascend into heaven with Jesus? Should we give her honor and glory? Why doesn't your church have statues? What is faith? You talked about having the 'right kind' of faith this morning. What does that mean? And what about…"

Calvin raised his hand. "Slow down, buddy. Did you write these down?"

"Not all of them. Some just came up in class."

"Let's start with the ones I can answer."

Ronnie took a paper from the back of the book. Calvin chose the question about statues first. "Let's look at Exodus 20:4-5 where it talks about idols."

"Are you saying statues are idols?"

"You decide after reading it. I want you to know where this comes from. The first verse says, 'And God spoke all theses words.' This came directly from God Himself."

"I believe that."

"Good. It says, 'You shall not make for yourself an idol in the form of anything in heaven above or on the earth beneath or in the waters below. You shall not bow down to them or worship them; for I, the Lord your God, am a jealous God, punishing the children for the sin of the fathers to the third and fourth generation of those who hate me.'"

"I learned the Ten Commandments in school, but I never heard that one. Can I see your Bible, please?"

Calvin passed it to him. Ronnie read all the commandments, then shook his head. "The statues of Mary, Joseph, and the other saints qualify as a form of something in heaven and we do bow down to them. I don't worship them, but I'm just as guilty as anyone for bowing down. Heck, Calvin, it was taught *and* required. I had to."

"I understand."

Ronnie held the book in his lap, examining it further. Since Calvin's Bible was a study Bible, something caught Ronnie's attention on the next page. "What's this here?" Ronnie asked as he pointed to the article.

Calvin looked where he was pointing. The article asked, Why did God require sacrifices? "Why don't you read it and find out for yourself." Calvin correctly presumed Ronnie was not used to reading the Bible for himself, but there was no time like the present to start.

Ronnie silently read the article. "This brings me to the question I had about communion. You call it the Lord's Supper, right?"

"Yes, we do."

"Your Bible says that 'the innocent can substitute for the guilty.' I'm glad we don't sacrifice animals anymore, but I'm glad we continue to offer some sacrifice."

"Isn't that what Christ did for us on the cross?"

"Yes, we remember it every time we take communion, right?"

"Let me show you something in Hebrews 4:14." Ronnie gave the Bible back to Calvin.

Calvin found the place, then returned the Bible to Ronnie.

"Why does your Bible have a capital D by the word priest?" he asked after reading the verses.

"It means the word's in the dictionary. Look it up, my dictionary's marked."

Ronnie found the word and its definition. "This says Jesus is our great high priest and that the body of Christ is a holy priesthood. What does that mean?"

"Does it give a verse?"

"Hebrews 4:14 and 1 Peter 2:5."

"Since we've already read Hebrews, let's go to 1 Peter."

Ronnie returned the Bible so Calvin could find the verse. After reading it, he began to understand that sacrifices were no longer necessary. Jesus was the final sacrifice.

"Remember what my Bible said earlier about the innocent can substitute for the guilty. That's exactly what Jesus did for us. He became the innocent substitute for our sins. Romans 3:23 says that all have sinned and fall short of the glory of God. Based on that, is there any doubt you and I are sinners?"

Ronnie hung his head. "No, sir."

"I'm not telling you these things to make you feel bad, son." Calvin placed a large, calloused hand on the young man's back.

"I don't feel bad. I realize I have a lot of soul searching to do."

"I have a question for you, but I don't want you to answer out loud. Is communion really necessary every week?" Calvin gave him a few minutes to consider the question before continuing. "As far as being able to tell you what the priest is doing and saying through communion, I don't know. I'm not an expert on Catholicism. I know there are books that would answer that for you. Years ago I read one called *Conversations with Catholics*. I think the whole book would benefit you. I'll ask Amanda to get you a copy of it. She loves any excuse to go into the Christian bookstore. Mind if I ask her to get you a Bible, too?"

"That would be great. Besides, I wouldn't know what to buy. And it's kind of hard for me to get there. My boss works me from sunup to sundown."

"I've heard *terrible* things about him."

"Back to business. Mary is the next subject on my list." Together they looked over Ronnie's questions.

Calvin did his best to find answers to the young man's questions. He had no trouble proving that Mary was not always a virgin from Matthew 13:55-56. Ronnie was shocked to discover that Jesus had four brothers and at least two sisters. Calvin couldn't think of where to find any evidence of who Mary's mother was, so he suggested they skip that question. He did show Ronnie in John 19:25-27 where Jesus commanded John to take Mary as his mother. Calvin asked Ronnie to consider why Jesus would've said that if Mary had been going with Him.

Calvin looked over the questions again. "I'm sorry. I missed this question about why our church doesn't have statues."

"I figured it out on my own."

"Where to next?" Calvin asked as he returned the paper to Ronnie. He was sure the congregation had finished the last song before the preaching would begin, but was unconcerned about missing the entire service if necessary. He felt God working through him.

"I can figure out the rest myself once I get a Bible and the book you recommended. But…" Ronnie paused, searching for the right words. "I've always been *told* what I had to do to get to heaven. What do you think it takes to get to heaven?

"I'll tell you what I believe, but I want you to understand something first."

"Sure."

"It doesn't matter what I believe. The only thing that matters is what the Bible says."

"Okay."

"I believe God gave us ten basic laws to abide by. If, and that's a big if, we kept every one of them, we still wouldn't get into heaven. Obeying all the rules is religion, accepting Jesus into your heart is a relationship. We must have a personal relationship with Jesus Christ. Romans 14:10 says 'We will all stand before God's judgment seat.' If we stand there and say 'I was a good person and obeyed all your laws' but we didn't have a relationship with Jesus, we won't be admitted. If we go there and had a personal relationship with Jesus, then God will cover our sins with the blood of Jesus and we'll be admitted."

"So you're saying that all my good works and even my best attempts at being good will have been for nothing?"

"Ronnie," it was Calvin's turn to search for the right words, "I want to share a verse with you that will summarize what we've just been talking about." Calvin turned his Bible to Ephesians 2:8-9. "I'd like you to read it for yourself. Not just once, but several times. Let it sink into your soul."

Ronnie accepted the Bible and read the verse aloud, not for Calvin's sake, but his own. The second time he read it silently. The third time he barely made it through because of the tears in his eyes. Calvin knew how the young man felt. He'd felt the same way when he read it.

"Why did God give us such a gift?" Ronnie asked with tears in his eyes.

"John 3:16 tells us that God so loved the world that He gave His only begotten Son, that whosoever believes in Him shall not perish but have everlasting life."

Calvin helped him find the book. Ronnie's calloused hands shook as he found the chapter and verse. After reading the verse, he cried even harder. "He did this because He loved me? I don't even have kids of my own, but I can't imagine sending my only son to do this."

"Yes, Ronnie, He did this for us. While we were yet sinners, He sent Christ to be the innocent sacrifice for us."

"Boss, I want a relationship with Jesus. I don't wanna try to get into heaven on my own anymore. What do I do?"

"Acknowledge you've sinned. Ask Him for forgiveness. Then ask Him to come into your life to live. That's all you need to do."

"That seems too simple."

Calvin chuckled. "Yes, I know. That's why so many people miss it. They probably think that an all-powerful God must have some system you have to go through. He doesn't. It really is that simple. I'll help you if you want."

"I want to be on my knees. Some old habits die hard."

"That's okay. It shows God you're humble." Both men knelt on the carpeted floor.

Ronnie began to make the sign of the cross, then decided against it. He cried as he prayed, "Dear God, I am a sinner. I've learned there's nothing I can do by myself to cover up my sins or take them away. Please forgive me for not being all that You want me to be. I'd like to invite Your Son into my heart right now. I want Him to be my friend and my guide to eternity with You. Thank You for the gift You gave me so we could be together forever." Ronnie paused.

Calvin finished the prayer for him. "Father, I praise You for Ronnie coming to You today. I thank You for letting me be a part of Your introduction. I ask that You send Your Holy Spirit to guide and direct my new brother in Your ways. I pray You'll continue to use me to help him on his walk with You. In Jesus' name we pray, amen."

After standing up, the two men exchanged a look, and then Calvin extended his arms to embrace the new member of God's family. "Welcome to the family, my friend." Calvin gave him a hearty hug and a strong pat on the back. "Why don't we go tell the rest of the church what you've done?"

"What?"

"Don't you usually share good news with someone?"

"Yes."

"I can't think of any better news, and there is a whole group of people upstairs right now ready and willing to help support you in your walk with Jesus."

"They don't even know me."

"That doesn't matter. You're an adopted child of God's family."

"Adopted?"

"I'll explain later," Calvin said as he heard the music begin.

"Then let's go." As they got to the steps, Ronnie stopped and looked at Calvin. "What do I call you now, boss? Brother or friend?"

"All of the above," Calvin smiled.

Together both men slipped into the pew next to Amanda and Judy just as the congregation began the second verse. As the song ended, but the organist played softly, the pastor invited anyone with prayer concerns or praises to join him. Ronnie looked at Calvin, who nodded. Calvin squeezed Amanda's hand that he'd taken when he joined her, then followed Ronnie up front.

The two men made their way to the front of the building where Calvin introduced Ronnie to the pastor and briefly explained why they'd come. The pastor motioned for the organist to stop playing at the end of the verse. When the song ended, Pastor Nichols handed a microphone to Calvin. He explained to the congregation how he and Ronnie had spent the last hour discussing the requirements for entrance into heaven and that Ronnie had decided to ask Jesus into his heart.

Several yahoos and many amens echoed in the building. Laurinda looked as calm as ever on the outside, but inside she was filled with excitement.

Calvin returned the microphone to the pastor. "Welcome to the family," the pastor told Ronnie as he shook his hand. "Amanda, please come and join us. After the closing prayer I'd like to invite everyone to come forward and welcome Ronnie to the family." Pastor Nichols asked one of the deacons to close in prayer.

When the prayer was finished, Ronnie began shaking hands and accepting hugs from people he'd never met before and a few he'd just met. Jimmy was the first person he recognized. A few people behind him at the end of the line stood the other person he recognized and wanted to get to know better, Laurinda Bowman. He shook hands with strangers that asked how he knew Calvin, but he never let her out of his sight as he explained the connection.

When she finally arrived, Ronnie's mouth went dry. When he regained his ability to talk, they both spoke at once. "You look beautiful today."

"Welcome to the family of believers."

They both said thank you at the same time.

Calvin interrupted them. "If you two stop talking at the same time, it might work better." He gave Ronnie another hug, then gave Laurinda a peck on her cheek and said good-bye before he and Amanda left to rejoin Judy, who'd waited for them at their seat.

"I'm buying lunch if you're interested," Calvin told his wife's best friend.

"What about Ronnie?"

Calvin looked over his shoulder and smiled. "I think he's in pretty good hands, don't you?"

Amanda smiled.

Chapter 8

Calvin parked at the Flap Jack Shack while his passengers continued talking. He was sure they did that nonstop whenever they were together. He wondered how women found so much to talk about. He and his friends usually said so little when they were together.

The trio was seated, and Calvin began to look over the menu while the women continued to talk. "Excuse me," he finally interrupted. "But have you forgotten I'm here?"

The two looked at each other across the table and laughed. "If you were paying attention, you'd have realized we've been talking about *you!*"

Calvin looked at Judy, who nodded her head in agreement.

"We were wondering where you are." Amanda put her arm through his and held his hand.

"I'm thinking about tomorrow and Ronnie mostly. Could you do me a favor tomorrow?"

"Yes."

"I told Ronnie I'd ask you to get him a Bible and a book I read about Catholics. I think it's called *Conversations with Catholics* but I don't remember the author. McCarthy, I think. Ronnie had questions this morning I couldn't answer since I don't know much about Catholicism."

"What kind of Bible?"

"A study Bible like mine would be great. While you're there, get this lovely lady a Bible, too. Have you talked about the Bible study yet?"

"On the way here." Amanda snuggled close to Calvin.

"I'm looking forward to it, but she doesn't have to buy me a Bible."

The women made plans to visit the Family Christian Store the next day between Judy's appointments.

"I've been thinking about something," Calvin said after they dropped Judy off at the church. "I was wondering if I could help you do laundry today."

"Why?"

"Earlier I wanted to offer so that you wouldn't have to do it alone tomorrow. But now that you and Judy have plans, it would give you more time tomorrow."

"What are your qualifications?" she asked. "The last time I remember you doing laundry was after Jessi was born. Was that you," Amanda teased, "or was that my mother? I don't remember."

After his first and only trip to the laundromat, he asked his mother-in-law if she would do it if he dropped it off to her. He offered to pay her. She did the laundry, but refused payment. It'd been a family joke ever since.

"I can carry baskets and fold, you know."

"You know I don't work on the Lord's day."

"You know I don't either, but just this once I don't think He'd mind. Besides, it's not like *you're* actually working."

Later, after Calvin placed a full basket of clothes on the floor, Amanda sorted them, then started the washer.

"You do such a great job with the laundry, I don't care if I ever learn how."

"Keep the compliments coming and you'll never have to." Amanda paused, thinking about their daughters. "Jessi wanted to learn. Then again she wanted to do everything I did." Amanda was near tears. Calvin drew her into his arm. "I wonder if she follows her new mommy around." Tears rolled down her cheeks. "This isn't fair. If someone would tell me what I had to do to get them back, I would do it. I feel powerless."

Calvin held his crying wife close. "I know this has been harder on you than me because you were with them so much." Calvin stroked her hair and prayed, asking God to strengthen his wife through this rough time. As he prayed, Amanda relaxed and stopped crying. She touched his shirt where her tears had soaked it. "It'll dry," he said as she sniffled. He reached into a pile of dirty clothes and grabbed a sock and handed it to her. "Blow your nose."

"You're sooooo thoughtful. I believe I'll find a tissue."

"Suit yourself." Calvin tossed the sock back onto the pile.

*   *   *

With his tongue less tied, Ronnie asked Laurinda what she was doing for the afternoon.

"I'm visiting my grandma in Jackson at the nursing home. I usually go every Sunday between services."

"Between services?"

"There's a more casual service at six."

"Should I go to that, too?"

"I'd like it if you did." Laurinda blushed. The lights in the auditorium flickered. "That's our cue to leave."

"I could drive you if you want," he blurted out.

"I'd like that, but I don't want to be any trouble."

"No trouble. It'd be my pleasure to take you to see your grandma if it's all right. I don't want her to get the wrong impression about meeting me." Ronnie wished he could take back his words before they left his mouth.

"I'd love for you to meet Grandma Meredith, and I'm sure she won't get the wrong impression." Laurinda already hoped Ronnie would meet all of her family and become a part of it, God willing. "Is it okay if we stop for lunch on the way? I'm starving."

"Me, too." He extended his elbow to her to escort her out of the building. She draped her hand over it and together they went out to his car. She released his arm so he could unlock the passenger door and open it for her. He grabbed an empty pop can from the floor board and tossed it into the back seat, then took off his jacket and placed it on the seat.

"What'd you do that for?"

"I don't want you to get your dress dirty."

"I don't want you to get cold."

"I never get cold. I only wear my jacket because every morning I hear my mother telling me to put it on."

"You still live at home?"

"No. I hear her in my head. She was always afraid my brother and I would get sick and she wouldn't be able to afford the doctor bill."

"Oh," Laurinda said, hoping to learn more about him.

"Dad left when my brother was three and I was five. We haven't seen him since. He never paid Mom any child support. Since she's Catholic, she refused to remarry, so she raised my brother and me alone. Sometimes she worked two or three jobs just to make ends meet. When I was old enough, I got a paper route. She quit her night job and got a full time day job that offered benefits. I don't think she ever got over those first few years though. The only good thing Dad ever did for us was sign off the title to the house we lived in. I don't think he was trying to be nice, I think he was getting out of his responsibilities all together."

Laurinda touched his right hand that was resting on the console. "I'm sorry."

"I'm over it." He thought for a moment, then added, "Well, maybe not completely, but I think what happened to me this morning will help. I don't know how I'm going to explain this to my mother. She lives in Chicago and I only see her at Christmas, so I've got a while before I *have* to tell her."

"Don't you talk to her between Christmases?"

"Yeah, but this isn't something I'd tell her over the phone."

"I guess you're right. I'd think she'd be upset to know you're not going to a Catholic church anymore."

"Upset would be an understatement. I'm pretty sure she knows I haven't gotten back into the church."

"Back?" Laurinda questioned.

"I'll explain in a minute. Where would you like to eat?"

"I'm sorry. I've been listening to you so I forgot I was hungry."

"That's funny. I was busy talking and I forgot I was hungry." They both laughed.

"I'll eat wherever you want."

"Nope, today's lady's choice and I'm buying."

"I'll choose, but you don't have to buy."

"It would be my pleasure to treat such a beautiful woman to lunch."

Laurinda blushed. "Since we were both starving before we started talking, why don't we just hit the next fast food restaurant that we find? Right now, I'd eat just about anything."

"So would I." He saw an Arby's so he changed lanes and made his way there.

They placed their orders, and when the lady asked if it was for here or to go, Ronnie looked at Laurinda. "It's up to you. If you are in a hurry, I can eat and drive."

Not wanting the afternoon with him to end too soon she chose to eat there.

Once they were seated, Laurinda bowed her head to pray. Ronnie dropped the French fries he was about to dip in the catsup and bowed his head, too. Laurinda wanted to reach across the table and hold his hand but decided that might be too forward and too soon. She said a simple prayer aloud of thanksgiving for the food and company, then closed in Jesus' name.

Ronnie said amen and almost made the sign of the cross.

"You were going to tell me what you meant by *back* to the Catholic Church."

"I figured Calvin told you about my bad boy days."

"No, he hasn't told me anything about you. He's a private man and shows that respect to other people as well. Trust me, anything you've told him, he kept to himself. I take that back, he probably told Amanda, but that's as far as it went. If you want me to know something about you, you'll have to tell me yourself. The same applies to me. If you want to know something about me, just ask. Please explain your bad boy days."

"Let me start out by saying it could've been worse. I didn't get into any legal trouble and the hardest drug I ever used was alcohol. I hung out with a gang for about a year before I got smart and left Chicago. Mom was both disappointed and relieved when I moved here. I have a distant uncle in the area. She thought he might help me out once I got here, but I prefer to do things for myself. I think that's because I grew up without a dad. I was the man of the house for a long time. When I got here, I flipped burgers for a year before Joe came in and started talking up this great construction company he worked for and he got me an interview. The rest you know about."

"Do you miss your mom and brother?"

"Yeah, I miss 'em." He covered her hand with his. "But, I'm so glad I came here."

Laurinda blushed and pulled her hand out from under his so she could pick up her sandwich. His touch stirred feelings she wasn't ready to deal with.

His attention returned to his own meal and nothing more was said until they were leaving. "I don't know how to get to Jackson, so I'll need you to navigate."

"No problem," she said as he opened the car door for her.

Once he was behind the wheel, she gave him directions for the next few miles. She finished by saying, "I'm glad you came here, too." He smiled and his heart skipped a beat.

"You haven't told me anything about yourself. It's your turn."

"What do you want to know? Get on the highway there on the right."

"Okay. You can start by telling me which grandma we're going to see, and a little about her."

"She is my father's mother. My grandpa died six months ago and her health went downhill right away. Mum says it's probably because she loved him so much that she doesn't want to live without him. I hope to find someone I can love like that."

"With my past, I'm afraid I'll never find anyone to love me like that."

"You don't have a past anymore. You've been born again."

"What does that mean?"

"The Bible says anyone who accepts Christ into their lives is a new creation. I don't know the exact verse."

"That's okay. I don't know much about the Bible except that it has an Old and New Testament. And what little I learned this morning with Calvin. He's going to ask Amanda to buy me a Bible tomorrow while I am at work. I was a horrible student, but I'm looking forward to learning all I can about God. This morning Calvin pointed out a few of the differences between what I was taught and what the Bible says."

"I'm sure she'll get you a study Bible. Those are awesome. I have a study Bible. Now about your past. God says that He will forget your sins as far as the east is from the west. So I'm certain you got a fresh start at life this morning." She looked out the window as she said, "I know you got a fresh start with me today."

He couldn't believe his ears. "What do you mean by a fresh start with you?"

"If you hadn't become a Christian this morning, I wouldn't have gone anywhere with you today, or ever for that matter."

"This is a bonus for me. I join the family of God and get the pleasure of your company, too."

Laurinda blushed but he didn't see it because she was still looking out the window.

"Tell me more about your grandma."

"She's almost seventy. I think she's beautiful in spite of what the stroke has done to her. The doctors think the stroke was brought on by Grandpa's death. They were married when she was sixteen and he was twenty. To live with someone that long, then in a blink of an eye lose them had to be rough on her."

"What happened to your grandpa?"

"He had a heart attack. We all thought he was healthy, but we were wrong. He was ready to go. He lived a good life and served the Lord well. He and Grandma raised ten kids. My father is their youngest son. I guess this is where you'll want to bail."

"Why would I want to bail?"

"Because I have a very large extended family. It's scared away more than one boyfriend." She blushed and quickly turned her head toward the window again. *I can't believe I just said that.*

Did she just say boyfriend?

"I, I..." Laurinda stammered, "I didn't mean to imply that you're a boyfriend. I just meant," she stammered even more.

He reached over and touched her arm. "It's okay. You don't have to turn away from me." She turned to face him. He stole a look at her, then back at the road. "Besides, I think you're even more beautiful when you blush."

"Thank you." She continued to tell him about her extended family in an attempt to recover from her embarrassing comment. "My own family is another story. I'm an only child. I was a little hard on my mother when I was born so they decided not to have any more children. My father always wondered what it would be like to be an only child and I've spent most of my life wondering what it would be like to be one of many. Maybe not nine siblings, but at least two or three. If I ever have children of my own, I hope I handle it better than Mom did, because I want a house full." She thought for a minute, then added, "But I'll be happy with however many God gives me, if any."

"I've never given children any thought. In fact, Laurinda, is it okay if I tell you something very personal?"

"Are you sure you want to?"

"Yes. For some reason I feel like it is something you need to know about me. I don't know what you are looking for in a man, but…" His voice trailed off. This time he spent a few minutes looking between the front and side windows.

"You'll be coming up on the town in just about a mile. Before the first light you will need to get on another highway headed west. Take the first exit, then turn right and follow the signs. You can't miss it."

"Okay." He looked at her briefly, thankful for the distraction of directions. He was still set on telling her but still didn't know exactly how to say it without sounding forward.

Laurinda's mind raced with wonder about what he could possibly tell her that was so personal he had trouble saying it. "Maybe what you want to tell me can wait until the ride home. It's obviously something very important to you or you would have just come right out and told me. Turn here."

"You're right. It's nothing I'm ashamed of. In fact, I'm personally kind of proud of myself considering the times we live in and the pressure young men are under these days."

Now Laurinda really wanted to know his *secret* if that was what it was.

"You might want to continue to help navigate. I've become a bit distracted."

"See that yellow building up there on the left? Turn there. Then go down three blocks on the right. You can't miss it."

"You might be surprised." He didn't require any further instructions until he asked her where she'd like him to park.

"In the back parking lot if you don't mind. Grandma's room is in the back of the building and we can check in with the nurse's station to let them know we're here."

Ronnie did as instructed and quickly found a spot two spaces from the door. He parked and killed the engine, then made his way around the car to open the door for Laurinda. She'd reached for the door handle but remembered he'd opened the door for her every time so far today. She placed her hands in her lap and waited for his extended hand.

Grandma Meredith's face lit up when she saw Laurinda walk through the door. Ronnie waited in the hall so Laurinda could make sure her grandma was ready for nonfamily company.

"Grandma, I have someone I want you to meet," Ronnie heard her say. He stepped through the door and Laurinda introduced the two.

"This is Ronnie Colthorp. The young man I told you about. He's the new guy at work."

"Nice to meet you, Ronnie. Come over and sit down. I'd like to go for a walk with you today, but I'm worn out from having to go to lunch," she said to Ronnie. "Linny, I do wish you would tell them to just bring me my lunch. You know it's hard for me to get around."

Ronnie placed a chair beside Laurinda, who was sitting by her grandma on the bed.

"Yes, I know, Grandma. They want you to get some exercise every day so you keep up your strength."

"What do I need my strength for? My work is done. I'm ready to go home. I want to be with Grandpa. He left without me and I need to find him."

"I know, sweetie. But we want you to stay with us a while longer. Grandpa is being well taken care of and we're doing the best we can for you."

Grandma crossed her good arm over the one paralyzed by her stroke. "I know you are, but Grandpa needs me," the elderly lady insisted.

Laurinda steered the subject away from Grandma leaving by telling her about Ronnie's first visit to church today. They discussed Ronnie becoming a new creation in Christ and Laurinda asked Grandma if she knew the verse where Paul talked about that.

"Of course I know, sweetie. Paul wrote so many books. I loved them all."

Ronnie doubted that she really knew. Her thoughts seemed to have been affected by the stroke as much as her body.

Grandma looked out the window as if she had forgotten Laurinda had even asked her a question. Then she looked directly at Ronnie and said, "2 Corinthians 5:17 says, 'Therefore, if anyone is in Christ, he is a new creation; the old has gone, the new has come.' You no longer have a past, except to learn from it and tell others what God has saved you from." With that, Grandma closed her eyes and went to sleep.

Ronnie looked from Grandma to Laurinda. She motioned with her head toward the door. He put the chair back while Laurinda kissed her Grandma good-bye. She joined Ronnie at the door and they walked to his car in silence.

After Ronnie started the car, he said, "I like her. She tells it like it is."

"She sure does, always has. She says, 'I like you as you are, so you like me as I am, then we'll get along.' I'll miss her desperately when she's gone, and I'm afraid that won't be very long from now."

"I know how you feel. Why didn't you tell me your nickname was Linny?"

"Usually only my grandma calls me Linny. She says Laurinda is too stuffy, even though she helped name me, and I am anything but stuffy."

"I like it, and I agree with her…" He stole a sideways glance at her, then said, "Linny."

She liked the way it sounded when he said it, so she didn't object. "I forgot to warn you that she would probably fall asleep on us like that."

"That's okay. I spent a lot of time at the hospital with my mother's parents before they passed. I got used to a lot of strange things. I figured they were old and had lived their lives, so they could pretty much get away with anything."

"It's a little early to head back. Would you like to stop for an ice cream cone?"

He smiled at her. "Isn't it a little cold for ice cream?"

"Never!" she exclaimed, and then gave him directions to the Parlor.

Over a shared banana split, they talked about the church's upcoming singles get-together on Friday. Pizza and games sounded good to him, but being with her was his motivation for saying he'd go.

Back at church, the usual crowd was present, plus two more. Ronnie greeted Calvin and Amanda at the door as they walked in.

"I thought I saw your car back in the parking lot," Calvin said to Ronnie as he shook his hand. "I feel bad that Laurinda had to stay here the whole time by herself though," Calvin teased him.

"Well," Ronnie started. "She and I...well," he started again, "I...ah...I took her to see her grandma. And we had lunch together. She invited me to the singles get-together this Friday." He paused, looked at his own feet, then said, "Boss, I'd go anywhere with her."

Calvin laughed. "Just don't go anywhere too fast. Okay, buddy? I care a great deal for that young lady. I think of her as a little sister if you get my meaning."

"I hear you loud and clear. I have only the best intentions if she'll have anything to do with me."

"It sounds like she wants something to do with you since she invited you to the singles get-together. I haven't been to one of those in years. The short time Amanda and I went, I didn't feel single. I'd had my eye on her for a few years, so my heart was already gone. I just had to wait for God to tell me it was right."

"What do you mean by that?"

Calvin explained to Ronnie about asking God to help him in every decision in his life, from the little ones to the big ones, especially who to marry.

Chapter 9

Monday morning on the way back to the job site, Calvin tuned the radio to the local Christian station. Just before he pulled into the parking lot at the gas station the song "Butterfly Kisses" started. Because of the song's lyrics, Calvin usually turned the radio off until he figured the song was over. This morning he didn't. He couldn't. For some reason his hand just wouldn't reach for the button. Instead he sat glued to the seat. Tears streamed down his face just as they had Amanda's the day before. His heart ached as the song played on.

Neither of the girls had ever baked him a cake or taken a pony ride, but there were other memories that gripped his heart, like the time the three of them built the swing set in the backyard. As Bob Carlisle sang about his sweet sixteen-year-old, Calvin was overcome with disappointment, knowing he might not see his daughters turn sixteen. He'd given them butterfly kisses, prayed together, and then hugged and kissed them every night.

By the final verse, Calvin's body was shaking from his sobs. "Lord, I'll never walk them down the aisle to their waiting husbands. Amanda's right, it's not fair. I've done a lot of wrong and I know I didn't deserve them, but I don't think I deserved to lose them, either. Please," he begged, "bring them back to us. Please." Calvin cried out in anguish, draped his arms across the steering wheel, and rested his head on them. He felt extreme anger toward the people who'd stolen so much from him and Amanda. In that moment, he felt they had taken not just the girls, but also his life.

Ronnie was the first to notice Calvin was back but had not gotten out of his truck. He decided to check on him. As Ronnie got closer to the truck, he could tell Calvin was crying by his posture and the way his body shook. Ronnie opened the door of the truck. "What's wrong, brother?"

Calvin looked at Ronnie. "The song," Calvin managed to say.

By the time Ronnie opened the door, "Butterfly Kisses" was over. "This song?" he asked, then reached in and turned the key so the radio would be silent.

"I miss my girls. I wish I could find 'em. I want 'em back for me... for Amanda," Calvin said through tears.

Ronnie knew little about his boss, but he'd heard a great deal about what had happened to his daughters. "Why don't you get out of the truck and come inside where it's warm? I'll get you a cup of coffee and we can talk."

As Ronnie helped Calvin from the truck and into the building, the rest of the crew went about their work as if they hadn't noticed. Ronnie directed Calvin to the back room, sat him on a plastic chair, and went to get him coffee.

By the time he was handed the steaming cup, Calvin had stopped crying. "Man, I'm sorry about that. I guess I've just held it in as long as I could. The song "Butterfly Kisses" really did me in this morning."

"It's all right to cry. Anybody that says different has never lost someone they love. I cried like a baby when my grandmother died."

"But I don't want you to think I can't handle this situation. You're a brand new Christian and looking to me as an example. I don't want you to think I..."

"Look, boss, I've only been with you a few months and I don't know the whole story, but I've heard things. If what I've heard is correct, you've done very well under the circumstances. Everyone talks about your faith in God and how strong you are."

"I don't feel very strong right now."

"Sounds like you're mourning the loss of your daughters. *No one,* including me, is going to think any less of you if you grieve. You are one of the greatest guys I know. You and I both know you didn't have to hire me. I certainly didn't fit into the pattern of the people you employ. Maybe you saw something in me that I didn't even know was there. Even when I challenged you, you didn't lose your cool. Everyone told me it was because you're a Christian. I've watched you, and you've proven yourself to be more of a Christian than I ever thought about being. You live your faith. That's why I talked to you yesterday. You've helped me get my life on track and for that I thank you. I understand you've been there for everyone on this crew at some point in your relationship with them. It's time to accept our help. Why don't you go home and spend the day with Amanda?"

Calvin sipped the hot beverage. "I'd do that but I'd be all alone if I went home. She and Judy are shopping, for you in fact. Then she's going to her mother's for the day. Being here will help me more than being in an empty house. I'm beginning to understand why Amanda stayed sad so much. A few weeks after the girls were kidnapped, Amanda straightened their rooms a little, but for the most part they still look the same as they did the last morning I looked in on them before leaving for work. Sometimes we close their bedroom doors so we don't have to see in. You were right, people have no idea how painful it is to lose someone they love until it happens to them. I pray for them morning, night, and sometimes in between. It would be different if they'd died. At least then we could have visited their graves. But this," he ran his hand through his hair, "this is hell on earth. I know they are out there, I just can't find them." Waves of tears came over him again.

Ronnie took his coffee from his hand and set it on the floor. He placed his right hand on Calvin's shoulder and waited for the tears to stop before asking, "Have you hired a private investigator?"

"One here and one in Chicago. They collaborated with the police to find the house in Chicago where the girls stayed for a little while. The local guy asked Amanda questions that jogged her memory about the woman the airline attendant described. With his help, Amanda remembered talking to the woman in the mall a few days before the girls were stolen. She'd commented to Amanda about how beautiful the girls were, and they talked as they walked through the mall together. Amanda beat herself up for a while after that because she thought she should've remembered sooner. The PI told her that sometimes information like that stays buried until someone knows where to look for it. Unfortunately, the information didn't make any difference. Both men are still on the case, but we haven't heard anything from them in a while. Sometimes, I think our daughters just vanished into thin air."

"It was tough losing my grandmother and I know where she went. I don't have kids so I can't begin to imagine how painful this is for you and Amanda."

Joe stuck his head into the back room. "Excuse me for interrupting, I could use your help out here, boss."

Calvin looked at Ronnie. "See, I can't go home, you guys do need me. We've taken up enough time, let's get back to work. The busier I stay, the better I feel. Busy hands help keep a man's mind off his troubles, my father always says." Calvin shook Ronnie's hand and embraced him in a hug. "Thanks for listening, brother."

*　　*　　*

Amanda showered and dressed, leaving her hair down as instructed. She ate a bowl of cereal, then cleaned up the kitchen and started to vacuum the living room. As she pushed and pulled the vacuum across the floor, she remembered the time Calvin had gotten a new pair of work boots. Katrina thought the box was the best toy every created. She'd sit in it as Calvin pushed, pulled, or sometimes shoved the box around the room as she squealed with delight. Amanda laughed out loud as she replayed the scene in her mind.

Not having vacuumed the girls' rooms in a while, Amanda decided to try it today. She touched the handle of the door leading into Jessica's room, then turned it and let the machine and herself in.

She breathed deeply, as if trying to breathe her daughter back into her room where she belonged. She gazed at the bed remembering the many nights she and Calvin had stood at the door and watched her sleep. She laughed as she remembered the many times they had to put Jessi back in bed after thinking they had her there for the night. Once she told them, "I just want to be with you." Since neither parent could argue with the comment, they allowed her a few extra minutes with them before explaining that mommies and daddies needed quiet time together. Amanda said to the empty room, "I just want to be with you."

She ran the vacuum across the middle of the room, then under the bed as far as it would reach. As she did, she recalled how Jessi stretched every morning. She remembered a morning when she'd sat beside the bed and watched her daughter wake up. Jessi's face lit up when she turned over and saw her mother beside her.

"Good morning, Mommy," she'd said as she reached for Amanda and snuggled her little still-baby face into her mother's neck, her blond curls tickling Amanda's nose. Amanda stood up, holding her close.

Presently, Amanda switched off the machine and sat down on the bed, then picked up the white stuffed clown bear that Amanda's uncle had sent Jessi for her first Christmas. She looked into its smiling face and gently tugged at the red ball hanging from the tip of its floppy hat. She looked up toward heaven. "God, please watch over them, and if it's in Your will, please bring them back to us." She kissed the bear's little black nose, then replaced it on the pillow and left to vacuum Katrina's room.

It was easier to vacuum under the baby bed. Amanda stopped her sweeping, this time to stand beside the bed and look in. Kat was like Jessi in her sleeping and waking.

Amanda ran her hand along the rail of the bed, then reached in and picked up the Raggedy Ann doll that Maria had given Jessi for her second Christmas. Some months later Jessi gave the doll to Kat. When Amanda asked her if she really wanted to give it to her sister, Jessi said, "I want her to have something of mine to hold in case I'm not with her." Tears swelled in Amanda's eyes. She kissed the doll, then returned it to the bed. Amanda smiled and brushed away tears with her hands.

She left Katrina's door open as well. After replacing the vacuum to its spot in the closet, Amanda returned to the living room and stood looking into each of her daughter's room in turn. She signed and thanked God that He'd eased her pain. She felt that in some way she'd let go of the girls, truly giving them to Him. At that very moment she understood what the Bible meant by peace that surpasses all understanding.

Amanda checked her watch, then put on her coat and boots. She knew Judy was busy and she didn't want to keep her waiting, so she hurried out the door.

Amanda didn't recognize the car in the drive, but she thought she recognized the lady who passed her in the doorway as she was going in. "Good morning," she told the lady before stepping inside the warm house. Judy hugged her before she could get her coat off. "What was that for?" she asked.

"I wanted to thank you for last week when you didn't let up on me about my relationship with God."

"Was I pushy?"

"Not you! Did you recognize the lady that just left?"

"Maybe. Do I know her?"

"That's Elizabeth Parks, our waitress last week."

"Oh yeah."

"Sit down so I can do your braid."

Judy sprayed a mist of water on her friend's hair. "Elizabeth's had a tough life. Her parents divorced when she was young. Her older sister beat up on her every chance she got and was mean to her. Her self-esteem was pretty much nonexistent. She got pregnant and married after high school last summer. He was an alcoholic who abused her to the point she miscarried the baby. The hospital staff recognized the situation for what it was and turned him in to the police. She's scared to testify against him, but feels like it's the right thing to do."

"You said this happened recently?"

"Yes. She said if she hadn't lost the baby, he would've killed it after it was born. She moved here two months ago to get away from her hometown where everyone knew what had happened. She said she's going back for the trial. I gave her the name of my lawyer and one of the business cards Peggy gave me for the Council Against Domestic Assault. You remember Peggy, don't you?" Judy brushed the snarls from Amanda's hair as she talked.

"She was in a similar situation, wasn't she?"

"Yes, she was. She stops here from time to time. You should see her now, self-confident *and* self-sufficient. She runs her own company and travels a lot. She does speaking engagements about domestic violence. That's why she gave me those business cards." Judy thought for a minute, then added, "I wish I could have recovered like that."

"You have your own business. I'm proud of the way you picked up your life after your divorce."

"Which one?" Judy asked sarcastically as she put a rubber band into Amanda's hair to hold the braid in place.

"I've told you before, make God the head of the search committee and you can't go wrong if you ever decide to try again."

"I gave men up a long time ago, you know that." Judy twirled the chair around so Amanda could look in the mirror. "What do you think?"

"I think it looks great, as usual." Amanda stood up and reached for her coat where she'd placed a twenty dollar bill. "Are you going to let me pay you today?"

"Naw, that's what friends are for. You helped me in a way I can never repay, so it's the least I can do."

"Maybe it's the least you can do, but I think you're already doing the most you can do."

"How so?"

"If I know you, and I do, you talked to Elizabeth about your life and told her more about Jesus." Amanda slid her arms into her coat and smiled.

Judy smiled, "She's coming back next week so we can talk some more. I was hoping you'd be early today, but you weren't, so I went ahead without you. You'd have been proud of me. I prayed with her."

"That's awesome."

"She hugged me and said it was just what she needed. That's why she's coming back next week."

Amanda hugged her friend. "I'm proud of you…no matter what you do."

"Let's get out of here. I'm ready to shop."

"Some things never change."

"And they never will." Judy wrapped her arm through her best friend's arm and practically dragged her to the door. "Is it okay if we take your van since it's already warm?"

"Sure."

They arrived at the Family Christian Store a short time later and were the first customers of the day. Aimie offered her assistance and it was gladly accepted as they looked through the Bibles. Amanda picked a study Bible just like Calvin's, only a different color for Ronnie. She gave Aimie a piece of paper with Ronnie's full name written on it so she could engrave it on the front of the Bible while she and Judy continued looking for her Bible. They had several Bibles spread out on the table when Aimie returned. Amanda gave her approval of the engraving as Judy decided on a soft covered woman's study Bible.

"I need to bother you for one more thing if you don't mind," Amanda told Aimie.

"What's that?"

"I need a book called *Conversations with Catholics*, but I don't know the author."

"I'll check the computer to see if we have it in stock. If we do, I'll have it at the counter." Aimie insisted she put the unselected Bibles away so the ladies could continue shopping.

"Thank you, Aimie," Amanda said.

Together Amanda and Judy found the section of Kay Arthur study books. Judy was glad Amanda was there since she couldn't remember the name of the book she needed to buy.

"Do you think Elizabeth would want to do this, too?" Judy asked as Amanda took a book off the shelf and handed it to her.

"I don't know. She only waited on me once. You tell me."

"I guess what I was really saying was, would you tutor us both?"

"Yes, if you want her to join us. There isn't anything I wouldn't do for God, even lead a mini Bible study."

After Judy took a second copy of *Lord, I Need Your Grace to Make It* from the shelf, they headed straight to the checkout. As they passed by the music, Amanda remembered that she still needed to get a song for church.

"Do you have time to listen to a few songs with me? Miss Ruby asked me to sing. I didn't find anything last week when I was here. Maybe a new set of eyes will help."

Judy checked her watch and decided she had time. The two sat down at the listening center and just started picking different songs. A short time later, Judy found a song she really enjoyed called "On My Knees." She stopped the CD Amanda was previewing and took it out of the player. Amanda didn't question her, instead she waited for Judy to replace it with the CD she was holding. Amanda listened and smiled. Though she didn't recall hearing the song before, she enjoyed it and agreed with Judy when she said *this* was the song.

"It just sounds like you," Judy told her once she'd listened to all of the song and removed the headphones from her head. Judy looked closely at her friend. "See, I told you it was you. You're crying."

"So, what's your point?" Amanda asked as she wiped the tears from her eyes and smiled at her friend.

They returned the unselected music they still had out, and then pushed in the chairs and made their way to the cash register.

Judy picked up a bag of Testamints and added them to her pile. "I always keep candy in the dish on the table. It may as well have an impact."

"Good idea."

Aimie gave Amanda the book she'd requested as Amanda presented her family perks card. Judy filled out the application for a card while Aimie rang up Amanda's purchases. Aimie gave Amanda her change and some stickers.

"What are those?" Judy asked.

"For every five dollars you spend you get a sticker. Once you have twenty stickers on a card like this," Aimie showed Judy a card, "you bring it back in and get five dollars off any purchase."

"I turn them in to the church office so we can build up the library," Amanda told Judy.

"Amanda, your next trip should get you your twenty-five percent off coupon," Aimie said enthusiastically.

"I see that."

"Do you have just a minute more? There's something Michael asked me to mention to you."

"Well, I have to get Judy back to work, but you still need to ring up her order, so if you can talk and ring at the same time, I have time."

"Last week when you were in you mentioned that you weren't as busy as you once where. I told Michael and he asked me to talk to you about coming to work for us part-time."

Amanda was dumbfounded by her comment. She hadn't thought about going back to work since she and Calvin decided she wouldn't go back to Edwards Construction.

"I'll pray about it and talk it over with my husband."

"I'll tell Michael. Here's his card. I know he'd like you to call him and let him know pretty soon. He mentioned having you do a story hour on Saturday mornings and maybe helping out in the store a couple of days a week."

Amanda tucked the card into her purse. "I'll call as soon as I decide, I promise."

After Aimie finished Judy's purchase, the three women said their good-byes.

As Amanda unlocked the van doors and both women climbed inside the van, Judy said, "I think you'd be great for a story hour."

"Yeah, but it might be rough. Like I told Aimie, I'll discuss it with Calvin. We'll pray about it." Amanda started the van and drove back to Judy's.

After dropping Judy off, Amanda stopped by the grocery store for some things, then went to the gas station Edwards Construction was renovating.

Calvin met her when she pulled into the drive. He thought she was there to see him, but instead she came to bring Ronnie his

Bible and the book she'd bought him. He escorted his wife into the station and over to where Ronnie was cleaning up from some earlier destruction.

Ronnie took his gloves off and extended his hand when Amanda handed him the box containing his new Bible. "Calvin told me your full name. I hope you don't mind that I had it engraved with that instead of Ronnie."

"I don't mind. I just think Ronald Edward Colthorp is a little stuffy for me." He examined the Bible inside and out. "This is beautiful. Thank you both very much." Ronnie took his wallet from his back pocket and began to take money from it.

"That won't be necessary, the Bible is a gift from Calvin and me. I wrote that inside the front. Here is the book you and Calvin talked about." Amanda handed him a small bag with the book inside.

Ronnie hadn't put his wallet away, so he offered to pay for the book at least.

"Just pass it on someday, young man," Calvin told him. "Now get back to work, ye scallywag."

"Aye, aye, Captain. Thank you again, Mrs. Edwards," he said as he shook her hand. "I'm gonna set this stuff over on the counter."

Calvin walked Amanda back outside so he could have her to himself for a few minutes before she left. Since it was cold outside, Calvin suggested they get into the van so they could talk.

"Judy and I had a good time at the store this morning. I miss spending time with her."

"You two should get together more often then."

"Maybe, but that might be a little difficult if I take the job."

"Take what job?"

"Aimie told me Michael, the store manager, asked me to consider coming to work there. They want me to do a Saturday morning story hour. That might be a little rough, but every day I feel stronger. Besides, there isn't anything I won't do for God." Amanda realized she had just told Judy the same thing.

"Michael is a smart businessman."

"What do you mean?"

"With a beautiful woman like you in his store, he will have every man for thirty, no forty, miles around in the place."

"Cut it out." Amanda playfully jabbed at him. "Coming back to work for you isn't an option, and doing your scheduling doesn't keep me busy. Please pray about this so we can give him a decision soon."

"I'll do that," he promised. Calvin picked up Amanda's hand and placed a gentle kiss on the back of it.

"Mom and I are going to look for some new curtains for the front window of the apartment. It seems the cleaning did them more harm than good. Since there's a sale going on, would you care if I pick up those two throw pillows I've been wanting for the couch?"

"If that makes you happy. Do you need any money?"

Amanda rolled her eyes at him. "Honey, I have your good name, that's all I need."

"You mean my credit card," he teased her back. "Just don't spend too much."

"Define 'too much.'" she said as she smiled and batted her eyelashes at her handsome husband. "I've got to go get Mom. I'll see you at dinner."

"You aren't getting out of this parking lot without kissing me good-bye. It could be *hours*," he exaggerated the word, "before I see you again."

They leaned together for a kiss. He got out of the van and walked around to her window, which she rolled down. "Better give me just one more kiss. I don't know how much time Mother and I will spend shopping today." He gladly kissed her again through the open window. When they finished, she added with a smile, "Or how much I'll spend." Calvin laughed as she rolled up the window and drove away.

Chapter 10

Calvin opened the back door to the wonderful smell of pork roast. The smell was good, but it was his wife he was eager to see. He found her sitting on the couch watching a home video of their family. Though she looked like she'd been crying, she wasn't presently. She was laughing at the silly antics of their children caught on tape.

Amanda heard Calvin come in, but decided to stay where she was, waiting to tell him about her afternoon and what had been laid on her heart while shopping.

"Hi," she said as he walked into the room. "Stay right there. I have something I need to tell you." Calvin leaned against the wall and waited as she paused the video and resumed talking.

"You know how tough it is for me to shop at the mall, right?" Without waiting for a reply, she continued, "Well, something changed today. It started this morning when I vacuumed the girls' rooms. It felt like I let go of them. Then while shopping this afternoon, the Lord laid something on my heart regarding the pain we've endured these past months. I was thinking about what you'd said about remembering the girls with gladness, not sadness. I'm *choosing* to do just that. I started this morning without the usual sadness." She paused, gathering her thoughts before continuing.

"If I live my life hating the people who stole our daughters, it only destroys me, not them. They stole our children, but we still have each other. Neither they, nor anyone else for that matter, can ever take away our place in heaven. Or the love that Jesus has for us.

We already have everything we need in Him. They have stolen our daughters, but they can never steal our joy, because that comes from within."

As she spoke, tears formed in Calvin's eyes so that by the time she finished speaking, they flowed freely from his eyes. Amanda closed the distance between them so she could comfort her best friend. He opened his arms and she molded herself to his embrace. "I didn't mean to make you cry," Amanda whispered. He hugged her tighter to himself, unable to form the words he needed to say.

"You don't understand," he began, his voice shaking and barely audible. Amanda tried to take a step back so she could see his face, but he didn't release her, only a new flood of tears.

"This morning in the truck I broke down crying because of the song "Butterfly Kisses." Manny, I was *so* angry with that woman and those two guys that I couldn't think straight. I hated them all for what they've done to our family. Mostly for taking the girls, but also what it's done to you. I love you *so* much. I can't stand to see you hurting." He kissed the top of her head before continuing. "I felt like they stole my very life from me. I have no doubt that the lesson He gave you was the lesson I needed to hear."

Calvin relaxed his arms so he could look directly into Amanda's eyes. "I thank God for you daily." He placed a gentle kiss on her lips, then another and another until their pain gave way to passion.

*   *   *

On Tuesday, Ronnie came to work with his new book in hand. "If you have time later, boss, I have more questions I'd like to ask."

At lunch, Calvin offered thanks to God for their food, and then he and Ronnie shared lunch and a lively conversation around whose responsibility it is to prepare oneself for heaven.

"I read that evangelical Bible-believing Christians accept that Jesus died on the cross to save them from their sins, and they ask Him to forgive them of their sin. They believe it is up to them to prepare themselves for heaven through sermons, classes, scripture reading, and memorization according to *Conversations with Catholics*."

"I agree with that," Calvin said.

"Catholics, on the other hand, rely on the church to prepare them for heaven." Ronnie shook his head. "I've never looked at salvation this way before." Their food was gone, but the conversation and remodeling continued.

On Wednesday, Ronnie told Calvin, "I'm sure my mother won't approve of my decision to follow Christ in a different way, and I ain't looking forward to telling her."

They stopped what they were doing. Calvin placed his right hand on Ronnie's shoulder and prayed, "Father God, we come humbly before Your throne and ask that when the time comes for Ronnie to share You with his mother, that You will soften her heart and make her receptive not only to her son's decision, but also to carefully consider what he shares with her."

Calvin released Ronnie's shoulder and resumed working. Ronnie opened his eyes and looked at Calvin disbelievingly.

"You didn't say amen," Ronnie said.

"Because I'm still praying," Calvin told the younger man.

The two men discussed how hard it could be for Catholics to make the conversion to being evangelical Bible-believing Christians.

On Thursday, Ronnie told Calvin he had a question for him that he wanted to discuss in private. The two men excused themselves from the group and made their way to Calvin's truck. When they were seated, Calvin tentatively suggested Ronnie give thanks for their meal. Calvin was aware that praying aloud was new to his young brother so he added, "If you're comfortable praying aloud."

"No problem. I've been learning from the best," Ronnie replied, referring to the times he'd heard Calvin pray. "Dear God, thank You for this day and the many blessings You've given us. Thank You for Calvin and Amanda's willingness to share with me. Thank You for this food we are about to receive. Let our bodies be nourished by it so that we may bring glory to You. In Jesus' name I pray, amen."

"Amen." The two men addressed Ronnie's question as they ate their lunch.

"On Sunday we talked about the Lord's Supper. Do you believe the bread and juice become the body and blood of Christ?"

"No," Calvin answered.

"This book says that the Catholic Church teaches that through 'mystical reality' the bread and juice actually become the body and blood of Jesus. I've known and believed this for years. Now after reading this, I have my doubts." Ronnie handed Calvin the open book and pointed to the highlighted area. "See?"

"I see, and remember. So you doubt that the bread and juice are truly Christ's body?"

"Yes," Ronnie hesitated. "What do you think? Is it or isn't it?"

"Remember that I told you on Sunday what I believe doesn't matter. It's what God's Word says that matters."

"I remember. The book says that Catholics support this by what the Bible says in John 6:51-55. Jesus says He is the 'living bread' and that the bread He gives for the life of the world is 'My' flesh. That seemed pretty convincing to me."

Calvin paused for a moment to let the young man's thoughts sink in and to pray for guidance for himself and understanding for Ronnie. God's presence was with Calvin as he spoke. "Do you know what parables are?"

"Yes, stories that Jesus told."

Calvin reached for the Bible he'd placed in his truck that morning in anticipation of needing it during lunch, then turned to the dictionary until he found the word. "It says that a parable is 'a saying or story that drives home a point using illustrations from everyday life; a comparison of two objects for the purpose of teaching.' Jesus told many parables during the course of His life on earth." Calvin turned to the book of John, chapter 6. "Look at verse 35."

Ronnie took the open Bible and read the verse aloud. "Then Jesus declared, 'I am the bread of life.'"

"Far enough," Calvin interrupted, and indicated that he needed the Bible back. Calvin then turned to John, chapter 10. "Read verse 9."

Ronnie again accepted the open Bible offered to him, then read the verse aloud. "I am the gate; whoever enters through Me will be saved."

"Far enough," Calvin interrupted again. "Now verse 27."

"My sheep listen to My voice; I know them and they follow Me."

"Turn to chapter 15 and read verse 5."

"I am the vine." Ronnie stopped himself this time. "I think I know where you're going, boss."

"Really?"

"Jesus used parables to explain who He was to His people, or His sheep as He called us. He's not a gate, a vine, or bread. He was giving His disciples examples they could understand."

Calvin was so filled with the Holy Spirit that goose bumps covered him. "You've got it!" Calvin exclaimed. He not only meant that Ronnie understood the concept of communion, but he also thought that Ronnie had the Holy Spirit in him.

When he told Ronnie so, he smiled and agreed. "I believe you are right." He raised his left sleeve and showed Calvin his own goose bumps.

As they ate, Ronnie told Calvin that he'd questioned his mother about communion once as a teenager, but she said that's the way it is and we don't question the church. That ended it for Ronnie, until now. They discussed whether Jesus had deliberately tried to confuse his followers by the use of parables. They decided he hadn't, but rather had used them to make things clearer. Lunch was finished but the discussion followed them inside.

"In Matthew 13:9, Jesus says, 'He who has ears, let him hear,'" Calvin told Ronnie as they worked side by side. "Didn't people in Jesus' day have ears?"

"I'm sure they did," Ronnie replied.

"What do you think Jesus meant by that?"

"Maybe He meant hearing isn't just about having ears. It's about understanding as well."

"It's like the parable Jesus told in Matthew 13 about the seeds that fell on three different soils. Those who understood and followed His teachings were the good soil. I didn't think of this outside, but Jesus goes on to say…" Calvin stopped what he was doing to aid his memory. "He explained why He spoke in parables. He said, 'This is why I speak to them in parables: though seeing, they do not see; though hearing, they do not hear or understand.' There is more to what He said, but I don't have that part memorized. I know He went on to say something about hearing but not understanding, and seeing but not perceiving."

"How do you have so much of the Bible memorized?"

"I don't think I have nearly enough memorized. In Psalm 119:11 it says, "Thy word have I hidden in my heart that I might not sin against Thee.' So I figure that's a good reason to memorize verses. I know a lot more verses than I know the reference for, but I'm working on it."

"I only know John 3:16. My family didn't study the Bible. It was 'fed' to us."

"Just because that's what was, doesn't mean that's what has to be, my friend."

Friday's lunch discussion included Joe and Kenny and was eaten inside the gas station despite the dust. Calvin explained that he and Ronnie had been going over the book *Conversations with Catholics* this week. Neither man had read the book but they joined them anyway.

Ronnie told them he'd read a part about prayer. "The subtitle was called *Mechanical Worship* and it was about the ritualistic focus of the Catholic Church. It said Catholics don't speak to God in their prayers, but rather just recite the prayers. I had a prayer book like the author talked about. We learned prayers. Yesterday I told Calvin that the only verse I'd memorized was John 3:16, but I was wrong. I also know the Lord's Prayer. Only I don't know where it's found."

"Matthew 6:9-13," Kenny told him.

"Thank you. My book had prayers for morning, night, before and after meals, before and after communion, for the living and the dead, the confession of sin, and to honor Mary. This book calls them ready-made prayers. I can quote you all of those prayers, but I won't because now I understand they were just another way for the Church to take hold of us. I know this now because the book said going to Mass is *not* voluntary. I knew that first hand. There were even special days we *had* to be there above and beyond Sunday. The Church made it easier on us by offering Saturday Masses. Lots of my friends went on Saturday so they could get drunk and not worry about getting up early on Sunday. Are we obligated to go to church?"

Joe answered, "Brother it's not required, but it is highly recommended. The Bible says not to forsake the assembly with other believers."

Calvin asked if Ronnie knew the Lord's Prayer.

"Yes."

"Do you know what it means?"

Ronnie shrugged his shoulders.

Calvin turned in his Bible to the book of Matthew where Jesus introduced what is now referred to as the Lord's Prayer. He handed Ronnie the Bible and asked him to read the verses he'd previously circled.

"Our Father in heaven, hollowed be Your name, Your kingdom come, Your will be done on earth as it is in heaven. Give us this day our daily bread. Forgive us our debts, as we also have forgiven our debtors. And lead us not into temptation, but deliver us from the evil one."

"You missed a part of verse 9," Calvin told Ronnie.

"I did?" Ronnie looked up at Calvin with a confused look on his face, and then looked back down at his Bible.

"Yes, look closer."

"I guess I missed the part that says 'This, then, is how you should pray.' What does that mean?" Ronnie asked.

"Back up to verse 5 and read from there."

"'And when you pray, do not be like the hypocrites, for they love to pray standing in the synagogues and on the street corners to be seen by men. I tell you the truth; they have received their reward in full.' Six says, 'But when you pray, go into your room, close the door and pray to your Father, who is unseen. Then your Father, Who sees what is done in secret, will reward you.' Seven says, 'And when you pray, do not keep on babbling like pagans, for they think they will be heard because of their many words.' Eight says, 'Do not be like them, for your Father knows what you need before you ask him.' You have something highlighted here on the side that says 'Prayer was never intended to inform God of something he doesn't already know. The point of prayer isn't merely to get what we want, but to nurture our relationship with God."

After he finished reading, Ronnie asked Calvin, "Now, what do you mean when you ask what does the prayer mean?"

"Remember that Jesus taught in parables. In a way, this is a parable as well. Jesus teaches us to call God our Father. When He says hallowed be Your name, Jesus teaches us to show respect to God. When He says Your kingdom come, Your will be done on earth as it is in heaven, He is telling us to align our will with God's will. Our daily bread refers to our daily general needs. We are to forgive others who sin against us just as God forgave our sins against Him. God does not lead us into temptation; we are quite good at getting into that by ourselves. But we do need Him to deliver us from evil. We need his protection not just from temptation, but from everything evil."

Joe and Kenny nodded in agreement as Ronnie considered what Calvin said.

"What you just said isn't in your Bible. How'd you know all that?" Ronnie asked.

"Like you've been devouring the book *Conversations with Catholics* the past few nights, I've devoured other books over the years. Plus I heard a sermon on it once or twice," Calvin informed the small group.

"I listened in church, but I never heard a sermon on this," Ronnie said.

"If I'm not mistaken," Calvin said, "I believe the Catholic Church has a three-year rotation. They preach on the same subject once every three years. That way they cover the whole Bible, or so you're led to believe. Maybe they preached on the Lord's Prayer, but not the way I heard it explained."

"There are a lot of differences between what the Bible says and what the Catholics teach. This book is going to take a while, I can tell," Ronnie said as he ran his hands through his hair in mock exasperation.

"You're just a baby in Christ. You have a lot to learn. Remember, you have to crawl before you can walk and walk before you can run," Joe told him.

"I know." Ronnie looked at his watch as he finished his drink. "Now we better get back to this project." He winked at Joe and Kenny. "Because you know how the boss gets on us if we get behind."

"Yeah," Joe and Kenny agreed as they began to clean up.

"I'll make you guys a deal," Calvin told them. "If we get this section right here," he gestured in front of him, "done before we leave today, you can all have Sunday off," he teased them.

"Whatever you say, boss," Kenny said as he threw a piece of his trash at Calvin and smiled.

The lunch hour lasted longer than a hour, but Calvin was unconcerned because he knew that their priorities were in order. Work progressed at what could be described as a blessed rate afterward. By the end of the day, the section Calvin mentioned after lunch was complete, just as he knew it would be.

"Since you all did such a great job today and we're ahead of schedule, you can all have tomorrow off as well."

As each man said good-bye to the other, Ronnie asked Calvin to wish him luck for the night. "I don't really believe in luck, Ronnie, but I'll pray for you," Calvin told him. "Why, what is going on?"

"I forgot old married men don't go to singles parties anymore."

"I may be married, but I am not old!" Calvin exclaimed. "I suggest you try to go home to clean up first. You're a mess."

"Thanks. I deserved that after the old comment."

"Yes, you did. Are you picking Laurinda up?"

"I'm meeting her there so I better hurry." The two men shook hands and parted ways.

* * *

The church parking lot wasn't as full as it was Sunday morning, so it was easy to see that Laurinda was already there. Ronnie found a parking spot, and then made his way into the warm building. He'd forgotten to ask exactly where in the church they'd be meeting, but he could tell by the lights, the smell, and the sounds that everyone was downstairs. Laurinda was talking with two women when Ronnie came in through the door closest to the food table. She excused herself and made her way to him.

"Fancy meetin' you here," he said to her.

"I invited you, remember? Come on," she said as she took him by the hand and led him over to where she'd been talking when he came in. "I'll introduce you to everybody. They probably shook your hand on Sunday, but I doubt you remember them." Laurinda didn't let go of his hand while introducing him to her friends. As they exchanged small talk, Pastor Dave called for everyone's attention.

"Now that we're all here, let's go to the Lord in prayer." He gave everyone in the room time to join hands with the person next to them. Since Laurinda and Ronnie were already holding hands they stayed together and joined others in a circle around the room. Once everyone was settled and all heads were bowed, Pastor Dave began to pray. "Heavenly Father, we give You thanks and praise for who You are and for this day that You've given us. We thank You for this time together with our Christian brothers and sisters for a time of food and fellowship. We dedicate this night to You. We pray that our wills will be aligned with Yours this night and we will do nothing in speech or deed that disappoints You. Thank You for this food, may it nourish our bodies so we may continue to praise you. These things we pray in Jesus' name, amen."

Laurinda continued to hold Ronnie's hand as she directed him back toward the table covered in pizza boxes. "You get to be first in line since this is your first time here."

"Not unless you stay with me."

"Don't worry. I won't go anywhere without you. I know what it's like to be new. I've only been coming here for about a year."

Once they'd served themselves and found a seat, Ronnie asked if they had been waiting for him. Laurinda said they had been, but no one was in a hurry since everyone liked to get caught up.

"I'm sorry. I wish you'd told me. I wouldn't have talked so much at lunch today."

"What does lunch have to do with anything?"

"All week Calvin and I have been talking about the book *Conversations with Catholics* that Amanda got for me. Calvin read it years ago and suggested I read it. Today Joe and Kenny joined us. It's challenging everything I learned growing up. We spent more than an hour for lunch and didn't get cleaned up to leave until six. I was so dirty I had to go home and shower. The good thing is, we're ahead of schedule so Calvin gave us tomorrow off. I'm planning to study Sunday's lesson since I spent all week reading the book."

Another couple joined them at the table and they began discussing what happens after dinner. The three of them agreed to teach Ronnie how to play euchre. Sometimes the girls played against the guys, but tonight Laurinda wanted to be Ronnie's partner. She smiled to herself as she thought of being his partner, even if it was just for cards. She remembered Amanda's comment about praying about the relationship so she did, right then.

Ronnie caught on quickly to the game and they beat their opponents by four points. The group agreed to move to a different game and selected Scrabble so they could include the only person who'd been left without a partner.

Later, when Ronnie thought the evening was winding down, Laurinda disappeared into the kitchen. Within a few minutes she reappeared holding a five gallon bucket of cinnamon swirl ice cream and a scoop. "If anyone wants some, I suggest you get a spoon and a bowl. Otherwise, I'll just eat this all myself."

Everyone, including Ronnie, ran past her to the kitchen and got a bowl and spoon from the counter, then quickly returned to where she was still standing, scoop poised and ready to take the first bite.

Ronnie playfully wrestled the scoop from her hand and tossed it to Phillip. "If we want any ice cream, we better put you in charge of this."

Laurinda set the bucket on the table and slid it toward Phillip. "He's right, you know."

Everyone in the room laughed. Laurinda was notorious for her ability to eat a lot of ice cream. She made sure there was ice cream at every gathering. Everyone liked her choice this evening. Ronnie offered her the bowl and spoon he had gotten for her while in the kitchen getting his own.

This time when the couple sat down at the table they were alone. "I have something to tell you," Laurinda began in a very serious low tone of voice. "It's about my past, and I think it's very important that you know this about me."

"Yeah, me too. If you remember from Sunday, there is something I want to tell you, too." He spoke equally low. "But are you sure this is the place to reveal deep dark secrets?" he asked.

"Well, it is if it's not a dark secret," she replied.

"You mean yours isn't dark?"

"No. You mean yours is?"

"No, I was just being so serious because you had been. Go on, tell me what your secret is and then I'll tell you mine."

"No, you go first. You've been waiting longer than I have."

Ronnie searched his memory for a prayer from his childhood that would help him through this moment, but then remembered he didn't have to rely on someone else's prayer. He could talk to God just like a friend. He prayed he could talk to Laurinda like a friend right now, too.

"Linny." He used her nickname to lighten the mood. She raised an eyebrow at him, and then smiled.

"Yes."

Ronnie shuffled his feet and twirled his spoon in his ice cream trying to figure out the best way to tell her what he so desperately wanted her to know. How to say it without appearing too forward was beyond him. He ran his unoccupied hand through his hair, looked at her, and then looked back into the cinnamon swirl ice cream.

"I don't understand why this is so hard for you, but it is obvious you are still not ready." She gently touched his left hand when he put it back on the table. "I don't have to know tonight, either. Besides, what I have to tell you is not even serious. I just want you to know where I get my love for ice cream."

Ronnie breathed a sigh of relief, and Laurinda was sure it was his first breath in a while.

"When I was a baby, and even to this day, my Dad has had a bowl of ice cream almost every night before he goes to bed. When I was a baby, my mum thought I was tucked in for the night so she went to the living room to join Dad. About a minute later I'd be up shaking my bed and yelling 'Creamy, Mommy, creamy.' I don't remember it but it has been a big joke in my family ever since."

"I wish I had fond memories like that of my parents. But since I don't, I'm looking forward to making them with my own family someday."

Laurinda smiled.

Chapter 11

Saturday morning at ten o'clock the Edwardses' phone rang. It was Ronnie.

"Amanda, I'm sorry to be calling you so early and at home. I really need to talk to Calvin, please."

"I'll get him."

"Thank you."

"Honey, Ronnie's on the phone. He sounds anxious," Amanda told Calvin when she found him in the basement.

"Thanks, sweetheart," he told Amanda as she handed him the phone. "Hey, buddy, what's up? Amanda said you sounded anxious."

"I'm sorry for calling you at home. I got your number from Laurinda. She said I should call you. I didn't mean to interrupt your Saturday."

"Ronnie, stop apologizing and tell me what's wrong."

"I have to go to Chicago. My aunt called and told me my mother's in the hospital. She slipped on some ice and fell. They took her to the hospital to be checked and found a spot on one of her lungs while taking the X-rays. I am scared. She's the only parent I got." Ronnie was crying.

"What can we do to help? You know we'll be praying for you both."

"I don't know. I don't know anything right now 'cept that I wanna to be in Chicago. I wanna say good-bye and tell her I love her. Calvin, I don't want to lose her." Ronnie was crying almost uncontrollably.

"Listen, Ronnie, there is no reason to assume the worst."

Ronnie was silent except for crying. Calvin heard him take a deep breath. "She's smoked for years and my brother and I kept tellin' her to quit, but she wouldn't listen. I blame my dad for her smoking. She didn't smoke before he left. After she realized he wasn't coming back she started. It's his fault, I know it is."

"Calm down, brother. We all make choices in life, some good, some bad, but they're our choices. We can't hold anyone else responsible. Maybe this is nothing and you won't know until more tests are run. If she's anything like you, she's a tough lady who can handle a lot."

Ronnie calmed down and stopped pacing the floor as Calvin spoke. "You're right about her being tough. She handled two rowdy boys by herself and we weren't easily handled, especially in our teens. I don't know exactly when I'll be back, but I know I can't stay long. I've got bills to pay and they don't get paid if I don't work."

"Don't worry about that. Just go and be with your mom."

"I hope I won't put us behind on the gas station."

"You just let me worry about that."

"I would boss, but you don't worry, you pray."

Calvin laughed. "Now I know you listen to some of what I say."

"Oh, I listen to everything you say, especially when it comes to Laurinda. Boss, she offered to drive to Chicago with me, or maybe she offered to drive for me. I'm not really in any condition to drive right now. Should I take her up on the offer or is she just being polite?"

"I know Laurinda's very polite, but I also know that she doesn't do things just for that reason. Since she only works part-time for us during the winter months, I don't know if her other job can spare her like we can. She wouldn't necessarily have to be back to do payroll on Friday since Amanda can do it. Speaking of payroll, do you have enough cash for the trip or do you need an advance?"

"I can't believe you asked me that. I was wondering how to ask if I could just get a hundred dollars that would get me there and back for gas and food."

"That's not a problem. If you decide to take Laurinda up on her offer, she knows how to get here. If not, then I'll give you directions."

"You were no help. I wanted you to tell me if I should take her up on it, and all you say is you can spare her and she doesn't do things just because she's polite."

"I can't make that decision for you. But I can tell you that she's not rich and wouldn't be able to afford a hotel room, so you'll have to think of somewhere she can stay that won't cost her anything, or compromise her or you."

"I already thought of that. I have to call my aunt back before I leave so I thought I'd ask if she can stay there. With her kids gone, I know she'd enjoy the company. My uncle won't retire, so she's at home all day and some evenings by herself. I know she'll say yes. I can stay in my old room at Mom's unless she's changed it into something else."

"It sounds like you've already made up your mind about accepting her offer if you're making plans for her to stay with your aunt. Just remember what I told you about her being like a little sister to me and moving slowly with her."

"Yes, sir. I better call her back before she changes her mind."

"All right, we will see you soon."

"Calvin, thanks for listening and helping me calm down."

"You're welcome, but the only thing I did to help you calm down was pray for you the whole time."

"I should've known. 'If you're going to worry, why pray? If you're going to pray, why worry?' Did I get that right?"

"Yes, good-bye."

Ronnie laughed. "Good-bye."

After the two men hung up, Calvin explained everything to Amanda, and Ronnie called the girl of his dreams.

One hour later the pair of travelers arrived at the Edwardses' front door. Calvin had already made a run to the bank to withdraw two hundred dollars for them.

"Come in out of the cold," Amanda said when she opened the door. "I'm sure you're eager to get on the road so I'll go get Calvin. He sneaks off to his workroom every chance he gets. I think he's working on a surprise for me," she said over her shoulder as she made her way to the top of the basement stairs. "They're here."

When Calvin reached the trio, he withdrew the two bills from his pocket and placed them in Ronnie's hand. "There's a little extra in case you need it."

Amanda went to the kitchen, returning with a cooler filled with drinks, sandwiches, and snacks. "It's getting close to lunch and I doubt you'll want to stop to eat so I threw together a few things for you." She hugged Laurinda and then Ronnie. "Have a safe trip and call when you get there."

"We will. Thanks so much for the lunch, Amanda, it was very thoughtful." Laurinda spoke for both of them. She hugged Amanda again, then Calvin.

Ronnie offered his hand to Calvin. As Calvin took Ronnie's hand in his, he pulled him close into a hug as well. "We're family, remember? I'd like to pray before you leave." The small group joined hands as Calvin prayed for their safe journey and Ronnie's mother. Everyone hugged once more after the prayer, and then Ronnie and Laurinda left.

Ronnie started the trip by driving for the first hour. They ate the sandwiches Amanda packed, and afterward they switched drivers. When they arrived in Gary, Indiana, they stopped for gas since Ronnie hadn't thought to fill up before leaving.

"This city stinks," Laurinda commented as she got out of the car to go to the ladies room.

"Yup, it's a big industrial area. I don't like the smell myself. It's even worse in the summer. Why don't you stay inside until I get done here. We'll get a candy bar." He laughed, and then added, "Or maybe ice cream."

"Cute! I'll wait for you," she called over her shoulder.

When Laurinda had finished in the bathroom, she looked around the station at the knickknacks for sale. As she browsed, she noticed two little girls and their mother rush toward the bathroom. She smiled at the girls and nodded at the woman as they passed, and then continued to browse. When Ronnie finished filling the car, he joined her and they picked out ice cream treats, and then waited to pay for their purchases.

While they waited, the woman and little girls passed Laurinda again. This time she looked closer at the girls, and then their mother. She thought it strange that the girls didn't look very much like her. She wondered what her own children might look like as her gaze turned to Ronnie. As if he could hear her thoughts, she quickly looked away. The oldest little girl wanted to stop and look at the pretties, but her mother told her they had to get going if they were going to get to their Grandma Smith's house on time. Laurinda overheard the child say, "She's not my grandma. My grandma's Sandy and..."

The woman cut her off. "Daddy's waiting in the car and we're in a hurry."

Laurinda prayed the little girl wouldn't get into trouble once she returned to the car.

"All set?" Ronnie asked her, pulling her from her thoughts.

"I'm sorry, yes. I was praying that little girl doesn't get into trouble because of what she said to her mum."

Ronnie held the door open for her. "What'd she say?"

"That Mrs. Smith wasn't her grandma. Her grandma was Sandy."

"Wonder what that meant."

Laurinda shrugged her shoulders. "I don't know. The girls didn't look like her. Maybe she's their step-mother." Laurinda looked around for the girls. Except for a few cars at the pumps, the lot was empty. "Do you want me to keep driving?"

"I'll take over. You've done most of the driving and we only have a little more than an hour before we'll be there. Besides, it will be easier for me to drive it than explain it." Ronnie unlocked the passenger door and let her in.

"I was getting a little tired of looking at the lines in the road. Besides, now I can eat my ice cream with both hands," Laurinda said, and they laughed.

"Are you going to want to freshen up or is it okay if we go straight to the hospital?"

"I'm fine. When's your aunt expecting us?"

"I told her about six o'clock. She said she'd have dinner waiting for us."

Laurinda looked at her ice cream and then at Ronnie. "Why didn't you tell me that before I got the jumbo ice cream sandwich," she exclaimed.

"I think you can handle it." He smiled at her, started the car, and then pulled away from the pump.

When they arrived at the hospital, Ronnie knew his aunt wouldn't have dinner ready for them since she was still at the hospital. Katherine's face lit up when her son walked into the room.

"What are you doing here?" she exclaimed.

"I had to come and check on my favorite mother," he told her.

"How many other mothers do you have?"

"Wouldn't you like to know." He leaned over and kissed her, and then introduced Laurinda to them. He sat down on the bed beside her. "You tried doing a little ice ballet, did you?" he asked her as he picked up her hand to hold it in his own.

"I have to do something to keep myself busy since my boys left me to go and find the finer things in life." She looked directly at Laurinda and smiled.

"Have they told you what the spot is yet? When was the doctor last here, and when will he be back? Are you in any pain?"

She raised her free hand to make him stop talking so fast. "The spot was so tiny I hardly saw it when the doctor showed it to me. He said because it was so small, they'd just keep an eye on it for now. He was here this morning, and will be back tomorrow to check me out of this place. Yes, I am in pain, but not because of the *spot*, but because of the fall. I ache from head to toe. I'm not as young as I used to be. They told me it'll take a while to recover.

Now tell me about this lovely lady."

"This is Laurinda. We work together."

"It's a pleasure to meet you, Ms. Colthorp," Laurinda said as she extended her hand to Katherine.

"Glad to meet you, Laurinda."

Aunt Dorothy suggested she and Laurinda give mother and son some time alone. "I'll take her to see the indoor atrium the hospital added last summer. We won't be long," Dorothy told Ronnie.

The two women left Ronnie and his mother alone. Ronnie explained that he and Laurinda worked for the same company but not really together. He told her about going to the singles party the night before, carefully leaving out the part about it being at her church. The last thing he wanted to do right now was upset his mother with the fact that he'd left the Catholic Church forever. They discussed the trip over and she caught him up on his younger brother. Before they knew it, an hour had passed and his stomach began growling. "I'm going to go see what Aunt Dot's done with Laurinda. They must be getting hungry, too." He kissed his mother's

131

cheek, got instructions on how to find the atrium, and then left the room.

He didn't make it to the atrium since the two women got off the elevator he was waiting for. "I know I told you I'd have dinner waiting, sweetie," Aunt Dorothy said, "but my plans changed. I'll take you two out to dinner if that's okay with you."

"It's okay with me if it's okay with Laurinda."

The trio told Katherine their plans, and she agreed it had gotten too late for Dorothy to cook anything. After Dorothy and Ronnie kissed Katherine good-bye, she extended her hand to Laurinda indicating she expected a kiss from her as well. Laurinda gave her a peck on the cheek, and then the trio left.

"Get some rest, Mother," Ronnie said just before leaving.

"Don't worry about me."

Ronnie thought about what Calvin always says about worry, but he didn't mention it to her. He only waved good-bye.

Ronnie and Laurinda followed Aunt Dorothy to the restaurant.

"Did you mention to Aunt Dot that I've become a born-again Christian?" Ronnie asked Laurinda as soon as they were alone.

"No. It's not my place to tell her. I mentioned that we went to the singles party last night but not where. Why do you call her Dot?"

"My Uncle Eddie gave her that nickname a long time ago and it kinda stuck with her." Ronnie rubbed his hands across the steering wheel, then reached over for her hand and picked it up from her lap. He brought it to his lips and gently kissed it, then returned it to its place on her lap.

"What'd you do that for?" she asked.

"You are incredible," he told her. "Do you believe God puts people together for a reason?"

"Yes. I believe you were brought to Edwards Construction so Calvin could share the gospel with you and you would come to know the Lord in a personal way." She wanted to say that she hoped it was also to bring them together but decided against it.

"That has certainly been an awesome outcome of my being at Edwards. But I was thinking about you and me," he said as he stole a look at her face in the light from the street lamps. "I didn't mean to make you cry."

"I…well, it's just that I was…" she stammered. "Get out of my head," she told him.

"I wasn't in your head. I've been right here driving the whole time," he said as he smiled at her. "So you were thinking it, too?"

"Ronnie, I've been thinking about you since the first day I met you. Fortunately, Amanda reminded me of what I already knew— that I needed to pray about you. Like I said before, there's no way I would've had anything to do with you, except work, if you hadn't become a Christian."

"Any other requirements I need to meet?"

"Actually, you've already met another one and you didn't even know it."

"I didn't know I'd met the first one. So what's the second?"

"You treated your mother and aunt with respect. That shows you love her very much. You teased your mother, but she teased you right back."

"I don't remember a lot about my dad, except that he treated her horribly. When I became the man of the house, I decided to treat her better. One good thing I learned growing up Catholic was to respect human life."

"Then would you join me in October for the Life Chain?"

"Lady, I'd go anywhere with you. What's the Life Chain?"

"Obviously, I'd go anywhere with you." She gestured out the window at the city and laughed. "Life Chain is an organized way to help stop abortion. I've been a part of it every year."

"If it's important to you, pretty lady, then it's important to me. I'll be there."

"Thank you," Laurinda said as she smiled at him. "I have a confession."

"We don't have time to stop at the parish," he teased her.

"Not that kind of confession. My confession is strictly for and about you," she paused, gathering her thoughts. "I wanted to come here to see how you treated your mother. And if I hadn't come, I wouldn't have gotten to experience how bad Gary, Indiana, stinks."

"If I had my way, you would've experienced Gary someday."

"You have to remember, you shouldn't want to do things your way anymore. Someday you'll learn that it's better to do things God's way." This time she took his hand into hers and held it. "Pray about us and be sure whatever you do is in God's will."

Before he could ask her how he would know what God's will was, Aunt Dorothy turned her blinker on to enter the restaurant parking lot, so he followed.

Once inside, Ronnie helped both women remove their coats and then hung them on the coatrack. As they waited for a table, Ronnie called Calvin to let them know they'd arrived safely and his mother was fine. As the hostess took them to their table, Ronnie leaned over to Laurinda, "There's something I need to ask you later."

Once they were seated, Aunt Dorothy started asking questions. "What's been going on in your life, Ronnie, besides this pretty lady?"

"Working mostly, trying to make ends meet."

"There's something you're not telling me. You look different."

"I got my hair cut a few weeks ago."

"That's not it and you know it. There's a glow about you."

Ronnie looked at Laurinda with pleading eyes as if asking for help. She smiled at him and raised her eyebrows as if to say, no time like the present.

"You're right, Aunt Dorothy. You always could see right through me. You know I used to hate that," he told her. "I never could lie to you."

"You look too happy for a man who's just trying to make ends meet. I've lived with a man who's been trying to do that for as long as I've known him, and even though he accomplished it long ago, he still doesn't look as happy as you do."

The waitress took their orders.

"Laurinda told me that she told you about the party we were at last night. What she didn't tell you was where." He paused to make sure he worded the next part correctly. "We were at her church."

"What parish does she belong to?"

"Aunt Dot, she doesn't belong to a parish. She isn't Catholic."

"I presumed she was Catholic because you were raised that way. I'm living proof that Catholicism isn't for everyone. What church does she belong to?"

"Friendship Baptist Church," Laurinda said.

"I didn't mean to leave you out of the conversation." Ronnie looked to Laurinda as he felt for her hand under the table and grasped it in his own. "It's a really cool church, and I had a wonderful time at the party."

"That's good, but that's not it, either," Aunt Dorothy persisted.

"If I tell you, you have to promise not to tell Mom. I don't want to upset her right now."

"Depending on what it is, it may upset her no matter who tells her, so I promise to let you do it. I don't want her to shoot the messenger."

"A couple of weeks ago I talked to my boss about church. He invited me to join him and his wife at Friendship Baptist Church. I planned to attend their Sunday school class so they gave me a copy of the book they were studying. We didn't work that Saturday because of freezing rain. Anyway, I spent all day getting caught up in the book. It really challenged me to think about everything I learned growing up Catholic. I went to the class with a list of questions for Calvin. That's our boss. After class we stayed behind to talk. By the end of our conversation I realized that I didn't know Jesus as my personal Savior."

"Go on," Aunt Dorothy urged him.

"I realized Jesus died for us, once and for all. We don't have to keep crucifying Him at every Mass, and attending Mass isn't required to get into heaven. I found a lot of things we don't have to do to get to heaven. More importantly, I found out what we have to do to get into heaven." He checked her reaction before continuing. "I confessed my sins, asked Him to forgive me, and asked Him to come into my heart to live forever."

"I'm so happy for you. I've been praying about this for years. You know how hard it was for your mother when I first left the Church, but over the years she's come to accept it. Is that all?"

"What do you mean is that all?" Ronnie said, a little louder than he meant to. "That's everything!" he exclaimed. He lowered his voice, then said, "I hope she accepts my conversion quicker than she did yours. You know how important it is to me that she accepts me as I am."

"I'm not discounting your acceptance of Jesus, really. I'm thrilled for you." Aunt Dorothy paused, "I was afraid you were going to tell me that you and Laurinda had to get married because she was pregnant."

Laurinda blushed. "Aunt Dot, I've never even kissed her on the mouth. And I don't plan to until we are married, either." He wished he could take the last part back before the words were completely out of his mouth. When am I ever going to learn to think before I speak, he thought.

"Oh, honey, I'm sorry. I didn't mean to insult either of you. It's just that I overhead him tell you that he had something he needed to ask you, so I thought maybe he was going to propose. I never meant to imply that you two were sleeping together." Fortunately for Aunt Dorothy, the food arrived just then and everyone turned their attention to the waitress.

When the waitress left, Laurinda reached across the table and placed her hand over Dorothy's and said, "Aunt Dorothy, I'm not offended by your assumption. I might have done the same thing." Everyone ate in silence for a while.

"Did I tell you I've even been trying to get your mother to read the Bible I gave her last Christmas," Aunt Dorothy said, breaking the silence.

"I remember she asked what she was supposed to do with it. Didn't she say she got all she needed from Mass?"

"Yes. Now back to telling your mother. I agree now's not the time to tell her, but I'm sure Christmas won't be either. Let me work on her for you, then sometime during the summer you and Laurinda can come back and tell her. I'll stay in touch and keep you posted on how I'm doing."

"You'd do that for me?" Ronnie asked.

"No, honey, I'd do that for her!" She laughed. "Of course I'd do that for you. I love you. Now tell me about this book you're studying. Maybe I'd like it."

Ronnie told her about their Sunday school book and the book *Conversations with Catholics*. He told her that he and Calvin had spent every day last week studying at lunch. The group alternated between talking and eating until their plates were empty.

When the waitress asked if they wanted dessert, even Laurinda declined. "What, no ice cream tonight, Linny?"

"Are you kidding. I'm so full you may have to roll me out to Aunt Dorothy's car. I'm also very tired."

Aunt Dorothy paid the bill while Ronnie and Laurinda got their coats, and then moved Laurinda's things from Ronnie's car to Aunt Dorothy's.

Once outside he kissed both women on the cheek and bid them good night, promising to pick Laurinda up in the morning to go back to the hospital.

The following morning Ronnie slept later than usual and might have slept later had he not been awakened by the phone. Afraid it was the hospital, he ran to the kitchen. It was Laurinda. She and Aunt Dorothy had gone home and prayed with his Uncle Eddie about the situation. Uncle Eddie suggested that everyone join them at church the following morning. It wasn't Baptist, but neither was it Catholic. Ronnie agreed to join them because he wanted to be in church. They gave him directions and only twenty-five minutes to be ready.

Ronnie didn't bring dress clothes. He didn't think he'd need them. He looked in his old closet and found some clothes his little brother had left there. After a shower, he found something that fit, then put on his tennis shoes. He slipped on his coat and drove to the church.

He found his aunt, uncle, and Laurinda just inside the door waiting for him. Laurinda looked beautiful and he let her know he thought so while he shook his uncle's hand.

"Good to see you, young man," Ronnie's Uncle Eddie said as he shook the younger man's hand. "Your Aunt Dorothy tells me you've been making some changes in your life. I hope this delightful young woman is a permanent part of those changes."

"From what everyone's telling me, that's up to God, not just me. But I'll go along with Him if He says it's okay."

"You're right, it is God's will be done," Uncle Eddie agreed. The group made their way inside the sanctuary to sing and hear God's word.

The two couples traveled in their respective vehicles for brunch. Ronnie was eager to get to the hospital even though he told his mother on the phone earlier that the four of them were going to church and out for breakfast afterward. Ronnie and his uncle talked about the gas station he was renovating and about his uncle's job as a communications salesman. The women discussed the Edwards children being stolen. Aunt Dorothy had read about it so she asked if there'd been any progress. Regretfully, Laurinda said no. Laurinda thought of the little girls she'd seen at the gas station, but brushed the thought aside to give Aunt Dorothy her full attention.

When the party arrived at the hospital, Katherine was waiting for them since the doctor had discharged her. It was decided that she would go home with Dorothy and Eddie so Dorothy could take care of her. They also decided that Ronnie and Laurinda would keep the same sleeping arrangements for the night and leave in the morning after breakfast.

After a light dinner at his aunt and uncle's house, Ronnie shook his uncle's hand, kissed the women good-bye, and then returned to his childhood home. He changed from the uncomfortable dress clothes into his old boxers. He brushed his teeth, and then lay down on the bed that seemed a lot smaller than he remembered. He lay staring at the ceiling until an idea hit him. He knew his mother would be short on money since she was told not go back to work for a week, so he took one of the hundred dollar bills from his jeans pocket and placed it under her pillow with a note telling her how much he loved her.

He returned to his room, but instead of immediately lying back down, he knelt beside the bed and prayed like he'd never prayed before. He poured his heart out to God about everything from his mother and Laurinda to the Edwards children to sins he'd committed years ago. By the time he finished, he was crying and emotionally exhausted.

When the two vehicles arrived at Katherine's house, Uncle Eddie had breakfast ready. When he prayed before their meal, Katherine noticed Ronnie didn't make the sign of the cross before or after the prayer, but she didn't say anything. She was glad to be out of the hospital, and as soon as she could convince Dorothy to let her go home, she would. Before leaving for home, Ronnie made her promise to stay the whole week before trying to go back to work or even home. "God will supply all your needs," he told her as he hugged and kissed her good-bye. It was a tearful good-bye for them, not knowing when they'd see each other again.

Ronnie filled up the car with gas before they left his hometown so the only reason to stop was for a bathroom break. The need to go hit Laurinda just before Gary so they stopped at the same gas station as they had before. Ronnie waited for her in the car. She hurried into the bathroom, but on the way out she looked down where the little girl had been two days before and realized there were elephants on the shelf where she'd been looking. Maybe they just put those there, she thought to herself. The idea bothered her so bad, she asked the clerk if the elephant display had been there on Saturday. She said yes.

"Do you still have any time left on the calling card?" she asked Ronnie when she returned to the car.

"Yes, do you need it?"

"Yes." She paused. "Maybe…no." She paused again. "Never mind. I think this is something I need to tell Calvin in person."

Chapter 12

Amanda changed clothes four times before settling on tan pants and a purple turtleneck sweater. She pulled her hair into a half ponytail. She knew she'd be on her feet a lot so she and Calvin purchased a pair of nurse's shoes on Saturday. I'm glad Michael suggested I only work two hours today, she thought.

She'd been both excited about and dreading this since she and Calvin decided it was God's will for her to work at the Family Christian Store. She called Michael to accept the job on Wednesday and filled out the paperwork on Friday. All she had to do today was learn her job. What if I can't help the customers, she thought. "Every time I've asked someone there about a book or a song they knew exactly what I wanted. I don't have that much knowledge, and this morning I doubt I ever will. This is where faith comes in, she thought as she slipped on her jacket and went to the van.

As Amanda put the van in park, she said, "I can do all things through Christ, Who strengthens me."

Michael showed her around the building, pointing out the sections and talking about the displays. He asked for ideas on how she'd reset the displays. She shared a couple of ideas off the top of her head. He laughed when she asked how much budget was allotted for changing the displays. "We use our imaginations around here a lot more than our checkbook. Don't despair, we have lots of stuff in the back from old displays. I'm sure you'll do something creative to make it look new."

He pushed the door to the back room open and let her go in front of him. "Here's the time clock and your time card. Go ahead and punch in. I'll make a note that you've already been here for ten minutes. I should have brought you back here first. Sorry."

"That's okay," Amanda told him. "I'm so nervous that I won't be able to help your customers that I didn't even think of punching in. I've never done that before."

"Don't worry, someone will always be here with you if you can't find something. We have a great team of employees here."

They left the office and stepped into what Michael kept referring to as the back room. "Generally, we get all the books on the shelves after they're entered into the computer, but there's no way we can get all these pictures on the walls. So we keep them up here." He pointed above the pictures. "And this is where we keep the overstock cards."

"Are these Christmas cards for this year or last year?"

"Last year's. Sometimes we send them back to the company, but this year we are putting them in our clearance section in July."

"Do people buy Christmas cards in July?"

"Oh yeah, they do, just like they buy Easter cards in December. People love to buy things at a discounted price. Which reminds me, did I mention you get a twenty-five percent discount off everything you buy?"

"No, you didn't, but I like that! Calvin will be thrilled. He says I spend more money here in a year than some families spend on food for a year."

"That's the reason I suggested you come to work for us." He paused. "If you don't mind me asking, have you learned anything more about your daughters?"

"I don't mind you asking. I'm afraid we haven't."

"I'm so sorry to hear that. I'll continue to pray for you and them."

"I appreciate that. Prayer is what has gotten us through this far."

"All right then! Let's make your name tag and get you out on the sales floor."

"I'm in no hurry. I'm afraid I won't be able to help people as well as you and Aimie do."

"If you can't answer someone's question or can't find what they're looking for, remember you can come and get one of us and follow along until the question is answered or the item is found. That way, in the future, you'll know where to look. The computer helps a lot even if they only know a part of the name of a book or song. Here, put this on and we'll go up front. I'll show you how to use the cash register and computer." He handed Amanda her name tag and she pinned it to her sweater. "You can stick it into the cork board every time you leave or you can take it with you, but when you're on the sales floor you must have it on."

"I can be forgetful at times, so I'll leave it here when I go." Amanda paused. "Unless I forget to take it off."

Michael laughed and opened the door so they could return to the sales floor. After a while at the computer Amanda felt completely illiterate. She was certain she'd never get the hang of it. Sensing her frustration, Michael suggested she help Aimie with pricing and stocking the books. Aimie explained how each piece of merchandise has its own number. After the merchandise is priced, she or Michael will enter the information into the computer in the back. "The computers are shut down at night so in the morning they update automatically with the information from the back computer." Aimie took a book from the pile that Amanda had just finished pricing.

"Let me show you what information this little tag gives you. It will make looking things up on the computer easier." Aimie proceeded to show her what she could learn from the bar code and the price tag.

At the end of her two hours Amanda left with a better opinion of the computer system. Even though she was still slightly frazzled and her feet hurt, she promised to come back the next day.

Michael laughed.

Amanda was setting the table when Calvin arrived home several hours later. "Dinner will be a few minutes if you want to take a shower and change clothes. I have to fold a load of laundry," she informed him after they kissed hello.

They both turned toward their bedroom, but only made it as far as the living room before the doorbell rang. "I'll get it if you want to go fold the clothes," he said as he winked at her.

"Okay, but you know where I'll be if you want to help me."

"You know I will," he said before she left the room.

Calvin opened the door to discover two weary travelers. He was about to call to Amanda until Laurinda held up her hand to stop him.

"I need to talk to you first," Laurinda told him.

Calvin extended his right arm to motion she go first into the living room. He gave Ronnie a quizzical look.

Ronnie shrugged his shoulders.

Both men sat down while Laurinda paced around the room until she came to the chalk drawing Calvin had given Amanda recently. "Who's that?" she asked.

"It's what the girls might look like now. A guy Jimmy knows did it for me."

Tears swelled in Laurinda's eyes and a lump formed in her throat. She gazed at the curio cabinet that held what she guessed was over one hundred elephant figures. "Where's Amanda?"

"In the bedroom. Do you want me to get her now?"

"No. May we go outside. I can't breathe in here."

Once outside, she looked at Ronnie for strength. If what she suspected was true, she'd feel even worse than she did not knowing.

"Calvin," she began, then stopped. Her hands were sweating despite the cold, so she wiped them on her jeans. She took a deep breath and tried again. "Calvin, I think…I think I saw the girls this weekend."

Calvin stared at her. Moments dragged on for what seemed like hours before he said, "Did you just say you thought you saw *my* daughters *this* weekend?" Tears welled up in his eyes and his hands began to shake as he looked at his bookkeeper, friend, and sister in Christ.

"Yes. On the way down we had to get gas near Gary, Indiana. I'd been driving so I needed to get out, stretch, and use the bathroom. When I came out of the bathroom I waited inside for Ronnie. A lady with two little girls came in and went toward the bathroom. I looked at them but didn't really see them. While we were waiting to pay, they came out and the oldest girl stopped to look at a display near me. I looked at them again but only thought to myself how they didn't look like their mother, at least the woman I presumed was their mother. She tried to hurry the oldest girl because the woman said they were late getting to Grandma Smith's house. The girl said something about Mrs. Smith was not her grandma, that Sandy was her grandma. She was about to say something else, but the woman told her that her daddy was waiting. I prayed the girl wouldn't get into trouble for what she'd said. I told Ronnie about it. I figured the woman was probably a step-mother and that Mrs. Smith was her mother. I could see where that would make a child a little hostile toward the step-grandmother. If hostile's the word I want to use.

"Today we stopped at the same place again. As I walked toward the exit, I passed by the display the girl had been looking at. It took my breath away, and then I thought maybe it was a new display since Saturday. I asked the clerk, but she said it wasn't."

Laurinda looked at Ronnie for support, then said, "Calvin, it was a display of elephants." That being said, Laurinda began crying uncontrollably. Ronnie took her into his arms.

At first it seemed Calvin hadn't heard a word she'd said. He didn't speak or move for what felt like an eternity. Ronnie wasn't even certain he was breathing.

After clearing his throat, Calvin spoke. "Thank you for suggesting we come out here. I don't want to get Amanda's hopes up. I'd like you to call this man," Calvin pulled a business card out of his wallet and handed it to Laurinda "and tell him everything you just told me. Now let's go inside where it's warm. Amanda has dinner almost ready so you should stay and eat with us. After dinner, you excuse yourself and use the phone downstairs so the charge is on our bill." Calvin rubbed his forehead as he looked at Laurinda. "You saw our babies."

Laurinda dried her eyes and tried to control her emotions. "Calvin, I'm so sorry I didn't realize it was them. I had to go back to the spot to get a clear picture of them in my mind. I'm afraid I don't remember the woman's face. Her hair must have been dark because I thought the kids didn't look anything like her."

Calvin looked like he was somewhere else. "We better get inside before Amanda gets suspicious."

Fortunately, Amanda remained in the bedroom while they were in the garage and hadn't heard the door opening and closing. Calvin took their coats and suggested they go to the living room. He gave Ronnie instructions on how to start the gas fireplace in the living room before he made his way to his bedroom.

"I'm so rude. I was hogging all of Ronnie and Laurinda's time. I figured you'd be done sooner."

"Ronnie and Laurinda are here?"

"Yeah, and boy they've got some stories to tell. I hope you don't mind but I invited them for dinner. I trust we have enough."

"I'm sure we will. Besides, if anyone doesn't get enough, we can always have ice cream." They laughed about Laurinda's love for ice cream.

"May I help here so we can get out there?" Calvin nodded his head toward the living room. "I don't want to leave those two alone in front of our fireplace for long." He put his arms around her waist. "You know it sometimes gets too hot in there for us." He kissed her earlobe, then down her neck. His heart ached, but he didn't want her to know it.

"If you don't stop that, it'll be too hot in here. The rest are towels. I don't care if they wrinkle."

Over dinner, Ronnie and Laurinda shared their weekend, excluding the gas station, except that they thought it was in the worst smelling city ever. Calvin and Amanda agreed to pray that Ronnie's aunt and uncle would be able to soften Ronnie's mother's heart before he tells her about his recent decision. Laurinda said they'd love Ronnie's aunt. She was straightforward and didn't pull any punches when it came to getting information, even if the information she got wasn't what she expected. Ronnie told them about how his aunt had thought Laurinda was pregnant.

"That reminds me," Laurinda said to Ronnie. "You said you had something to ask me. That was the reason Aunt Dorothy thought I was pregnant. What did you want to ask me?"

"Remind me what we were talking about and I'll tell you what the question was."

"We'd been talking about how you had already met two of my requirements in a potential boyfriend."

"I remember," Ronnie said. "I actually had two questions. What are the other requirements, and how do you know that what you're doing is in God's will?"

"I'm glad you didn't remember that until we got here. We can discuss the first question on the way back to my car. As for the second question, I have a tough enough time dealing with that myself." She paused. "I just feel it in my spirit. I know the obvious things to not do, but sometimes the not-so-obvious stuff is a lot harder.

"Maybe Calvin and Amanda would have a better answer for you. Right now I need to make a phone call." She looked at Amanda. "Is it okay if I use the phone downstairs?"

"Sure, go ahead. We'll entertain Ronnie with our dating history and how Calvin was sure I was the only girl in the world for him." She winked at her husband.

He pointed to Amanda. "Yeah, what she said. We'll entertain him with our dating history. Take your time. It'll take us a while."

Ronnie stood up when Laurinda did. "Where ya going?" Calvin asked.

"Nowhere. Don't you know that when a lady leaves the table you are supposed to stand up?"

"Yeah, what he said," Amanda teased him. When she stood up to clear the table, Calvin practically tipped his chair over trying to stand up, too. Everyone laughed.

"And I'm usually such a gentleman." He placed the back of his right hand on his forehead and dramatically asked, "Wherever did I go wrong?"

"Okay, Shakespeare, enough of the dramatics. Tell me how you know that what you're doing is in God's will. I think Linny…"

"You know her nickname? Honey," he called to Amanda, "this is getting serious."

"Knock it off, boss. As I was about to say before, I think Laurinda was right when she said it's easy to know the biggies. I don't, usually, have any problem restraining myself from hurting people." He smiled at Calvin. "And I don't desire to have another man's wife or his donkey or his male or female servant." Calvin looked impressed with his knowledge of the commandment. "One night last week when I got home from work, I looked up the Ten Commandments again. That one was funny, so I remembered part of it. Please tell me how you know about the little things and about the big ones, like who to marry."

"When we talk to God, we use our voices. He hears us in spirit. He uses our spirit to speak to us. He also uses other people. I believe everything happens in this world for a reason." Ronnie looked directly at Calvin and nodded in agreement, certain he was referring to the trip to Chicago.

"When we pray, God hears our spirit more than our words. He listens to and looks at our hearts. When the prophet Samuel went to Jesse's house to anoint David as the new king of Israel, he looked at all of Jesse's sons in terms of the flesh. The Lord told Samuel not to consider appearance or height, because God does not look at outward appearance, He looks at the heart. In Proverbs, I believe chapter 27, it says "as water reflects a face, so a man's heart reflects the man." What I'm about to say is going to cause you to ask another question. Get to know the heart of God."

"Okay. How do I get to know the heart of God?"

"Read, little brother, read. The books Amanda got you are good, but no where can you really get to know the heart of God better than in His word. I suggest you read the book of John first."

"I feel like all I ever do is work and read, work and read." Ronnie exaggerated his words. "Occasionally, I work in a little sleep where I can. I'd like to spend a little more time with that beautiful woman in your basement."

"We might be able to arrange a little time in the basement for you with her," Calvin teased. Ronnie laughed. "Seriously, in a way I envy the ability to just work, read, and sleep. Paul was right when he said it's better if you can remain unmarried. When you're married, your priorities are different. I'm married to Amanda and our company, but I wouldn't trade them for anything in this world." Calvin thought for a moment, then said, "Actually, I would trade the company to have our daughters back, but you know what I mean."

"Yes, sir."

"I used to do what you are doing now, only I was also going to high school, too. It got easier when I went on work-study. I believe because I put God first in my life during that difficult time, everything I did was blessed. The Bible tells us to seek God first, and then all the desires of our hearts will be added to us."

"If you'll excuse me then, I'm going to go find God because Laurinda is truly the desire of my heart," he teased Calvin. "Seriously, I want to be all that God wants me to be, kind of like the Marines commercial, huh? I don't ever want to get into anything over my head again. For now, I'll continue to work, read, sleep, and be content to see her when I can."

"One of the things Amanda and I did was stay with a crowd, whether it was at church or with each other's families. I realize it's harder for you to do that with your family so far away, but we're here for you if you want to hang out with us old married folks."

"Thanks, I appreciate that. Why don't you go check on Linny, while I help your wife with the dishes?"

"Sure, but we have a dishwasher. Besides, she left for the bedroom five minutes ago to finish folding the clothes."

"Oh. I wondered why she stopped coming over to the table."

Both men made their way to the basement just as Laurinda concluded her conversation. Laurinda gave the detective her home and cell phone number in case he needed anything else, then thanked him for his time and hung up.

"How did it go?" Calvin asked.

"I repeated everything three times. At first I just thought he was dense, but then I realized you wouldn't hire anyone like that. He told me that each time I told him the story, he picked up something new. I couldn't remember the exit number, but once I told him about the other businesses near the gas station, he knew exactly where I was talking about. He asked me to visit the police station so I could describe the woman to a sketch artist. I told him I didn't think it would help because I can't remember what she looks like. He told me to wait one week, and then go to a local gas station, the same kind if possible. I know right where I'll go. Anyway, he told me to have the drawing faxed to him when it was complete."

"I remember Amanda trying so hard to remember the face of the lady she thought might have taken the girls. When she stopped trying so hard, it finally came to her. So don't try to remember until you go to the gas station. I'll even buy you a tank of gas."

"That's not necessary," Laurinda assured Calvin. "You do so much for me, this is the least I can do." She looked at her hands lying idle in her lap. She felt like she'd been as idle in Gary as her hands were now. Tears sprang to her eyes as she apologized again to Calvin for not recognizing his daughters. The small group heard Amanda leaving the bedroom and making her way back to the kitchen. Laurinda willed herself to stop crying so Amanda wouldn't ask questions she didn't want to answer. She excused herself to freshen up and buy some time.

Within a few minutes Amanda did join the men. Laurinda rejoined them a short time later. Since everyone had to be up early the next day, the party promptly ended.

Later in bed, Amanda mentioned that she thought the phone call upset Laurinda. "Do you know what's bothering her?" she asked Calvin.

Since he couldn't lie to her, he said, "Yes, but it's not my place to tell you about it. When the time is right, I'm sure Laurinda will share with you. Maybe you shouldn't press the issue for now."

Amanda agreed to wait for Laurinda to come to her.

In the car on the way back to Ronnie's apartment, Laurinda resumed crying.

In the most loving way possible, Ronnie said, "Linny, I want you to stop crying before you get out of this car. Crying could make you wreck if you're driving."

"You're right. I just feel awful that I didn't recognize the girls. I've known those girls since before they were born."

"Haven't they been gone for six months?"

"Yes."

"Linny, kids change so fast when they are young. Please stop beating yourself up. At least you can give a new description to the police of the girls and the woman who has them."

"If I can remember what she looked like."

"There you go beating yourself up again. I don't wanna see anyone hurt you, even you!"

In the dark she found his right hand rubbing the steering wheel and she gently took it into her own. There were many things she wanted to discuss with him, but as Grandma Meredith would say, she shouldn't put the cart before the horse, so she just held his hand until he pulled into his parking lot and asked for her keys.

"You wait here until I can get your car started. I'll be right back to wait with you while it warms up. Remember, I'll need your keys." He paused. "And my hand." He reminded her since she had made no effort to retrieve the keys from her purse. Instead she sat silently praying.

"Oh yeah, I guess they might help," she said as she reluctantly released his hand and reached for her purse. She would have been content holding his hand all night, but she knew he had to be at work early so she released it so he could get out of his car.

"I promise I'll be right back."

"I know. I was enjoying the moment. Your hand feels good wrapped around mine." I pray your arms will someday feel as good, she thought.

As promised, he returned as soon as her car began to hum.

"Is there another singles get-together this Friday?" Ronnie asked.

"No, we only have one a month."

"You mean I have to wait a month to see you again?"

"If your intention is to only see me at the singles parties, then the answer is yes."

"That's not my intention, Miss Bowman. I'd like to see you every night for the rest of my life, but I have some things to take care of first. I want to get myself right with God and be sure of who I am and where I belong in this world. It may surprise you to know this, but I don't plan to work for Edwards Construction the rest of my life. I want to own my own business someday. It may be construction, it may not be. I have too many questions in my own life to bring someone else into it on a permanent basis right now."

Laurinda looked out the window, afraid he was telling her he didn't want to see her anymore.

"If you think I don't want to see you anymore, you're thinking wrong."

"Get out of my head."

"Never." He kissed her hand that he held in his own.

"For now, I think it best for me to get out of your car."

"You should get home, it's getting late. Thank you so much for going with me to see my mother. After learning that it helped me pass one of your requirements, I am even more grateful you joined me."

"I would have gone even if you hadn't passed one of my requirements."

"You haven't answered my question about your requirements yet."

"Sorry. What's your question?"

"I'm wondering about these requirements. Do you have them written down or do you just make them up as you go along?"

"That's for me to know and you to find out," she said as she practically bolted from his car.

He shut off the engine, wishing he could shut off his body like he had the engine. She was already in her car before he could say good-bye again, so he just waved.

His phone was ringing when he got to the door of his apartment. He unlocked the door and got to the phone just before his answering machine picked up. "Hello, mother," he said, knowing it was her from the caller ID.

"You sound winded. Are you all right?" she asked.

"Yes. I was rushing to get in to answer the phone, that's all. How are you feeling?"

"I'm going to go crazy here at Aunt Dorothy's. I can't wait to get back home to stay."

"But you will stay there until the doctor says okay to go back to work, right?"

"Yes, dear, since it seems someone left some money under my pillow for me. You knew I wouldn't go over there without my pillow. I'll pay you back when I can."

"No, you won't. At least I won't take it if you try."

"Thank you."

He told her to thank God, not him, and said good-night.

Chapter 13

Work steadily progressed on the gas station and by mid March the job was finished ahead of schedule. The owner was thrilled to be reopening early so he offered free gas to the crew. The owner gave Calvin the go ahead to start the Jackson store whenever he was ready. The two men discussed dates and shook hands before Calvin left for home to surprise Amanda.

Ronnie's relationship with the Lord grew, as did his relationship with Laurinda. Since the Edwardses had begun holding a Bible study at their home on Wednesday evenings, the two saw each other at least twice a week and on Friday or Saturday night.

Amanda's job at the Family Christian Store became a bright spot in her life. While the first story hour she did was difficult for her, each week it became easier. She mastered the computer and learned a great deal about the various types of books and their sections. She continued to avoid the Bible section since she was not as familiar with them. The children's section was her favorite. She was given free reign with decorating the various shelves. Once Michael saw what wonderful work she did, he gave her the same freedom with the front window. Michael and Calvin teased her about how well she recycled her paycheck.

One morning a week Amanda, Judy, and Elizabeth worked their way through the book *Lord, I Need Your Grace to Make It*. Judy and Elizabeth became good friends, so when the time came for Elizabeth's husband to stand trial for spousal abuse and the murder of their unborn child, Judy accompanied her to her hometown for moral support. With the testimony of the hospital staff that treated her, Elizabeth didn't have to testify. After the assistant prosecuting attorney wrapped up the State's side of the case, he asked for a directed verdict and received it: Guilty. Elizabeth cried as her husband was taken back to the county jail to await transport to prison for the rest of his life. Judy treated Elizabeth to ice cream on the way home. Elizabeth moved into Judy's spare room and the two became inseparable. Together they began attending church every Sunday and joined the Bible study at the Edwards home on Wednesday nights. After much prayer, Elizabeth filed for divorce.

Laurinda gave a description of the woman she'd seen in Gary to the police sketch artist. Unfortunately, after three weeks there'd still been no news. Calvin continued to keep the information from Amanda, not wanting to get her hopes up now that she was doing so well at getting on with her life.

*   *   *

Calvin pulled into the driveway, but didn't open the garage door. He didn't want to give Amanda any warning that he was home. He dropped the mail he was carrying onto the table before sneaking around the house to find her. He sniffed the air for the smell of fabric softener. Finding none, he ruled out the basement. He went to the living room and looked through the fireplace to see if she was in their bedroom. He looked in both girls' rooms, then went back to the top of the stairs to see if he'd missed seeing a light on in the basement. He returned to check their bathroom. She wasn't there, but he heard the water running in the adjoining bathroom. Not wanting to scare her by going directly into the girls' bathroom, he made noise before getting there.

Steam seeped out of the crack created when he opened the door. The only sound in the room was the running water. He could tell by the steam that she'd been in the tub for quite a while.

He saw her feet resting on the wall of the shower enclosure near the spigot. He heard her singing but couldn't make out the song. Despite the noise he'd made, she still hadn't heard him. He closed the door behind him, hoping that she wouldn't hear him now. He waited to see if she'd acknowledge him, but she didn't. Perplexed about how to let her know he was there without scaring her in the process, he decided to go out and come back in, a lot louder this time. His departure went unnoticed, and once the door was closed, he prayed his wife was all right. This was the first time since the girls were stolen that she'd been in the bathtub. He stepped back and called her name. Getting no response, he walked closer to the bathroom and called her again. This time she responded.

"I'm in here," she called as she shut off the water. "I'm in the girls' bathroom," she said to clarify her location.

He opened the door and walked right in, knowing he had her full attention. "Hey there." He tried to act casual, like it was normal to find her stretched out in their daughter's bathtub.

"Hey there, yourself," she replied as she laid back in the tub. "I bet you're wondering what I'm doing in here."

"Yes, I *am* rather surprised. You're usually at work right now, aren't you?"

"What day is it?"

"Friday," he responded.

"Well then, I think it is I who should be wondering about your appearance here at eleven thirty on a Friday. I seldom work Fridays. You, on the other hand, work every Friday."

"I worked today," he replied with a smile. He sat down on the side of the tub and lazily twirled his finger in the water beside her. "So," he said as he began to flick water playfully at her, "are you going to tell me what a busy woman like yourself is doing lounging around in the bathtub at eleven thirty on a Friday morning?"

"What if I said I didn't want to tell you," she teased.

"Then I would have to increase the volume of water that I throw at you," he teased back, then stuck the rest of his fingers into the water.

"This would bother me how?" She rolled her eyes at him. "I'm already wet."

"Good point. Maybe I should try another approach." He stood up and began to take off his shirt. "If you won't tell me why you're in there, maybe I'll join you."

"I'll talk." She sat up pretending to guard her territory, and then turned serious. "I thought it was time to conquer my fear. While cleaning today, I started thinking about my fear of this room, so I looked up fear in the concordance of my Bible. The first place it sent me was Psalm 140. I think it was verses 1 through 11, or maybe it went to 12. I don't remember.

"Anyway, it started out with David asking God to rescue him from evil men. David called God his strong deliverer and his shield in battle. David called on God to do some pretty nasty things to those who'd hurt him. You and I have talked a lot about that and have decided not to pray for vengeance. The commentary on the side said that even admitting our fears can bring honor and glory to God. It said something like David's fears actually brought him closer to God. I wanted to be free from my fear of this room, but even more I want to be closer to God. I gave God my fear, and got naked and filled up the tub."

There were no tears, only a solemn look on Amanda's face as she spoke. He could tell that her heart was sincere and her fear was lifted. He longed to hold her, but decided against getting himself all wet and opted for a kiss on her forehead.

"Well then, I believe this is a very much deserved bath and I'll leave you to it."

"So you won't be joining me?"

"Not unless you want me to. You know I take up a lot of room in there."

"I've been here for a while. I was adding warm water just as you came in."

"You didn't hear me the first time I came in?"

"I heard you come in after you bellowed my name twice if that's what you mean."

"I came in before that, but since you didn't hear me, I went back out so I wouldn't scare you."

"You are becoming a very good little, I mean, big Indian. I'm proud of you and glad you didn't scare me when you came in. I've been praying and thinking about other things I can use or give up to bring God glory." She reached for the water release, and then stood up and asked him to pass her the towel she'd brought with her.

She blushed as his gaze swept over her and a smile crossed his face. "If you must cover up that beautiful body, I'm not going to stick around to help you." He placed the towel into her hands and headed for the door, knowing they would not get anything done for quite some time if he didn't leave right then. She'd directed his mind to the Bible, but at that moment the only verse that came to his mind was where it admonished husbands to delight in the wife of their youth. He closed the door behind him and made his way to the kitchen.

She joined him in the kitchen just a few minutes later, wrapped in only her old green housecoat. "You hungry?" she asked when she found him bent over and looking aimlessly into the refrigerator.

She smelled so good, he tried to focus his attention on her question and the empty feeling in his stomach instead of the desire growing within him. "As a matter of fact, I'm starving," he informed her.

She wrapped her arms around him and hugged him. He righted himself, closed the refrigerator door, and turned around. "Woman, I don't think you have a clue what you're doing to me."

She tipped her head up at him and looked into his eyes. "Show me," she said as his lips met hers.

*   *   *

A while later as Amanda cleared the table for lunch, she thumbed through the mail. Two letters caught her eye so she set them to the side and continued to sort the junk from the mail that would need her attention. Calvin returned to the kitchen and noticed the two pieces of mail she'd set to the side. One was from her aunt in Janesville, Wisconsin, the other from the private investigator in Chicago. The air seemed unusually thin in the house right then and nonexistent in his lungs. He looked at the envelope and then at his wife. It was obvious she hadn't opened it, and it was too late for him to remove it without her questioning him. He chastised himself for not looking through it, while at the same time he was grateful he was home when she found it.

"Honey, I need to talk to you about something."

She set the mail back on the table in the two piles she had created beside the two pieces that interested her the most. "Can it wait until I open these two pieces of mail?" she asked, uncharacteristically oblivious to his uncomfortable state of mind. "I'm not sure which one to open first."

"Why don't you open the one from your aunt and I'll get the other one. It's probably a bill."

"No, it's not a bill. Those come in a different kind of envelope. You read that one, I'll read this one, and we can discuss them over lunch."

"If we are both reading," he pointed out, "who will fix lunch?"

She swiped first one letter, then the other, with the letter opener and handed the appropriate envelope to him. "Whoever finishes first," she teased, knowing her aunt wrote long letters.

"Deal," he said, grateful to get the letter before she did. Calvin removed the letter and quickly read its short contents. Usually no news meant good news, but not this time. The detective had circulated the picture of the woman in the area and filed it with the local police without any luck. He said the area was cold, and would try again in six to eight weeks. He closed by saying he'd continue to pray for them.

Calvin looked up to find Amanda still reading her letter. A smile spread across her face. She felt him watching her and looked up. "This is good."

"Tell me about it while I fix lunch." He paused, then asked, "What's for lunch?"

She laughed. "I'll fix it while I tell you about my letter," she said as she stood up.

As he sat down, he was relieved she hadn't asked about his letter and hoped she'd forget it since she seemed pretty excited about hers.

He was wrong. "But first," she started, "tell me about your letter."

He swallowed hard, prayed a quick plea for help, then took her hand and pulled her onto his lap.

"I'm not sure where to start." He paused. "With the letter or the visit to Chicago."

"You went to Chicago?" she asked.

"No, I didn't go to Chicago. Ronnie and Laurinda did."

"Almost four weeks ago. So?"

"While they were in Gary they stopped at a gas station and Linny saw two little girls about Jessica's and Katrina's ages with a lady. She didn't think anything of it at the time. When they got back here, she saw the pictures I had drawn for you and she recognized them as the kids she saw in Gary. She called the PI and she told him everything she could remember. A week later she went to the police station and described the lady to the sketch artist. They sent the picture to the PI and he's been looking in the area of the gas station for four weeks." He paused to check her response. She sat motionless on his lap, her eyes fixed on him. "The letter says the area is cold. The woman is obviously not wanted for anything locally, otherwise she'd be in their database of pictures. I'm sorry I didn't tell you sooner. I didn't want to upset you."

"Four weeks ago it might have crushed me, but a lot has happened to and in me since then, including today." She kissed him on his forehead as she stood up and went to the refrigerator. "I'm sorry they didn't find anything, but I'm grateful to know the girls are alive." Tears formed in her eyes, making it difficult to focus on the contents of the refrigerator. She squeezed her eyes shut and tears fell to the floor. Her voice cracked as she asked him if he wanted ham or turkey.

In a moment, he was behind her, turning her toward him, enclosing her in his arms. "I'm so sorry, honey. I wish this had been better news." His voice cracked as he thought about how close they might have been to getting their daughters back. They held each other for a while before realizing the refrigerator was still open.

"Let's get some lunch and you can tell me about Aunt Cindy's letter." Calvin kissed her on the nose and released her from his arms.

Amanda wiped her eyes and face with her hands and returned to the task of making lunch. "You didn't tell me if you want ham or turkey."

"Whatever you're having is fine with me."

She made sandwiches while he got drinks. When they sat down, he gave thanks for the food and prayed for their daughters' return to them.

Amanda's sandwich was forgotten as she told Calvin about her aunt's letter.

"She and Mom have been discussing having a fiftieth wedding anniversary party for my grandparents. She wants me to help."

"But your aunt's in Janesville. What can you do from here?"

"Help with the guest list, find invitations, address them, and help with other decisions, like should we cater it or have everyone bring a dish to pass. You know, the usual party plans."

He wrinkled his brow at her. He knew little to nothing about party planning. Over the years he'd left party planning in her capable hands while he got things she needed.

"Where's the party gonna be?"

"Since Grandpa has trouble traveling, I presume it will be in Janesville."

"That's what I thought, too. So if you help plan it, I presume you'll want to go," he teased her.

She took a bite of her sandwich and nodded yes.

"When is it?"

She took a drink of milk. "June, but Aunt Cindy isn't sure of the date yet. That's something she wants to discuss with Mom and me. She knows it will be hard for us to get away so she wants to make it as convenient for us as possible. She said the date is up to us." She stood up and got the calendar from the wall so they could look at the weekends in June. Not knowing what jobs he'll have, or what progress would have been made, they picked the third weekend until they realized that was Father's Day weekend.

"Do you think we should have it that weekend?" she asked.

"You'd be with your dad. Your mom, Aunt Cindy, Uncle Bill, and Aunt Paula would be with their dad, and lots of your cousins would get to be with theirs. I think it's the perfect weekend."

"But you wouldn't get to be with your dad and," she said and paused, "this is the first Father's Day you'll be without the girls. Are you sure you want to be so far from home?" She covered his strong hand with her own and looked into his eyes.

"I've been away from my father on Father's Day before and we can celebrate with him another Sunday. As long as we're together it doesn't matter where we are."

"You're right, as long as we are together and God is with us, we'll make it through anything. He's brought us this far, hasn't He?"

Calvin smiled at her. "You're *so* right. Father's Day weekend it is for us if it works out for everyone else. Why don't you call your mom and get started on this planning thing you do so well."

"I'll finish my lunch, and then call right afterward."

He cleaned up the kitchen, kissed her, and went downstairs to play a video game until he could have the kitchen table for working on the most recent requests for bids he'd received.

Amanda finished her lunch, put away her dishes, and called her mother and left a message. She then went downstairs to watch Calvin for a little while. On her way, she stopped in her sewing room and picked up some embroidering she'd been working on before the girls were stolen. The pillowcases were to be a gift for her parents, but she'd lost interest in everything so she stopped working on them. She considered making them a gift for her grandparents, but decided to finish them and figure out later what to do with them. She settled herself at the end of the couch opposite Calvin.

When he noticed what she was doing, he asked, "Finally going to finish those?"

"I thought I might. I hope I'm better at this than you are at that game," she teased.

He huffed at her with a smile, then pushed resume.

An hour later, the couple returned upstairs, he to the dining room table and she to the couch to continue sewing. A short time later when her mother called, Amanda asked Calvin if he wanted to join her parents for dinner later. He said that was fine and returned to his work.

Just before dinner the Edward's arrived at Amanda's childhood home. Over final dinner preparations the women discussed the third weekend in June for the anniversary party and decided Sandy would call Cindy so she would have an answer for Amanda tonight by the time they arrived for dinner. Amanda told her about the letter from the PI and how Laurinda thought she'd seen the girls on the way to Chicago.

"Mom, it's good to know they're alive, but difficult knowing that someone else is watching them grow up. It was difficult when Katrina turned two ten days ago and we weren't together. Did I tell you I baked a cake on her birthday and took it to the job site?"

"Yes, you did."

"Anyway, I consoled myself by thinking that even though I wasn't with her, that without me, she wouldn't have had a birthday in the first place. I pray for them daily, so in a way it's like I am helping raise them even if I'm not there."

"I pray for them every day, too. I hadn't really thought I was still helping raise them, too," her mother said. "When did you get so smart?"

"I didn't know I was." Amanda laughed. "Maybe it was when I prayed for wisdom."

"Maybe. What time can you be here? You've got to see what Judy did with my hair today."

"I can't wait. How about six thirty? That gives us a little time in case Calvin wants to change clothes, or maybe if I'm lucky, clean off our dining room table." The two women laughed, agreed on six thirty, and said good-bye.

At six thirty, the Edwardses arrived at the Steinman's. Over dinner the women discussed Sandy's conversation with her sister and that the idea of Father's Day weekend for the party met with her approval, while the men discussed the route they'd take even though they wouldn't be traveling together. Amanda heard them

165

saying it would take about seven or eight hours to get there. She and Sandy's conversation stopped when Frank mentioned Gary, Indiana. Sandy hadn't told Frank about the latest development regarding their granddaughters before their guests arrived. Everyone's conversation revolved around that for the remainder of dinner.

After dinner the couples played cards until ten when everyone decided to call it a night.

"I know it's a little early to ask, but would you like to join us for Easter dinner this year?" Sandy said as the younger couple prepared to leave.

"I don't see why not," Amanda replied. "If it's all right with Calvin," she added.

"I'm inviting his parents so he wouldn't have anywhere else to go even if he wanted to," Sandy said.

Amanda laughed. She knew how much her mother loved to host parties. If there was such a thing as a party gene, Amanda was sure she'd inherited it from her mother.

Calvin smiled at his mother-in-law over the top of his wife's head. "I know my parents will accept your invitation. Mother knows you throw a good dinner party."

"I hoped you'd say that." After hugs, kisses, and handshakes, the Edwardses were on their way home.

"Easter is just a few weeks away. Mom said she'd call tomorrow to discuss detailed plans for that and for the anniversary party," Amanda said as they walked to their van.

"Yes, and I'm sure it will be a very long call," Calvin said as he opened the door and helped her into her seat.

"What do you think about the food?"

"There should be plenty."

"You know there'll be plenty. I meant should we cater it or make it a dish-to-pass type of thing?"

"Easter or the anniversary party?"

"Both," she smiled at him.

"Bring a dish-to-pass for Easter, cater the party."

"That sounds good. You're a better party planner than you give yourself credit for."

"No, I just complete you like you complete me." Calvin reached over and took her hand into his own. "We were meant for each other from the start." He moved their hands to his lips and placed a soft kiss on hers. "I love you, Mrs. Edwards."

"I love you, Mr. Edwards," she replied, feeling giddy inside. She loved it when he called her that.

Chapter 14

Calvin was correct when he teased Amanda that the conversation between her and her mother would be a long one. Many things were discussed, few actually decided. More phone calls between the aunts and uncle would have to be made, and lists exchanged. One thing was decided, however, and that was the party would not be a surprise for the guests of honor.

Amanda was sure her mother hadn't gotten her party gene from Grandma Schavey since she didn't throw parties. It wasn't that she disliked them, Amanda decided, it was probably because Grandma's life had been more about working than parties. With eight children and a sixty acre farm, there was no time for parties.

After the call ended, Amanda thought about some of what her grandparents had lived through and decided she'd rather carry her own cross. They'd already outlived four of their own children, two that died before the age of twelve. They'd struggled to keep the farm during the tough times, and even now struggled with developers who called them daily wanting to buy it. If her Uncle Bill hadn't taken over the farm, they probably would have sold it a long time ago.

As Amanda wandered through her house, she smiled thinking about her and Calvin celebrating fifty years together. She thought about the stolen moments, because their own children might not be there with them. She cried because of the many stolen moments they'd already missed with their children, like Katrina's second birthday, which she may or may not have even celebrated yet.

Amanda presumed the people who have her wouldn't know her exact birthday.

She recalled going to get each of the girls' birth certificates after they were born. She'd loved being the bookkeeper for Edwards Construction, but her favorite job had been being a mother to her two beautiful daughters. It's true what people say, Amanda thought, when someone is gone—you only remember the good things about them. Amanda hardly remembered when the girls had fought. She was certain that they had fought, but that wasn't what she chose to remember. Instead, she chose to remember last Easter when Jessi insisted the girls be dressed alike. Amanda had no problem getting exact matching dresses for them, but had to settle for a dress that was only similar to theirs for herself. The girls had new matching hats and shoes. Amanda passed on a hat for herself and wore a pair of shoes she already owned.

She remembered how excited they'd been when they found their Easter baskets just outside their bedroom doors. Because Katrina was so young, there wasn't much candy in her basket. After she discovered how good it tasted, she tried to take Jessica's. Amanda recalled, with all the candy excitement, how difficult it had been to explain the true meaning of Easter to them. Jessica asked if the Jesus who died on the cross was the same Jesus who was just born at Christmas. Calvin said Jesus was the same person, but it was many years after His birth. For weeks, Jessi pretended Katrina was baby Jesus. She would tell her that when she grew up she would have to die on a cross to save all the people.

Tears streamed freely down Amanda's cheeks as she stood with her back against her bedroom door, staring into her children's empty rooms. She thought about how an empty tomb once held her Savior, and how He was the main reason she'd gotten through every day of the past seven months. What a price He paid for her to be free. In some ways she felt free, in other ways she still felt bound. The pain that once bound her was slowly diminishing, though she still felt bound by helplessness. She was certain *she'd* never find her children, and equally sure she couldn't do anything to help anyone else find them, either.

She wanted to send Ronnie and Laurinda back to Chicago so they could see them again. When she and Calvin discussed it, he agreed that would be great, but not practical. Since the private investigator hadn't found anything in three weeks, he was certain the woman had been passing through rather than living in the area. They briefly discussed that they themselves would be passing through Gary in just three months. They agreed to stop at the same gas station at about the same time if possible.

Calvin called to her from the dining room where he was finishing the bids from the previous night.

"I'll be right there," she called back. She went into the girls' bathroom and splashed water on her face to wash away the tears. She wasn't trying to hide her tears from him, it just made her feel better when the tears were washed away like my sins, she thought.

Calvin was done with the bids and suggested they find out if Ronnie and Laurinda were busy. He also suggested pizza and a video at the house.

"Are you taking over as the social planner of the family?" she asked.

"Never!" he exclaimed. "That's always been, and always will be, your job. I'm getting bug-eyed here and need a break. We could go out if you'd rather."

"No. I think it's a great idea. I'll call her, and then you can call him."

"And what makes you think they aren't already together?" Calvin asked.

"Good point," Amanda replied.

He was right.

Ronnie and Laurinda agreed getting together would be a great idea. Calvin called in an order for two pizzas, and then paid for them over the phone so Ronnie and Laurinda could stop and pick them up on the way over after they stopped for the video.

Over pizza the men discussed the bids Calvin just finished working on and the kitchen job they'd be starting on Wednesday. Ronnie told him how grateful he was that he hadn't been laid off this year. He updated them on his mother's condition, and he and Laurinda's plans to go see her the first weekend in June if they weren't too busy at work.

"Amanda and I will be leaving on Friday morning before Father's Day, so maybe that would be a better weekend if Linny can stand not being with her father that day," Calvin told the couple.

Ronnie was grateful for the advance notice. He looked at Laurinda with a quizzical look on his face. "What do you think, *Linny?*"

"I think we can definitely talk about it. It's a good thing I love you two guys, otherwise I wouldn't let you get away with calling me Linny," Laurinda exclaimed.

The foursome discussed the recent letter from the private investigator. Laurinda cried as she apologized to Amanda for not recognizing the girls right away.

"I'm so grateful to know they were alive and together," Amanda assured her. "It appears God has given us an opportunity to go through Gary, Indiana, in June. We plan to stop at the gas station on the way there, and on the way back if we aren't successful on the way down. I know it's a long shot, but one we have to try."

Calvin got the exit number and directions to the gas station.

They stopped eating and took a moment to pray that the girls would be there on the way down. After the prayer, they also discussed how wonderful it would be to take their children to the anniversary party, and what an awesome anniversary gift it would be for her grandparents to see their great-granddaughters again.

During the video, Calvin's mother called to say they'd been invited to the Steinman's for Easter dinner and that they'd accepted. "I think Amanda told me they were going to invite you. I'm glad you accepted. I don't mean to be rude, Mother, but we've got company tonight, so we'll see you tomorrow night. I love you."

"I love you, too."

After Calvin's phone call, the couples finished the movie and played a few hands of cards before saying good-bye for the night.

*   *   *

"This is our final week of Lord, I Need Your Grace To Make It. Does anyone have any thoughts on this final chapter?" the leader of the Sunday school class asked.

"If anyone had told me I was a saint before I read this chapter, I would've told them they were crazy," Ronnie said. After several amens from his classmates, Ronnie continued, "I've never been in prison, thank God, but I have been imprisoned by my sins. I used to believe that if God loved me, he wouldn't have let me join a gang in the first place. Now I understand it wasn't His fault I joined the gang, and it wasn't His responsibility to get me out of it. I know that He was always with me. That's probably why I'm alive and here today. Laurinda says He isn't finished with me yet."

"Have you considered signing up at the youth center as a mentor," a middle-aged man asked.

"What youth center?"

"I'll take that as a no. See me after class and I'll give you the details," the same man said.

"Over the past few weeks I've told you all about being in a gang and how bad I was. What makes you think I'd be a good mentor?" Ronnie asked.

"You're not in a gang any more, are you?" the man asked.

"Of course not. My boss man there," he pointed at Calvin, "would bust my chops if I was."

"Then you have a story to share about how God worked in your life. Your story might help the kids steer clear of ever joining a gang."

"I hadn't really thought about that."

"Does anyone else want to share what they thought about this final chapter where Kay reminds us that God's grace is sufficient for all our needs?" the leader asked.

Amanda waited, hoping someone else would speak first, but when no one did, she said, "I find it very difficult to say what Paul said about being content with weakness, insults, distresses, persecutions, and difficulties. I don't have any obvious physical weaknesses. I don't remember ever being insulted or persecuted. But sometimes I think I've had more than my share of distresses and difficulties. I was glad to read that having grace doesn't mean we will soar above our troubles, but rather it makes it possible to plod through them. I continue to expect great things from God. And now I'm able to attempt great things for Him. One of the greatest things I do is simply get out of bed every day. I struggled with Mark 10:2-30. We didn't give up our daughters willingly, they were stolen from us, but I believe there was a reason and pray daily that it will bring God glory when they're returned to us."

"I think you've been a tower of strength," a lady said. Several others said amen. "I can't imagine how difficult it must have been for you when they were first stolen. I don't think I would have made it. Your faith is an inspiration to me."

Tears ran down Amanda's face. "I can't believe I'm an inspiration to you. You're so kind."

"When my kids are driving me crazy with their petty fighting, I think about you and I thank God for my children. I also ask Him to return your daughters to you and give you strength until you do get them back. I pray that *often*." Everyone laughed.

The two women couldn't have stayed in their seats even if there'd been glue on them. They got up and hugged each other tight. "Thank you for your prayers. I thought everyone had forgotten and stopped praying for us."

The room fell silent. Calvin knew Amanda was stronger than she gave herself credit for, but only by the grace of God. The two women broke their embrace to find everyone in the room wiping their eyes.

"I believe Mrs. Edwards has shown us here today what true reliance on God's grace is all about. Not one of us would want to walk in her or Calvin's shoes. God has given each of us different trials. But like the apostle Paul told his readers, God's grace will get us through it. He reminds us to run with endurance the race that is set before us, fixing our eyes on Jesus, the author and perfecter of faith. On day seven, Kay reminds us that God's goal for each of us as His children is to be conformed into the image of His Son. This can be accomplished through our trials. Jesus didn't take one step here on earth without consulting His Father. He came here to do God's will, not His own. That is what we need to do as well," the leader concluded.

"We need to take a final vote on the next book we are going to study." He listed the options.

Someone near the back of the room suggested they restudy the current book. "Sometimes I read the same chapter twice and I discover something new every time."

"I agree. We need to be reminded daily about God's grace," someone else added.

"We can revisit it again if you'd like, but I think we need to move on to another book. God has so much to teach us. I like to take advantage, as it were, of the author's perspective of the subject. Even though it is not a study book, I'd really love to share the book by John Ortberg called *If You Want to Walk on Water, You've Got to Get Out of the Boat*. I know the name is a mouthful, but I've read it and I think you'll be just as challenged by it as I was."

"We know the options," Jimmy said. "Everyone in favor of trusting the leader God has placed over us say amen."

Everyone said amen.

"I kind of thought you'd think this way. The books are under the sheet over on the table. Pick one up on your way out if you'll be joining us. A free will offering will be taken next week to offset the costs. Jimmy, since you seem to be the ring leader at the moment, will you close us in prayer?"

A few people laughed, then everyone bowed their head in silence.

"We thank You most gracious Heavenly Father, for the ability to come into Your house to worship You. Father, we thank You for Your grace. As a class, we thank You for Jeff, who led us through this study about Your grace. We ask Your blessing on each person in this room, Father. And we ask that You would continue to bless our class as we endeavor to learn more about You and become more like Your Son. It is in His name we pray. Amen."

Amanda asked Calvin for his handkerchief to dry her eyes. Many people stopped and hugged them, patted them on the back, or simply reminded them they were loved and being prayed for in their time of trouble. An older gentleman Amanda didn't recognize hugged her and whispered in her ear, "You'll get them back," before quickly moving on.

At first Amanda wasn't sure what he'd said, but then it became clear to her as if he had said it again. She excused herself to go freshen up before the service. She looked up and down the hall, but didn't see the elderly man. She couldn't believe he could have gotten very far as old as he appeared.

A short time later when she joined Calvin upstairs, she searched the crowd for the man, but still couldn't find him. "Did you see that older man who hugged me downstairs?" she asked Calvin.

"What older man?"

"The one with the gray jacket. Didn't you see him?"

"No, honey, I'm afraid I didn't, but I was talking to Jimmy and Ronnie."

Amanda asked others from the class. No one had seen him hug her. In fact, no one saw a man in a gray jacket. Amanda began to wonder if she'd really seen him or if she'd imagined the whole thing.

The organist began to play the prelude so everyone made their way to their seats. Amanda sang and listened to the sermon, but when it was over she couldn't remember what was sung or said. She was preoccupied with the old man in the gray jacket. On the way home she told Calvin what happened. Again he said he hadn't seen an old man in a gray jacket. He assured her she wasn't losing her mind. She was glad at least one of them thought so.

After lunch and two challenging games of backgammon, Calvin and Amanda retired to their favorite pastime. Only this time Amanda couldn't concentrate on the book in front of her so she joined Calvin as he looked over the bids he'd completed the day before. He was listing them in order of size and man-hours when Amanda joined him. He arranged them so that a certain part of the crew could be at one job, while the other group could be at another job. He showed Amanda his plans, provided he got the bids, for the next twelve weeks.

"This job is starting Wednesday." He showed her the plans for Mrs. Robinson's new kitchen. "If I've done this right, we would be in and out of there by the following Wednesday. I know from past experience how difficult it can be to go without a kitchen, so I'd like to keep their downtime as short as possible. She told me not to worry about the kitchen being out of commission on Sunday because they always go out to lunch after church and then go to one of their children's homes for dinner. They go to a different child's house every week. Then on the seventh week they all get together back at their house. They have *six* grown children. I thought two kids was a handful, I can't imagine having six."

"My Grandma Schavey had eight kids for a while."

"I think I was like having eight kids for my parents," Calvin joked.

"I've known you a long time, Calvin Edwards. I don't believe for a second your parents thought that at all." She smiled at him. "I, on the other hand," she paused, "think you're like having ten kids around here."

He raised his left eyebrow at her, then reached over and began tickling her until she cried for mercy. "This only proves my point," she said after she stopped laughing.

"You love it and you know it."

"Maybe," she cooed.

As he rose from his chair, he kissed her on the tip of her nose, and then ran his right index finger from her chin downward slightly, then back up again. He tipped her chin up with his finger and brought his face close to hers. She could feel his breath on her nose again. He circled her throat with his finger and continued to hover just above her nose. He moved his finger to her lips and she kissed it before he lowered his lips next to hers. She closed her eyes, sucked in her breath, and held it in anticipation of his kiss. Then suddenly, she felt the tip of his tongue on her eyelid, and then on her cheek. He began licking her face like a puppy would do for attention. She opened her eyes, and then rolled them at him as she pushed him away.

"You are incorrigible," she told him. "Worse than a child or a puppy. I can't believe I fell for that."

He barked and pretended to wag his tail as he went back and forth between her and the basement door. "Can I play video games before church?" He didn't wait for a response before adding, "Can I, can I, pleeeease?" He used his big blue eyes to plead with her as his bark changed to a whimper.

"If that's what you really want to do."

She joined him in the basement and began working on her pillowcases while watching him play video games again. She was glad she'd married a man who still knew how to be a kid sometimes.

After he'd played several games, Amanda checked her watch. "I think we better get moving or we'll be late for church. I wouldn't want the pastor keeping us after for being late."

They arrived at church with plenty of time to spare and stood around talking with some of their friends. Amanda was getting caught up in Elizabeth's divorce proceedings when Brother Jim, the director of music, approached them.

"Excuse me, Amanda, may I interrupt you a moment?"

Amanda excused herself and gave her attention to Brother Jim.

"Miss Ruby said you've agreed to let me put you back on the music schedule, is that right?"

"I did tell her that. I wanted to find a song and practice it first. I've got the song picked out, but I haven't perfected it yet."

"I've known you your whole life, young lady. I've never heard you mess up a song, and I don't believe it takes you months of practice to get it right, either."

"Thank you, but this is a song I'd never heard before. Judy picked it out a few weeks ago. I've been rather busy so I haven't had much time to practice it. How about you put me on the schedule for two or three weeks from now and I promise to have learned it by then."

"It's okay with me if it's okay with Miss Ruby. I'll put you on for the week after next. That should make her happy."

"Who's Miss Ruby," Elizabeth asked after Jim left.

Amanda visually searched the church for her, but heard her before she saw her. "That sweet lady right over there," she said as she pointed in the direction she'd heard Ruby's voice. "She's the one standing up over there. She's the life of any party. She has a heart of gold. I think she must be tone-deaf, though, because she likes my singing."

"Judy told me how beautifully you sing. I can't wait to hear you. I won't miss that Sunday!"

The organist began to play, so everyone left standing at that point made their way to a seat. The Edwardses took their usual place as Ronnie and Laurinda, and Judy and Elizabeth joined them in the same pew. Amanda smiled and thanked God as she thought of the recent chain of events that had taken place bringing the people in this row together. It could only have been You, Amanda thought.

Before they knew it, services were over and Calvin and Amanda bid everyone a hasty good-bye. On the way to his parents' house, Amanda told Calvin, "It's been great to not have to cook very much this weekend."

"Don't get used to it," he said with a wink. "I still prefer your cooking over anyone else's, even my mother's."

*   *   *

Delilah Edwards was in the kitchen still working on dinner when Calvin and Amanda arrived. Howard Edwards met them at the door and took their coats. He shook Calvin's hand, and he and Amanda exchanged a light kiss on each other's cheeks.

"Mother's been cooking all afternoon. She's going nuts wondering what you two have to tell us. I couldn't begin to speculate what it is, so I didn't try. She's been speculating all kinds of crazy things."

"It's nothing crazy, Dad."

"Let's get into the kitchen so you can ease her mind."

Calvin kissed his mother's cheek, and Amanda did the same. "Please don't keep me in suspense any longer."

"Why don't we all sit down and we'll tell you everything," Calvin suggested.

When the two couples were seated in the living room, Calvin told them about the events of the past three weeks. "It is good to know the girls are alive and together. We believe God had provided us with a reason to go through Gary, Indiana, ourselves."

His mother interrupted him. "I don't mean to interrupt, but Sandy told me about the anniversary party in Janesville when she invited us over for Easter dinner. That sounded exciting, but this is even more exciting."

"Mom, remember there's no guarantee we'll see the girls, much less come home with them."

Amanda told them about the elderly man she alone had seen and what he'd said to her. She reiterated, "There are no guarantees."

Howard and Delilah agreed there were no guarantees. They promised to pray more often for the safe return of their granddaughters.

Just then the timer when off, indicating it was time for dinner. The two women went to the kitchen to get the food ready for the table. Calvin would have helped if they'd been at home. Howard wouldn't think of helping with a meal. On the same token, his mother never had anything to do with his business dealings. While Amanda's parents adjusted their schedule to help each other when they could, Calvin's remained strong believers that each had separate roles in the family and those lines should not be crossed.

Calvin felt awkward sitting alone with his father. Growing up he rarely saw his father during the week because he was always busy building his investment business. All his hard work was now paying off financially, but there was little emotional connection with his son as a result. Sometimes as a child, Calvin often wondered if his birth had been an accident as far as his father was concerned. He was beginning to soften as he got older, and Calvin saw noticeable changes after the girls were taken. Even with that, he felt closer to Amanda's father than he did his own. They waited in silence to be called to the table.

When Amanda told them dinner was ready, Calvin practically ran to the table. He told everyone it was because he was starving for his mother's cooking. Amanda knew better from the long discussions they'd had regarding his relationship with his father.

Howard hadn't appeared emotionally bothered by the disappearance of his granddaughters, but they knew he cared. He suggested offering a reward, then offered the money to back it for leads that might help find their granddaughters. It wasn't until recently that Calvin and Amanda discovered he'd paid their private investigators $5,000 each.

Calvin vowed a long time ago to not be just a paycheck father. He loved his father, but he just couldn't relate to him. Some of the things Calvin did or didn't do as a father and husband were the result of conscious decisions on his part. Being available for both his wife and children was very important to him. Summer months were a little harder on him time wise, but when he was home, he was completely there. He thanked God he'd grown up in the church so he could watch some of the other dads with their children. It gave Calvin a better perspective of the type of father he wanted to be and the type of father God is.

Over dinner, the two men discussed projects Calvin had lined up for the summer, while the two women discussed the trip to Janesville and Amanda's new job. Amanda was eager to share the news about Judy, Ronnie, and Elizabeth with her mother-in-law, whom she rarely saw. Even when the elder Edwardses were in the area, they seldom spent time with the younger couple.

Amanda's family made Calvin uncomfortable at first with all their socializing and hugging and kissing whenever they got together. Over time he'd come not only to accept it, but to look forward to it.

After dinner, Amanda helped Delilah clean up the kitchen before the younger Edwards couple bid them good night and left for home.

Chapter 15

The following morning Amanda was given permission to decorate the front window at the store however she wanted for Easter. She spent part of the morning looking through the boxes of decorations from past years. She didn't find what she wanted, but then decided she didn't really know what she wanted. She went outside to look at the current display. She prayed for inspiration as she pondered the window and how to best use it to express Easter.

She went back inside behind the counter and looked at the current sale flyer. In the corner of one page she noticed a cross covered with a simple purple cloth. "Thank you," she told her Heavenly Father.

She went to Michael's office and showed him the picture. "This is what I'd like to do to the front window if it's okay with you."

"It's okay with me, but we don't have any of the supplies and I don't have a budget for it. Maybe you could keep looking."

"Or maybe I could have my husband build the cross and I could pick up the cloth at my favorite fabric store," she told him a little more excitedly than she meant to, and then added, "If it's okay with you."

"It's okay with me, but we don't have the budget for it," Michael reminded her. He was disappointed to tell her that because he saw how excited she was about it and how it would have to come out of her pocket if she wanted to do it.

"Since I was supposed to spend the morning working on the window but can't, should I go home?"

"That's up to you. I have the budget for you to work up to thirty hours this week. When you do the window is up to you as long as it's done by close on Saturday."

"I think I'll go for now. I really want to talk to Calvin about this and maybe I can get the fabric on the way."

"Okay. Let me know when everything's ready and I'll make time to help you. Do you know that removable shelves create the ledge you're currently setting things on?"

"No, I didn't!" Amanda exclaimed with excitement. "That helps me know how big of a cross Calvin can make. I was hoping for a big one! I'm sure he'll want to take measurements so maybe we'll be back later today."

"You two stop by for measurements whenever it's convenient for him."

"Thanks. I'll tell him." On impulse, Amanda hugged Michael. "I'm so glad you invited me to work here."

"Me, too," he said as he hugged her back.

After picking up four yards of royal purple cotton fabric, Amanda headed home, certain she would find Calvin there. She was right. He had the table covered in paperwork. He was on the phone when she came in so he motioned that he'd only be a minute more.

When he concluded the conversation, he stood up, stretched, and then wrapped his arms around his wife, welcoming her home but not realizing she was home from work early. He was glad to have her in his arms.

"Tough day at the office, honey?"

"Yeah. It's not my favorite thing to spend so much time on the phone. But, alas, I must do it if I am to keep the bill collectors from our door."

"I doubt we could make it on my paycheck."

"I'm sure we couldn't the way you recycle it back into the store. By the way, what are you doing home?" he asked as he looked at his watch, realizing she was home earlier than she said she'd be.

She recounted the morning's events to him, including her request to have him build a cross.

"What kind of wood would you like it made from?" was all he asked.

She hugged him closer as she thanked him and said she didn't know what kind of wood. "That's for you to decide. Are you ready for lunch or do you have more calls to make?"

"Depends on what's on the menu." He squeezed her bottom.

"Not me!" she exclaimed. "We both have work to do. Actually, besides the laundry, I don't have much to do. I'd help you with phone calls, but since we only have one line, I can't." She wiggled out of his arms. "I'll start the laundry, and then come back and fix lunch and a batch of your favorite cookies if we can go get the wood for the cross when you're done with your calls."

"Sounds like a plan. I've got the next three weeks scheduled starting with the kitchen I told you about for this week. Since the guys aren't working today, I don't think they'll mind working Saturday. I know Ronnie will be there with me."

"I was thinking, have you talked to him about tithing?"

"No. He'll ask when he's ready. Besides, I'm sure one of our pastors will preach on that subject before long."

Amanda laughed at his comment before turning to gather the laundry. "I'm sure you're right," she called over her shoulder. "Now get back to work so we can go shopping." Amanda dragged her last word out so long, he was sure she was still saying it as she got to the bedroom.

With the laundry started, Amanda began to soften the butter and get the eggs to room temperature for the peanut butter-chocolate chip cookies Calvin loved so much. They decided to eat lunch at the counter so he didn't have to clear the table.

Over an unusually leisurely lunch they discussed the size of the cross and the type of wood. She suggested it would be a good idea to make the cross easy to break down since they had so little storage space in the back room of the store. Afterward, she showed him the fabric she bought.

"Michael said we could go to the store to measure anytime that works for you. What if we stop there before we buy the wood? Maybe you can discuss what type of wood to use with Michael."

"That sounds good to me. I'll be done with my calls in a little while, so I'll be able to sample those cookies for you whenever you're ready."

"You are so self-sacrificing. Whatever would I do without you?"

He returned to his phone calls while she cleaned up their lunch dishes and began to measure the dry ingredients into a separate bowl. When she needed to use the mixer, he moved to the living room to continue his calls. A short time later, his nose brought him back into the kitchen with the phone still on the side of his head.

He poured himself a tall glass of milk and waited for the timer to go off as he finished his conversation, promising to call back the next afternoon.

"I thought only dogs were trained that well, and I thought they used a bell or something," she told him after he got off the phone.

"What are you talking about? I was almost done with that call and I was thirsty," he said with a sheepish grin on his face. She was not convinced.

"So drink your milk and be on your way," she teased.

He wrapped his arms around her waist from behind her. "But remember, I'm the self-sacrificing one who is going to sample your baked goods."

"If you don't let go, I won't be able to get any more cookies into the oven."

"Take your time. I can only eat one pan of cookies at a time. My mother did teach me *some* manners."

"*Some* would be correct," she said as she playfully pushed him away from her so she could have the next batch ready to go into the oven as soon as the first batch came out. She wasn't concerned with getting them out since her husband already had an oven mitt on and had placed two pot holders on the counter. He stood somewhat patiently beside the oven waiting for the timer to go off.

"I wonder where you'll be when it comes time to clean up this mess." She gestured toward the scattered measuring cups, spoons, and bowls.

"On the couch, holding my stomach because I ate too many cookies," he replied. When the timer went off, he opened the oven and took out the cookies. "I suppose you want me to put these on the pot holders I set on the counter."

"Unless you want to burn your tongue or lips, you better let 'em cool off a bit."

He set the pan on the counter, then moved over to his wife. "If I burnt my tongue or lips, I wouldn't be able to do this." He kissed her full on the mouth.

"Are you trying to cool off the cookies and heat up the cook?" she asked after he released her.

He smiled, took a plate from the cupboard, and then scooped four hot cookies off the pan onto his plate. "Actually, I was distracting the cook." He turned to leave, but added, "I'll be back," in his best Arnold Schwarzenegger voice.

He finished off the first pan of cookies, but declined to try any from the second or third pans. By the time all the cookies were baked, the kitchen had been cleaned. A few minutes later, they were walking out of the house on their way to the Family Christian Store with a container of cookies to share with her fellow employees.

Calvin and Michael discussed the type of wood for the cross, and estimated some measurements since the shelves were full of the current display. Amanda showed Aimie the fabric she'd purchased. Aimie was excited that Amanda had taken over the window decorating. It gave her more time to do the office work she preferred.

When the cookie tin was empty, Calvin was ready to go shopping. Shopping wasn't so bad, in his opinion, when it involved building supplies. He could live the rest of his life, he always told Amanda, without ever stepping inside a clothing or grocery store again.

The couple made their selection of wood and were on their way home again in no time. "See, honey," Calvin said as they drove home. "That's how you're supposed to shop. Get in, get what you need, and get out."

"You know I do that," she smiled at him, batting her eye lashes, "*most* of the time anyway. We can stop at the mall on the way home and I'll show you."

"Do you need something specific, or would it be one of those times you look until you find something you want?"

"You can breathe easy, I was just kidding," she told him. "Besides, I did some shopping while you and Michael were talking about the cross project. Did you notice how many times he reminded you that we have no budget for this project?"

"I didn't keep count, but I know it was a lot. What were you shopping for this time?"

"I was looking at invitations for the anniversary party. Mom asked me to pick out five options for her to choose from. You know as well as I do that if my mother saw all the options, it would take forever before she decided on one."

"Good point. What'd you find?"

"I found a cream colored one with a gold cross on the front that I'm sure she'll love." She looked over at Calvin, who was concentrating on his driving. She just stared at him for a few seconds before he felt her watching him.

"What are you looking at?"

"Just the best-looking guy I know. However, I'm not so shallow as to only think of how handsome you are. I also thank God you're in my life and for how much you love me."

Calvin reached for her hand, brought it to his mouth, and placed a tender kiss there. "That goes for me, too, you know. I think you're gorgeous, and I thank God you're in my life and love me as much as you do."

"Anyway," Amanda said and pulled her hand back and placed it on her lap, "I'm sure Mother will go with my suggestion. I'm so excited about this party. I haven't planned or helped plan a party since Jessi turned four. I miss planning parties." She got a bit teary-eyed and looked out the window. "I miss them."

He reached for her hand again and held it tight. "I know, sweetheart, I know." He kissed her hand again. "I wish I could love you enough to fill the void."

She used her free hand to wipe away the tears that made their way down her cheeks. "Do you think there'll ever be a time when I don't miss them so much?"

"I'm sure there will *never* be a time when you don't miss them so much until they come home to us." He'd never said the last part to her before, but the words seemed to take form on their own and felt natural to say.

She continued talking about the invitation as if she hadn't heard him. A few minutes later as they pulled into their driveway, she said, "You've never said that before."

"I'm sorry," he said, not apologizing so much as saying he didn't understand why she said what she'd said.

"You said 'until they come home to us' just now. Why'd you say that?"

He pulled into the garage and killed the engine. "To be honest, I'm not sure. It just rolled off my tongue like it was natural. I hope it didn't upset you."

"No, of course not," she said as they both reached for their respective door handles to get out. She turned to look at him. "But the timing is a little strange after what that man told me at church."

"Maybe God is telling us something."

"And maybe that's Him calling on the phone right now." She scurried out the door and into the house, reaching the kitchen phone just before the answering machine picked up. "Hello."

A familiar voice responded the same.

"How are you, Mrs. Bowman?" Amanda asked. Silence, then, "Oh, Mrs. Bowman, I am so sorry to hear that." Then more silence from Amanda as she listened to Laurinda's mother.

"Let me check with Calvin to see if he knows where she might be." She covered the phone and asked Calvin, who had joined her in the kitchen, if he knew where Laurinda was today. He suggested she might be with Ronnie and that he'd be happy to call him to find out. Amanda relayed his suggestion to Mrs. Bowman and said she'd call her back after Calvin had talked to Ronnie. Mrs. Bowman thanked her and the two women said good-bye.

Amanda explained to Calvin why they needed to find Laurinda. Afterwards, the couple took a minute to remove their jackets and pray for Laurinda's family. Calvin handed Amanda the purple cloth he brought in with him, and then called Ronnie.

"What are you up to today, little brother?" Calvin asked casually.

"Your beautiful bookkeeper and I were just about to leave the community center." Ronnie winked at Laurinda and she blushed. "Why, what's up?"

"Are you driving or is Laurinda?"

"I am. Why?"

"Do you know where Laurinda's parents live?"

"Yes, I've been there before," he chuckled. "Why?"

"Can Linny hear you?"

"Yes. Tell me what you need me to do and I'll do it, sir."

"Okay. Her mother just called here. I need you to take her home. Mrs. Bowman will explain when you get there. I'll tell you this much, it's not good news."

"I figured as much." Ronnie's voice sounded calm, but inside his heart was breaking for his girlfriend. "I'll take care of that for you. Thank you so much for calling me. I'll let you know how it goes."

"Let us know if we can do anything. I'll call Mrs. Bowman and let her know you're on your way."

"Okay, thanks. I'll let you know if I need any help. I'll talk to you later."

"I look forward to hearing from you."

When the men hung up, Amanda suggested she cook enough dinner for six people and take it over to the Bowman's house in about an hour. Calvin agreed that would probably be a welcomed gift.

"What was that all about?" Laurinda asked.

"I have to take you home if you don't mind. Boss needs me to do something."

"This late in the afternoon?" she asked. "If Calvin needs you, it must be pretty important. Is it anything I can help you with?" she asked.

"No," was his simple reply.

A short time later Ronnie pulled into her parents' driveway, turned off the engine, and then went around to open her door. Ronnie was grateful only her mother's car was in the driveway.

He opened the door for her and then followed her in. Laurinda knew right away something was wrong because she could see that

191

her mother had been crying. Mrs. Bowman took her daughter by the hand and led her to the couch where the two women sat down.

"Honey, I have something I need to tell you." Mrs. Bowman picked up her daughter's other hand and covered it with her own. "The Lord called Grandma home about an hour ago. She's finally with Grandpa."

"Oh, Mama!" Laurinda exclaimed as tears instantly streamed down her face. "I'm sad, but I'm happy. I'll miss her so, but I know she wanted to be with Grandpa."

Ronnie reached over to the table beside Laurinda to the box of tissues, pulled two out, and handed one to each of the women. "Thank you," they replied in unison.

"I'm sorry, I didn't mean to forget you," Laurinda said. "Sit here on the coffee table across from me." She picked up his hand and held it in hers as she wiped the tears from her eyes with the tissue in her left hand. "Did you know why you were bringing me here?"

"Yes, but it wasn't my place to tell you."

Laurinda squeezed his hand. "Does Daddy know yet?"

"No. I just got the call about twenty-five minutes ago. He'll be home from work any minute. I didn't think I needed to call him any sooner. There's nothing we can do right now anyway." She wiped her nose with the tissue Ronnie'd given her. "There was so much to do when Grandpa died, but there won't be this time. Grandma convinced us to make her funeral arrangements at the same time we made his. That was strange, not just making the plans at the same time, but also that she had the wherewithal to suggest it. I thought she was too distraught to think logically at the time."

"Didn't she even tell you what dress she wanted to wear?"

"Yes. It's at the nursing home hanging in her closet. When Daddy gets home, we," she motioned to Ronnie as to include him, "can all go down there."

As if on cue, Mr. Bowman pulled in the driveway and parked next to Ronnie's car. He'd grown accustom to seeing the car in the driveway and knew Ronnie was off work today, so he thought nothing of seeing it parked there. He knew something was wrong the second he walked through the door. Mrs. Bowman stood up and made her way to her him. "What's wrong?"

"Mother is gone, honey."

"Okay," he said almost casually. "She was ready. She told me again yesterday. We'll leave as soon as I can get cleaned up." He hugged his wife, gave her a kiss on the cheek, and then sat down on the bench to take off his boots. He unlaced his right boot and tugged at it.

"Mother was so practical to have us make her arrangements," he said as he got his first boot off. "She was always such a practical woman." He unlaced his second boot and then removed it. With that chore out of his way, he stood up, draped his left arm over his wife's shoulder, and made his way to his daughter.

Laurinda and Ronnie had stood up when her mother did, but had waited to say anything until her mother had told him. Seeing him brought a new flood of tears for Laurinda, and tears to Ronnie's eyes. Mr. Bowman wrapped his right arm around his daughter and pulled the two women close to him so he could comfort them and himself with their closeness.

Ronnie cried as he watched the exchange, remembering how sad he'd been when his grandparents passed away. This was the first loss in his life since he'd become a born-again Christian.

Mr. Bowman picked his head up from where he'd rested it on the two woman's heads and motioned for Ronnie to join them. Ronnie took a few steps toward them. Laurinda left her father's embrace and wrapped her arms around her boyfriend.

"Thank you for staying," she muttered against his chest.

"Unless you ask me to leave, I'll be right here for you."

"Thank you," she managed to say through another flood of tears. "I'm going to miss her so bad."

"I know, sweetie. It was obvious how much you adored her and her you."

Mr. and Mrs. Bowman walked past the couple on their way to their bedroom so he could shower and she could get his clothes ready. Just as they entered the bedroom, the doorbell rang. Mrs. Bowman called over her shoulder and asked Laurinda to get the door, saying she would be back in just a few minutes.

Laurinda opened the door and was not surprised to see Calvin and Amanda, both of them with their hands full of containers of food. "Hello, kids," Calvin said, "we brought you a little something to eat."

"Hello, yourselves," Laurinda said as she opened the door wide for them to enter. "It looks like you brought more than just a *little* something to eat."

"When my wife cooks, she goes all out," Calvin said as he shrugged his shoulders.

Mrs. Bowman returned in time to hear Calvin's comment. "Hello," she said as she acknowledged them. "You didn't have to bring anything. Having you help find Linny was plenty of help tonight. We appreciate the way you take care of our baby girl."

Laurinda blushed at her mother's comment. "I'm not a baby," she injected, then playfully stomped her foot to lighten the mood a bit. Everyone laughed.

"We figured you'd be going to Jackson and didn't know if you'd want to eat before or after, so we decided to bring it over as soon as it was done," Amanda told Mrs. Bowman.

"You're so thoughtful. Let's take these things into the kitchen. No sense standing here at the door. I don't know if we'll eat before we leave or when we get back," she told Amanda as she took the containers from Calvin and went to the kitchen with Amanda behind her.

"It's warm now, but it will warm up very easily," Amanda said.

"You knew?" Laurinda asked Calvin.

"Yes. Your mother told us when she called our house looking for you."

"That's why you called Ronnie?"

"Yes. I am so sorry to hear about this. Didn't your grandfather pass just last year?"

"Yes, he went home almost seven months ago. You know the doctors thought Grammy's stroke was brought on by his death. She began developing Alzheimer's, then just gave up living. She wanted to be with Grandpa and her Lord. I'm sad, but that's only because I'm a selfish human being. I'm also happy because I know she's where she wanted to be, and she has no more pain and no more sorrow."

"She's right where she wanted to be," Mrs. Bowman said as she and Amanda returned to the living room.

"Praise God," Calvin said. "It's hard for now to have her gone from us, but it comforts us knowing she's with the Lord."

Mr. Bowman joined the group just after they'd all sat down to reminisce about his mother. Calvin stood up and shook the older man's hand, offering his condolences.

"Thank you," he said. "Please, sit back down."

Mrs. Bowman told her husband about the food the Edwardses brought.

"It would make sense to eat before we leave because it might be late when we get back. There's really nothing we have to do. I'd just like to go down there," Mr. Bowman said.

"I figured you'd say that. Amanda and I didn't put anything in the refrigerator so we can eat right now if you're ready."

"I am. The sooner we eat, the sooner we leave." Mr. Bowman stood up to make his way to the kitchen. "I hope you'll stay and eat with us since I'm sure you cooked enough for a small army," he said as he patted Amanda on the back.

She looked at Calvin for an answer to Mr. Bowman's question. He nodded. "We'd love to stay. When we're finished, you all can leave and Calvin and I will clean up the kitchen and then lock up behind us."

Mrs. Bowman hugged Amanda. "You're so thoughtful. That would be sweet of you."

The group rose to follow Mr. Bowman to the kitchen. Once the food was placed on the table and plates were ready, everyone bowed their head as Mr. Bowman began to pray. "Our most gracious Heavenly Father, we give You thanks for the food, the friends, and the end to my mother's suffering. I ask for strength as our family adjusts to life without our loved one until we met again." Everyone joined him as he said amen.

After dinner Calvin and Amanda walked the sad group to Mr. Bowman's car and waved good-bye. They returned to the kitchen and cleaned up as promised. When they were finished, they locked the front door and prayed for their friends as they headed for their earthly home.

Chapter 16

Ronnie opened the door for Laurinda, and she slid all the way over to the other side of the car so Ronnie used the same door to get in. He laid his hand, palm up, on the seat and Laurinda placed her hand into his. They stayed that way for the hour drive.

Conversation was limited as each person dealt with the loss of their loved one and friend in their own way. The closer they got to the nursing home, the more Laurinda and her mother cried. Ronnie was grateful Amanda had handed him a box of tissues as they were leaving. Amanda is such a thoughtful woman, he thought as he passed two tissues up to Mrs. Bowman. Laurinda wiped at her tears with her free hand, unwilling to let go of Ronnie.

Mr. Bowman parked in the back where Ronnie and Laurinda had parked every Sunday after church since the first time. Ronnie spent all week looking forward to their drive to Jackson, their leisurely lunch on the way, and the time they spent with Grandma Meredith, however short. He'd miss it all, he thought as he got out of the car, opened Mrs. Bowman's door, and then made his way around to Laurinda's.

"Thank you, Ronnie," Mrs. Bowman said as she got out. She remembered when she and Tom were young—he'd done the same for her. Now it seemed they were in such a hurry she usually just got her own door.

Mr. Bowman thought, I should be getting Eva's door for her. He thought of how his parents were so close. His father doted on his mother. His mother always knew she was loved. Tom tried to remember the last time he'd told his wife he loved her. He met her at the front of the car, wrapped his arm around her shoulder, and whispered "I love you" into her ear. She smiled and snuggled closer to him.

The younger couple followed them in, hand in hand, Laurinda clutching tightly to Ronnie with one hand, a fist full of tissues with the other.

Tom went to the nurse's station closest to his mother's room.

"Our deepest sympathy, Mr. Bowman," a young nurse told him. "We'll miss your mother a great deal. She was a blessing to all who knew her."

"Thank you. Were you with her when she passed?" he asked.

"No sir, but I was the first one to discover she'd gone on. I came in a little early for my shift, and when I made my first rounds, I found her. At first I thought she was sleeping. Then I realized she looked too peaceful to just be sleeping. I checked her pulse and found none. I believe she took a nap after lunch and just never woke up on earth."

Tom was once again grateful his family had been able to get his mother into the Christian facility. "I appreciate everything you've all done for my mother. I know she loved it here."

"We loved having her. All of the residents that knew her thought highly of her as well. Did you know that one of the ladies down the hall came and sat with your mother for hours at a time? Mrs. Ingram was one of our non-Christian residents. After your mother talked to her about the Lord, she asked us for a Bible. It wasn't long before she and your mother were having lively discussions. Your mother told me yesterday that she'd led Mrs. Ingram through the prayer of salvation."

By this time both Laurinda and her mother were crying all over again. Grandma was famous for saying the only thing you can take with you to heaven is your friends and family. They were glad to know that Grandma didn't stop sharing the Lord with those around her.

"Actually, Ronnie and I knew about Mrs. Ingram," Laurinda commented. "Grandma asked us to pray for her a week ago yesterday."

"When Mrs. Ingram found out about your mother, she came and sat with her until the people from the funeral home came for her about twenty minutes later. We gave them the dress you left here for this special occasion. If you'd like to take anything from her room, you're welcome to," the nurse continued. "But there's no hurry to clean out the room. If there is anything we can do, please just let us know." She smiled at each of them with a mix of happiness and sadness in her eyes. A buzzer behind her sounded so she excused herself as the family turned to make their way to the small room.

"Linny, Grandma told me last week that she wanted you to have this group of pictures," Mrs. Bowman told her daughter.

"She knew how much all these pictures meant to me." She picked up a frame and showed Ronnie a picture of her and a cousin sitting on her grandfather's lap as babies. Laurinda explained that she hardly ever saw this particular cousin anymore, so the picture meant a great deal to her. She looked forward to seeing her at the funeral if she could make it back. The nurse's words came back to her, *special occasion,* she thought. "Grandma would be mad at us if we act sad," she said through tears. "But I just can't think of this as a special occasion." She held the frame close to her chest as Ronnie put his arm around her for comfort. "I can't celebrate my loss." She turned and buried her face in Ronnie's shoulder.

Ronnie remembered the times Calvin had told him that he prayed for strength and wisdom, so he did just that as he held his girlfriend. "We won't be celebrating our loss, sweetie, we'll be celebrating heaven and your grandma's gain. She's no longer in pain."

"But I am," she replied through more tears. Ronnie feared he'd said the wrong thing until Laurinda's mother spoke.

"Ronnie's right, honey. Remember how she was when Grandpa died?"

Laurinda nodded against Ronnie's strong chest. He smells good, she thought.

"She was like a rock. She recalled the good times while she laughed and cried with her family and friends. She knew it was just a matter of time before she'd see him again."

"I don't have that knowledge. I look forward to going to heaven someday, but I'm not in a hurry." She pulled her head back and looked up at Ronnie. "There's so much I want to do with my life before I go."

Ronnie touched her face to wipe away the tears. He wanted to kiss her on the tip of her nose like he'd seen Calvin do to Amanda many times. His heart welled up with love for the woman tucked securely against him. He thought of how many times Calvin had cautioned him to keep their relationship pure.

Tom sat down in what was once his father's favorite easy chair to look through the photo album that rested on the table beside him. "Look at these bathing suits," he said, pointing at a black and white photo, trying to lighten the mood. "Ronnie, wouldn't you just love to go to the beach with one of these suits on?"

Ronnie moved his arm to Laurinda's back and around her waist, and then together they took a few steps to see the picture her father was talking about. Laurinda laughed at the silly antics of her grandpa in a bathing suit that she could only describe as a baby's onesie. "He looks like a clown in that outfit. But then again, Grandpa always was a bit of a clown."

Eva looked at the pictures. "Remember when you'd climb up on his lap while he was sitting in this very chair and feel his face with your little hand. Most of the time he was clean shaven, but once in a while you would say, 'Grandpa, you need shabe.' Of course he'd laugh. Once he started laughing, you couldn't help but laugh with him. I think I have a picture at home of one such occasion. In fact, I probably have more than one.

"He thought the sun rose and set in you, and you thought the same of him. Grandma thought the same thing. I think you were her favorite grandchild, but I'm sure she would have said she loved you all the same."

"Do you remember the summer I spent with them and I stepped on a bee? I was holding a stick in my hand, grabbing my foot, and asking one of them to pull it out. Because the bee was long gone and they couldn't see the stinger so well, they thought I meant the stick. Grandma pulled the stick out of my hand. I stopped crying just long enough to tell her that I'd stepped on a bee. After the stinger was removed, it wasn't long before I was being nursed back to health with a chocolate-dipped cone from the ice cream shop around the corner."

"I'm sure that the ice cream remedy was Grandpa's idea," Eva suggested. "I don't recall the event, but I know you wanted to spend the whole summer with them, every summer."

"Next to Grandma's cooking, ice cream was by far his favorite thing to eat," Tom said. "My father seldom went to bed without a bowl of ice cream." He rubbed the arm of the chair with the palm of his hand. Everyone drew in a breath as if they smelled the elder Bowman's aftershave even now.

"Ronnie, I'll tell you why she wanted to spend so much time with my parents. They spoiled her rotten. If she wanted to own it and they could afford it, she had it. If she wanted to go somewhere, they stopped what they were doing and took her. Spoiled rotten, I tell you." Tom lovingly winked at his daughter.

"That's okay with me," Ronnie informed him. "I look forward to spoiling her myself." He squeezed her against himself. "God willing." He wanted to say that he looked forward to a great many things with her, but refrained for fear the comment would be taken the wrong way. Besides, as Calvin said, his will needs to be aligned with God's. He prayed right then to be shown God's will where Laurinda was concerned.

Eva began gathering a few of her mother-in-law's personal items and placing them in one of the bags she'd gotten from the nurse's station. Laurinda removed herself from Ronnie's grasp and joined her mother. Ronnie joined Mr. Bowman looking at the other pictures in the album while Laurinda picked up a bag and started cleaning out the bureau drawers. She lifted one of the hankies she found there to her nose. "May I have this Mummy? It smells like her."

Eva looked at her husband, who nodded his approval. "Yes, sweetheart. I know you'll cherish it. I'm sure Grandma would be happy for you to have it."

"Can you imagine buying a car for just fifteen dollars?" Tom asked Ronnie. He showed him a picture of his father standing in front of a car. His mother had written $15 above the picture. "I'm sure it was used, and a great deal of money to him at the time."

"My first car was used and it was a small fortune to me," Ronnie replied.

The two men looked through the book while the two women worked. A short time later Tom suggested they move on. He wanted to go to the funeral home even though he wouldn't be able to see his mother and all the arrangements had already been made. He wanted to be doing something, even if this was essentially doing nothing.

The group was walking toward the exit when they heard a feeble voice behind them calling out. "Mr. Bowman, Mr. Bowman. May I speak to you?" she asked after she had his attention.

The group retraced their steps so the elderly woman wouldn't have to walk so far. "You are Mr. Bowman, aren't you?" she asked once the foursome drew near.

"Yes, ma'am," he said as he extended his right hand to grasp her shaky, wrinkled one. "May I help you?" he asked politely.

"You can't do anything for me, sonny." She smiled at him, revealing a smile with few teeth. "I want to tell you what a blessing your mama's been to me these past weeks."

"Mrs. Ingram, I presume."

"Yes, yes, sonny. I'm Mrs. Ingram, and I'm a born-again Christian thanks to your mama. She prayed over me 'til I came to my senses, and then led me to the Lord. I'm a thick-headed old goat so I guess it took her a great bunch of prayin' on me."

"My mother would have been praying for you no matter what. No matter what size the prayer concern, she loved to pray," he told her. Laurinda and Eva nodded in agreement.

"I'm gonna miss sittin' with her and talkin' over them Bible stories she told me."

"I'm sure there are lots of people here who would love to discuss the Bible with you," Eva suggested.

"Not everybody accepts me the way Meredith did."

"I think many of your fellow Christians would accept you the way Jesus does," Laurinda said. "I know you have a good heart. Grandma could always tell that about a person." Laurinda stepped toward the hunched-over frail woman and gave her a hug.

Anyone watching might have thought Laurinda gave her a million dollars by the smile on the elder woman's face when the two separated.

"Maybe the rest of you Christians are more like my Meredith than I thought. I won't keep you. I know you have lots of arrangements to make. I wanted you to know I'll miss her very much."

"Thank you for telling us how much she meant to you. We don't have any arrangements to make since she insisted we make her arrangements when my father passed."

"I understand," Mrs. Ingram said. "I'm an old lady and can't do much for you…"

"You can pray for us," Laurinda suggested, not meaning to interrupt. "That would mean a lot to me."

"Then I'll do it, young miss." Laurinda felt the urge to hug her again and was certain it would be equally well received. This time she wasn't sure Mrs. Ingram was going to let her go. "He's a handsome one, that husband of yours," she whispered into Laurinda's ear before she let her go.

She blushed. "We're not married," she whispered back to her. She silently wondered, could this be a confirmation from God that we should be together? She kept her personal desire from everyone but the One who knew what would happen. Each time she had these thoughts, she reminded herself that it had to be God's will or it wouldn't work.

Mrs. Ingram winked at her before the group turned back toward the exit. When they reached the exit, Tom opened the door and held it until everyone was out.

"She's as sweet as Grandma described her to us, isn't she, Ronnie?" Laurinda asked after they were seated next to each other again in the back seat.

"I think so," Ronnie said as he reached over to hold her hand.

"I hope to be at least half the prayer warrior that Grandma was," she said.

Ronnie squeezed her hand. "Me, too, though you have a better start at it than I do. So I'm sure you'll make it."

"Remember, nothing is too large *or* too small to take to our Heavenly Father," Tom told him. "Never fail to pray immediately for someone when they ask for prayer. You can pray with them or by yourself for them. These two things will help you both be prayer warriors."

After he finished speaking, he silently prayed for the relationship between the two young people in the back seat, with each other and their Lord. He and his wife had discussed Ronnie's interest in their only child just a few nights before. They were aware of his past, yet felt confident about his future. Since his spiritual future was going in the right direction, they were more concerned with his financial future. They decided that if he asked for Laurinda's hand in marriage, they'd say yes.

The foursome arrived at the funeral home and made their way inside. Mr. and Mrs. Bowman spoke to the director for a few minutes while Ronnie and Laurinda looked around. A solemn-looking woman showed them where the elder Mrs. Bowman would be available for viewing the following evening. They discussed the visitation times and the expected funeral time in just two days. She said the prearranged obituary notice had been faxed to the Jackson and Lansing papers so it would be in both papers the next morning. Mr. and Mrs. Bowman joined the small group after the woman finished talking. Mr. Bowman suggested it was time to leave. Ronnie and Laurinda thanked her for her time, and the group returned to the car.

"Daddy, may we *please* go to the ice cream shop?" Laurinda asked when they were all in the car.

"With the warm spell we've had the past few days, you must have forgotten it is still winter," he teased her.

She leaned in between her parents' seats, as she had done so many times as a child, to plead her case about *needing* to have ice cream before she went to bed. She smiled at her father in a childish way and fluttered her eyelashes at him, though her father didn't see her face.

He looked at Ronnie in the rearview mirror. "Be careful of *that* look, young man, it works every time."

A little while later the foursome was at the Parlor. It was busy but it didn't take long to be seated. Each couple ordered a banana split to share. The three Bowmans told Ronnie several stories about their family visits here before the ice cream was delivered to their table. Since Mr. Bowman had already thanked the Lord for food and the time they had to be together before they ordered, they all dug right into their frozen treats when the waitress set them on the table.

"Don't forget, I don't like the cherry," Laurinda reminded Ronnie.

"You take the end with the marshmallow cream because I don't like it." He turned the dish so the marshmallow cream was on her end of the container.

"I can eat the half of the banana that's on the back of the serving dish, so he can have the one on the front."

"We could both work on the front banana, then turn the dish when it's gone, and then we can eat the half from the back."

"As long as all the marshmallow cream is gone before we turn it."

"Not a problem," she said with a smile. "I'll make short work on the marshmallow and to be *sure* it's all gone before we turn the dish."

When their spoons bumped together because they were both going for the same bite, they'd laugh and tell the other one to go ahead, and then smile at each other.

They seemed oblivious of her parents until finally her mother spoke. "You two remind me of Daddy and me about twenty-four years ago. This was one of the first places your father brought me when we were dating. I think he wanted to be sure that I loved ice cream, too."

Tom laughed. "I didn't even care if she could cook. I had to be sure she loved ice cream. She could learn to cook. She couldn't learn to love ice cream like I do."

The whole group laughed, and Laurinda blushed at the comparison her mother had just made. More confirmation about us being together, she thought. "That was not my motive for coming here tonight," she said in her defense. "I already know Ronnie loves ice cream like I do. We stopped here every time we visited Grandma."

She directed her attention to Ronnie and asked, "Wasn't it just yesterday we were talking about skipping lunch next time we came down and just coming straight here for ice cream? It's been such a long, full day it doesn't seem like we were here just yesterday."

"I know how you feel." He checked to make sure the marshmallow was gone, and then turned the dish so they could get to the other half of the banana. "We haven't even had a chance to tell you both what we did today."

"That's right," Laurinda injected. "I'm so proud of him."

"Well then, I think it's time you tell us," Tom said with a grin. "I thought you'd come and talk to me before you asked her, but if you want to do it this way, I'm okay with it."

Laurinda blushed because of her mother's comment earlier, but this time she almost passed out when the blood rushed to her face. "Daddy!" she exclaimed.

"I'm just teasing, sweetie. Relax." He patted her hand that was on the table across from his own.

Laurinda found it a little difficult to look at Ronnie right then. If she'd been able to look at him, she would have seen how quickly the blood rushed to his face, too. She played in the ice cream with her spoon for what seemed like an hour.

Eva broke the awkward silence by asking what they did.

When Ronnie found his voice, he said, "Laurinda worked for a little while this morning while I slept in for the first time in ages. Not that seven o'clock is late to the rest of the world, but it is to me.

"When she was done, we met for a picnic lunch. I'd never been on a picnic in March before. That was fun. Anyway, we went to the youth center and spent the rest of the afternoon there. At first I didn't think there would be anyone there because of it being school time and all. I didn't realize the youth center was connected to the alternative education building. We both signed up to become mentors.

"Last week a young couple requested mentors. After interviewing both of us separately, and then together, the lady decided we would be the perfect couple to help this pair, so they put us all together."

Laurinda liked the sound of "the perfect couple."

"They have a six-week-old adorable baby girl together. The girl, Melissa is her name," Laurinda clarified. "Her mother had very little involvement in her life while she was growing up and her father was gone by the time she was ten. I wasn't sure we were a match, because I can't relate to not having my parents involved in my life. You've always been very supportive of me. I pray this will work." Laurinda paused so Ronnie could take over.

"Jayson was a football jock who felt pressured by his friends to have sex. He says he loves her and wants to marry her someday, but neither of them is ready for that. He already has an athletic scholarship to Michigan State. He could have stayed at the high school and attended regular classes, but he didn't want to leave her with all the responsibility of the baby. Right off the bat I told him I understood that pressure from friends. I was pressured, too, but I didn't give in to it."

There, Ronnie thought, I've finally told her what I've been trying to tell her all along. After he said it, he began to wonder why he'd been so scared to tell her. Maybe it was because before he had tried to tell her while they were alone. That might have made it seem like he wanted to now.

Ronnie continued, "Second, I told him that I admired him for his commitment to Melissa and the baby. Most of the guys I grew up with would not only have stayed at school, they would probably have denied responsibility in the first place. I didn't go into any detail about my upbringing, I felt, we felt," he indicated toward Laurinda, "that it would be better to get their story first so we could begin to pray about how we could help them.

"We have one small problem. I have a full-time job that doesn't have a lot of down time. I can't be at the school during the day. I'm afraid most of the mentoring may fall on this beautiful lady." When he turned to look at her, she was grateful her normal color had returned. Her eyes lit up as he smiled at her. She smiled back.

"I don't mind helping them during the day when I can. The director knows that he works full-time and that I have two part-time jobs. She said we could have some early evening meetings with them if we need to." She spoke to her parents but didn't take her eyes off Ronnie. She directed her attention back to her parents before adding, "I spoke to the director about inviting the kids to church with us. She said she could not tell us yes or no about that as the director, but as a Christian, she was all for it."

"We mentioned it to them while we told them about us," Ronnie said. "They didn't get excited, but neither did they reject the idea."

"I told them about our wonderful youth programs and our nursery on Wednesday nights," Laurinda added. "I told her I don't know anything about being a mother, but I have been around lots of babies. I really look forward to being a mother someday."

"I look forward to having grandchildren someday, too, but I'm in no hurry," Eva said, smiling at her daughter and the young man she believed would someday be their son-in-law. She thought that she should discuss the idea with Laurinda after the funeral. She frowned, remembering why they were in Jackson, then remembered God has a plan for everything and smiled because they were all together.

Mr. and Mrs. Bowman finished their banana split and waited while both Ronnie and Laurinda playfully fought over who'd get the last bite of ice cream. She insisted he take it, while he insisted she take it. Finally, he won with the argument that he'd eaten more than her by having the cherry. She conceded and ate the last bite of banana. Tom picked up the check the waitress had left there earlier, so Ronnie dropped three dollars on the table. Both couples were very full as they made their way to the checkout. There was a line to pay so Tom handed Ronnie the keys to his car and asked him to bring it to the door for the ladies.

Ronnie took the keys, and then asked, "Are you sure?"

"I trust you with my daughter, who is far more important to me than a material possession."

"Good point." He moved his arm in a sweeping motion indicating for the two women to go in front of him. The ladies waited by the door.

He didn't need to adjust the seat as he and Tom were the same height. He let the engine warm up for a couple of minutes, and then pulled around to the door. When Ronnie started to get out, Tom suggested they sit up front and let the ladies ride in the back.

"Don't you want to drive back, sir?" Ronnie asked.

"No, you go ahead if you don't mind."

"No, sir, I don't mind. It isn't every day I get to drive a nice car like this. You've seen what I drive. This is a treat."

Laurinda sat behind her father so she could look at Ronnie at an angle and see his handsome face instead of just the back of his head. The two ladies discussed what they would wear for the viewing the next evening, while the men discussed the upcoming jobs Ronnie would be working on and the mentoring program. They were almost home when everyone fell silent, deep in their own thoughts about the situation they currently found themselves in.

Chapter 17

Tuesday morning started with the Edwardses on their knees. The difference today was that they were able to start it together. Calvin asked Amanda if she wanted to start the prayer.

"I'm afraid all you'd get from me is babble. I'm on an emotional edge, clinging to Jesus for strength right now."

"What a perfect place, besides on our knees, to start," Calvin told her.

Amanda wiped the tears from her eyes with the back of her hand, and then returned it to its place in Calvin's.

"Heavenly Father, my heart aches for the Bowman family. It's a mixed blessing to those of us left behind when a loved one that knows You passes from this life to the next. We have Your promise that we, Your children, will all be with You forever. Please let this knowledge be the strength the Bowman family needs to get through the coming hours and days that turn into weeks, then months without this one they love so much, just as You have provided it to me." Amanda squeezed Calvin's hand to let him know she was finished.

"Father God, I too lift up the Bowman family as they deal with the loss of their loved one. We know that what grieves us, grieves You. I pray they will be comforted in knowing that this loss is only temporary and in knowing that the family will be together again in glory someday.

"I'd like to thank You for this extra time that I've been given with the beautiful wife that You've given me. May we both be towers of strength to the Bowman family during this difficult time for them. Show us how we can be of Heavenly service to them. In Jesus' name we pray."

They both said, "Amen."

"I called Mrs. Robinson and told her about the funeral, and asked if she'd mind if we waited. I told her I'd bring reinforcements on Saturday to keep us on track. I'll see if Jimmy can help," Calvin told Amanda over breakfast as the couple discussed their plans for the next two days.

"Unless there's an unexpected ice or snow storm, I'm sure he'll say yes. Are we going to the viewing tonight or do you just want to go to the funeral service tomorrow?"

"Both," he replied.

"I figured you'd say that. Do you want me to have your suit cleaned? If so, I need to get it there within the next half hour so they'll have it back by about nine o'clock tomorrow."

After putting their dishes in the dishwasher, Amanda walked past Calvin. He reached out to capture her and pulled her onto his lap. "Woman, why do you bother the master of this castle with such trivial matters?" he playfully growled as he nuzzled her neck with his day-old beard.

"Because," she said as she placed the back of her right hand on her forehead and laid back, "you have to tell me what to do, or else I would be a damsel in distress."

"And don't you forget it," he growled again as she wiggled out of his arms.

"I'll go check your suit and make this extremely important decision on my very, very own. Then I will jump like a bunny into the shower. If your suit doesn't need to be dropped off at the cleaner's, you are welcome to join me." She knew from years of showering with him that it always took longer when they were in there together.

He began to follow her while acting like a little puppy one second, a gorilla the next, then a strange combination of the two animals after that. "You are incorrigible," she fussed at him, trying to shoo him away.

She made her way to the closet to check the suit. After close inspection she decided that it didn't need to be cleaned. Her puppy-gorilla husband panted, then scratched under his arm pits, while nodding toward the bathroom. Amanda tried to ignore him, but instead she laughed and shook her head at his antics.

"Come on, goofball. Let's see if we can't tame the savage beast in you with a shower and a shave. Emphasis on the shave part."

He raised his arms above his head, exposing the hair while continuing to behave more like a gorilla than a man.

Amanda suggested shaving under his arms would remove the savage beast in him. He adamantly shook his head from side to side. "I'll be good," he said, and then barked.

Amanda recalled the many times this type of behavior had driven both of their daughters into fits of laughter. Even though Katrina was very young, she still understood when Daddy was being silly and when he was serious. She smiled as she remembered some of the times his antics had made one or both of their daughters run toward her and wrap themselves around her leg if she was standing, or her neck if she was sitting. She remembered the smell of each of them as they snuggled up close to her for protection from the "daddy monster."

"You okay?" Calvin asked as he wrapped his arms around his wife from behind.

Since they were standing in front of their bathroom mirror, she could see his face, and then she looked at herself. She hadn't realized she was crying.

"I was just remembering the many times you drove the girls crazy with your silliness. But it wasn't a sad memory. I didn't even realize I was crying." She turned around to face him and snuggled against his chest.

He reached down to her chin and lifted it so he could look directly into her eyes. "I'm so glad that you're not as sad anymore. I know we've both had our moments, but I praise God that yours are less now."

"Me, too," she agreed with him. He placed a kiss on the tip of her nose and gently on her lips.

When the sweet kiss ended, she wiggled out of his arms and began preparing for her shower. "Can you give me just a few minutes by myself in there?" She nodded toward the shower. "I need to knock down the jungle on my legs."

"I can get you a really sharp knife from the kitchen if you like."

"I believe the shaver you gave me last Christmas will do just fine. But thank you for your generous offer. Now if you'll excuse me, I need to get done here so I can get to work in a couple of hours." She started the water, undressed, and then stepped into the shower. "Hey," she called from behind the curtain, "would you mind running out and getting the paper before you join me?"

"What if I've already gotten undressed?"

"Just tie a towel around your waist and hold real tight so you don't give the neighbors a thrill if it falls off," she teased him. He poked at her through the shower curtain, causing her to squeal.

A few minutes later he pushed the curtain open at the corner and joined her. Before she could even ask, he told her the viewing was scheduled from two to four and six to eight in the evening. Since she was done with her legs, she offered to shave the back of his neck for him.

"If you think it needs it, then shave away."

Later when Amanda was ready for work, she kissed Calvin good-bye and promised to be back by noon.

"I promise to have the table cleaned off so you'll be able to set my lunch right in front of me," he playfully growled at her.

* * *

Laurinda had picked up a few things at her apartment on the way home from Jackson Monday night so she could stay in her old room and be with her parents.

"This feels kind of like Thanksgiving or Christmas morning because Daddy is home," Laurinda told her parents over a lite breakfast.

"I guess those were pretty much the only weekdays that I did stay home," Mr. Bowman said. He apologized to two of his favorite women. "I wish I could get back some of those missed days with the two of you."

"We know you were taking care of us," Mrs. Bowman said.

"Yes, Daddy," Laurinda said, "we understood."

Their conversation was interrupted when the doorbell rang the first of many times throughout the morning as friends and neighbors brought food to the grieving family. Laurinda was grateful when she opened the door and found the tall handsome man, who she was beginning to love so deeply, at the door. Just seeing his smile lifted some of her sadness.

On the way to the couch to sit down she told him, "It's really strange to think that I only have one set of grandparents left."

Ronnie handed her a tissue as the tears welled up in her eyes again. She thanked him, then blew her nose. "I'm not as close to Mom's parents as I was to my Daddy's parents." She looked at him with sadness in her eyes. He looked at her lovingly. "I'm not saying that I won't miss them when they go, it's just that..."

"I understand," he said as he picked her left hand up and held it in his own. They fell silent, both of them looking at their intertwined hands. He imagined what her small hand would look like with a diamond on it. He thought of the savings account he'd opened with the bonus money from the gas job to save for her ring. If it is God's will and she'd have me, he thought. He turned her hand this way and that.

"Is there something wrong with my hand?" she asked him.

"No, of course not, I was just thinking. I hope I didn't hurt you."

"You didn't hurt me. I just wondered what you're doing."

Just then her mother came into the room. "I didn't know you were here, Ronnie. I guess Linny was keeping you to herself. I think her lack of sharing comes from being an only child. We tried to get her together with her cousins as much as we could before she started school so we wouldn't have this problem. Now I see it didn't work." Eva extended her hand to the young man. "Why don't you come with me and we'll get you something to eat."

Ronnie stood up, took her hand, and followed her into the kitchen, leaving Laurinda sitting on the couch with a pouty look on her face and an objection on her lips. "But, Mummy, I share. Really I do!" she exclaimed.

Eva playfully ignored her daughter's protests as she led Ronnie into the kitchen. "There's plenty here. If you don't see something you want or like, just check the refrigerator. I'm sure you'll find something there. If you still don't find anything you want, let me know and I'll cook something for you."

Ronnie was amazed at all the food on the counter and in the refrigerator when he peeked inside it. He took the milk out and asked for a glass. Eva showed him where the glasses were kept. "If you're going to become a regular around our home, you may as well know where we keep things." She went on to show him where the other dishes were kept, along with the silverware and other items she thought he might need to help satisfy his hunger pains.

Laurinda joined them as they both began to fix plates of various fruits and baked goods. "May I join you or is this a private party?"

"Come on in," her mother said, "the food is fine."

"So is the company," Ronnie said, smiling.

Tom joined them a short time later.

Just then the doorbell rang and Tom excused himself to answer the door. He thanked his coworker for the food and invited her in. She declined, saying she had to get to work and she'd see him this evening.

The foursome ate a hearty breakfast after giving thanks for the food and fellowship time. Since there was plenty of time before they needed to be at the funeral home, they looked for pictures for the display board beside the casket.

Laurinda picked one of her favorite pictures of Grandma and herself that Grampa had taken when she was five. Laurinda didn't remember the story firsthand, but she lovingly remembered it being told time and again by her grandparents. It wasn't a story about the fish that got away, it was about the little girl who almost did.

Eva told the story. "They'd gone fishing that summer and she caught her first fish. It was too little to keep, so Dad took this picture, and then threw the fish back into the water. After that, Linny became bored, lay down at the back of the boat, and fell asleep. Grandma covered her with a towel so she wouldn't get sunburned. When Linny woke up she had to pee. Since there was no bathroom on board, she took it upon herself to create one. She pulled down her bathing suit bottom and tried to climb onto the side, and said 'somebody hold me.' Grandma and Grandpa laughed so hard it was hard to remember that they had to hold her or she might fall into the water."

Laurinda blushed as Ronnie smiled and said, "I see now you've been an independent spirit since an early age."

After the group looked over the pictures they'd picked out
and the ladies were happy with their selections, the pictures were
carefully taped to the poster board Eva had left over from her Sunday
school supplies. After the pictures were cleaned up, and everyone had
a light lunch, Tom announced it was time to go. Everyone became
more somber as they readied themselves for the trip.

*   *   *

Amanda arrived home to find lunch already on the table. "I
thought you said you'd have the table cleaned off when I got back,"
she teased Calvin.

"I said I'd have *my* stuff off the table. But if you want me to
remove all this yummy food, I'll be happy to do that for you, too."

"Oh no, the sandwiches look great. Did you add the garlic salt to
the chicken?"

"I knew I forgot something. I thought it was chili powder you put
in." He helped her remove her coat and laid it across an empty chair
in anticipation of needing it again shortly.

"Whatever you want to put in is fine with me. I can eat yogurt for
lunch if you really put chili powder in it."

"Would I do that to you?" He wrapped his arms around her waist
and pulled her to him.

She looked into his eyes. "No," she barely said. "We need to eat
lunch. We have a long drive ahead of us."

"You wanna take the truck?"

She rolled her eyes at him as they sat down. Calvin prayed for
a blessing on the food, and strength for their friends today and the
days to come.

*   *   *

The Bowman foursome arrived at the funeral home and made their way inside to begin receiving their family and friends. Calvin and Amanda arrived about an hour later. Laurinda was the first to notice them. She and Ronnie talked with the Edwardses for a while until her parents joined them.

"We were hoping you'd be here today," Mrs. Bowman said. "We have a favor to ask of both of you. One may seem bigger than the other, but they're of equal importance to us."

"We told you we'd help in any way we can," Amanda reminded her.

"Obviously, we had time to think, talk, and pray on the way down here today. The fact that you have such a beautiful voice came up and we discussed the fact that we have no one to sing at the funeral." Mrs. Bowman gave Amanda a minute to let the idea sink in before continuing. "We were wondering if you would sing "Amazing Grace" for us."

"Do you want it with or without accompaniment," Amanda asked.

"You'll do it?"

"We said we would do anything to help. I know I meant it."

Mrs. Bowman hugged her tight. "Thank you so much." She released her from the embrace, and then added, "Either way is fine. Just let me know what you need and we'll make arrangements for it."

"If it really doesn't matter to you, then I'll do it without accompaniment."

Mr. Bowman extended his hand to Amanda. "Thank you very much. It was my mother's favorite song. I don't know why we didn't think of it earlier to give you more time to adjust to the idea. I really appreciate you doing it on such short notice." Mr. Bowman shook Calvin's hand after he released Amanda's.

"You said you had a favor to ask both of us. I know you don't want me to sing," Calvin said.

"It would be all right with me if you did," Mr. Bowman told the younger man.

"You've obviously never heard me sing," Calvin chuckled.

"I'll take your word for it. We were also talking about one of Mom's nursing home friends, Mrs. Ingram. We met her last night while we were there. Mother was very special to her. I was wondering if it'd be too much trouble to ask you to pick her up and bring her here for the funeral tomorrow. If she wants to come that is."

"Give me directions and we'll take care of that, too. Amanda will need a few minutes to warm up and she can do that in the van on the way down."

"I'll call Mrs. Ingram from here and be sure she wants to come. I'm certain she'll say yes. I'll get back with you as soon as I've talked to her."

"That's fine. We'll be here a while."

Tom excused himself to make the phone call. When he returned a short time later he found Calvin and Ronnie talking about Jayson, the boy Ronnie's mentoring.

"Would it be okay with you, boss, if I ask Jayson if he has any construction experience?" Ronnie asked Calvin.

"We could use all the help we can get with the kitchen project we're starting later this week. Sure, go ahead." As Ronnie was about to walk away, Calvin told him to make sure Jayson had a work permit.

"Will do, boss man," Ronnie said.

Just then Tom returned. "I don't mean to interrupt, gentleman. Calvin, Mrs. Ingram would like to come to the service tomorrow. She'll be ready an hour before the service and waiting for you any time after that."

"I'm sure Amanda will want to be here early, but I don't know how early."

"Whatever works best for you. We really appreciate this."

"We're happy to do it."

Mr. Bowman extended his right hand to Calvin and placed his left hand on his shoulder to thank him again. Then he leaned in toward Calvin and said, "I appreciate you bringing this young man into the company as well. I've never seen Linny happier, and Eva and I think the world of him."

"You know God brought him to us in the first place. So I can't take any of the credit."

Mr. Bowman patted Calvin's shoulder. "I know." He spoke again, this time so Ronnie could hear. "I'll give you directions to the nursing home so you shouldn't have any trouble tomorrow."

The two men went to find some paper and Ronnie excused himself to find Laurinda. Once the directions were written, Mr. Bowman said, "I guess we'll be seeing you tomorrow then. It's getting late and we need to get some dinner before the second viewing tonight."

"Yes, sir. I think Amanda is ready as well. She looks a little tired." The two men shook hands again as Amanda joined them. "Are you ready, honey?"

She nodded her head. Mr. Bowman thanked them for coming and the couple went to say good-bye to Mrs. Bowman, Ronnie, and Laurinda.

* * *

Later, as Calvin and Amanda lay in bed, Amanda began talking about her plans for the front window at work. Even though she was so tired, she talked nonstop for ten minutes. Finally, she said, "I guess we should stop talking and get to sleep."

"I'm confused."

"About the window?" Amanda asked him.

221

"No. You said we," he said and paused. "I haven't said a word."
Together they laughed, and then cuddled up like two spoons in a
drawer before falling asleep.

* * *

Morning brought with it a somber mood. "I didn't ask how many
verses they want me to sing."

"I'm sure there'll be time to ask when we get there. If everything
goes as planned when we pick up Mrs. Ingram, we'll be over a half
hour early."

"You're right."

Amanda practiced all five verses of "Amazing Grace" several
times as they drove to the nursing home. Calvin wondered how she
managed to make it sound *so* beautiful every time. He smiled and
thanked God again for bringing her into his life.

When they arrived, everything went smoothly in getting Mrs.
Ingram checked out and into their van. Amanda offered her the front
passenger's seat but she refused.

"Don't get me wrong," the elderly woman said. "I'd love to be seen
with such a handsome man, but he's your husband and it wouldn't
be right for me to take your place up there," she told Amanda after
she was seated in the back seat. "I'd rather sit back here with the little
ones anyway."

Calvin's head jerked as he looked at Amanda. "Mrs. Ingram, we
don't have our children with us."

"Oh, I know that, sonny. When they come back, you can tell
them about the crazy old lady who sat where they usually sit."

Calvin and Amanda wondered if someone had told Mrs. Ingram
about their situation. Amanda recalled Laurinda saying yesterday
afternoon that they'd all just met Mrs. Ingram the night Grandma
Meredith passed.

"Children are such a wonderful gift from God. I outlived both my children. One died at birth and the other died before she got grown. I have no one left to take care of me. That's why I'm in the nursing home, all alone. My sister is in a nursing home in Illinois. We write each other because it's too expensive to call."

"We're sorry you've lost so much, Mrs. Ingram," Calvin said for the both of them.

"Nonsense, my boy. I've recently been given everything. Meredith introduced me to the new Man in my life."

"Would that be Jesus Christ?" he asked.

"Indeed. As for your children, God works in mysterious ways sometimes. I knew that even before I knew Jesus. Take me losing my Pearl, for example. When she died in my arms, I thought I couldn't go on. Then it wasn't long until her sister was born. Now, if I had given up when Pearl died, I wouldn't have had my Margaret. Margaret was such a delight, always singing and dancing around our house, even when there was no music. We only played our radio at night to hear the news, to save electricity. We were dirt poor back then. Then my husband, Veryl, he got into some business dealings that at first I didn't like. But when he came home driving a new car and told me we were moving to a nicer neighborhood, I began to believe in those business deals. I didn't ask where the money came from, I just enjoyed the pleasures it brought.

"He stopped working at the factory so we didn't have any insurance when little Margaret got so sick. I thought we had enough money to take care of everything we ever needed, until then. She should've had an operation. The doctors said it might have saved her. We never had the chance to find out. She died before we could get together enough money to pay for it."

"I'm so sorry, Mrs. Ingram. Our daughters have been missing for seven months and in some ways it's like they died, but there is nowhere to go and sit with them. And we never got to say good-bye," Amanda explained as she wiped tears from her eyes.

"So you're the couple I heard about last summer? I remember Meredith saying something about it. Do you know she prayed for you every day?" she asked without awaiting a response, and then added, "She kept telling me you'd get them back sooner than later." From that point on, Amanda didn't hear anything else Mrs. Ingram said. Her mind was spinning.

A short time later, they arrived at the funeral home. Calvin pulled up to the door and parked. He helped Mrs. Ingram inside and then returned to get Amanda who hadn't moved a muscle. He opened the door and extended his hand to her. She took it and got out with a blank stare on her face.

"Are you all right?" he asked.

"Yes, I'll be fine," she said as she stared forward. She finally turned to look at him with tears in her eyes. "They're coming home."

"Honey, please don't get your hopes up because of what Mrs. Ingram said. We can't be sure."

Before that moment, Amanda had never questioned Calvin's faith. "She's the second person to tell me that in less than a week. You believe what you want and I'll believe what I want." With that, she turned and walked inside to Mrs. Ingram, leaving her husband with nothing to say and no one to say it to.

She wiped her eyes, helped Mrs. Ingram with her coat, and then took off and hung up her own. "I need to practice the song I'm singing. We should find you a seat."

"Oh no, I'd rather stay with you and Calvin."

"But if you stay with me, you'll have to hear the same song twice in a short period of time."

"What's the song?"

"'Amazing Grace.'"

"I believe I'll stay with you."

"All right, but don't say I didn't warn you. Let's go find Mr. and Mrs. Bowman so they know we're here."

The two ladies found Mr. Bowman first, and he also suggested Mrs. Ingram might want to sit down and wait for the service to start. She declined. Amanda asked where Mrs. Bowman and Laurinda were and he pointed them out near the casket and excused himself to greet more new comers.

Amanda hugged first Mrs. Bowman and then Laurinda. Mrs. Ingram did the same. "I am grateful you invited me and helped me get a ride."

"We're glad to have you," Mrs. Bowman said. "Would you like to have a seat and wait for the service to start?"

"Why does everyone keep asking me that? Don't you think my hips have spread enough from all the sitting I do in that ol' nursing home?" She patted her thigh and smiled.

Mrs. Bowman apologized, and when Mrs. Ingram started laughing, she realized that she had been kidding with her.

"I'd like to stay with Amanda and that handsome husband of hers. Besides, I believe that a girl should dance with the one what brought her to the party. Speaking of handsome husbands, where is yours, Laurinda?"

Laurinda blushed. "Remember I told you Monday night he's not my husband? Ronnie is around here somewhere."

To help Laurinda out of the embarrassing moment, Amanda asked if there was somewhere she could practice one last time. Laurinda offered to show her and Mrs. Ingram to a room where she could practice.

"Thanks for this break. It feels like I've been here forever. I hate seeing Grandma lying there lifeless," Laurinda said as she walked ahead of the two ladies. "Amanda, did you get a copy of the order of the service?"

"No, I was only focused on practicing."

"I'll go get you one and be right back with it. Here's the room." She opened the door in front of them. "When you're done, come and find me so I can show you where to sit."

"Thank you, dear," Amanda said. Mrs. Ingram's words still swirled in her mind, but she had a job to do and needed to prepare for it, so praying for strength, she pushed everything else aside.

Laurinda left to get the order of service for Amanda and find Ronnie. It'd been a while since she'd seen him and she wanted him by her side until everything was over. She got the paper she needed for Amanda, and then looked for Ronnie. He was in a different part of the home where someone else's body could have been but wasn't. He was crying.

Laurinda sat down beside him and put her arm around him. "It's okay, I'm here."

He'd been so involved with his own thoughts that he hadn't heard her come in. "I'm sorry," he blubbered. "I'm supposed to be supporting you, not the other way around."

"Right now you're the one who needs supporting. Do you want to talk about it?"

"Even though she's been gone a while, I still miss my grandmother so much."

"I'm sure the same thing will happen to me from time to time. Like when I hold her hankie close to me. I think I'll wear it tucked inside my dress somewhere when I get married." She couldn't believe she just said that. "I...I," she stammered. "That is if I get married."

He took her left hand into his and fumbled with it just as he'd done the day before. "I'm going to do my best to be sure you do." He raised her hand to his lips and kissed it gently.

Her eyes began to tear. "So that's why you were holding my hand like that yesterday?"

"This is a conversation for another day. Today is a day for new beginnings, but not ours. It's a time for your grandma to be welcomed into the house of the Lord."

"I believe that happened the moment after she took her last breath."

"I agree. I'm just saying it's her new beginning today, not ours. That will come in God's time."

Laurinda looked at her hands and remembered the paper she was supposed to be delivering. "We better get this to Amanda or she'll be looking for me."

Ronnie wiped his nose on the tissue in his hand, and then stood up and extended his other hand to Laurinda. "Then let's get going."

The couple stopped short just outside the door as they heard the beautiful sound of "Amazing Grace" sung by Amanda on the other side. Tears welled up in both of their eyes as she sang the final verse.

"She's an awesome singer. No wonder your parents asked her to sing today."

"Grandma would have loved to hear her sing. I'm not sure the two ever even met. Such a shame."

"Do you think Grandma will hear it from heaven?"

"I don't know, but what I do know is that I'll get into trouble if I don't get us seated before the service starts."

Laurinda managed to get everyone seated with time to spare. At the appointed time, Amanda stood up, prayed for strength, and sang "Amazing Grace" from the depths of her heart and soul. There wasn't a dry eye in the place.

After the service everyone followed the hearse to the graveside where Mrs. Bowman was laid to rest beside her beloved husband. After a short service, family and friends went to the church where the ten Bowman children grew up, and enjoyed a meal prepared by the ladies there.

Chapter 18

"That was the most beautiful rendition of "Amazing Grace" that I've ever heard," Mrs. Ingram said after she was once again in the back seat of the Edwardses' van.

"Thank you, Mrs. Ingram. It's my favorite song."

"I think it meant more to me today because I have a relationship with the Man you were singing about. I understand grace better."

"I'm glad you were able to come with us," Amanda told her. "I've truly enjoyed your company."

"And I, yours."

As they were about to leave Mrs. Ingram in her room, she asked them to wait just a minute. After Calvin helped her get her coat off and she'd hung it in the closet, she scratched her head, trying to remember something.

"Meredith told me something and I think you should know about it. It didn't make since to me at the time, but now that I've met you, it does." She thought again for a moment. "She said something about how God sometimes allows things to happen so He can show His glory. If the something was bad, then He shows His glory by settin' it right." Mrs. Ingram paused. "I don't know why I felt compelled to tell you this, I'm sure you already know it. I'm not going to keep you. I know you have a long drive ahead of you. Thank you again for carting this old woman around."

"You're welcome. It's been our pleasure to get to know you," Calvin said. "Mrs. Ingram, don't be surprised if you say things to people about God. He uses willing vessels to spread His word. I'm sure this is something Amanda and I both needed to hear. Thank you."

Mrs. Ingram's face lit up as he encouraged her.

Both of the Edwardses hugged her good-bye and she told them not to be strangers—they were welcome anytime.

Calvin held the door open to their van for his wife to get in. She turned to him and said, "I believe I will be back to see her. How about you?"

"I think we might work it into our schedule," he said as he winked at her.

"What do you think about the other thing she said?" Amanda asked once he was in the driver's seat.

"I think she was saying something Meredith told her that she, or God, thought we needed to hear. Think about it. God has been glorified since our babies were taken. Look how strong you are now compared to before. You read to kids every Saturday morning, work at the Family Christian Store, and you're witnessing to people almost every day." He reached for her hand. He waited to speak again until she was looking directly at him. "You truly are a shinning example of God's strength. I'm so proud of the woman of faith that you're becoming."

Tears streamed down Amanda's cheeks. Before she could object, Calvin placed his finger on her lips to silence her.

"Don't argue with me." He kissed her hand, started the van, and drove them home.

*   *   *

"You really do have a big family," Ronnie told Laurinda on the way back to her parents' house. "I hope you don't expect me to remember all your aunts, uncles, and cousins' names."

"No, you don't have to remember everyone's name. I can't even keep track of all my cousins' children anymore. My dad is the baby of the family. I have cousins who are much older than me."

"I know you introduced me to a lot of people, but I don't remember you pointing out the cousin that was in the picture with you. Was she there?"

"No. My Aunt Dorothy told me that Michelle couldn't get away from work. I'll call her this week and talk to her."

"Speaking of talking to someone, what do you think about coming back down here to visit Mrs. Ingram?"

"Get out of my head."

Mr. Bowman looked at his daughter in his rearview mirror. "He does that to you, too?" he asked her.

"Yes, Daddy, he does. I think he climbs right into my head and sees what I'm thinking."

"Your mother does that to me all the time. My ears are so big because she crawls in and out whenever she wants."

"It seems we have a lot in common with you and Mum."

Everyone laughed.

"That's one of the requirements," she whispered to Ronnie.

He smiled from ear to ear.

"Daddy, Mum, what would you think of Ronnie and me visiting Mrs. Ingram? Amanda said she has only one living relative, a sister in Illinois, who's also in a nursing home."

Mrs. Bowman said, "I think it'd be greatly appreciated and a great way to continue to show her Jesus' love."

"Yeah, what she said," Mr. Bowman said as he reached over to hold his wife's hand.

"Well, since we all seem to be of one mind on this matter, I guess it's settled. The only question is how often?" Laurinda asked.

"I think it's a wonderful break from what we both do everyday, so I suggest every Sunday. Since she's able to get out, maybe we could take her with us to get ice cream sometimes," Ronnie responded.

"Sounds good to me," Laurinda said as she squeezed his hand, feeling as giddy as a schoolgirl. *Stay calm. God's will, not mine.* She smiled at him.

The pair discussed when they'd be able to get together with Jayson and Melissa. "I told Calvin about Jayson and suggested he might be able to work for him after school and on Saturdays. Calvin needs to know if he's had construction experience."

Laurinda offered to call the school in the morning and leave a message for Jayson to call her when he got the chance.

When Ronnie told Mr. Bowman about the job they'd be starting in the morning, Eva said she'd love to have her kitchen remodeled. "If that's what you want to do, sweetheart, call Calvin or just ask Ronnie to do it."

"I would do it myself, but I won't for two reasons. First, I wouldn't take the work from Calvin, and second, it would take too long for me to do it myself. I can mention it to him if you like."

"We'll discuss it and I'll let you know. I'm pretty sure I know where to find you." Eva smiled.

Everyone was laughing as Mr. Bowman pulled into their driveway. "It's going to be tough getting up to go to work in the morning," he said. "The only thing worse than having to go to work tomorrow is not having any work to go to."

"I hear that," Ronnie said.

* * *

"I'm grateful you needed the extra day before you started. I had to finish cleaning everything out of the cupboards," Mrs. Robinson told Calvin and the crew as they assembled in her kitchen to begin disassembling it. "I'm sorry for the reason."

Ronnie spoke for the group and the family. "Thank you, Mrs. Robinson. I'll tell the family you send your sympathy."

"Thank you, young man. Now if you'll excuse me, I'm going shopping for new curtains this morning."

"Yes, ma'am," everyone said.

Once she was gone the destruction began. By lunch time the old cabinets, countertop, and cupboards were gone. After some lively discussion about this week's Sunday school lesson at lunch, the team pulled up the carpet. Calvin called the company where he'd ordered the hardwood flooring to confirm delivery the next day. While he confirmed the delivery time, everyone else worked on cleaning up the dust from the floor removal. Some time was spent replacing the sections of rotted subfloor, making it safe to walk on.

Everyone but Calvin was gone when Mrs. Robinson returned. She was flabbergasted by the emptiness when she walked in. Calvin explained they'd needed to repair some of the subfloor, which he pointed out to her. Since that hadn't been a part of the original estimate, he told her how much more it would cost. She said she didn't care about the cost as long as everything looked great and was safe.

"We'll be here at eight tomorrow to continue the floor. The flooring should be here between eight thirty and nine o'clock."

"I'm going to Novi tomorrow. I didn't find curtains today so I'm going there to look."

"I'm sorry you didn't find what you wanted."

"Are you kidding? This is just an excuse to go to the Novi mall," she said and laughed.

"You're starting to sound like my wife." He extended his right hand to shake hers and said good-bye.

"I'll leave the door unlocked for you. If I'm not back by the time you need to leave, just lock up behind you."

"Very well. Have fun tomorrow."

"I will," she said with a smile

*   *   *

Calvin arrived home a short time later to find dinner on the table waiting for him. "Everything smells awesome."

"Thank you," Amanda said with a glowing smile on her face.

Normally, he would have just thought her smile was a result of his compliment, but this time he could tell it was something different. "What's up?" he asked.

"Nothing. Now hurry and get washed up so we can sit down and eat before it gets cold."

"I'll do as you asked," he teased her, "but then you must tell me what has caused your face to be all aglow."

"I'll do as you ask after you do what I ask. Besides, it's Wednesday and we have people coming here for Bible study in case you've forgotten."

He walked over to the kitchen sink and began to wash his hands. "Actually, I had forgotten. I wouldn't be surprised if Ronnie forgot, too. Today felt more like Monday than Wednesday since it was our first day of work this week."

She handed him a towel. "Will you hurry up, for goodness sake?"

"For goodness sake or for yours?" he teased her as he dried his hands. She ran to the table and sat down when he started to roll the towel as if to snap her with it. Instead he threw the towel on the counter and joined her at the table. "I'd let you ask the blessing for the food, but I'm afraid you'd only say 'Rub-a-dub-dub, thank God for the grub.'"

"Then you don't know me as well as you think you do. I might go on and on listing my blessings."

Calvin said a short, respectful prayer blessing the food.

"Are you going to tell me the good news or keep me waiting?"

"I had a very special visitor in the store today while I was working," she began. "You'll *never* guess who it was, not in a million years."

"I'm sure our dinner would be pretty cold by then, so why don't you just tell me who it was and we can start eating."

"Go ahead and fix your plate. I can wait until after dinner to tell you."

"In what lifetime would you be able to keep good news to yourself that long?"

She ignored his teasing and began her story. "Michael went to the other store to pick up something. I don't even remember now what it was. Anyway, while he was gone I got a phone call from the manager of one of the most awesome female Christian singers I've ever heard. He said they were in our area and wanted to stop by and hang out for a while. I explained that I was the only person in the store, but that didn't bother them.

So I ran and got a copy of her latest CD and opened it so I could have her sign it. Imagine my surprise when her husband was with her! I got a book he'd written and asked him to sign it as well. Of course I paid for everything before I left the store. Oh my gosh, Calvin, I was so excited. They left before Michael got back so I felt bad I was the only one in the store. Not even a single customer came in while they were there."

Amanda finally took a breath, giving Calvin a chance to talk. "That's awesome, honey. Could you put some names with this story?"

"I'm sorry. She was none other than Cindy Morgan and her husband is Sigmund Brouwer. He's written lots of books, but I chose *The Carpenter's Cloth*." Amanda jumped up and got the CD and book from the counter and showed him. "The really cool thing is that the CD and the book go together. They're both about Easter." Amanda became more solemn. "I read the whole book this afternoon and wished I could have shared it with the girls. Most of it would be over Katrina's head, but Jessica would have understood some of it. I know they'd have both loved the music."

Calvin reached out and covered her hands with his. "Be strong, sweetheart. Let's pray they're being lovingly cared for and are being taught about our Lord and Savior."

Through tears she nodded her head and muttered, "Okay."

"Dear loving and gracious Heavenly Father, Amanda and I come before You asking that while our daughters are away from us, but not You, that the people who have them will teach them about Your love and will love them as we do, bringing no harm to either of them. We pray this with confidence knowing that nothing touches us without passing through Your hands first. We pray this in Jesus' name, amen."

"Thank you. I thought I was over crying like this, but I know that will probably never happen. Having you here and being able to pray helps so much."

"You pray without me?"

"Yes, but it's not the same."

"I understand."

"I've gone on so long our dinner is cold and people will start getting here in thirty minutes. We better hurry up and eat."

"You're right."

"I did have another visitor today—Judy. Good thing it was after Michael got back and I was working on a book display. By the way, she loved what we did with the window."

"It was your idea. I just delivered and helped set up."

"Delivered, helped set up, *and* made the cross. Anyway, she had some interesting news for me. On Sunday I noticed her talking to a man after church, but with the funeral and everything I haven't had time to call and ask her who he was. She said he's a widower with three small children. They just moved back to the area to be closer to his family. His mother takes care of the children while he's working. He was talking to someone else, she told me who, but I forgot who she said. Anyway, he said he needed a haircut for himself and his two boys so whoever it was suggested Judy, and then introduced them. He was holding a beautiful six-month-old baby girl in his arms. He scheduled an appointment for Monday late afternoon so he'd have time to get to his mom's after work and pick up the boys.

"He and the boys came over and he told her his recent life story. His wife was pregnant with the little girl when her car was hit by a drunk driver. She was kept alive until it was safe to deliver the baby." Amanda wiped the tears from her eyes. Calvin waited for her to collect herself.

"The day the baby was born was the day his wife died. Judy said he told her the doctors said they could keep her alive for one more day if he wanted them to, but he declined. As a Christian, he was able to see his wife's death as a mixed blessing. He'd lost her, but his Heavenly Father now had her in His arms and he had a beautiful little reminder of her in his arms.

"This is the part of the story where Judy broke down and cried. You and I both know what she chose to do with the baby God gave her. It wasn't until she dedicated her life to Christ recently that she realized He holds that baby in His hands. Meeting someone who lost his wife but got a baby really hit her hard. I took her into the back room and sat her down until she stopped crying. He told her all this after she'd cut the boys' hair and they'd gone upstairs to watch a video in her living room."

"I know she has a way of getting you to talk a lot while in that chair of hers. She practically threatened me with great hair harm if I didn't tell her what I had planned for you on Valentine's Day," Calvin told her.

"She said it wasn't like that at all. She said he just opened up like they'd known each other for years. They stayed for dinner after he called his mother to let her know. While she cooked, the boys watched the rest of the video and he kept her company and kept talking.

"He told her he tried to stay in their hometown, but without family around it was too difficult for him to try to work and take care of the kids. He called his parents and asked if he could come home. She said they agreed immediately. He is waiting for the house there to sell. Until then he plans to stay with his parents. He said he couldn't imagine leaving his kids with anyone besides his mother. Judy said that just after he said that, the oldest boy, she told me his name but I can't think of it right now, came up to her and politely asked for a glass of water. When she gave it to him, he gave her a hug and thanked her.

"Judy thought the poor boy must be starving for attention, but then remembered they were living with their grandparents so that probably wasn't true. Bill, oh, that's the dad's name, said the little boy didn't usually have anything to do with strangers, and he certainly would not have hugged one unless he felt comfortable around them.

"She said they prayed holding hands like we do. Judy's not used to that but she didn't feel uncomfortable. She said she really liked it and she was glad Elizabeth had been at work. He might not have opened up as much if she were there.

"If I didn't know any better, based on the dreamy look in her eyes today, I'd say she's falling for him. I didn't say anything because she didn't, but I'd bet you anything they end up together."

"You better not be doing any of your matchmaking, Mrs. Edwards. Let the good Lord take care of that," Calvin teased.

"Calvin Edwards, I wouldn't dream of doing any matchmaking," she said sheepishly. "Besides, the only thing I know about him is what Judy told me and that really isn't much. His parents go to our church but I didn't recognize the name. I'm sure I would know them if I saw them. She didn't mention what he does for a living."

"As long as he's not the competition for Edwards Construction, I don't care what he does. I hope he doesn't want Judy to be the woman he replaces his wife with. I don't want to see her get hurt," he said in a very fatherly tone.

"I've told her to put God in charge of the search committee for husband hunting if she ever decides to remarry. I think she's finally decided to try again and He's brought someone right to her doorstep. That's all I've got to say about that."

"For the moment," he teased her, "we better eat our dinner or put it in the fridge for later." He looked at his watch.

"You're right. Do you want me to warm it up?"

"Naw."

"Do me a favor. Don't say anything tonight unless she does, and pray she *will* put God's will before her own."

"That sounds like two favors," he said as he took a bite of his cold dinner. "I can handle both of them."

Amanda finished her dinner in record time and began cleaning the kitchen when the phone rang. She answered it so Calvin could get cleaned up.

"Hello. I didn't expect to hear from you until I saw you tonight. What's up?"

"I was wondering if you had room in your Bible study group for one more."

"I believe we can find a folding chair somewhere in the house if we need it. Do you have someone specific in mind or are you planning to pick someone up from the street?"

"I thought…well." Judy paused, trying to find the right words. "I didn't tell you today that on Sunday I told Bill about the study at your house. I sort of, well, I asked if he'd want to join us. I hope you don't mind."

238

"Don't be silly. We'd love to have him. The more the merrier. Are you riding together?"

"Yes, he's coming to get me. Elizabeth is working so she won't be there tonight. I hate that she can't be with us, but at least we three are able to keep up our girls weekly study. Have I told you lately how much I love and appreciate you?"

"No. Maybe. I don't remember. My mind isn't what it used to be, you know." Amanda toyed with her friend.

"Then I'll be sure to tell you more often. Since I knew you were working today, I took the liberty of making dessert for tonight."

"Please tell me you made your banana split cake."

"I did."

"Are you trying to win your way to Bill's heart through his stomach?"

"You know me so well." They laughed. "I keep listening to the way you boss Laurinda around about following God's will first, so I'm going to try to do the same thing. I figure if it's good advice for Laurinda, it's good advice for me."

"Am I too bossy?"

"No. It's exactly what I need to hear. But hey, I've gotta go so I can finish doing my hair. We'll be there shortly."

"Thanks again for making the dessert. I was so excited about *all* my visitors today that I wasn't even thinking about dessert when I got home. Go make yourself more beautiful. We'll see you when you get here."

"See ya."

Amanda joined Calvin in the bedroom where he'd just finished dressing. "We have a new person coming tonight."

"The more the merrier," he said with a twinkle in his eye as he swept her into his arms. "What's for dessert?"

"Judy's bringing it," she said as she wiggled out of his arms when the doorbell rang.

"Who's the new person?" he asked, following her toward the door.

"Bill," was the only thing she had time to say before opening the door to let in Ronnie and Laurinda.

Amanda and Laurinda sat on the couch to talk about their day while Ronnie and Calvin stayed near the front door.

"Laurinda left a message for Jayson today and he called her back," Ronnie told Calvin. "He said his only construction experience was in shop class. He did say he was a hard worker and a quick learner. She also asked him about his grades. I was a little surprised at the answer—his GPA is 3.78."

"Wow!" Calvin exclaimed. "That's great. Did she ask him if he would be interested in working?"

"Yes, she did and he is."

"Ask her to call him back tomorrow and have him call me tomorrow night so I can talk to him about the job and get him set up to come over Saturday."

"Sure, boss. No problem. I welcome any opportunity to talk to that beautiful lady and you know it." Calvin raised his eyebrow at the boy and then excused himself to answer the door again.

After the banana split cake was placed in the refrigerator, the group began their introductions to the newest member of their group. Bill introduced himself, but said little about his background.

Calvin opened with prayer, thanking their Creator for the group's ability to get together and worship Him, and for the newest member to their group. He also prayed that everyone would take from this Bible study what He wanted them to learn. He closed in Jesus' name and everyone said amen.

"Last week we finally finished with chapter 3 in the book of James," he said with a laugh. "Remember we picked this book to study because it was so small. Good thing, otherwise we might be stuck in one book for years the way we pick a chapter, and sometimes a verse, apart."

He looked directly at Bill. "I don't mean to scare you or anything, but we're all so passionate about the Bible that we all seem to have a lot to say about it and how it has, or will, affect our lives."

"Then I'm afraid your Bible study may take a little longer than before," Bill said.

Everyone laughed.

"Then let's get started. Does anyone want to read the first twelve verses or do you want me to?"

"I'll read them," Bill offered. "I have the NIV version, in case my text doesn't match yours."

"We all have the NIV version," Judy told him. "Calvin or Amanda probably gave everyone in this room their Bible." She winked at Amanda. "Actually, Amanda only helped me pick mine out."

"Okay, then I'll begin." He cleared his throat and read from God's word. Judy hung on every word for two reasons. First, because he was reading from the Bible and she'd developed a true hunger for it, and second, because of who was reading. She loved to hear him talk. They'd already spent several hours on the phone since his haircut.

Amanda was the first to speak when he finished. "I don't mean to skip verses 1 through 6, but I love verses 7 and 8. 'Submit yourselves then, to God. Resist the devil, and he will flee from you. Come near to God and He will come near to you.' I love to think of coming near to God. I'm amazed that we can do that."

Everyone shared stories, and the verses were discussed until finally the time came for dessert. Three couples nearly finished off a 13x9 inch pan of Judy's famous banana split cake before closing their fellowship time in prayer and calling it a night.

After everyone left, Amanda began to clean up the mess the group had made in the kitchen. "What did you think of Bill?"

"He seems like a nice guy and he sure knows his Bible well. He must think a lot of Judy to have opened up to her like he did. He didn't really talk much about his life tonight."

"I think I saw a connection between them like with you and me. She's really been trying to learn God's word, so Bill will be a good influence on her."

They looked at one another, then, despite her wet hands, joined hands and hearts to pray for their friends, both the new and the old ones.

* * *

Saturday morning Jayson joined Edwards Construction as they installed the new cupboards for Mrs. Robinson. Someone helped him work a level. Someone else showed him the best way to put the screws into the cupboard so they won't fall down. Calvin noted everything he did and how he took to everything.

During the lunch break, the crew discussed the upcoming Easter service the following week. Ronnie invited Jayson to the service. Calvin suggested he not wait for Easter, but suggested he and his family could join them the next day. Since Calvin offered to buy dinner afterward, he was pretty sure Jayson would be there.

At the end of the day, the only thing left for the crew to do Monday was install the countertop and make cuts for the cooktop and sink. Even the new curtains Mrs. Robinson had purchased were hung.

"I'll see you tomorrow," Calvin said as he shook Jayson's hand and thanked him for a good day's work.

* * *

The following morning, Calvin and Ronnie were pleased when, just before the first song, Jayson, Melissa, and their daughter came into the sanctuary. Since Calvin was ushering, he was able to seat them next to Ronnie and Laurinda.

Calvin stood at the back of the church for a few extra minutes before he went to join Amanda. He looked out over the crowd and saw Ronnie and Laurinda, Jayson and Melissa, Jimmy and Beth, Judy and Bill with his children and Elizabeth beside them, and Amanda a few rows ahead of them. He smiled as he thought of how God had been working in all these people's lives, and how honored he felt to be a part of it in one way or another. He went to join the one who meant the most to him.

After church, the Edwardses, Ronnie and Laurinda, and Jayson, Melissa, and their baby, Suzie, caravanned to breakfast.

Chapter 19

"Good morning, everyone," Pastor Nichols greeted the congregation from the pulpit.

"Good morning," the congregation replied.

"Isn't it great to be in the house of the Lord this glorious Easter morning?"

"Amen," the congregation replied.

"Did your children get enough candy in your Easter baskets this morning?"

"No," some of the children replied as many of the parents said they'd gotten too much.

"We're going to do something different this morning. I need the children to help with today's sermon. Do you kids think you can help me this morning?"

"Yes," they eagerly replied.

"There are many plastic Easter eggs hidden in the sanctuary today. Most of them have a piece of candy in them, but some of them don't. The eggs with numbers on them have something extra special inside. When the deacons pass the offering plate to your parents, I need each child to find one egg. Once you get your egg, go back to your seats and wait for me to tell you what to do next. All the eggs are in the sanctuary, so don't leave the area. And don't open your eggs until I tell you it is okay to open them."

"Okay," the eager children replied.

"We better not keep them waiting long. Brother Jim, please come and lead us in a song of worship."

"We're only going to sing one song and then go right to the offering to give Pastor Nichols more time to preach. I'll have you stand since it may be a while before you get to do so again." The congregation laughed as they stood and then joined him in song.

After the offertory prayer, Pastor Nichols told the children to start looking for their eggs, reminding them only one egg per child. Once the deacons were moving, so were the children. Once every child had their egg and was seated next to their parents, Pastor Nichols said, "I need the children whose eggs have a number on them to come up and sit in the front row. I know it's not like us Baptists to sit in the front row, but I think the kids can do it just this once."

The congregation laughed as all twelve children made their way to the front row.

The pastor went down the steps to stand in front of them. "Who knows what we're celebrating today?" he asked the children.

"Easter," they all said.

"And who can tell me what Easter is all about?"

"Jesus," some replied.

"Right. Who has the egg with the number one on it?"

"I do," a little girl said.

"Come on up here and let's take a look at what's inside your egg."

The little girl opened her egg and took out its contents.

"Why don't you hold it up so everyone can see what it is?"

The little girl complied and held up a small, plastic toy donkey for everyone to see.

"You can sit down now. When the kings of Jesus' day returned from battle, they road into the city on horses. When Jesus, the King of kings, went into the city the day of Passover, He demonstrated His humility and gentleness by riding a lowly donkey.

"Who has the egg with the number two?"

A boy about thirteen shyly stepped forward, embarrassed to be the biggest and oldest child in the group. "Here you go, Pastor," the boy said as he extended his hand with the open egg in it to the pastor.

"Would you like to tell everyone what you have there?"

"A dove."

The pastor took the dove and the boy sat down.

"When Jesus entered the temple that morning, He found money changers and buyers and sellers where they didn't belong. He overturned the benches of those selling doves and other items necessary for the Jews to make sacrifices. Jesus told them, 'Is it not written, "My house will be called a house of prayer for all nations"? But you have made it into a den of robbers.' Jesus returned the temple into a place of worship and healing. Because of this, the children shouted, 'Hosanna to the Son of David.' Even they recognized Jesus as a son of David.

"Who has egg number three?"

"I do," said a little girl, her voice barely above a whisper.

"Bring it up here." The pastor squatted down to the girl's level, reassuring her it was all right to come up to him.

She opened it above his hand so the object landed in it. "Do you want to hold it up or do you want me to?"

"You," she whispered.

"The third object is a little twig not much smaller than many of my helpers this morning. You all must be thinking I'm crazy. Jesus was beaten by leather whips with rocks and metal woven in them, not by a little twig.

"You'd be right," he said and paused, "about the twig versus the whip that is."

He waited for the laughter to stop. "A twig was important to Jesus during the week leading up to His death on the cross. When He left the temple, He went out of the city of Bethany for the night. Early the next morning He saw a barren fig tree on the side of the road. He said, 'May you never bear fruit again.' The tree died immediately.

"I'm not sure the tree wasn't already dead, like so many of us, when He got there. We claim to be Christian and think we're bearing fruit, but really we're dead. If this is true of us, Jesus tells us in another parable, He will cut us off. His lesson here was one of faith for the disciples, and us. He told us that with faith we can move mountains. Faith and belief, coupled with prayer, equals mountain removed, just as three nails plus one cross equals forgiven.

"I need egg four, please."

A little boy with four on his egg marched up to the pastor. "Here you go," he said. "I peeked inside my egg. It's a book. I have lots of books," he informed Pastor Nichols. Everyone laughed at the little boy's candor and honesty.

"Thank you for your help. I'll take the book and you can have a seat." Pastor Nichols was pleased with how well all the children were behaving, but knew he had limited time and had better hurry.

"Jesus was very good at telling stories. You'd think that He'd be doing more important things than telling stories with only a few days left on earth. Teaching His disciples was an important thing to Him. He taught the parable of the two sons, the tenants, and the talents. He taught us to pay our taxes."

Several members groaned.

"He taught us there'll be no giving or receiving in marriage in heaven, and that God is the God of the living and not the dead. He taught us to love the Lord our God with all our heart, soul, and mind. He said love your neighbor as yourself. His job on earth was not only to save us, but also to teach us.

"Who has egg five?"

A little boy jumped up and ran to the pastor's side. "I came right up 'cause I knew you wanted me to."

"I did want you to. You're a very quick fellow. Now what do I need you to do?"

"Open the egg 'cause you can't." The congregation laughed.

"What's in your egg?"

The little boy twisted the egg until a tiny box fell onto the floor.

"That's why everything in the eggs are unbreakable," Pastor Nichols told the congregation. "Hold it up to show everyone."

The little boy picked the box up from the floor and held it as high over his head as his small frame allowed.

"For those of you in the back, my helper here is holding a box. You can sit down now. Thank you for your help.

"There was a woman who brought an alabaster box of very precious ointment into the home of Simon the Leper where Jesus and His disciples were having dinner. She broke the box and poured the ointment over Jesus' head. Some in the room were upset she'd wasted the expensive ointment. Jesus saw it differently.

"Egg six, please."

A little girl came forward with her egg almost open.

"Haven't you been up here already?" he asked.

"No, swilly! That was my sister. We're twins. We look alike, but we don't sound alike." The congregation laughed.

"Now I hear the difference. What's in your egg?"

She held up a shiny silver coin as high as she could. "I like money," she told the pastor. "Can I keep it?" Everyone laughed again.

"When we're finished you can have it back."

"This is one of the more obvious parts of the Easter story. Judas Iscariot went to the chief priests and asked what Jesus was worth to them. We had only one coin in our egg, but Judas was given thirty pieces of silver for betraying Jesus. We might say this was the first time the priests had actual faith. I'd have been leery of giving thirty pieces of silver to one of Jesus' closest friends. I wonder how they were sure Judas would do what he said. Maybe they were sure because *he* came to them. Or maybe it was because they recognized the devil, but missed the Savior.

"Who has egg seven?"

"I do," said a little girl as she walked up to the pastor. "My egg has a crouton in it." She placed the crouton into the pastor's outstretched hand. "You can keep it, I don't want it."

When the laughter died down, Pastor Nichols explained the crouton. "This is another obvious part of the Easter story. The night He established the Lord's Supper, Jesus washed the disciple's feet, predicted His betrayal and Peter's denial, and gave the disciples a new command.

"I said a new command, not a new commandment. This command, in my own life, is harder than the top ten. He told us to 'love one another as I have loved you.' Ouch. There He goes teaching again.

"I need egg eight."

A little boy brought the item but left the egg at his seat. "It's a pillow," he announced. "I'd rather have candy," he said as he dropped the object into the pastor's hand and returned to his seat.

"Don't worry, kids or parents, the kids who got something in their eggs besides candy will get a piece after the service. Let's talk about this pillow. Don't get excited. We're not having pillows installed on the back of the pews as headrests." When the laughter died down, he continued. "Is there anything more comforting than laying your head down on a soft pillow at night?

"I say there is. Jesus knew His disciples would be afraid when they could no longer see Him. He told them about a Comforter like no other. Even those down feather comforters don't hold a candle to the One I'm talking about. We know Him as the Holy Spirit. Jesus referred to Him as the Counselor. A counselor is someone who comes alongside someone else in their time of trouble. When I was young and couldn't get to sleep, I'd lay down on my pillow with my arm underneath my ear so I could hear my own heartbeat. Then I'd imagine climbing up on God's great big lap and curling up there. I found comfort in God's lap, nestled against His chest and listening to His heartbeat. I can't tell you the number of times I fell asleep like that. Try it. It's better than any sleep aid I've ever had and it has no ill side effects in the morning. In fact, just the opposite is true.

"I need egg nine, and I see by the clock I better hurry or every wife with a ham in the oven will be after me when the service is over."

The congregation laughed.

Egg number nine held two hands folded in prayer.

"In the final hours of His life, Jesus is teaching us once again. He taught us to pray, to be sure. But it's what He says in His prayer that we all need to learn. Brother Fox, please read John 17:1-5."

Brother Fox stood up and spoke into the microphone provided to him ahead of time. "After Jesus said this, He looked toward heaven and prayed: 'Father, the time has come. Glorify Your Son, that Your Son may glorify You. For You granted Him authority over all people that He might give eternal life to all those You have given Him. Now this is eternal life: that they may know You, the only true God, and Jesus Christ, whom You have sent. I have brought You glory on earth by completing the work You gave Me to do. And now, Father, glorify Me in Your presence with the glory I had with You before the world began.'"

"Thank you, Brother Fox. Jesus goes on to pray for His disciples, and us. He asks God to protect us from the evil one and for God to let us be one with Him. He asks God to let us, lowly creatures of the earth, be allowed to see His glory.

"Talk about a prayer request. Sometimes I pray just to have Him help me through the day. I can't imagine asking to be allowed to see His glory, too. Teenagers understand this aim-high type prayer. When they ask to borrow the car, they usually ask for money for gas and other expenses they might incur while in *your* car. Am I right parents?"

Several amens arose from the crowd.

"Who has egg number ten?"

"I do," a young girl with blonde ringlets sticking out from under her Easter bonnet said. She handed a pebble to the pastor. She motioned for him to bend down to her level so she could whisper in his ear. "I thought it might save time if I just brought it up." She didn't realize she was very close to his lapel microphone and that everyone heard what she said anyway.

The congregation laughed and Pastor Nichols smiled. He thanked her as she sat down.

"While in the garden of Gethsemane Jesus prayed even more. I think the best tidbit we can take from this prayer is that we, too, need to be in earnest prayer over matters that are bigger than we are.

"I don't know about you, but that covers about everything in my life. There've been times in my life when I've wished God would let a cup pass from my lips. But we must be like Jesus and remember, God is in control. He has our best interests at heart, and He has a plan.

"Egg eleven, please." The content of egg was placed in his hand, and the child who brought it made a hasty retreat. The content was so small that he lifted the cross for everyone to see.

"We all know the morbidity that went along with the three nails. I'll skip that for today. Instead, I'd ask that you take a moment to look at the larger cross behind me and think about what it's meant in your life."

As the congregation did as he asked, he motioned for the last child to bring up the final egg and stand beside him. His son, Stephen, stood beside him, looking out at the congregation.

"Honestly, folks, this was not planned. I'm kind of glad it is my own son since I wouldn't want to have any of the other children disappointed by what is in the last egg."

251

Pastor Nichols looked down at Stephen. "Go ahead, son, open it up."

The boy did as he was told, but was a little surprised when nothing came out of the egg. He tipped both parts of the egg toward his face, hoping to find something stuck to the inside.

"I wondered why almost everyone else's eggs made noise, but mine didn't." He looked up at this father. "Daddy, why is my egg empty?"

"Your egg represents something we all need in our lives."

"What's that, Daddy?"

"Hope, son." Pastor Nichols was speaking directly to his son, knowing what a hard time he was having trying to fit into his new school where everyone knows he's the son of a preacher.

"Because the tomb where Jesus was buried is empty, like your egg, we have hope." He turned to address the congregation. "Hope not just here on earth, but hope for a future in heaven. Hebrews 11:1 tells us that 'Faith is the substance of things hoped for, the evidence of things not seen.'"

He looked back at his son, who had tears in his eyes and running down his cheeks. The father bent down to his son's level and the boy wrapped his arms around his neck.

"Thanks, you're the best dad ever."

Silence fell over the congregation as they observed the exchange between father and son. Since the pastor's microphone was still on, they heard the comment the boy had thought was private.

Pastor Nichols straightened himself, picking his son up with the boy's arms still wrapped around his neck. "Folks, it doesn't get any better than this, this side of heaven. God wants you to do the same thing my son just did to me. Wrap your arms around God, tell Him He's the best Dad ever," the pastor said through tears.

"The kids can go back to their parents. Jill and Candy, you'll need to come and get your girls. They fell asleep on me.

252

"I was rather passionate about this sermon. I'm sorry I've kept you so late. We need to sing a song, but right now I can't recall which one Brother Jim had picked out. So I'll turn the service over to him. If you'd like to come down front to pray, the altar is open," he told the congregation. "Brother Edwards, will you come and be here if anyone needs you?"

The song title and number were announced as Calvin made his way down front to be available to anyone who needed prayer. He agreed to close the service in prayer when the time came.

Elizabeth Parks sat unmoving during the service but had been very moved by the sermon. Tears streamed down her face as she made her way to pray. Judy followed for support. Calvin met her and offered her tissues and a listening ear.

As the congregation continued to sing, Elizabeth poured her heart out to the Lord as Calvin and Judy knelt beside her.

"I'm such a horrible person," she finally said to Calvin and Judy. "I have done nothing but mess up. I can't do this alone anymore." She cried out in anguish, "I need Jesus. Please give me Jesus."

Judy comforted her. "You're not a horrible person. You've just had some horrible things happen to you."

Elizabeth had been learning about Jesus at the Bible study with Judy and Amanda. In spite of that, and everything Judy told her about what Jesus had done for her, she only thought of Him as a good person, not the One who could help her. When Amanda heard Elizabeth cry out, she went to the front to join the kneeling trio.

After Brother Jim closed in prayer, the musician continued to play, and several people continued singing while others prayed for the woman who was obviously in a great deal of emotional pain.

Pastor Nichols joined the small group, as did his wife and several others. The ones closest to Elizabeth placed their hands on her shoulders, with the people behind them placing their hand on those people's shoulders.

Calvin suggested she pray for forgiveness. He led her through it, and when they said amen, so did everyone else around them.

Elizabeth emerged from the semicircle with swollen eyes and tears still streaming down her face. Any other time in her life if she'd looked like this, she would have died of embarrassment if anyone had seen her. Today, she thought, it doesn't matter. I'm born again!

The crowd dispersed after everyone hugged her. She and Pastor Nichols made plans for getting together the next day to discuss her baptism. Everyone went their separate ways to enjoy Easter dinner with family and friends.

Chapter 20

"Honey, there is something I'd like to talk to you about while it's just the two of us," Eva Bowman told Laurinda as they worked in the kitchen preparing the family's Easter dinner.

"It must be serious based on your tone. Am I in trouble?"

"Did I call you by your full name or raise my voice?"

"No, but I thought you sounded very serious." Laurinda finished peeling the potatoes and began washing them. "What are we doing with these?"

"Mashed."

"Mashed is one of my favorites."

"Every potato is your favorite. This isn't a subject you want to avoid, honey."

"I'm not trying to avoid it."

"Sounds like you are."

"I'm sorry, go ahead."

"Daddy and I've been talking about you and Ronnie." Eva paused. "Are you thinking about marrying him?"

Laurinda almost dropped the knife she had in her hand. "Would that be bad?"

"Not at all. In fact, we've been praying about what to do if he asks our blessing to marry you."

"You have?" Laurinda exclaimed.

"Honey, we've been praying about this subject since you were born. Now we have a name and a face to go with our prayers."

"Are you saying you want me to marry him?" Laurinda paused. "If he asks?"

"No, but we want you to know we've been praying about this for a long time. We like Ronnie a great deal, but what's important is whether or not you like him and how well you would work together in life. We want you both to be sure it's God's will. Marriage is hard enough inside God's will." Eva began slicing onions for the salad. "Did I ever tell you what Grandpa Bowman told me on our wedding day?"

"I don't remember."

"He said, 'If I could have chosen a daughter-in-law, I would have chosen you.' I cried when he said it. I felt the same way on our ten year anniversary when he told me he'd chosen well. He made it sound like he'd really been the one to pick me. When I told your dad, he said he didn't know anything about it. That's when he told me his parents had been praying about me when we started dating."

"That's cool what Grandpa said to you." She looked down to avoid her mother's eyes. "I was thinking about it, Mom," she said as she stopped slicing the potatoes, "even before he became a Christian." Laurinda hung her head as if she felt ashamed.

Eva walked around the counter and placed a reassuring arm around her. "It's okay, honey. I know you would've walked away if he hadn't become a Christian."

"Amanda helped me remember that on Valentine's Day when I got my hair permed. That was before you knew about Ronnie."

"Amanda gives sound godly guidance. I'm glad you work for her and Calvin. I'm proud of you. Don't ever forget it." The two women hugged and returned to their work.

A short time later the ladies had the table brimming with hot, delicious food. After prayer, Laurinda told her parents about Elizabeth wanting to get baptized.

"Have you been baptized?" Tom asked Ronnie.

"I was as a baby."

"That was your parents' choice, wasn't it?" Laurinda asked.

"Yes. Isn't it the same thing?"

"No," Tom said. "As Christians, we believe two things about baptism. First, it's a public profession of our faith in Jesus, and second, that baptism means total immersion in water. I believe as a Catholic you would have been sprinkled. Is that correct?"

"I was. My mother hung my brother's and my baptismal certificates on the living room wall with our school pictures." Ronnie lowered his eyes. "Now I realize she did it to remind us of our religion, not our relationship with Jesus," he said, saddened by the idea.

Laurinda reached over to cover his hand with hers. Eva covered his other hand with hers and patted him reassuringly.

"I don't know how I'm going to tell her I've left the Church," he said through tears.

"Ronnie, let's pray about this," Tom suggested.

"I don't want to hold up our dinner."

"We don't mind," all the Bowmans said at once.

"It's always the right time to pray," Tom said as he extended one hand to his wife, the other to his daughter.

They all joined hands and prayed for strength for Ronnie and the right words to tell his mother about his new life in Christ. When they finished, they returned to their dinner and the topic of baptism.

"What do I have to do to be baptized?" Ronnie asked.

"Go see Pastor Nichols. He'll talk to you about it in great detail. I'll tell you the short version," Laurinda said excitedly.

"I'm all ears," he said as he took another piece of ham from the platter.

"Not *all* ears," Eva said, and everyone laughed.

"You need to bring shorts, a T-shirt, and a towel to church the morning you're going to be baptized. You'll go into a little room off the side of the baptismal and change into the shorts and T-shirt. When it's time, you'll step into the water where Pastor Nichols will be waiting for you. He'll have you stand in front of him. He'll talk for a few minutes, pray for a few minutes, and then dunk you under the water."

"I hope not for a few minutes." When everyone stopped laughing, he continued, "Why do I go all the way under?"

"It symbolizes your death, burial, and resurrection in Jesus," Tom told him.

"This sounds like something I want to do," he said with great enthusiasm. "Linny, will you call Pastor Nichols for me tomorrow and schedule an evening appointment with him? If you have time, that is."

"Is there anything else you want to talk to the pastor about?" Tom asked him with a twinkle in his eye.

"Daddy!" Laurinda exclaimed.

Tom smiled, "Pass the potatoes, please."

"We're thinking about going down to see Mrs. Ingram after dinner," Laurinda told her parents after her natural color returned to her face.

"Would you like to join us?" Ronnie asked.

"What a wonderful idea," Eva said. "What do you think, honey?"

"Sounds good to me."

"Should we call first?" Laurinda asked.

"I think it's a good idea just in case. It is an hour drive from here," Tom said. "The Parlor will be closed today. Do you still want to go?"

"I don't have to have ice cream *every day* of my life!" Laurinda exclaimed.

Everyone laughed.

*　*　*

"I thought Maria, Don, and the kids were going to be here," Amanda said to her mother after they hugged and kissed.

"She called yesterday to say they all have the flu. I must have been so busy with dinner preparations that I forgot to mention it to you. I'm sorry."

"I would fuss at her for not calling me, but since they're all sick, I'll forgive her this time. I just talked to her," Amanda thought for a moment, "Thursday night. She didn't say anything then about being sick."

"She said everyone was fine until yesterday morning. The kids started fighting over their bathroom, and she and Don were taking turns in theirs. I told her I'd come up tomorrow if she wants me to, but she said she didn't want to infect me. Maybe I'll make some chicken soup and take it up there, leave it on the porch, ring the doorbell, and run." The two women laughed, knowing she'd never do such a thing.

"Is my little sister sick, too?"

Sandy Steinman was about to answer her when Doreen appeared in the doorway. "I better not be sick or Mom and Dad will throw me out."

"I'd take you in and you know it," Amanda said as she and her sister wrapped their arms around each other.

"I miss you all so bad," she said as she choked back tears.

"You can drop out of college and come live with us anytime you want to."

They broke their hug as Sandy scolded Amanda for telling her sister such nonsense. "She'll finish her degree like you did, and then find a wonderful job just like you did."

"She didn't find a job, Mom. She married one!" The three women laughed. "Speaking of Calvin, where is he?" Doreen asked.

"I'm sure he's around here somewhere," Amanda replied.

"If there's food involved," Doreen said, "I know he's close by."

She almost jumped out of her skin when Calvin walked up behind her and poked her with a finger in each of her sides. "Were you talking about me, little sister?"

She spun around and poked him in his taut belly. "I guess all that food you eat isn't catching up with you yet."

He wrapped his strong arms around her in a hug. "And it never will. I've work hard for a living all my life. I didn't get to go off to some cushy college."

"Hey, college is hard work," she said as she pushed out of his grip. "But you're looking pretty good," she paused, "for an *old* man."

"Ha!" he said as he tickled her. "Where's that guy of yours?"

"He went home for Easter, too. He left right after class on Thursday. Since he doesn't have to work, he was able to take an early flight out. He was joining his parents, and then going to Costa Rica for a family reunion."

"Sounds like you might be marrying into money there, little sis."

"You know I had no idea he had money when we met. Sometimes I wish he didn't have so much of it, because other people don't understand why we are together."

Calvin lifted her left hand. "Nothing yet?"

"We're not ready. Certain requirements must be met and you know it. I have to be in my senior year before we'll even begin to make plans for a wedding, and I don't want a ring on my finger for more than six months before we get married."

"Is that so you can still play the field? A beautiful lady like you could have many offers of marriage if she wanted them."

"Thanks for the compliment, but I don't want any other offers. You know he's a godly man. And good looking."

"Not as good looking as me."

She ignored his comment, which she knew bugged him worse than responding to it. "He never dated his whole freshman year. He said there wasn't anyone he wanted to date until his sophomore year when I came onto campus. He said it was love at first sight."

"That's why he didn't ask you out for six months," Calvin teased Doreen.

"He didn't want it to be just love at first sight. He wanted it to be from God. So he spent those six months getting to know me on less personal dates and praying the whole time. You know he's going into the seminary when he's out of school."

"I can't believe you're considering bringing a preacher into this family. We all know what horrible sinners we all are. We don't need him to remind us."

"Yes, we're all horrible sinners, but thankfully every sinner has a future and every saint has a past. I happen to think this family is pretty much on the saint side." She looked thoughtful for a moment, and then added, "Except maybe you Caaaaalvvvvvin."

He poked at her again. "Hey now, I know where you sleep and it would not bother me in the least bit to short-sheet your bed."

"You better not!"

Calvin and Doreen continued their banter until the doorbell rang. Calvin excused himself to answer it, already knowing who was on the other side of the door. Amanda wiped her hands dry and quickly joined him on his way to the door.

They welcomed his parents with hugs, kisses, and handshakes. Frank Steinman was joined by his wife and daughter as he also went to greet their guests. After more hugs and handshakes, the elder Edwardses' food joined the rest on the table and everyone sat down to share a meal.

Everyone joined hands as Frank set aside his usual silliness to pray.

"Father God, we come humbly before You this Easter Sunday requesting further blessings from Your glorious hand. I ask that You be with every person here with us today and with those in the family who are not with us."

Calvin and Doreen, who were on either side of Amanda, squeezed her hand to comfort her, both knowing how difficult Easter was for her without the girls.

Howard squeezed his son-in-law's hand and his wife's hand to comfort them.

"We pray You'll bring a quick recovery to those in our family who are sick. We thank You so much for the gift of Your Son that You gave to us and for the ability to worship You freely. We pray for the troops who are still fighting for freedom all over the globe and that You will bring them home safely to their families. Now we ask that You bless this food to our bodies so that we may be able to best serve You. In Jesus' name, amen."

Everyone said amen and began passing dishes and filling their plates. In spite of those family members missing from the dinner table, everyone enjoyed themselves, the company, and the food. Conversation was light and lively. Doreen asked where Marie and her family were. Sandy explained.

"Mom," Amanda said, "I have a question for you. I was thinking about my older and younger sisters. Were you mad when you named us all?"

"No. What makes you ask that, honey?"

"Marie, Amanda, Doreen. Our first initials spell out 'mad.'"

Everyone laughed.

"You obviously have too much free time on your hands if that's all you have to think about," Sandy said. "I'd never thought of that, but you're right, it does spell mad."

"That's like that silly kid's joke about why you're never suppose to use the letter D around ma," Amanda said.

"Why not?" Doreen asked.

"Because D makes 'ma mad,'" she explained.

Everyone laughed again.

Doreen said, "I never make you mad, do I, Mummy?"

"Of course not, honey, you're my favorite," she paused, "youngest daughter."

Everyone laughed again.

Chapter 21

Monday morning Amanda told Michael she couldn't bear to take down the Easter window display. When he gave her permission to leave it up another week, she skipped away, eager to work on a display in the children's section.

Several busy hours later, Amanda was at home about to start dinner. Before she could start the oven, she heard Calvin open the garage door. She checked her watch, noting it was just five o'clock. She left the oven and waited by the door for her beloved.

"You're the most wonderful sight to come home to," he told her as he swept her up in his arms as soon as he was through the door and set his lunch box down. "I am so blessed to have you." He placed a gentle kiss on her lips.

"Wow!" she exclaimed. "That was some welcome home and I was here first. What's gotten into you?"

"You, woman, you've gotten into me and I never want you to leave."

"I never will, except to make your dinner…if you'll put me down."

"Well, little lady, I'm afraid I just can't let you do that," he said in his best John Wayne impersonation.

"Aren't you hungry?"

He looked at her with a big smile. "As a matter of fact, I'm very hungry. That's why I came home early." He raised his left eyebrow at her. "But I have everything under control. If you'd be so kind and as to unwrap yourself from me and get out two plates, two forks, three serving spoons, a set of tongs, and plenty of napkins, I'll be happy to explain."

"First of all, I'm not wrapped around you. That would be the other way around. Secondly, you need not explain now that you've mentioned plenty of napkins. I know what you've done. However, I must ask why you've kept me waiting for my surprise."

"My most humble apologies, my love. I wasn't sure," he said with a grin, "that you'd approve."

She playfully pushed him away. "Are you out of your mind!" she exclaimed as if she actually meant it. "Get out of here and bring me my Kentucky Fried Chicken, you silly boy."

He bent over and kissed her on the tip of her nose just before she made her getaway to the kitchen. She squealed as he playfully slapped at her bottom as she escaped. "I'll be back," he growled in his best beast impersonation.

Amanda squealed again, reminding them both of the many times his growl sent their daughters into her arms, a topic they discussed over Amanda's favorite meal when Calvin returned with it.

While they cleaned up, the phone rang. Amanda managed to say hello before Judy took complete control of the conversation. Before she knew what had been said, she was hanging up and telling Calvin that Judy was on her way over.

A short time later, Amanda opened the door to allow Judy to enter. She began talking before Amanda closed the door behind her. "You're never going to believe what Bill and I talked about after Easter dinner. Oh, hi, Calvin," she said before continuing, "Bill and I had a very long talk."

The two women sat down on the couch facing each other. Judy picked Amanda's hands up and began rubbing the back of them with her thumbs, a habit she started in junior high whenever she was nervous or heard bad news. Usually, she only rubbed her own hand.

Tonight she held Amanda's hands, hoping to make sense of what she wanted to tell her.

"On the phone I thought you said this was good news."

"It is." She drew in her breath. "I think."

"Then why are you acting like you have something bad to tell me?"

"What?"

"You're rubbing my hands, and with you that usually means bad news or you're nervous about something."

Judy looked down and realized Amanda was right. "I'm sorry. I really can't decide what kind of news this is. I haven't had time to digest it, even though I've had all day to think about it."

"Why didn't you just come to the store today if it's this important?"

"Of all days, I had back-to-back appointments starting about the time you got to work until I called you."

"I would've thought you'd be busier before Easter than after."

"I was busy before, too. I had two perms, with several haircuts and sets in between. I was surprised I could work at all with everything Bill said to me racing through my head."

"Are you going to tell me?" She looked at Calvin, who was still in the living room, much to her surprise. "Us?" she corrected.

"He asked me to…" She shook her head in disbelief. "I still can't believe this." Judy looked at Calvin and then Amanda. "He asked me if I'd consider marrying him."

The two women screamed simultaneously, exactly like when Amanda told Judy that Calvin had asked her to marry him and both of Judy's previous proposals.

Calvin stuck his index finger into his right ear and wiggled his finger as if trying to regain his hearing. As the two women hugged, Calvin asked Judy if she said yes.

"Honey, that's not important right now," Amanda told him. "He's such a beaver," she reminded Judy. "Did he have a ring?"

"He wanted to be sure I'd say yes first."

"What exactly did he say?"

"We'd been talking for about two hours so it was kind of late by the time he finally said, 'I have something very important that I want to talk to you about.' He had this real serious look on his face. I almost freaked out, especially after all the other serious things we'd been talking about."

"Like what?" Amanda asked.

"First, we talked about God and our relationships with Him, then about our previous marriages. We discussed what we learned and what we'd do differently if we ever remarried. He asked if I'd considered remarrying. I said I'd considered it, but dismissed it just as quickly. He looked sad when I said I didn't see myself married again because I'd messed up both times before.

"He said I married the wrong men. I told him what you said about making God the head of my search committee. I said I'd do that if I ever thought about getting married again, but that I hadn't decided to search.

"He frowned, then said he'd already made God the head of his search committee. He said he and his wife discussed what they'd do if they lost each other and the kids were still young. She told him she wanted him to find a helpmate for the children, but even more so for himself. She said she knew how much love he had and he wouldn't be whole if he didn't have someone to share it with. He jokingly asked if she already had someone in mind. She said no. She told him not to wait forever, but instead to pray for guidance from God and He would lead him to the right woman.

"It was creepy the way he said she talked about it as if she somehow knew she'd be leaving him. She wasn't even pregnant with little Emily yet. He made her sound awesome. If I agree to marry him, there is no way I can live up to her memory." Judy's eyes teared up.

"I've only met Bill once, but I don't think he's the kind of man who'd compare you to his deceased wife. Do you, honey?"

"No," Calvin said in a supportive tone.

"Would you compare him to your ex-husbands?" Amanda asked.

"Even if I did, he'd come out way above them both. I scraped the bottom of the barrel both times. One was an alcoholic woman chaser, and the other was an abuser. A gorilla would be better than either of them. Bill would be like living with a saint."

"You know I love Calvin, and in my opinion, he's the best husband there ever was, is, or will be, but even I know he's no saint." She looked at Calvin. "No offense, honey."

"None taken."

"So you know he's no saint because, at best, he'd be a close second to Calvin," Amanda said with a big smile on her face.

"But he seems perfect," Judy swooned.

"There was only one perfect Man that ever walked the earth and they crucified Him. Don't get starry-eyed on me. He's just a mortal man who puts his pants on one leg at a time," Amanda reminded her friend.

"As if their conversation about him remarrying weren't enough, guess what else he told me?"

"What?"

"He said that as his wife, he'd want me to adopt his children so in case he died, I'd be able to keep them with me."

Amanda gasped. "He's really been thinking about this."

"He said he had been since the first night we talked."

"That was about a week ago wasn't it?"

"Exactly a week ago. Can you believe that?"

"When a man knows what, or who, we want, we don't mess around," Calvin said.

"It took you a while," Amanda said.

"I had a plan and it took time."

"Yeah, yeah, we," Amanda pointed to herself, then Judy, "know all about you and your plans."

"You have to admit, once I was sure it was you, I didn't let anyone else take you from me."

"That's why it feels like we've been married longer than we've actually been." She directed her attention back to Judy. "Go on."

"He said he'd been praying that God would bring a lady into his life. I almost choked when he said I was that lady. I've never thought of myself as a lady, even before my abortion and two failed marriages. You do know we've been talking every night since we met, right?"

"I think you mentioned it last Wednesday when the two of you were here. I know what prompted this. He ate your banana split cake and was hooked."

"Yeah, that's it," Judy said with a weak smile.

"We both know better than that," Amanda said. "He sees you the way God and I have seen you for years as a beautiful, smart, loving, wonderful woman. Even though you hadn't decided to search, I've been praying that God would send you someone wonderful. I think, from what I've heard, Bill could be the one."

"Would you answer my question now?" Calvin asked. The two women looked at him like he'd grown a horn in the middle of his forehead. "What did you tell him?"

"I told him I had to pray about it. He suggested I seek godly council from my friends. Naturally, I thought of Manny first." She winked at Calvin. "Manny, what should I say?"

"I'm going to let the name comment go and address your question instead. We need to pray. Right here, right now." Amanda looked at her spiritual leader. "Will you lead us, please?"

"I'd be honored." Calvin sat down on the coffee table across from the women. They all joined hands once he was seated.

"Father God, we come humbly before You in need as we so often do. We need Your wisdom and guidance in our lives always, but especially now for our sister Judy." Calvin squeezed her hand slightly. Unbeknownst to Calvin, Amanda did the same thing at the same time. "We know that in everything she's done, You've always been with her. We pray that You will be with her now by giving her Your wisdom and guidance in this situation with Bill. None of us, except You, really knows who he is or very much about him. Judy will need clear direction from You to know Your will. If marrying him is what You want for her, please give her the peace that surpasses all understanding. We thank You for what You're doing, and will do, in Judy's life. We praise You and thank You that she's in our lives. We place this situation into Your hands, knowing that Your will, will be done in all things, including this one. In Jesus' name, amen."

Judy was crying when he finished. "I didn't mean to make you cry," Calvin said as he handed her a tissue from the box on the table.

"You said so many wonderful things about me. How could you do that and not expect me to be a blubbering idiot when you finished?"

Amanda hugged her. "You are not a blubbering idiot, never have been, never will be. What you are is my second best earthly friend in this world."

"So does the peace that surpasses all understanding feel like the weight of the world has just been lifted from your shoulders?" Judy asked.

"It can," Amanda and Calvin said together.

"That's what happened to me when I was weighing whether or not to start dating Amanda. I knew I wanted to date her, but I wanted God's will, not mine." He picked up his and Amanda's still joined hands and kissed hers. "I'm one hundred percent sure it was the right decision, then and now." He kissed her again and then released her hand. "I'm going to go do some manly thing now while you two do your girly thing if that's okay with you."

"That's fine with us." Amanda smiled at him.

"You'll keep me posted on the outcome, I presume," Calvin said as he stood up to leave.

"We will," they said together.

He bent over and kissed Amanda on top of her head and then left them alone.

"I just thought of something!" Judy exclaimed.

"What?" Amanda asked.

"If we do get married, he and the kids would probably move into my house since he currently lives with his parents. I've managed to keep that house through two divorces. I don't want to lose it now." Judy thought for a moment, then added, "But now that we've prayed, I don't think that will be a problem. My other concern was I'd have to ask Elizabeth to leave, and I hate to do that."

"I'm sure she'd understand." Just then the phone rang. Amanda excused herself to answer it.

"Edwards residence. Yes, Calvin is here. Just a minute and I'll get him." Amanda laid the phone on the counter and went to the top of the stairs to let Calvin know the call was for him. He acknowledged her so she went back to the phone to listen until he picked up.

Once she heard the click, she hung up and returned to the couch. "I'm not a hundred percent sure, but I think that was Bill."

Judy's eyes widened. "What?"

"The caller only asked if Calvin was available, but it sure sounded like him."

"I wonder why he'd be calling Calvin."

"I'm sure whatever it is, if Calvin thinks it's okay, he'll tell us all about it when the conversation is over."

The women discussed how Judy's three-bedroom home could be divided among five people. Obviously Judy and Bill would share a room, so that was easy. Justin and Christopher would share a room, and little Emily would be in the smallest bedroom. Judy wondered what she'd do with all the junk she'd accumulated in that room over the years. Amanda suggested a yard sale.

Calvin appeared a few minutes later. "You'll never guess who that was."

Together they said, "Bill."

"Okay, so you guessed that. But you'll never guess what he called for."

"I believe you have us there, Mr. Edwards," Amanda said.

"He wants you to build a house for us so I don't have to have a yard sale," Judy guessed teasingly.

Calvin smiled. "Close, but not quite."

Judy's jaw dropped and her eyes widened. "What?"

"He didn't say anything about a yard sale."

Judy pretended she was about to fall off the couch.

"He does want to talk to me about a new house."

Judy fell off the couch. Everyone laughed. Amanda looked between Judy and Calvin, then back again, and again. Calvin extended his right hand to Judy to help her up off the floor. With his left hand he touched the bottom of Amanda's chin to close her dropped jaw.

"If I'd known you two were going to react this way, I would've kept the news to myself."

"We, I, just, it's," Judy stammered as she accepted Calvin's hand and allowed him to pull her up off the floor.

"Complete sentences would be very helpful," Calvin told her.

Judy repositioned herself on the couch, and then gathered her thoughts. She took a deep breath and asked him to tell them what Bill said.

"He's gotten an offer on his house in Tennessee. If they can work out the details, Bill wants to buy a house here. He's already been looking around and thinks he's found one. He's meeting the realtor tomorrow after work. He asked if I'd join him so I can examine it for defects," Calvin explained.

Judy rubbed her forehead. "I guess he really is serious. When he sees something, or someone, he wants, he goes after it."

"Or her," Amanda said with a smile.

"He told me the time and the address. If it's the house I'm thinking of, he may be surprised that I find all kinds of things wrong with it."

"Why would you say that?" Amanda asked.

"It's the one in Okemos we built just before you got pregnant with Jessi. It was the job that enabled us to build our house sooner than later. The owner was a lawyer, or someone like that, the rich, spare-no-expense type."

"I do remember the house, and it was a doctor. I wonder why they're selling."

"The realtor told Bill he's taking a job somewhere down south."

"I'm certain you won't find anything wrong with the house. I know you, your crew and subcontractors do a wonderful job," Judy said.

"By the way, I wouldn't have told you all this if he hadn't said it was okay. I told him you were here and that you'd both ask questions. We laughed because we both know how nosey women are."

"No nosier than you men," Amanda pointed out. "As I recall, you hung out up here to find out what was going on with Judy."

"So I did," Calvin acknowledged. He looked right at Judy. "Bill asked me to invite you, too, if you weren't busy."

Judy looked like she was going to fall of the couch again. "I haven't said yes and it looks like everything in his plan is going forward anyway."

"Judy." Amanda took both of Judy's hands into her own. "When a man gets a plan in his head, he moves. I'm certain he's been praying about this, maybe even since just after his wife passed into heaven. When something comes together like this seems to be, it's usually from the hand of God."

Calvin nodded his head in agreement. "You were kind of right about Bill asking me to build him a house. I've already built the house, now it's up to you, Bill, and God to build a home."

Tears ran down Judy's face. Amanda hugged her. "Keep praying and trusting God," Amanda whispered into her ear.

"Thank you both so much," Judy said when she and Amanda stopped hugging. She wiped her tears away with her hands. "I think I'll go home now and keep praying, and trusting." She looked at her watch. "Elizabeth should be home soon and I have a lot to tell her." Judy thought for a moment. "Maybe I won't have to ask her to leave after all. If she got a roommate, they could rent my place from us."

"That's a great idea," Amanda said. "What about your beauty shop?"

"I've built a beauty shop before, I could do it again…should the need arise," Calvin said with a wink and a smile.

Judy hugged Amanda, and then stood to hug Calvin as well. "You two are my two best friends in world. I'm blessed to have you both. Thanks for everything."

"You're welcome," the couple said together.

"I'm so happy for you," Amanda said.

Calvin wrote the time, address, and directions on a piece of paper for Judy before she hugged Amanda one more time and left.

Once she was gone, Calvin looked at Amanda, "I'd like you to join us so we can all go out to dinner afterward."

"Aren't you just the social planner these days?"

"That will never be my job. I lost my head there for a minute when Bill offered to take us out."

"Did you tell him you built the house?"

"No. I couldn't remember the exact address. It's been a while since we did that job, in case you've forgotten."

"I haven't forgotten that it's been a while, but I've forgotten the address, too. No worries," she said in her best Australian accent, "we can look through the books and figure it out."

"Once a bookkeeper, always a bookkeeper!"

"Well-kept books help you," she said with a smile on her face as she poked Calvin in the chest, "find what you're looking for."

He caught her finger before she could get away and used it to pull her close to him. He kissed her full on the mouth, leaving her frustrated when he stopped. "Thank you in advance for finding what I need."

Amanda used her right hand to fan herself. "Keep that up and I'll forget what I'm looking for."

He grinned and moved out of her way so she could get to the computer they kept in the kitchen nook. Once the program was running, Amanda searched by address for the house. She'd been right about the doctor. Calvin had been right about who built it.

Across town Judy arrived home to find Elizabeth soaking her feet. As soon as Judy walked in, Elizabeth told her she had something very important to talk to her about.

A half hour later the Edwardses' phone rang. Since Amanda had begun reading after Judy left, Calvin answered the phone. "Oh my gosh," was all the female voice on the other end said over and over. Calvin thought it was Judy so he called Amanda to the phone.

"It's either Judy or a prank call. Either way, you're more than welcome to it," he said as he passed her the phone.

"Hello?" Amanda managed to say in between her friend saying, "Oh my gosh." "Judy, what's wrong?"

After one final "Oh my gosh," Judy calmed down enough to relay what Elizabeth had told her.

"When I got home, Elizabeth was here soaking her feet. She said she had something important she wanted to talk to me about. I was afraid it was something awful. But, Amanda, it wasn't. It was something…something from the hand of God.

"She told me one of the girls she works with is having landlord trouble and wants to leave her current apartment. She can't leave until the end of next month when her lease is up. Anyway, she asked Elizabeth to consider renting an apartment or small house with her. I told her within a month my house might be available for rent. She asked why and I told her. She screamed with excitement. I know how she felt. I wanted to do that, too, when Bill first mentioned it. It gets better. The girl is working at the restaurant while she's putting herself through beauty school, which she finishes in June.

"Amanda, she'd be able to use the salon in the basement after she gets her license. If I rent the house to them, I wouldn't have to worry about getting the rent because she's going to keep working at the restaurant until she has a good enough client base to stop working there. Can you believe all this?"

"I can, and do, believe all this. I believe God still works in mysterious ways and He's always in control…when we let Him be. Remember Pastor Nichols told us yesterday that God has our best interests at heart and He has a plan?"

"I remember. I've been talking to Elizabeth since I got home so I haven't called Bill yet to tell him everything God's doing."

"I feel special. You called me first."

"You are special, but we always wait until after nine before one of us calls the other."

"Then I better get off the phone so you can call him. I'm so happy for you."

"Me, too." Judy paused. "Amanda, I love and appreciate you so much."

"I love you, too. Now call your boyfriend."

"He's beginning to sound more like a fiancé."

"I agree. Call me tomorrow."

"I will. Good-bye."

"Good-bye," Amanda said, then hung up and told Calvin what had happened.

Chapter 22

Tuesday morning the Edwardses' phone rang just after Calvin left for work. "Hello," Amanda said.

"Hello to you, too," Judy said. "I hardly slept last night after talking to Bill. He picked up a flyer about the house on his way home from work yesterday. He described the house to me. It sounds huge. I don't know what we'll do with all that space if we actually buy the house."

"I forgot to tell you last night that Calvin did build that house for a doctor. It cost quite a bit to build and I doubt that the price has gone down. Do you think Bill can afford it?"

"He told me the offer on his house will give him a sizable down payment for this one. He also told me if this house isn't big enough for us, we can live in it until he can talk Calvin into building us a bigger one."

"Judy! It has four bedrooms plus a master bedroom that's almost the size of some people's whole house. I didn't see it after it was completely done, but I remember it was huge. Did he mention it having two staircases to the upstairs?"

"Yes!"

"Now I know I'm thinking of the right house. Calvin's only built a handful of houses over the years. He says they take too long for him. He likes to help as many people as he can. That's part of the reason they got done early with the gas station job recently and that got him another gas station job down in Jackson."

"You're so proud of him. I hear it in your voice."

"I'm sure you'll be equally proud of Bill if you two decide it's God's will for you to marry. Everything I'm hearing sounds like God is already blessing your marriage."

"I agree. I told Bill about the new renter becoming a beautician. He mentioned her being my competition. I said I wasn't worried about it. He offered to put a salon in the new house or open up a shop somewhere in town. Then he gave me a third option that I hadn't considered."

When Judy paused, Amanda asked, "What?"

"He said I could stay home and be a full-time mom. Since neither of the boys are old enough for school and he works full-time, he asked if I'd consider being a full-time mother for all of them."

"What did you say?"

"I told him I'd have to get back with him on that since I've never been a mother before, and the one time I could have been a mother I chose to end my child's life."

Both women were silent for a moment.

"That's in the past, Judy. You really need to leave it there."

"I can't forget it."

"God has forgiven you and forgotten it. You need to let it go, sweetie."

"Another problem is that I didn't have a very good example in my own mother. She won't even know that she has grandchildren if I marry him."

"Do the things that she did that you liked. Don't do the things she did that you didn't like. Most of all, don't worry and do what comes natural to you."

"I could never be as good a mother as you…" Judy stopped herself, unsure if she should say "was" or "are."

Amanda accepted her sentence as complete and moved on. "Being a mother is something you learn partly from your own mother and grandmother, partly from other mothers, but mainly from doing the job," Amanda explained. "One of the most important things I learned from my granny was to make mud men. At the time I thought it was just about playing in the mud with her, but later I understood it meant she valued me so much, she'd take time to spend with me even though she had lots to do. I also learned it's the little things, like playing in the mud, that builds memories."

"I saw you do stuff like that with your girls. Remember the time I came over in the middle of the day and found you three playing with green pudding? I didn't even know green pudding existed. You made it, put wax paper on your counter, and then the three of you played in it. I was grossed out, but not you three. You were all having a ball."

"I added food coloring to vanilla pudding. And yes, we were having fun that day. Remember the time we called you to see if you wanted to stop over and eat dirt with us?"

"I wouldn't leave my house until you assured me it wasn't *real* dirt. Didn't we even eat a few worms that day?"

"I believe we did. It's doing things like that and loving the kids," Amanda swallowed, fighting back tears, "like there's no tomorrow, because sometimes there is no tomorrow." Tears rolled down her checks. She wiped at them with the back of her hand.

"I didn't mean to make you cry. I think you're *the* most wonderful mother I've ever known. I wanted to get your advice on what to tell Bill about this."

"I can recommend a great preschool for the boys for this fall if you two are interested. The oldest one isn't ready for school in the fall yet, is he?"

"No. Justin won't be five until January."

"What I'd do if it were me is put him in the three-day-a-week program and the younger boy in the two-day-a-week program. I know that means you'd be driving to school every day, but here's why I'd do it that way. Since Emily...it is Emily, right?"

"Yes. Emily's the baby's name. She'll be one in late October. Christopher will be three in early October. I don't expect you to remember all this right away. It's taken me all week and I cheated. I got pictures of each of them. Bill said he hasn't had one of the three of them taken together yet."

"That's too bad. He's missing a wonderful opportunity. Maybe that's something you could offer to do for him for Easter."

"Maybe. You were going to say something about Emily."

"She still takes naps and will for a while. While she naps on Monday, Wednesday, and Friday mornings while Justin's at preschool, you'd have quality one-on-one time with Christopher. Then on Tuesday and Thursday you'd have one-on-one time with Justin."

"That sounds like a great idea, but September is still five and a half months away. What if we aren't married by then?"

"As quickly as Bill is moving with the house, I think he'll probably move just as quickly with getting married. Even if you aren't married, you could spend a little time alone with each of the boys at least once a week. They knew their mother, so you'll have to work your way into their hearts. With Emily, you'll be the only mother she's ever known."

"Listen to you talking like this it's a done deal, like I'm going to marry him." Judy sounded upset.

"I didn't mean to upset you. I thought we were talking what-ifs here."

"We were and I'm not upset. I'm scared. *What if* I'm a bad mother?"

"Be your usual loving self and you'll be fine. They must already like you or Bill wouldn't have asked you to consider marrying him."

"I suppose you're right. I'm not keeping you from anything, am I?"

"It's a little late to ask me that now, don't you think?" Amanda laughed.

"Blonde moment, sorry."

"Blonde isn't *just* a hair color, it's a state of mind," Amanda told her. "I have blonde moments, too, you know."

"*Do I?* I've been your best girlfriend for many years." The two women laughed.

"The answer is no, you're not keeping me from anything. Since I worked yesterday, I'm doing laundry today."

"Is it easier for you if it's not Monday, or doesn't the day matter?"

"I'm better since I gave the girls to God. I thought you knew I've been having less trouble with depression for a while now. Most of the time I'm my usual happy-go-lucky self. There are still occasions, like Easter, when I lose it. We came home from dinner at Mom's and I cried myself to sleep. I was tucked safely in the arms of my loving husband so I knew I'd be all right. Maybe that will be the only other time I'll cry this week."

"Sorry about making you cry earlier. You know that wasn't my intention."

"It's okay."

"I better let you go. I have a client coming over in ten minutes and I haven't gone downstairs yet today. Maybe I could get used to not working."

"Trust me, if you marry Bill, you *will be working*. A husband and children are the most full-time job you'll ever have, but you'll never find a more rewarding one."

"Good point. I remember how much work a husband creates. I can't imagine three kids on top of that. Thanks for the advice. I really needed it."

"Don't mention it. That's what friends are for. I'll see you tonight at six in Okemos. I'll be the one with the really good-looking guy."

"*I'll* be the one with the really good-looking guy."

"We'll both be with really good-looking guys. See ya then."

"See ya."

Amanda finished the laundry with time to spare before Calvin would be home, so she made cookies.

"It smells mighty good in here," Calvin said when he walked through the door. He kissed Amanda. "Why don't you put a couple of those in my hand? I'll taste test 'em for you. If I'm going to die from them, then I'll be in the bathroom and won't make a mess on your clean kitchen floor."

"You might die from eating my cookies someday, mister, but it will be from overeating them, not just from eating them," she played back with him.

She handed him two cookies and he popped one into his mouth as he bent over to unlace his work boots with his empty hand.

"If you'll sit down right there, I'll take your boots off for you."

He grabbed two more cookies from the cookie sheet and sat down. "These are hot," he mumbled with his mouth full of the second cookie she'd given him.

"That'll teach you to take them right off the pan. The two I gave you had cooled a while before you got them. I just took those out of the oven before you walked in the door."

"Oh," he said, before he stuck a hot one into his mouth.

By the time she had his boots off, he'd eaten all four cookies. He got up, took two more cookies, and then headed to the shower.

"Calvin Edwards, you amaze me," Amanda called after him. He smiled at her before disappearing into the bedroom.

Amanda cleaned up the kitchen, eating a cookie herself now and then until Calvin rejoined her.

"Amanda Edwards, you amaze me. You fuss at me about how many cookies I eat, then as soon as my back's turned, you eat just as many." He wrapped his arms around her and pulled her close. "You are as bad as I am when it comes to being a cookie monster, and you know it."

"I most certainly am not!"

"You are, too," he said. "Admit it, and nobody gets hurt."

"Am not," she insisted.

"Are, too," he insisted back as he began to tickle her.

"No, I'm not," she tried to say between laughter.

"Admit it. Cookie monster," he said in his funny Cookie Monster voice as he continued to tickle her.

"Okay," she squealed, "I'm a cookie monster. I'm a cookie monster. Now stop tickling me. Pleeease."

"Confession is good for the soul," he said, grinning at her. She would have stuck her tongue out at him, but it was currently covered in cookie, so she rolled her eyes at him.

"Milk," she tried to say. "I need milk," she mumbled as she made her way past him to the refrigerator with a cup in hand.

She poured the milk and drank it all. "Look what you've reduced me to. I talked with my mouth full and had too much cookie in my mouth. Mother would be appalled at my behavior."

"You're right, right after she stopped laughing at you. Why, I bet she'd even send you to your room." He winked at her as if to say they could go there together.

"No, "We have friends who'd be wondering where we are if we don't get out of here very soon."

"I know," he said as he picked up three more cookies.

She eyed him suspiciously.

"I need them for the road. You wouldn't want me to grow weary as I'm driving down the road. I might crash the truck."

"Well, that wouldn't be my problem," she said, trying to act serious.

"Why not?" he asked as he held the door leading to the garage open for her.

"Because *I'll* be riding in the van."

"That you will, my lady," he said as he opened the van's passenger door to let her in. He bent at the waist and then popped another cookie into his mouth.

All three cookies were gone by the time they reached their destination.

"You did a wonderful job on this house. I love it even from the outside," Amanda told him.

The realtor was already there standing at the door. Amanda thought she looked like she was posing for a picture rather than waiting for her clients. Bill and Judy pulled in right behind the Edwardses so the four of them walked up together with Bill and Calvin in the lead.

"I can't believe how big this is," Judy told Amanda.

"Just wait until you see inside," Amanda said.

"Welcome, Mr. Cummings. Calvin, always a pleasure to see you." She shook both men's hands in turn, and then looked past the men. "And a pleasure to see you again, Amanda. You must be Judy." She shook Amanda's hand and then Judy's. "Bill told me all about how wonderful you are. I'm surprised we haven't met before now since you obviously already know the Edwardses."

"I don't get out much. I own a home-based business."

"Oh really, what do you do?"

"I'm a beautician. I own Judy's Cuts and More."

"Oh," she said in a condescending way. "Why don't we get inside and take a look around?" She opened the door. Judy was the first one inside the house with Bill close behind her. She stood in awe of the size and the beautiful decorations.

Directly to their right was a formal dining room. Directly in front of them was one of the two staircases leading to the second floor. On their left was a doorway leading into the master suite. They chose to start there.

Judy knew immediately why it was called a master suite instead of a master bedroom. The suite took up the entire left side of the house. Judy walked into a closet the size of her current bedroom. Then they went into the bathroom that held a full Jacuzzi, an oversized shower, two sinks, and two individually enclosed toilets. The linen closet in the room was almost as big as Judy's salon. It held a stacking washer and dryer.

"The couple didn't use that much," the realtor explained. "They had a housekeeper that did all the laundry in another part of the house. We'll get to that later."

The realtor guided them back out to the sleeping area. "Don't you just *love* this view?" she asked as she gestured toward the french doors that opened up onto a balcony.

Bill took Judy by the hand over to the doors. "Do you think you could wake up to this view every morning?"

"I could do that," she said.

He looked directly at her when he said he'd love to wake up to this view every morning. Judy blushed, sure he didn't mean the view outside the window.

"Obviously, the exercise equipment doesn't stay with the house, but it gives you a better idea of how big this room really is," the realtor said.

They looked away from each other and at the exercise equipment the doctor and his wife had in front of the windows, positioned so they could see into the backyard.

"I can't tell you how many deer we saw out here while working on this place," Calvin told them. "I used to get here early, hoping to see them."

"Oh, Bill, the kids would love that," Judy said.

"I agree."

"They'll love the playroom, too, then. It's not actually a child's playroom, but it could easily be converted. It's in the basement with the maid's quarters. Would you like to go upstairs, downstairs, or stay on this floor?"

Bill looked at Judy. "It's up to you, honey."

Judy blushed again. No one had called her honey in a long time, and when her ex-husband called her honey, it was usually associated with a request for another beer. "Wherever you want to go is fine with me."

"Let's finish this floor and then go upstairs."

The kitchen was everything Judy ever dreamed a kitchen could be. It had a cooktop with a built-in grill beside it, and two stacked convection ovens built into the wall. There was a breakfast nook at the back of the kitchen overlooking the same view as the master suite. The counter across from the sink was lower and there were three barstools tucked neatly under the counter.

"This would be a great place for the kids to eat breakfast and lunch," Bill told Judy. She nodded in agreement.

The refrigerator was twice the size of Judy's. Beside that was a built-in freezer. The walk-in pantry was bigger than her bathroom, with more specialty shelves, drawers, and various pull-outs than she knew existed.

Bill asked if Judy would mind cooking in this kitchen.

"I'd *love* to cook in this kitchen!" she exclaimed.

"Just getting her to cook will be a miracle," Amanda told him.

Judy rolled her eyes at her best friend. "I cook!" she exclaimed.

"Macaroni and cheese, pot pies, and TV dinners don't count," Amanda teased her.

Bill moved closer to Judy and put his arms around her waist, linking his fingers together in front of her. "I'm sorry we won't have a live-in maid that does the cooking for us, at least not right away."

She turned around in his arms and smiled at him. "That's okay. I really do know how to cook. It's just been a long time since I had a reason to."

"The kids love macaroni and cheese and pot pies. We'll have to order out on TV dinner night." Everyone laughed.

To the right of the kitchen was a masculine-looking study. "Unless you want to use this as a study," Judy said, "I'd rather this be the playroom. The kids are too little to be left alone downstairs to play while I make our TV dinners."

"What a wonderful idea. I'd rather have my study in the basement anyway. That way I won't know what's in my TV dinner until you pull the aluminum foil off it in front of me." Everyone laughed again.

Everyone returned to the kitchen. "At the back of the kitchen is the second staircase leading up and downstairs. Shall we go up?"

At the top of the stairs was a landing, and on the opposite side were the stairs that led to the formal dining room.

The upstairs was tastefully decorated but looked like no one ever went up there. Calvin explained that the doctor and his wife had no children but planned ahead for anyone who might buy it when he retired.

There were two bedrooms on either side of the stairs, each of equal size. Bill commented that that was good. When the kids got older they wouldn't argue over whose room was bigger. "There are four bedrooms and only three children."

"Perhaps you could use the spare room for a guestroom," the realtor suggested.

"Or, perhaps," he looked right at Judy, "we could have another child to fill that room."

Judy blushed redder than Amanda or Calvin had ever seen her blush before. She was speechless, something they'd *never* seen before.

The realtor suggested they return to the first floor the same way they'd gone upstairs so they'd be closer to the basement stairs. At the bottom of the stairs on the first floor, she showed them the formal living room with a fireplace in the corner.

"We'll have to get rid of this beautiful light-colored carpet right away," Bill said. "Kids and light-colored carpet don't mix well. And I refuse to tell my," he corrected himself, "our children they can't go into a room just because of the color of the carpet."

"I agree," Judy said. A second later she realized he'd said "our children." She felt lightheaded.

Amanda marveled at how like-minded they already seemed to be. Kind of like Calvin and me, she thought. She squeezed her husband's hand that she was holding.

The basement was the size of the entire first floor. Everyone agreed that the playroom was not for kids aged four and under, maybe even ten and under. The laundry room was equipped with an oversized washer and dryer. Again, Calvin pointed out that they had planned ahead for the future homeowner.

Judy and Amanda stayed in the laundry room for a few minutes longer than the rest of the group. "I was impressed with what you said about the playroom being on the first floor so you could watch the kids. I think you'll make a wonderful mother to those kids and any others you and Bill might have."

Judy blushed again, this time not as red. "I couldn't believe he said that."

"Why wouldn't he say that? You two are both still young enough to have children together. I think that would be great."

"There goes the guestroom. If we do get married, will you teach me how to cook?" The women laughed and rejoined the others.

After everyone inspected the maid's quarters, they'd seen it all. Calvin pointed out the egress windows in both the maid's quarters and right next to the stairs, telling everyone how having them there made it safe to have living space in the basement. Judy commented that the children would have to be taught early on that the windows were for emergency exit only, not for sneaking out of the house when she and Bill weren't looking.

Bill took her hand into his and entwined their fingers. "If we raise them right, and I'm sure we will, that shouldn't be a concern, much less a problem."

Everyone thanked the realtor for her time and Bill said he'd get back with her when he had more information about the sale of his house.

The foursome decided to meet at the Olive Garden, so everyone went to their respective vehicles.

Once Bill had Judy seated, he closed her door then walked around the car. He got into the car and started the engine. "I hope you didn't think I was coming on too strong in there," Bill said. "I felt like the realtor was coming on to me and I didn't want any part of it. I did what I could to make it perfectly clear to her that in my mind I'm already taken. I didn't think she was ever going to get the message, shy of me kissing you right there. And I didn't want to do that."

Judy's heart sank a little. After all he'd said inside she half expected him to kiss her when they got in the car.

"Believe me, I would have liked to have kissed you, but that was not the time, nor the place."

Her heart soared. She was looking forward to the day when the time and the place *were* right.

Chapter 23

Judy called Amanda Wednesday night when she returned from Bill's parents' house after having dinner with them. "Everyone loved my banana-split cake. It was a big hit with the boys."

Thursday night Judy called Amanda with another update. "I had dinner ready for them when they got here. Bill gave me the real estate update. He's made an offer on the house. The owners are considering it, but it's contingent on the sale of his home."

When Judy called on Friday night, Amanda told Judy she reminded her of a high school girl with her first serious crush on a boy. They laughed. "Why don't you bring Justin and Christopher to the Family Christian Store tomorrow for story hour if Bill doesn't mind?"

"I know he won't mind. Emily wouldn't get much out of it so I'll leave her with her grandma." Judy paused. "You'll never guess what I've started doing."

"Try me," Amanda said teasingly.

"I've started scheduling my client's appointments around things I want to do with or for the kids."

"That doesn't surprise me at all. Children have a way of getting into your heart when you're not looking." The friends said good-bye, each with a smile.

*   *   *

By the time Calvin got home at six o'clock Amanda hadn't started dinner yet. "We could go out to eat," he suggested after giving her a hello kiss."

"Or you could help me cook," she suggested.

"I haven't had enough time with you this week and I don't want you to cook."

"You could help me in the kitchen," she offered.

"I want some quality time with you. Not *kitchen time*," he emphasized.

"Well then, after pizza what will we do with our time?"

He smiled. She blushed.

"It's not what you think I'm thinking."

"Tell me, what are you thinking?"

"First we order pizza. When it arrives we eat. Then we go for a drive around the city."

Amanda noticed a little twinkle in his eye. "Do you have a particular destination in mind or are you just going to drive?"

"I do have a couple of destinations in mind. I'll tell you over dinner. You order the pizza while I take a shower."

Amanda agreed to order the pizza, and Calvin called over his shoulder on the way to their bathroom, "You can join me if you wanna. I'm sure my back needs to be scrubbed."

Amanda smiled and picked up the phone. Before she dialed, she looked through the junk drawer to see if she had any coupons. They weren't hurting for money, but she liked to save it when she could. She found what she was looking for and began to dial.

The voice on the other end of the line sounded familiar, but she couldn't quite place it. After talking with the girl and getting the order finalized, Amanda realized it was Melissa, the young girl Laurinda was mentoring.

"How have you been?" Amanda asked.

"I've been great since your husband gave Jayson a job and Laurinda helped me get this one. Laurinda and Ronnie are watching Suzie for me tonight so I can work. Next Thursday Laurinda is taking me and Suzie back to your church to look through the clothes closet. Suzie is growing so fast."

"That's wonderful, Melissa. It sounds like things are working out for the two of you. You're right, children grow like weeds."

"Mrs. Edwards, can I ask you something?"

"Sure, honey, whatever you want."

"Why are you, Mr. Edwards, Laurinda, and Ronnie helping us so much?

"Melissa, have you ever heard the saying 'God helps those who help themselves'?"

"No. I don't know much about God."

"Lots of people say that about God. Calvin, Ronnie, Laurinda, and I all believe a little differently about that saying. We believe God helps those who help others. He is a loving, caring God Who wants us to be like Him. If we only try to help ourselves, that isn't being like God. Let me give you an example. Once when we were first married and on a shoestring budget, our friend Bruce was in a motorcycle accident. The fall broke his neck. At the fundraiser we purchased a few things in the auction. We ended up spending more than we meant to, but we reminded ourselves it was for a good cause. The next day we got a check in the mail that we never expected to and it was more than enough to cover what we'd spent the night before."

"I get it. It's kind of like paying it forward, like the movie."

"Kind of. The awesome thing, Melissa, is you can never out give God. He has many, many blessings in store for us here on earth. We believe helping someone else, especially when it's hard for us, is taking a step of faith that God will supply our needs."

"Mrs. Edwards, already I see where our lives have been, what you called blessed, after meeting Laurinda and Ronnie. They're great."

Somewhere in the background Amanda heard someone yell at Melissa to take another call.

"I'm glad we had this talk. Hang on to our phone number and call me if you need anything."

"I will. Thank you for your order, Mrs. Edwards." Then she added, her voice a little lower, "Thanks for everything." Then she raised her voice again, "You have a great night. Thank you for choosing us. Our driver will be there in twenty-five minutes or less or your pizza is free."

Amanda had just hung up when Calvin joined her in the kitchen. "Was the pizza guy someone you knew?" He smiled lovingly at her. "You've got to be the only person I know who can take ten minutes to order one pizza."

"You have it *all* wrong," she playfully scolded him. "First of all, it wasn't a guy. Secondly, I was catching up on recent and future events. So there!" She pushed her right pointer finger playfully into his chest, pushing him backward a step.

"Well then, dear, sweet, wonderful wife of mine, who was it? What events of past and future did you learn about?"

She explained the conversation to him as he got a movie ready, and he told her one of the destinations he had planned for the night while they waited for the pizza.

"I talked to Ronnie today and found out Jayson's car tires are bald. Since it's not safe to drive the baby and her mother around like that, I was thinking of taking a gift certificate, which I picked up on my way home, over to the boy's house and leaving it in the door. Remember how we used to play the doorbell game as kids?"

"Maybe you rang doorbells and ran away, but I didn't!" she exclaimed.

"Okay, Miss Goody Two-Shoes," he teased, "I'm sure you've at least heard of it."

"Yes. I heard what you *bad* boys did at night for fun. I still say it was a good thing you and your buddies came back the next morning to clean up the toilet paper you hoodlums threw all over our yard the night before."

Calvin shrugged his shoulders. "We just happened to be in the neighborhood and thought it looked like a good community project. Besides, no one ever proved it was us." He kissed her on the cheek before getting off the couch to answer the door.

He paid for the pizza and gave the young man a sizable tip. He remembered what Amanda'd said earlier. He didn't recall anyone ever really putting into words how God wants us to be like Him in the area of giving. He didn't do it to get something, he did it to bless the other person.

He was smiling when he returned with their dinner. She knew what he'd done. They thanked God for the ability to help other people, and told Him they felt closer to Him when they did. They also prayed they'd go unnoticed on their expedition to Jayson's house later.

Two hours later the movie was over and the pizza box empty. "I thought it would have been a little darker than it is now that we're done with the movie," Calvin said as he stood up and stretched.

"The days are getting longer, you know. You're thinking we might get caught if it's not dark, aren't you?" she said, smiling at him. "Maybe we could add a few groceries to the drop."

Calvin agreed. After they cleaned up their dinner mess, they left for the grocery store.

Calvin pushed the cart while Amanda chose items she thought the young family could most use, including baby food and formula. Milk would have been good they agreed, but they couldn't be sure how soon Jayson would find the treasures. Amanda also included a daily devotional from the book section.

"Don't you feel kind of like a traitor, buying that book here instead of buying it from your employer?"

"Check your watch, Mr. Edwards. My employer closed fifteen minutes ago."

"Good point, Mrs. Edwards. My bad."

"My *what?*" Amanda exclaimed.

"I said, 'my bad.' It means I'm sorry. Jayson said it on the job site this week. I reacted the same way you did, only my voice doesn't have as high of a pitch as yours."

Amanda gave him a sideways grin and put some soup in the cart. "This is where we have to stop. We're getting into the perishable foods."

He eyed the sizeable amount of groceries in the cart. "Is there anything you missed?"

She tipped her head to the right and squinted at him.

"I'm just trying to help. We better hurry up or we'll be late to our destination after Jayson's."

"Oh, that's right, you said you had two destinations in mind. Are you going to tell me where else you're taking me?"

"No."

"I see how you are. At least tell me if I'm dressed appropriately."

"Yes."

"Will you give me a hint?" she asked as he began to pile the groceries onto the conveyer belt.

"No."

She began writing the check. "You're a man of few words tonight."

"Yup."

With the groceries in the back of the van, the couple was on their way to Jayson's house. When they arrived, the house was dark and there was a car in the drive but it wasn't Jayson's.

They placed the gift certificate in one of the grocery bags before it was placed on the front porch with a note that said *Jayson,*

Melissa, and Suzie. Amanda had written the note so Jayson wouldn't recognize Calvin's handwriting. Once they were on their way home, Calvin told Amanda they were going to meet Bill and Judy for a cup of coffee.

"There is only one problem with that," Amanda pointed out. "Neither of us drinks coffee, and I don't think Judy does, either."

"We couldn't exactly say we're going out for drinks, now could we? That wouldn't sound too good."

"You're right. Whose idea was this?"

"Bill's."

"Are you going to tell me why?"

"No."

"But you know why, don't you?"

"Yes."

"You're going to drive me crazy with these one word answers!" Amanda exclaimed.

"Sorry."

Amanda threw her hands up in playful disgust, and then laid them back on her lap. After a few more turns, she knew where they were going even if she didn't know why. Calvin parked and went around the van to open Amanda's door. They walked in together holding hands. The hostess took them to Bill and Judy's table where they were sitting side by side in the booth. Judy seemed to be crying while examining her left hand. Bill stood up to greet them when they arrived. Judy didn't stop looking at the ring Bill had placed there a few moments prior to the Edwardses' arrival. Bill motioned for Amanda to sit next to Judy. The two men sat across from them.

Amanda sat down next to Judy and got her attention. "Why are you crying? It's a beautiful ring."

She got Judy's attention. "I know," she said between sobs.

Amanda put her arm around Judy and asked to take a closer look at the ring. The three diamonds placed side by side sparkled with the light no matter how Judy moved her hand.

"So he asked you to marry him?" Amanda said as she held her friend's diamond-clad hand in her own.

"Yes," Judy said before she sobbed again.

"What did you say?"

At that very moment Judy really realized the significance of the situation. "Yes," she said with excitement.

The two women hugged and Judy finally stopped crying. The two men sat speechless during the exchange. They didn't understand females and silently decided they never would.

Bill was the first to speak. "I have some news I think you'll all find amusing."

"What's that, brother?" Calvin asked.

"Remember the family from somewhere up north that placed an offer on my house?"

"Yes," everyone else said in unison.

"Turns out that the family is not just any family. It's the doctor and his wife whose house we're buying up here."

"Oh my gosh," Amanda said.

"You're kidding?" Judy said.

"I thought the doctor and his wife wanted to downsize," Calvin said.

"Well, yes and no," Bill explained. "My house is smaller than theirs, but I have more property than they do here. He wants to have horses and my farm is perfect for them. We are currently negotiating an exchange of the two properties rather than a sale. We still have to pay a commission to each of the realtors but not as much as for an exchange."

"That's awesome, Bill," Calvin said.

"It means we'll have everything wrapped up within a week, two at the most. It also means I didn't have to wait another minute about asking this beautiful lady to marry me."

Judy blushed.

"I'm grateful she said yes. I invited you both because I thought she could use some moral support from her best girlfriend."

Judy and Amanda nodded. Amanda was thrilled to be involved with this wonderful time in Judy's life.

"I also thought I'd need moral support when I ask her if she will marry me *before* we close on the house."

Three sets of eyes looked at Bill as if he'd suddenly grown a horn on his forehead. Calvin knew about the ring, but not about the rest.

Bill reached across the table and picked up his fiancé's hand. "What do you think, Judy? If it's too fast, just say so and I'll understand."

At that moment everything cease to exist in Judy's world except for this wonderful Christian man who had not only asked her to marry him, but also said he wanted to marry her in the next two weeks.

"When you and I haven't been on the phone or together during the past two weeks, I've been praying about this. I loved it when you talked about having the den be a playroom so you could watch the kids, and then you asked if you could take the boys to Amanda's story hour tomorrow. I love your willingness to take the boys to preschool. Judy, I know you care about my children, and they absolutely adore you. I'd be an idiot not to snatch you up as quickly as I could."

It wasn't like you had a lot of competition beating my door down, Judy thought.

Bill placed his hand under Judy's chin and tilted her head upward so he could look her in the eye. "Honey, I need you to talk," Bill said gently.

Judy's eyes drifted away for a moment before returning to his. "Like I said when you asked me to be your wife—I'd be honored. I'll marry you tonight, next week, or next year, whenever you say."

Calvin and Amanda slipped out of the booth so both of their friends could do the same. They stepped out of the way as the couple embraced and Judy resumed crying. The two couples reseated themselves beside their loved one, and after a few moments, Judy stopped crying.

Bill turned to face Judy. "Here's what I am thinking. As soon as I get the date that we take possession of the house, we'll get married in front of the justice of the peace a day or two before. When we close on the house, we'll do so as a married couple. The house will be in both our names, but the mortgage will be in my name only based solely on my income, so you won't have to do anything but sign the papers as Judy Cummings.

"After we are settled in the house, we can have a church wedding and as big or little of a reception as you want. What do you think?"

"Okay," she said.

"Honey, don't just say okay, I need to know what you want to do. I don't want you to think I'm trying to rush you or run your life in any way." He placed his hand on top of her hands. "Tell me what you're thinking."

Amanda guessed what Judy was thinking. She and her first husband married quickly at his request, and that he'd turned out to be abusive. Amanda suggested Bill let them freshen up as she stood up. Bill released his hand from Judy's and said that would be a great idea. Judy got up in silence and walked with Amanda to the ladies' room. Amanda guided Judy to an overstuffed chair in the corner and then sat down in another chair beside her.

"Talk to me," Amanda said.

Judy looked right at her. "You know what I'm thinking."

"Probably, but why don't you tell me."

"My first marriage was a 'hurry up' thing and look how that turned out."

"I did know what you were thinking."

"And…" Judy's voice trailed off as tears streamed down her face.

"And this is extremely different. You were both very young, and you were very naive. Do you see any of the signs of abuse in Bill that you saw in him?"

"No."

"Did your first husband *ever* step foot inside a church?"

"No."

"Did he buy your engagement ring?"

"No. I bought both our wedding bands the day of the wedding."

"Did he buy you a house?"

"No, he moved in with me."

"Did he *ever* treat you as well as Bill does?"

"No."

"I bet Bill has never once asked you, much less *told* you, to get him a beer." The two women laughed.

"I don't want a big church wedding or reception."

"I'm sure that whatever you want will be okay with him."

The two women leaned forward and hugged. "I'm so happy for you, Judy. You deserved this man a long time ago."

"Better late than never," they said together after their hug.

Judy stopped to look in the mirror before going back out. "How could you let me sit there looking like this?"

"You didn't look like that at the table. You looked worse," she teased.

"Thanks!" After Judy freshened up her makeup the two women rejoined the men.

"Is everything okay?" Bill asked.

"It's better than okay, it's great! We're getting married in less than two weeks!" she exclaimed as she hugged her future husband. My final husband, she thought.

Judy told him she'd be okay with the justice of the peace for the wedding, and after they settled into their new home, an intimate reception at their new home. Bill loved the idea almost as much as he loved the woman.

Chapter 24

The following morning, after having gotten very little sleep the night before, Judy awoke at six thirty, two hours before she needed to be at Bill's parents' house to pick the boys up to take them to the Family Christian Store. She looked at the engagement ring again. In the early morning light she was sure it shined even brighter than it had last night.

She went over the evening again in her head as she lay looking at the ring. He had smelled so good when he got to her door last night. She couldn't ever remember him smelling that good. He'd been preoccupied on the way to the restaurant. He asked if she'd mind if he placed their order. She wondered if she'd be able to eat everything, but each course was light and seemed to take an unusual amount of time between each one. Thinking back, she realized he was stalling for time. He had to wait until just the right time to ask her. He couldn't ask too early or the Edward's wouldn't have shown up at just the right time.

When he returned her to her door, she had hoped he would finally think it was the right time and place to kiss her, but he didn't. As if he'd read her mind, he told her that although he wanted very much to kiss her, he was afraid he wouldn't be able to stop there. Her respect for him grew, as did her longing for their first kiss.

Suddenly, she realized their first kiss would be at their wedding. As she thought about their wedding, she realized she had nothing to wear. She jumped out of bed to call Amanda to see if they had time to go shopping for a dress before she picked up the boys.

She lay back down as she realized what time it was. She decided to ask Amanda about shopping after story hour and she'd returned the boys to their dad. As she lay staring at the ceiling, thinking about what kind of dress to buy, her phone rang. She was pleasantly surprised to hear Bill's voice on the other end.

"I hope I didn't wake you."

"No. I've been awake most of the night thanks to you."

"I'm sorry. Was it something I said?"

"No, it wasn't *something* you said, it was *everything* you said last night!"

"If it makes you feel any better, I didn't sleep much last night, either."

"I feel some better."

"When I got home, Mom had left me a note about the house situation."

"Is there something wrong?"

"No. Everything is right," he paused, "just like you and me."

Judy blushed.

"You know that all my furniture is still in my house, right?"

"I remember you mentioning it. You didn't have room for it here and you didn't want it in storage."

"Those reasons and the realtor said it would show better if people thought someone still lived in it. Well, it turns out that the doctor and his wife have had movers go in and get all of their furniture out of their house and it's on its way to my house. The movers have been told to keep it until my old house is empty. Turns out he didn't retire after all so they're taking a month's vacation before he starts his new job. There is no hurry for us to remove my things."

"That's good news."

"Yes. But I'm in a hurry to get my, I mean, our stuff up here. I'd like to fly down on Monday and get things moving." He laughed as he realized what he'd said. "You know, get things going for having our stuff moved up here."

"How long will you be gone?"

"A better question would be, how long will *we* be gone if you'd like to join me?"

Judy's face became red and warm. She'd only flown once as a kid and just the idea of flying anywhere excited her, but it excited her even more to think she'd be with him.

"Will you have time to go or are you booked solid for the next few days?"

"I've been doing a little less working since I met you. Seems like the phone isn't ringing like it was two weeks ago. Yet, I'm still paying all my bills. How long would we be gone?"

"Two or three days. If we leave early Monday before the close of business, we'd have time to make some arrangements. Anything we don't finish on Monday we should be able to finish on Tuesday. We can stay another day if you have time and would like to do any sightseeing or shopping."

"What on earth would I need to shop for?"

"Furniture, bedding, anything your little heart desires. The tax rate is less, and since cotton is big down south, many of the things made from or with cotton are less expensive there."

"Why would we need new furniture?"

"I want to donate my bed and get us a new one."

"Now that you mention it, I could leave my bed here for Elizabeth's new roommate." Judy was quiet for a moment. "What condition is your old bed in?"

"Very good condition. Why do you ask?"

"Would you mind shipping it up here with the rest of your stuff? Elizabeth's bed is something she and her ex-husband found on the side of the road. I'd like to give her your old bed if that's okay with you."

"I knew you were a wonderful woman the first time I met you. I'm not sure who loved you first, me or my kids."

Judy blushed again. She was thankful he couldn't see her blush or how bad her bed head was from her sleepless night. Suddenly, she realized in less than two weeks he'd be seeing her every morning for the rest of her life. The thought both scared and delighted her.

"Speaking of your children, do you have any plans for them after the story time?"

"No, do you have something in mind?"

"Actually, I do, but it doesn't really involve them," she paused, "or you directly. I was wondering if you'd mind if I spent some time with Amanda after I bring the kids back to you."

"You don't have to ask for permission to spend time with Amanda. I'll never control your life like that or any other way for that matter."

"Thank you. I wanted to call her when I woke up earlier, but it was too early. I need to find a dress for our wedding and I'd like her help."

"Do you need any money?"

"No. I'm all set. I'm not getting anything extravagant. Just something I can wear to church or out on a special night with my husband." The word nearly stuck in her throat. Either Bill didn't notice, or he chose not to say anything.

"Do you want to go Monday?"

"Do I want to? Yes. Can I? I don't know without looking at my calendar. I'll let you know when I come get the boys."

"That's fine. Would you rather I take the boys myself?"

"No. Amanda works until one, so I hoped to have lunch with my future family and hang out with them until she's done if that's okay with you?"

"It's more than okay. I look forward to every moment I spend with you. I'll let you go because I hear our little monsters waking up. I'll see you when you get here. I love you, Judy."

"I love you, Bill. See you at eight thirty."

Judy decided to take her shower and then call Amanda to see if she could go shopping with her. Judy was right. Amanda was scheduled to work until one. She was excited to help Judy shop for her wedding dress when asked a short time later. Judy said she'd have lunch with her family, and then come back to get Amanda so she didn't have to drive.

Judy went to the salon to check her schedule. Much to her disappointment, her schedule was full on Monday. The few appointments on Tuesday and Wednesday could be rescheduled for Friday.

Judy arrived at Bill's parents' house at the appointed time. She told Bill about her schedule. He told her they could leave after work on Monday and be back by Wednesday night. She said she'd call her clients after she and Amanda found the perfect dress.

The boys hugged and kissed their father and grandparents good-bye, and then raced to Judy's car.

*   *   *

When Judy returned to the Family Christian Store at one, Amanda was finishing up labeling some new books.

"Where are we going?" she asked Judy on the way to her car.

"I don't know. But I have something new to tell you on the way."

"Your life has gotten pretty exciting these past two weeks."

"Tell me about it," Judy said as she started her car. "Do you mind starting in that bridal shop in Dewitt?"

"I'm here to help. I'll go wherever you want."

Judy put the car in gear and pulled out of the parking spot. As she drove, she told Amanda all about her conversation with Bill. "He wants to buy a new bed just for us. I think that's so sweet."

"I think *he's* so sweet."

"Me, too," Judy said dreamily.

The first dress that she liked didn't fit right. The second dress looked better on the hanger than it did on her. Everything seems to be too "weddingish" she told Amanda.

"I want something simple so I can wear it to church sometimes."

"In that case, we shouldn't have left Okemos."

"What do you have in mind?"

"The second hand store by the dry cleaners."

"The second hand store by what dry cleaners?"

"On Grand River."

At their next stop Judy found the perfect dress, and then she realized she needed shoes.

Amanda called Calvin to tell him she'd be later than she thought. He told her he'd invited Ronnie and Laurinda over for pizza and a movie at seven o'clock.

By five o'clock Amanda was sure they'd been in every shoe store in the mall before Judy found the right pair of shoes. Later, when Amanda returned home, she told Calvin about their hunt for the perfect shoes. He thought the dress would've been harder to find than the shoes. Amanda laughed.

Ronnie and Laurinda arrived at seven o'clock with a movie, and ten minutes later the pizzas arrived. They prayed, then began to eat. They weren't as interested in the movie as they were about catching up with each other. Ronnie worked with Jayson during the day and he'd been ecstatic about finding groceries on the front porch of his mom's house, along with a gift certificate to a tire place with just the right amount for him to get four new tires. Since Ronnie had no idea Calvin and Amanda were behind the late night drop, Ronnie could honestly say he didn't know who did it, even though he suspected. He remembered when he and Laurinda had rushed to Chicago to see his mother and getting what he thought was an advance on his paycheck. To this day, he didn't recall any of it being withheld from his check.

After dinner, Ronnie suggested he and Calvin take care of the leftover pizza. Once in the kitchen, Ronnie took a small box out of his pocket and presented it to Calvin. Calvin tried to blush, but couldn't. Instead, he said, "I'm already taken."

"Just open it boss man and tell me if you think she'll like it." Ronnie paused. "Or more importantly if you think she'll take it?"

Calvin removed the lid from the box and then opened the lid to the ring box, and smiled. "I think she'll love and accept it."

"Boss, I'm so afraid that when I ask her, I'm going to mess it up completely. Do you have any pointers?"

"When do you plan to ask her?"

"Right this minute, five minutes from now, whenever. I just want her to be mine. I talked to her dad already and he said I could ask her whenever I was ready."

"Are you serious about right this minute? Don't you want to be alone with her at some fancy restaurant? Girls like that stuff you know."

"I know. But she knows I'm not the fancy restaurant type so she'd know right away if I took her to one. As far as being alone with her...well, that's not a good idea. It's becoming harder and harder to restrain myself from kissing her on the lips."

"Are you two okay in there?" Amanda called to the men.

"We're fine. We're trying to figure out how to burn the kitchen down."

"Okay, if that's all." She rolled her eyes at Laurinda. "Men!"

"Tell me about it. Ronnie has been acting weird all night. He acted like we had to get over here or he'd burst. We circled the subdivision three times before we pulled into the driveway so we wouldn't be ten minutes early."

Back in the kitchen, Calvin said, "Ronnie, I think I have an idea. Bear with me on this one."

"Sure, boss."

"Hey, ladies, we've decided we'd like a little ice cream for dessert. We'll run to the store and get some." Calvin handed the ring and its box back to Ronnie before returning to the living room.

"Any requests on what flavor?"

The two women looked at each other quizzically. "None, thanks. We aren't the ones craving for ice cream. You boys run along and do your thing. We'll be waiting right here when you get back," Amanda said.

"Okay. Love you, bye," Calvin called to Amanda.

"See ya, sweetie," Ronnie called to Laurinda

Once inside Ronnie's car, Calvin told him his plan. Ronnie liked it so they drove to the closest grocery store and bought everything they needed for the banana split that would change Ronnie's and Laurinda's lives forever. When the two men returned, they disappeared into the kitchen after telling the ladies they could not enter the kitchen. "We're making the best banana splits like you've never seen before," Calvin said.

"Are you making two or four?" Amanda called after them.

"You'll find out when we call you," Ronnie told her.

Ronnie was so nervous that he almost cut his finger instead of the banana. His scoops of ice cream seemed lopsided. His sprayed-on whipped cream didn't look right to him. He put that one to the side and decided to try again since he had to make two anyway. This time the banana was cut perfect, the ice cream was right where he wanted it, and the whipped cream couldn't have looked any better if a professional had done it. He placed a cherry on top of his, and a beautiful quarter-carat diamond ring on top of Laurinda's.

Calvin had everything but Laurinda's on the table by the time Ronnie finished it. Ronnie called to the ladies as he set the most expensive banana split on the table.

Laurinda walked into the kitchen first. "Ronnie, did you know that Judy and Bill are getting engaged?"

"No," he managed to mutter.

"Which one is mine?" Laurinda asked. Ronnie pointed.

She looked where his finger was pointing. She covered her mouth with both her hands. "You don't really expect me to be able to eat all that, do you?" she exclaimed.

Since she hadn't seen the ring, he said, "I think you'll be able to eat most of it. Why don't you sit down and eat what you can. Ladies first." He pulled her chair out for her and Calvin did the same for Amanda. When Laurinda looked at the top of hers, she finally saw the ring. No one said a word. Ronnie and Calvin looked at each other for a brief second, and then back at Laurinda who was crying.

"Wha…" She tried to speak. "Is…I…" she stammered. "Is this for me?" she finally managed to ask.

"It is if you'll have me to go with it," Ronnie said. He removed the ring from the whipped cream and wiped it off with a napkin Calvin had placed under her spoon, and then got down on one knee in front of her and asked, "Laurinda Sue Bowman, will you marry me?"

"Yes!" she exclaimed. "Yes, yes, yes!"

He slipped the ring onto her left ring finger and looked lovingly into her eyes. "I don't have a lot to offer you in the way of worldly goods, but I promise you with all my heart that I'll love you 'til the day I die."

Through tears Laurinda said that's all she wanted. He took her hand and they both stood to embrace one another.

* * *

"Do you realize that in the last twenty-four hours we've been witness to two engagements?" Amanda asked Calvin later after they were in bed.

"It makes me feel special. How 'bout you?"

"It makes me feel very special. I feel blessed just to be a part of these people's lives, and then they include us on their very special evenings." Amanda began to cry.

"What's wrong?" Calvin gently asked as he pulled his wife close to his chest.

"When the girls were first stolen from us, I never imagined I'd know happiness like this again."

"I'm glad you're happy." He kissed her and they fell asleep in each other's arms.

*   *   *

The alarm went off too early for Amanda the following morning. As soon as she finished praying, she told Calvin, who was already done praying, that she had to do a shower.

He looked at her with a quizzical look on his face. "What do you mean, you need to do a shower?"

"I have to give Judy a bridal shower. I doubt she needs any of the usual first-time bride shower gifts, but I can think of a few things she'll need."

"Cookbooks, I hope."

"Yes, cookbooks, and maybe some lessons, too. We've got to get to church. I'll need Laurinda's help, and maybe Beth's, too. Judy's leaving for a few days so I can make it a surprise for when she gets back. That way she can't object to me doing it."

Amanda was talking so fast, all Calvin could do was nod his head.

312

"What do you think of having it here next Sunday after church?" she called over her shoulder on her way to the shower.

"Whatever you say, dear," Calvin called after her.

"I'll ask Mom to bake the cake…" She kept talking but he couldn't hear her. He shook his head, thinking how he'd never understand how a woman could carry on a complete conversation all by herself.

By the time they got to church Amanda had everything under control for the shower—who to invite, the lunch menu, the cake design she wanted, and the color scheme. The hardest part would be keeping it a secret from Judy. At the end of the sermon, before the closing song, Pastor Dave asked if anyone had anything they wanted to share with the congregation.

Ronnie stood up first.

"Yes, sir, what would you like to share with us this morning?"

"First of all, as most of you know, I've become a born-again Christian. After talking with Pastor Dave and my girlfriend Laurinda's family, I've decided to make the public profession of what's happened on the inside of me. Soon as it can be arranged, I'm going to be baptized."

Many in the congregation said amen.

"And second," he paused to extend his hand to Laurinda to help her up to stand beside him, "I've asked this beautiful young lady to be my wife, and she said yes."

The congregation applauded.

Bill stood up as Ronnie and Laurinda sat down.

"I've been a born-again believer all my life so I've got that part covered. However, I believe it's time I moved my membership from my old home to my new home."

He extended his hand to Judy to help her up to stand beside him and continued, "And like Mr. Colthorp over there, I, too, have purposed marriage to a beautiful lady and she said yes as well."

"Amen and praise the Lord," people said as the applause grew louder this time.

"It looks like I'm going to be a little busy with weddings," Pastor Dave said after the applause died down. "I better get my best suit cleaned."

Everyone laughed.

The next person to stand was the last one anyone who knew him would expect to see in church, much less standing up to talk. Jayson cleared his throat and looked down at his girlfriend for courage.

"Two nights back while Melissa an' I was workin', somebody come by my mamma's house and left us some food and a piece of paper for some brand new tires for my ol' beat-up car. That's some real good news to us. I got tires yesterday after work."

He looked back down at Melissa, who smiled at him. "I'm real thankful to whoever would do that for us. Them diapers fit Suzie perfect and the formula was just right. Before I sit down I wanna thank Mr. Edwards over there for givin' me a job and a steady paycheck so I can take care of my girl and our baby." He turned toward Calvin and said, "Thank you, sir."

Many people said "amen" and "praise God." Many suspected they knew the benefactor of the gifts.

Once Jayson sat down, Pastor Dave thanked him for sharing. "Sounds like the Spirit of the Lord is alive and well here at Friendship Baptist Church. I guess the founders of this church named her well.

"Brother Jim, what song are we singing to close the service?"

"'When I Survey the Wondrous Cross,' but before we sing, Pastor, do you have time for a bit *more* good news?"

"By all means."

"As most of you know, I was diagnosed with cancer six months ago. The fact that I'm alive and with you now is a miracle since the doctors only gave me six months to live. But now, praise God, the cancer is in remission."

Many in the congregation echoed his praise to God. After that, Jim lead his fellow believers in one of his favorite hymns. At the end of the song and everyone was dismissed, many were still singing.

Amanda made her way to some of her and Judy's friends to tell them about the shower the following week at her house. Everyone agreed to come.

When Amanda got to Melissa, she asked, "Are you in a hurry or do you have time to go downstairs with me?"

Melissa looked at Jayson as if to ask if they had time. He said yes.

"You can join us if you want to, Jayson. I have a few baby clothes I want to show her."

"Sounds like woman stuff, Mrs. Edwards. I'll wait here for ya."

"I know you told me you and Laurinda would be here Thursday, but there's some things I," she swallowed, "want you to have for Suzie."

"Okay."

"I don't know if you know it, but our daughters were stolen from us last August. I recently found the strength and courage to sort through their clothes and I brought many of them here. I want you to take as much as you want, even if you think it's too big for Suzie now."

"Mrs. Edwards, can I ask you something?"

"Yes, dear."

"Did you and Mr. Edwards bring all that stuff to Jayson's house?"

"You may ask me anything but that."

"I understand." Melissa embraced Amanda. "Thank you, even if you didn't do it."

"You're welcome, even if we didn't do it." Amanda hugged her tight.

They looked through the clothing Amanda had brought in a few weeks earlier. Melissa took everything that wasn't already too small for Suzie. Amanda suggested she and Laurinda could spend their time Thursday looking for clothing for herself and Jayson.

Melissa agreed she and Jayson could use some new clothes. "I don't feel like I have anything good enough to wear to church. These are my best jeans, so that's why I've worn them here every time we come."

"Honey, God doesn't care what you wear to church and neither do the people here. You heard the pastor say this church was named correctly."

"I did."

"Are you busy next Sunday after church?" Amanda asked as they walked out of the clothing room into the hall.

"I don't think so. Why?"

"I was wondering if you'd be interested in joining a few of us ladies at my house for a surprise bridal shower for my friend Judy."

"I don't have no gift."

"Don't worry about a gift. I'll take care of that. Maybe you could come over early and help with set up and decorating if you have time."

"I'd like that very much. Me helping could be like my gift, right?"

"Right."

"Do you still have my number from when I ordered the pizza?"

"Yes."

"Then call me this week when you have some time and I'll give you the directions to our house."

"I can get 'em from the delivery guy. He remembers your house cuz your husband's a good tipper."

"Yes, he is, Melissa."

"And I know why," Melissa smiled at her.

Chapter 25

The week flew by and before Amanda knew it, it was Saturday afternoon. Melissa would be over in a few minutes to help with the food and decorations. Amanda hadn't wrapped the gift so Melissa could do it since it was from both of them.

Between Bill and Judy they had all the kitchen appliances a couple could possibly need. What they lacked, or more specifically, what Judy lacked, were the skills needed to cook. Amanda had been specific when each of the guests asked what to bring. Amanda was confident that Judy would be pleased with this outpouring of love from her friends, family, future family, and even some of her clients.

Melissa arrived without Suzie, much to Amanda's surprise.

"I thought Suzie'd be in the way cuz she wants all my time. It'll do her and Jayson good to spend time together. Besides, he has ta stay home with her, I got his car. Whoever gave Jayson them tires sure did him and me a big favor."

"I'm glad to hear that you're being blessed."

"I can only stay for about an hour since Jayson and me both gotta work and he drops me off first."

"I didn't know he had a second job. He must get pretty tired."

"He's used to working hard 'cause of football," Melissa said as she spread cream cheese on the slices of ham and then added a quarter of a pickle before closing it. "I've never had these before, are they good?"

"Help yourself. I'm sure no one will miss it."

Melissa took a bite of the appetizer she'd just created. "Not bad. Maybe I'll make these for Jayson. He loves pickles." She popped the balance of it into her mouth and then went to the sink to wash her hands.

"Are you done with those?" Amanda asked.

"That was my last one. What do you want me to do now?"

"Would you like to wrap our gift for Judy? I didn't wrap it so you could see what we got her."

"I hope someday I'm as thoughtful as you two are."

"You're already a very thoughtful person. You didn't have to come here today to help me. It's taking you away from Jayson and Suzie and you still have to work tonight. Where'd you say Jayson is working?"

"He's working for our competition, delivering. That's why them new tires are helpful. I wish he didn't work two jobs and go to school. He told me he applied for work study so he can work for Mr. Edwards more. He'd take classes in the mornin', then go to work from lunch on.

"I told him he should stay at school through lunch. We both get free breakfasts and lunches. He needs to eat since he wants to play ball in the fall for the university."

"I remember when Calvin was his age. He'd eat dinner with my family. My mother said she was sure he'd eat us out of house and home if she let him."

"But Mr. E. ain't fat or beefy like my Jayson."

"Everyone burns calories differently. Calvin has a high metabolism and he hardly ever gains weight. Drives me nuts. He can eat ten homemade cookies and not gain a single ounce. I gain a pound when I eat two cookies. It's not fair." Amanda smiled as Melissa nodded her head in understanding.

"This is beautiful. Ms. Judy's gonna love this robe and slippers, too. This the paper you want me to use?" Melissa asked as she fingered the end of the wrapping paper Amanda purchased when she bought the gifts.

"Don't you like it? I think I have other kinds in the basement, but I'm afraid it's mostly little kid birthday paper."

"I like it. It's so pretty I don't wanna cut it. I'm used to wrapping presents, when we can afford 'em in the funny papers my granma gives us. She thinks I still love to read 'em like when I was little. She means well, so I thank her for 'em. She's my favorite person in the world." Melissa stammered, "Besides Jayson and Suzie. Really I try to love them all equal."

"I understand. When our daughters were stolen from us, I don't think Calvin understood how much of me was taken with them. For a long time I thought he didn't think I loved him anymore, which was crazy thinking. But it was a crazy time for us."

"Ms. Laurinda told me she thinks she saw 'em someplace. Is that true?" Melissa stopped cutting the pretty paper so she wouldn't mess it up when she looked at Amanda.

"Yes, she thinks she might have seen them when she and Ronnie were on their way to Chicago to visit his mother. Our private investigator tried to follow the lead, but he came up empty-handed. You know, Melissa, I don't think he ever sent us a bill for the work he did on that. If he did, I never saw it."

"That's cuz you and Mr. E.'s always do nice things for everybody else. Somebody's gotta do nice for you."

"Pay it forward, right?" Amanda smiled at the teen.

"Right. I promise never to forget how nice you and Laurinda been to Jayson, Suzie, and me. I'll help someone else when we got ourselves a nice big house like this. I'll remember."

"I have no doubt you will, Melissa."

The two women worked in silence for a while until Melissa asked what Ronnie meant last Sunday when he said he was a born-again Christian and wanted to be baptized. The remainder of their time together Amanda explained the story of Jesus and how He came to earth to take away our sins. She explained why it was necessary to be born-again and why baptism was so important.

Before Melissa left, Amanda suggested she and Jayson look into the Wednesday evening youth group at church to learn more. "There would be people there closer to your age, and there's a nursery available for Suzie so you and Jayson could participate in the class."

"But, Mrs. E., nobody there has a baby like Jayson an' me. You know, not bein' married."

"You'd be surprised to know the teacher had a child out of wedlock a few years ago when she was in high school. She's married to a wonderful man now who isn't even the child's father. One girl that I know in the class had a baby and gave him up for adoption a year ago."

Her eyes widened. "Really?"

"Really," Amanda said. The two women hugged good-bye, promising to see each other the next day at church. Amanda suggested Melissa ride home with her so Jayson could keep the car. Melissa thanked her and said she'd talk to Jayson about the Wednesday night class.

Calvin came up from the basement after he heard the front door close. "Women sure talk a lot."

"We're very bossy, too. To prove it, I've left you a list of things I'd like you to do to help with the party."

"I've been working hard in the basement while you two ladies chatted. I could hardly concentrate with all the noise."

"Did you wreck your car again?"

He stuck his bottom lip out and looked at the floor like a hurt little child. "I did wreck my car, and I was sad."

"I'm sorry you wrecked your car, but playing video games isn't hard work, Mr. Edwards." She handed him a list of things she needed done.

"Will I get a cookie?"

"I'll give you the whole cookie jar if you get this list done quickly."

He was about to agree to her terms until he realized the cookie jar was empty. "That's a dirty trick," he said as he wrapped his arms around her in a bear hug. His scruffy unshaved face rubbed against her soft skin and she squealed.

"I'm gonna refill it, really," she said as she tried to squirm out of his grasp.

"Cookies first, work second."

"Work first, cookies second."

He growled close to her ear, sending shivers down her spine. "Work first, favorite cookies second." He released her and began studying the list. "Vacuuming is woman's work," he teased as he headed toward the closet. He growled, "Woman's work," then was gone.

A short time later the house was filled with the smell of chocolate chip cookies. The vacuuming was done and their card table and chairs were in the living room.

"Honey, your first batch of cookies is ready."

He joined her in the kitchen.

"Do you mind having pizza for dinner?"

"Yes, I mind having pizza for dinner tonight. I just slaved away making sure there wasn't a speck of dirt or dust in our living room and I'm not going to let you or your pizza mess it up. We *could* eat at the table if it weren't for all the party stuff you've got spread all over it."

"We could eat at the breakfast bar," she suggested.

"I'm too tall for the breakfast bar," he reminded her. "I'll take my legs off and leave them." He paused. "I don't know where I'd leave them. It might be messy."

"If you weren't so tall, your legs would fit under there. It suited our daughters just fine."

"So it did," he agreed, "and so it will again."

*   *   *

"Jayson, I hated lying to Mrs. E. 'bout where you was last night," Melissa said as she walked into his mother's house to get Suzie.

"A couple more jobs and I won't do it no more. I promise."

"You promised that last weekend and the weekend before that. Stop this weekend or I ain't gonna let you take Suzie no more 'til you do."

"I ain't using."

"And you better never start."

*   *   *

Sunday morning Amanda tried to concentrate on the sermon but had trouble. She was so excited for Judy, since the next day she and Bill were getting married. Judy asked Amanda to be her matron of honor and Bill asked Calvin to be his best man. After church, Amanda found Melissa and joined her as she went downstairs to get Suzie. Her heart skipped a beat when she saw Suzie in Katrina's dress.

"She looks beautiful."

"I hope seeing her wearin' it doesn't upset you."

"No. I'm glad you can use it."

"I'm gonna get her up to Jayson so we can go. What time is Ms. Judy 'posta be there?"

"One. Bill is dropping her off instead of taking her to lunch, which is where she thinks she's going with him after church."

"Where you gonna have everybody park?"

"Everyone will park down the street and around the corner from the house, everyone except my mom, who's bringing my two sisters with her. Judy won't think anything of my mom's car parked in my driveway after church."

Melissa delivered her daughter to Jayson and then joined Calvin and Amanda at their van. "It's nice of you to take me so Jayson doesn't have to. Thanks," she said as she climbed into the back seat.

"You're welcome," Calvin told her.

"You stayin' for the shower, Mr. E.?"

"Heavens no! I've had enough woman stuff in the past twenty-four hours to last me a long time. Since Laurinda's going to be at the shower, Ronnie and I are going to play pool while you ladies do your thing."

"He helped me with some cleaning and setting up yesterday after you left. He thinks of that as 'woman stuff.'" Amanda explained to her.

Melissa laughed. "Yesterday when I got to Jayson's, he'd been cleaning the oven without using any oven cleaner. His mom makes him clean the house on Saturdays."

"What will happen when we start working Saturdays?" Calvin asked her.

"I don't know. She knows we need the money for college and the baby so maybe she'll let him work with you and do the cleaning herself."

"Does he make good money delivering pizzas?"

"His tips ain't bad, but the hourly rate ain't good. He's puttin' all the money he can into a savings account. I don't think he has a hundred dollars yet."

"We'll have to see what we can do about that when the weather is a little more cooperative and we get back to working Saturdays. I've already told him that if he's interested, he can work for me full-time as soon as he's done with school this year. He said he'd be able to work until football practices started. If he's as good as I've heard he is, he could go pro."

"Oh, he's good."

Calvin pulled into the garage and parked the van. He got out and opened both van doors so the ladies could get out. "Nothing personal, ladies, but I've got to change and get the heck out of here. If you'll excuse me," he said once they were in the house, "I'm in a hurry."

The ladies hung up their own coats and then washed their hands and began setting the food out.

Calvin returned quickly, kissed Amanda good-bye, told them to have fun, and hurried out the door to the van. He had to wait for his mother and sisters-in-law to pull in before he backed out. He waved to them and was gone. The ladies walked through the garage and let themselves in. After hugs and introductions, they began helping getting ready for the party.

"Maria," Amanda said, "you must have skipped church this morning to be here with Mom."

"I did. But I think God knew I had a good reason."

"I'm not sure it did me any good to be there this morning. All I could think about was Judy, the party, how surprised she'll be, the wedding, the house, everything going on. Did Mom tell you that Ronnie and Laurinda are engaged, too?"

"Yes, she told me. Have they set a date yet?"

"No. I'm not sure it's even sunk in for her yet. He just asked her here Friday night using a banana split. I've never seen Laurinda as disinterested in a banana split as when she saw the ring."

"I can't wait to see it," Doreen said.

"Mom said he's getting baptized," Maria said.

"Yes, we're all very excited. Would you all pray for him? He still hasn't told his mother. I don't think it'll be easy for him from what I've heard."

The doorbell rang and several guests arrived at once. Melissa made sure everyone had something to drink while they waited. At five minutes after one, Bill and Judy arrived at the door. He told her he needed to stop here before lunch.

Judy figured out what was going on when she saw everyone in the living room and smelled the sloppy joes Amanda had warming in the Crock-Pot. She looked at Bill, who smiled and said he'd see her later. He gave her a kiss on the cheek and then left as quickly as Calvin had earlier.

"Surprise," Amanda said with excitement in her voice.

"I'd say so."

"I couldn't let you get married without having a shower."

Judy wanted to object since Amanda had already given her a bridal shower once before. Instead, she said thank you through tears.

Everyone enjoyed the abundance of food Amanda and Melissa had prepared the day before. The guests admired both Judy and Laurinda's new rings, and asked Laurinda when her wedding would be. She said no date had been set. After lunch, the ladies went to the living room so Judy could open her gifts.

Mrs. Cummings and Mrs. Steinman had each written down five of their family's favorite dinner recipes, along with a gift certificate for their time to show Judy how to prepare them. They both said they'd bring the necessary ingredients with them whenever she was ready.

Mrs. Cummings also gave her a pair of pearl earrings as a welcome to the family gift. "I hope they go with the dress you picked out for tomorrow," she said.

Judy walked over to hug her future mother-in-law. "They're perfect," she said.

Maria and Doreen gave her a negligee that matched the robe and slippers Amanda and Melissa gave her. Laurinda gave her a handmade centerpiece for her dining room table. She got the color scheme from Amanda. From her other friends and clients she received cookbooks and gift certificates for various restaurants. After all the presents were opened, everyone returned to the dining room for cake and an update on the bride's future.

Judy told everyone about their trip to Tennessee and how beautiful his home and land were there. "We picked out a complete bedroom set instead of just a new bed, and made arrangements for the new furniture to be picked up by the movers once they emptied the rest of the house."

"When we returned, the realtor had left a message about closing on both houses next Tuesday, so we applied for our marriage license that afternoon. We'll be staying at a local hotel tomorrow night, and then after breakfast we'll go to the closing."

Someone asked when the furniture would be in their house. "We had the keys to it last week so Bill gave one to the movers. Bill and I met with them to show them were to put everything. We're storing his old bedroom suite in the garage until I get my house ready for it. Since Elizabeth and her coworker will be renting my house, we're giving it to Elizabeth, and her roommate will get my old bedroom suite.

"I'll pack my personal belongings when I leave here today. Everything else will stay in the house."

"Are you keeping the salon open?" a client asked.

"Yes. Right now the plan is for me to take Tuesdays and Thursdays off so I can be with the kids. I'll be open all day Monday, Wednesday, Friday, and Saturday mornings. On the days I do work, Mrs. Cummings will keep the children for me. We'll see how that works for now. We still have lots of decisions to make. Everything is happening so fast. I feel like I'm in a dream. I'm afraid I'm going to wake up and find out that it wasn't real."

Mrs. Cummings put her arm around her future daughter-in-law. "It's real, darling. My Bill loves you very much, and I haven't seen him this happy in a long time."

Judy hugged her and cried.

Chapter 26

Monday morning Judy was awake before sunup. She hadn't canceled her regular appointments. In fact, she'd added Amanda and Laurinda.

What started as a small ceremony had grown larger than she anticipated. Maybe it was nerves, but right then she was having second thoughts. Her head felt like it was spinning.

As if someone had spoken to her, a single word came to her mind, pray. She asked, "Did you say pray?"

The word was in her mind again, nudging out the nervous feeling. To the voice in her mind she said, "Okay," then got down on her knees beside her bed. For a moment she thought about how last night was her last in her old bed that held more bad memories than she wanted to remember, and how it had been her last night to sleep alone again for the rest of her life.

She smiled and folded her hands, trying to remember how to begin. Didn't Amanda and Calvin say Father God? Maybe since she doesn't know Him as well, she thought, I should say something else.

Then as plainly as she'd heard the word pray, she heard "talk." She knew no one was in the room with her, yet she heard a voice. "Talk," she heard again.

"But I don't know what to say. I don't do this very often, and even less often by myself. Besides, I don't know where to begin. Everything's happening so fast. I feel like my life is out of control. I don't know if I've made the right decision. I've messed up so many times before that I'm afraid I'm doing it again.

"I'm not sure I was ever supposed to be married and here I am doing it a third time. I'm gonna be a mother to three children I barely know. Bill would like me to be a full-time mother to them. What if I mess them up? What if I mess everything up?"

"I'm here for you," the voice said.

Judy fought back tears with no avail. "I wanna be the best wife and mother I can be. I can't even cook. I am scared."

"Psalm 23," the voice said.

"I don't know Bible verses." She thought about the new Bible she'd gotten a few weeks earlier. "But I do have a Bible."

She stood up, switched on the bedside lamp, and found her Bible on the nightstand. She looked for the book of Psalms and found the chapter. Which verse, she wondered.

"All."

She picked up the Bible and climbed back onto the bed to read the chapter again and again until the words sank into her heart and soul. She felt a calm she'd never before experienced. Immediately Calvin's words came back to her. Peace that surpasses understanding. Is that a Bible verse? It must be if Calvin said it. Wherever it was, she understood it now.

She turned off her light, and holding her Bible, fell into a peaceful sleep. So peaceful she almost overslept. She rushed through her shower and didn't do anything with her hair.

The morning flew by and she was grateful when Amanda and Laurinda showed up at the same time, not surprisingly, in the same van.

"I'm glad to see you two."

They looked at her and understood. "Did you forget what today is, or are you trying a new hairdo for the wedding?" Amanda asked.

"It's called the 'jump out of the shower because I'm late' hairdo. Do you like it?"

"I've seen better," Laurinda told her. "I've tried it myself a time or two, so I can relate."

"Let's see what we can do for her," Amanda suggested.

"Let me get done with you two, then you can work on me."

"We aren't here to get our hair done. We're here to help you."

"But you booked appointments."

"I," Amanda began, gesturing between herself and Laurinda. "We knew you'd probably work someone else in and leave no time for you."

Judy hugged them both. "You're the best friends. Make yourselves at home. I'm going to try this shower thing again."

Within fifteen minutes, Judy was back with hair Amanda and Laurinda thought they could work with, with Judy's guidance. The ladies put her hair in rollers. Once it was done, Amanda set her under the dryer Calvin had placed there years before when she opened the salon.

Once her hair was dry and the rollers removed, Judy slipped into her wedding dress before they brushed her hair out. Judy reminded Laurinda that she'd be doing this same thing before long. Judy sat down in the chair and let Laurinda take the rollers out. She'd sat in this chair many times over the years, but this time it seemed different somehow. She had a nostalgic feeling that it would be the last time.

"Did I pull your hair?" Laurinda asked.

"No. What gives you that idea?"

"The tears in your eyes."

Judy wiped her eyes. "I didn't realize I was crying. I feel like this will be the last time I sit here. Silly, I know."

"It's not silly. You're being nostalgic and letting it get to you," Amanda said.

"Nostalgic or not, I know I'm doing the right thing," she said, and explained what had happened after she woke up the first time. "Do you think it was God?"

"Was it like Someone was talking to you in your head versus the way I'm talking to you now?" Amanda asked.

"Yes. Just like that," she said. "I knew it was Him. I had that peace Calvin talked about two weeks ago when this marriage stuff first came up. I was so at peace, I fell asleep with my Bible in my hands and stayed there until twenty minutes before my first appointment. I don't think I've ever slept so well in my whole life."

Laurinda turned the chair around and showed Judy what she'd done. "You could be a beautician? I couldn't have done any better myself. Thank you so much. I guess this mean it's time to go."

Laurinda looked at the clock. "It is time to go. We should have plenty of time to make that stop we talked about on the way over," she said to Amanda.

Laurinda helped Judy out of the chair. Once Judy was standing, everyone admired the bride, each one reflecting on her own thoughts. Amanda looked back on her wedding day, Laurinda looked forward to hers, while Judy said a prayer of thanksgiving for finally getting it right.

Amanda said, "We need to go."

Everyone made their way upstairs. Laurinda picked up the suitcase while Amanda helped Judy with her jacket.

A little while later Amanda pulled into the flower shop drive and Judy realized right away she hadn't thought about flowers. Amanda called earlier in the day to order a simple bouquet for Judy, a couple of flowers for herself, and boutonnières for each of the men. Laurinda and Judy waited while Amanda went in to get the order.

Judy thanked her for her thoughtfulness all the way to the courthouse. Amanda circled the parking lot to see if Bill was there yet. When she decided he wasn't there yet, she parked and hurried to get Judy inside.

A court clerk showed them where they could hide the bride until the judge was ready. Laurinda waited in the lobby for Bill, his family, Calvin, and Ronnie. She didn't wait long.

Laurinda went to get Amanda while Bill waited for the paperwork to be typed. Amanda arrived in time to sign as a witness, and then handed the pen to her husband who also signed.

"Are you ready?" the court clerk asked.

"I'm ready," Bill said with a big smile.

"I'm sure the bride is," Amanda told her.

"I'll take this to the judge and tell him you're ready." With that she turned to go down a hall and then disappeared through a door.

Amanda asked Calvin to take Bill and his family into the courtroom, explaining that she and Judy would be entering through a side door. She also told Calvin where to have Ronnie stand so he could get a picture of both Bill and Judy when Judy came in the room behind her. Ronnie had enjoyed photography in school and gotten very good with it, so he volunteered to be the official photographer for the wedding and the dinner afterward.

Amanda returned to Judy and Laurinda. "You can join the rest of the party in the courtroom if you want to," Amanda told Laurinda.

Laurinda hugged Judy one last time. She played with the ring on her finger as she thought of her own wedding day.

Bill about jumped out of this skin when Laurinda opened the door opposite where his bride was to come in. He swallowed the lump in his throat. "She'll come through that door." Calvin pointed in the opposite direction.

"I knew that," he said as he wrung his hands together. He looked at Calvin. "You've got the ring, right?"

"Yes." Calvin laughed. "But I think I've told you that about ten times."

"Sorry."

The door opened, so Bill and Calvin both directed their attention to it. Ronnie snapped a picture of the matron of honor. Then he positioned himself for a shot of the bride coming at him with the groom looking toward her. Unless there was two of him, there was no way he could get a shot of both of them at the same time any other way.

There was no music so Judy was unsure of when to come in. When the bailiff opened the door for her, she stepped through it without really realizing it. She heard a click sound but wasn't sure if it was the door shutting or the camera capturing this moment in time that would change her life forever. It was both.

Tears welled in Bill's eyes as he beheld his wife to be walking toward him. Breathtaking was all he could think about how Judy looked. He knew that if someone asked him what color her dress was, he wouldn't know the answer. His eyes were fixed on hers.

Judy was grateful Bill's eyes were fixed on hers, otherwise she might have run from the room in fear. What had she been thinking, trying this for a third time? She tried to remember the verse Amanda always said whenever she had something tough to do, like having blood drawn. The thought made her smile.

Bill smiled back at her. That was the last thing she remembered until he kissed her. She was certain she'd never been kissed like that before and silently prayed it wouldn't be the last time.

After the kiss, everyone began congratulating them. Ronnie took more pictures of the bride and groom together, and then with different family members and friends. He even made it into one with them and Laurinda. Judy was grateful he was capturing everything, but wondered if he'd ever get done.

She'd skipped lunch, which she now discovered was a big mistake, because she had a headache. Bill kissed her again and she forgot all about the headache. She just wanted to get through dinner and be alone with Bill.

After dinner at Red Lobster, Bill's parents took three very tired grandchildren home with them, and everyone else went their separate ways.

Chapter 27

The week following Bill and Judy's wedding seemed rather boring to Amanda, especially since they'd left for Key West after closing on their house. Amanda called Bill's mother to see if she could stop by and see the kids. Mrs. Cummings welcomed the help with her grandchildren, and Amanda got to know all of them better during the afternoon she spent with them.

Mrs. Cummings and Amanda discussed preschool for the boys. Amanda told her what she'd suggested to Judy and she loved the idea.

"We don't want to butt in on their business, but if you wouldn't mind getting a couple of applications, I could give them to Bill and Judy when they get back," Mrs. Cummings told Amanda.

That conversation is why Amanda presently found herself at Jessi's former preschool. Amanda parked in a familiar spot, and then numbly made her way to the door she'd used so many times the previous year. She knew she'd have to walk past Jessi's classroom to get to the office. *I can do all things through Christ who strengthens me,* she thought over and over. She smelled glue and paint as she approached the classroom. Tears welled up in her eyes before she realized it.

She stopped at the door and peered in to see the children learning through play. She recognized some of the children that had been in Jessi's class. She swallowed hard, trying to force the tears to stop running down her cheeks. She remembered Jessi sitting by the teacher, waiting for her to start reading. Story time was always Jessi's favorite part of preschool.

The teacher looked up and saw Amanda at the window. The two women had spent many hours together when Jessi was in her class. Mrs. Appleton nodded to Amanda with a slightly puzzled look. She'd been one of the many people who'd come by with food and prayer in the weeks immediately following the girls' disappearance. Mrs. Appleton motioned for her to come in.

Tentatively Amanda turned the handle. She quickly wiped the tears from her cheeks with the back of her hands. She didn't want to have to explain to the children why she'd been crying.

Mrs. Appleton stood up and hugged Amanda as soon as she was close enough. "It's so good to see you. What brings you in, Mrs. Edwards?"

"I have a friend who may want to bring her sons here, and while she's on her honeymoon, I thought I'd stop by and get the necessary paperwork for her."

"How old are her sons?"

"Justin is four and Christopher is two and a half."

"That's wonderful. Will you be joining them? I know the children loved it when you read to them."

"I don't think so. I have a job at the Family Christian Store now. I have story time there one Saturday a month. Maybe the kids could stop by there and hear me read."

"You're here now. Do you have a few minutes?"

Amanda never imagined Mrs. Appleton would ask her to read.

"I don't want to impose," Mrs. Appleton was saying as some of the children began pulling at Amanda's sweater and her hand, asking her to read to them.

Amanda looked at their little faces and decided that she could make it through one story. She certainly had time for it.

"All right," she agreed. "What would you like me to read?" she asked Mrs. Appleton.

"I was about to read an "Alice in Bibleland" book. It's Sandy's turn to choose the book today."

Amanda watched as a cute blonde girl with ringlets in her hair walked to the bookshelf, picked up a book, and brought it to her.

Mrs. Appleton motioned for Amanda to sit where she herself had been sitting when she saw Amanda. Sandy climbed onto Amanda's lap as soon as she was seated. Amanda'd forgotten that the book selector also had the privilege of sitting on the reader's lap. Jessi always wanted Amanda to come in when it was her turn to pick the book.

Amanda swallowed hard, successfully keeping back the tears. From the moment she opened the book and began to read, the children were entranced by the sound of her voice and she relaxed.

Once, Sandy snuggled so close to her, Amanda was afraid the girl had fallen asleep. She paused during the reading long enough to kiss her head.

For Amanda, story time seemed to drag, yet at the same time flew by too quickly. She loved to read and hold a child close when she did. Reluctantly, Sandy slid off her lap when the story was through.

"Mrs. Edwards," Sandy asked, "will you sing to us?"

"Sandy, I think we've asked enough of Mrs. Edwards for today. She came here to get something done and we're keeping her from it."

"That's very sweet of you to ask, Sandy, but Mrs. Appleton is right. I have to get some papers and get back home. Maybe I can stop by and read to you again." Amanda was about to stand up when she noticed Sandy's eyes.

Sandy's big blue eyes filled up with crocodile-sized tears. "I wanna you to sing." The little girl wasn't being whiny. Amanda sensed it was something more.

"What do you want me to sing?" she asked.

"'Mary Little Lamb.' You sing anyphing you want."

Amanda remembered Jessi pleading with her the morning they were stolen. Amanda'd been at the end of her proverbial rope that morning and had declined singing for her. Amanda wasn't going to make the same mistake again.

"How about "Amazing Grace"? Do you know that song?"

"Ah hugh," Sandy nodded.

"I'll need to stand up. I sing better standing up, and I'd really like it if you kids would sing with me if you know the words." Sandy stepped back and sat down with her friends.

Amanda stood up, cleared her throat, and sang the first, second, and third verses. The children sat as mesmerized when she sang as they had when she read. Mrs. Appleton and the children clapped when Amanda finished.

Mrs. Appleton reminded the children to thank Mrs. Edward for reading and singing.

After the children said thank you, Amanda made her way to the door. Mrs. Appleton joined her. "Thank you. That was beautiful."

"Why did Sandy ask me to sing? Was she in Jessi's class last year?"

"No, she wasn't. I don't know why she asked. Maybe because she knows a gentle, loving, giving, gifted person when she sees one.

"You're welcome here anytime as you can clearly see. Please don't be a stranger." The two women exchanged a hug and Amanda left.

Amanda hurried to the office and was greeted by more familiar faces. There was an awkward silence when she first stepped into the office, but it disappeared quickly when she told them why she was there. She left a short time later with the paperwork to enroll Justin for the remainder of the year and for both boys to start in the fall on opposite days.

* * *

Calvin took off his boots and set them on the floor mat. He smelled something cooking, but couldn't see the cook. "Woman," he playfully growled, "where are you hiding?"

"I'm down here," she called from the basement. "I'll be right up. I need to get this load into the dryer."

She joined him just a few minutes after the exchange. "I don't know what you're cooking in that kitchen, but it sure smells good. I hope we're eating soon."

"I need to fold this load of clothes and mash the potatoes. Then I'll have dinner on the table. You have time to take a shower if you want to," she said after she'd kissed him hello.

"Are you implying I stink?"

"Did I say that?"

"You didn't need to." He followed her back to the bedroom where she folded clothes. "How was your day?"

"Maybe we should wait 'til, during, or even after dinner before I answer that."

"Maybe you should tell me now. My shower, these clothes, our dinner can all wait." He took the clothes basket from her and set it on the bed. "You're more important than anything else on this earth to me and I want to know about your day."

Amanda sat down on the bed and Calvin joined her. She told him about the morning with Mrs. Cummings and the kids, and then the time she spent in the preschool class. He held her hand as she talked.

"As if all that wasn't emotional enough, I went to work and Mike asked me to start working on the window for Mother's Day. He could tell it upset me so he suggested Aimie do it. I said I could and spent the next two hours going through books I thought would make good gifts. I picked some really beautiful cards, too. Even with no budget the decorations were easy compared to having to select the stuff to go in the window.

"I'm not ready for Mother's Day without the girls." She began to cry.

"We'll get through it together, like we do every day."

She rubbed her eyes and thanked him for his support. Conscious of the time, she sent him to the bathroom and quickly folded the clothes.

Calvin had just shut the water off when the phone rang. Amanda turned off the mixer to answer the phone.

"Hello."

"Amanda is Calvin there?" Ronnie asked with urgency in his voice.

"He's in the shower right now. Is there something wrong?"

"I need to talk to him. Can you have him call me?"

"I'll have him answer the next time the phone rings. Why don't you give him five minutes to be safe?" Amanda was about to say good-bye and hang up when she heard Calvin open the bathroom door. "Hang on, Ronnie. I think I heard him open the bathroom door."

Amanda laid the phone down in the kitchen and went to the bedroom. She picked up the phone and handed it to Calvin. "It's Ronnie. He sounds upset."

Calvin took the phone from her and said hello. She returned to the kitchen to hang up the phone, and then returned to the bedroom.

Calvin paced the floor with his towel around his waist. He stopped in front of the closet and got a shirt, and then went to the dresser for jeans. Amanda got his socks and underwear out and set them on the bed. He was listening so intently he hardly noticed her.

Finally he spoke. "I'll be there as soon as I can. Stay put 'til I get there." Calvin hung up. He glared at Amanda as if he still didn't see her.

"I laid your socks and underwear on the bed," she said, hoping he'd finally notice her and explain.

He rubbed his forehead. "Thank you."

"Can you tell me what's going on and where you're going?"

"Jayson's been arrested."

Amanda gasped.

"He called Ronnie and asked him to bail him out. He wasn't given many details, but drugs were involved.

"I'm sorry about dinner," he said as he dressed. "I'm going to talk to Jayson and find out what what's going on. Depending on what he tells me, I may bail him out."

"I wonder why he didn't call his mother."

"I don't know. I'll know more when I get there." He pulled his shirt on and buttoned it. "I'll be home as soon as I can. Go ahead and eat when dinner's ready. I'll heat it up when I get back."

She followed him to the door and kissed him good-bye.

She'd just finished mashing the potatoes when the phone rang again. This time it was Melissa.

"Mrs. E., I hate to ask, but would you come get me from work? I wanna go to the jail to be with Jayson."

"I'll come get you, but there's no sense in going to the jail."

"I can't stay at work. I'm goin' crazy."

"I'll be there in a few minutes."

"Thank you."

Amanda cleaned off the beaters and then turned the Crock-Pot on low. When she reached the garage a few minutes later, she was grateful Calvin had taken the truck.

A half hour after Amanda left home, she and Melissa were back. On the way, Amanda learned that Jayson had been delivering drugs for someone he knew and he promised her he'd stop. The money was so good, he couldn't resist one last run. He justified what he was doing by saying she and Suzie had lots of needs. He wanted to be a good daddy.

Melissa told him he couldn't be a good daddy from prison. She sat on the couch and cried. Amanda handed the young woman a tissue.

A few minutes later the doorbell rang. Ronnie had picked Laurinda up and filled her in with what little he knew. They thought it would be a good idea to be at the Edwardses' when Calvin got home.

"Come in," Amanda said as she opened the door. They joined Melissa in the living room. Laurinda sat beside her and hugged her.

"We let you all down bad," she said through tears.

"No, you haven't," Laurinda said as she hugged her again.

Amanda sat down on the coffee table across from them. "Melissa, we've all made mistakes in our lives. We all learn from them and move on."

"I knew what he was doing but didn't tell no one. I didn't want him to get into trouble and he's in trouble anyway."

Amanda wished Calvin was there so he could pray. She wanted to ask Ronnie, but thought it might be awkward for him as a new Christian. Just as she was about to suggest they pray, he sat down next to her and suggested it himself.

Laurinda let go of Melissa, who wiped her tears with the new tissue Amanda offered her, and then they all joined hands.

Ronnie spoke with the same authority as Calvin when he prayed. Amanda remembered who'd been his prayer mentor.

"Heavenly Father, we come to You with heavy hearts. We're facing an uncertain situation with Jayson but we know nothing is uncertain for You. We're placing this situation into Your hands and asking You to give each of us Your peace. We know that all things work to the good for those who love You. There've been times in each of our lives where we haven't understood why something happened, but we always know that You're in control and You'll work it out to our benefit and Your glory." He squeezed Amanda's hand.

She squeezed his back for encouragement.

"Father, we thank You for everything You do for us. In Jesus' name, amen."

Everyone else said amen.

"Thank you," Melissa said. She didn't think prayer would help, but she didn't think it would hurt, either.

Amanda asked if anyone was hungry, offering to heat up the potatoes and finish the dinner she and Calvin were suppose to eat. She'd made extra, with plans for the leftovers, but at the moment she decided feeding more people seemed like a better idea.

Ronnie smiled. "I'm always hungry."

Laurinda nodded in agreement. "He's right."

Melissa sat on the couch in a daze.

"I'll help you in the kitchen so Laurinda and Melissa can talk," Ronnie offered.

For the second time tonight Ronnie surprised her. Amanda squeezed Melissa's shoulder, and then went to the kitchen. She showed Ronnie where the canned vegetables and can opener were kept. She got the potatoes out of the refrigerator and set a pan on the stove for the vegetables.

By the time the potatoes and mixed vegetables were warm, Amanda'd given Ronnie the job of slicing the roast she'd taken out of the Crock-Pot.

Just as the foursome sat down, the door opened and Calvin and Jayson walked in. To lighten the mood, Calvin said, "You weren't thinking of eating without us, were you?"

Amanda got up to get more plates, and Melissa got up to hug Jayson. He looked at her with tears in his eyes. "I'm so sorry, baby."

"I know," she whispered.

Once everyone was seated, Calvin gave thanks for the food and prayed again for the situation. Jayson asked Amanda if Calvin had been a lawyer in a previous life.

"I don't believe in a previous life, but no, he's never been a lawyer. Why?"

"You shoulda heard him, ma'am. He made me out like the perfect Boy Scout, course I'm not. He told 'em I'd help 'em get the guy I been delivering for if they'd go easy on me. He pointed out I ain't eighteen yet. He told 'em he'd be responsible for me 'til I get me a lawyer and we talk to the prosecuting guy. That's why we didn't stay there longer. Mr. E.'s got a real good name with them police. I can't thank him enough."

"Me, either," Melissa said shyly.

"It's what we do for friends," Calvin said. "Now let's eat this roast before it gets cold."

After dinner Ronnie agreed to take everyone home.

When Calvin and Amanda were finally alone, she asked, "Do you know why Jayson didn't call his mother?"

"He said that he tried, but she wasn't home. He said she works nights so he couldn't reach her. From what Ronnie told me about her, I suspect she was at home but already passed out for the night and he was afraid to call her. She might have made things worse for him and he knew it."

"What about his dad? I've never heard anyone talk about him."

"Ronnie said his dad left her when he found out his mom was pregnant with him. He doesn't know where he is."

"Maybe that's why Jayson's trying so hard to be a good father to Suzie. Do you think he'll have to go back to jail?"

"I'm going to try to keep him out if I can help it. I told the officer that I'd keep him working every day after school and Saturday all day long. Sunday's we may have him and Melissa come over here after church. I suspect Ronnie and Laurinda will be willing to help watch him, too. He has to bring me weekly progress reports from school so I know he's been there and trying. I'll keep the police updated."

"This sounds like a lot of work for both of you."

"It'll be harder for him than me. He has to contact the officer and let him know whenever he's contacted for another run. They want to get the dealer and buyer. If it goes higher than those people, the prosecutor might cut deals with them as well.

"We'll have to wait and pray."

"We've gotten good at that the past eight months." She gave him a weak smile.

"Yes, we have, darling." He gave her a hug. "It's been a long day, why don't we call it an early night."

"That's fine with me."

Chapter 28

"Do you want to do anything special tonight," Calvin asked Amanda after he kissed her hello.

"What do you have in mind?"

"I didn't say I had anything in mind."

"Judy stopped by the store today. She had Emily with her. She's such a beautiful baby. Reminded me of Katrina at her age. Anyway, Judy invited us over for pizza and a movie. I said I'd check with you when you got home."

"I asked you first." He gave her a sideways look. "Does that mean you don't want to go over there?"

"I didn't say that."

"But neither was it the first thing you said when I walked in the door or when I asked you if you wanted to do anything special." He reached out to her and pulled her into his arms. "Is something wrong?"

Amanda took a deep breath and then let it out against his broad chest. With moist eyes, she tipped her head back to look at him. "I'd rather take a sleeping pill and wake up on Monday."

He held her close. "I understand." He felt tears wet his shirt. "Honey, just because the girls aren't here doesn't make you any less their mother. You may not be able to care for their everyday needs and hold them in your arms, but you're still doing *the* most important thing any mother can do for her children—you pray for them daily."

"It's not enough," she sobbed, pulling him closer to her.

"I know." He stroked the back of her hair with his calloused hand and kissed her on the top of her head. "I wish I could love you enough to fill the void."

Amanda sniffled and pulled her head back to look into his eyes. "Usually you do, but this will be my first Mother's Day without them. I can't imagine how bad I'll feel on Sunday if I feel this bad already." She wiped her tears with the back of her hands.

Calvin reached into his back pocket and offered her his hankie. "It's not very dirty today."

Amanda looked at the piece of cloth. She thought she saw blood on it. "I believe I'll pass. Is that blood?"

"I scraped my knuckles today." He showed her his hand.

"Why isn't there a bandage on them?"

He shrugged and looked sheepishly at the floor. "Cause I didn't have one and didn't have time to stop and look for one."

"Did you wash it?"

He avoided eye contact with her. "Not exactly."

"What does that mean?" She didn't wait for him to answer. "You could get an infection!"

"Sorry." He wanted to say *mom* because she was in what he called *mother mode*. "Maybe you could clean and bandage it for me. I must warn you, I might fall in love with you."

She looked at him quizzically. "*Might* fall in love with me? What's that suppose to mean?"

"You know, the Florence Nightingale effect."

She stopped crying and rolled her eyes at him. "If you aren't *already* in love with me, Calvin Edwards, then I think we have bigger problems than your hand getting infected."

He smiled. They went to the bathroom to clean him up. Before they got there he said, "Are we going tonight or not? I need to know because if we're going, I'll take a shower. If we're staying home, I'll wait 'til morning to shower."

She stopped him as he walked into the bathroom. "You need a shower no matter what we decide to do tonight," she informed him. "I don't want a stinky man on my sheets."

"Ma'am, yes, ma'am," he continued to teased her. "I'll need help undressing. My hand hurts pretty bad."

"You're incorrigible," she said, but began unbuttoning his shirt anyway. "I didn't have anything planned for dinner because I didn't know if you were planning anything. I guess we could go to Judy and Bill's for dinner. I do have one other condition, besides you taking a shower."

"Anything for you, my love," he said as he grimaced when his shirt passed over his scrapped hand.

"Sorry. I think we should take dessert. I'm thinking cookies and cream cake."

"I agree. Why don't I finish up here and you call Judy. *Maybe* you'll be off the phone by the time I get out of the shower."

"Maybe, yourself," she said and turned to walk away.

Amanda said good-bye to Judy just as Calvin shut off the shower water. She sat on the bed waiting for him to come out. "See, I *was not* still on the phone when you got out of the shower."

He threw his towel at her. "Because you made the call from right there and knew when I shut off the water."

She was about to protest being hit with his wet towel, but decided the view was worth it. She redirected their attention to the night's plans.

"Judy said she thought the cake was a great idea. She warned me the movie would be G Rated. I told her We're okay with that, and then I asked if she wanted us to bring one of ours. They laughed."

One hour later Judy opened the door of her new home and life to allow her longtime friends to come in. After the cake was refrigerated, Amanda and Judy joined everyone else in the family room to help the boys pick a movie.

During the movie and dinner, Amanda watched the boys, trying to decide which personality types they were. Justin was clearly a beaver, always asking questions. When he announced everyone's napkins had to be folded a certain way, Amanda almost died laughing. She decided Christopher was mainly an otter. He was all over Bill and Calvin even during the movie, telling them about his day. When a character in the movie made a gesture that Christopher liked, he had to do it as well, and often. Emily was too little for a specific personality type. She sat on Judy's lap through most of the movie, cuddling.

After the movie the boys wanted cake. Amanda thought they were both more like bulls in a ring with a red cape. Then they charged into the kitchen with plenty of gusto.

Calvin caught Amanda's eyes as the boys waited eagerly for their cake. "Remind you of anyone?" he mouthed to her. She nodded, remembering the many times each of their daughters behaved the same way at dessert time.

After dessert, Judy excused herself and the children so she could get them ready for bed. They shared one room since everyone was so young. Amanda offered to clean up the kitchen while Judy was gone, so the two men retired to the basement to discuss Bill's ideas for creating an office.

A short time later, Judy returned to the kitchen down the back staircase. She called down to Bill and told him the kids were ready for him.

Judy explained, "I get the work out of the way and he prays with them. I don't get the boys all wound up the way Bill does when he gets them ready for bed. We seem to be making a pretty good team at this parenting thing."

"Calvin was the same way with the girls. Sometimes even after prayers I'd have to stay and get them settled down again."

"I hadn't thought about staying with them. The kids are with me and their grandmother more than they are their dad, so I thought it'd be better to give them some quiet time. I'll talk it over with Bill when we go to bed tonight.

"Speaking of going to bed, I don't think you've seen the new comforter and curtains in our bedroom."

The ladies left Calvin sitting at the table looking out the window while they went to see the new items.

"This has got to be one of the most beautiful beds I've ever seen. The comforter and pillows only increase its beauty. I'm not sure why you bought curtains. It doesn't look like you close them very much."

"I don't, but the windows needed something, and we planned ahead in case anyone builds off to our left."

"I suppose so. So, how's it going in the kitchen?"

"Oh my gosh! Before you said kitchen, I was afraid you were going to ask how it's going in here."

Amanda laughed. "That's none of my business, but the kitchen is a different matter. I've given you recipes and wondered if you needed any help with them."

It was Judy's turn to laugh. "I haven't actually tried any of them." She twirled her hair with her finger. "Bill's been doing all the cooking."

Both women laughed this time. "He's a really great cook. And me, well, you know how bad I am." They sat down facing one another in the chairs set in front of the window.

"You're only bad at it because you've never tried very hard."

"Maybe so, but it's better this way, really. I do help out. I cut up vegetables and stir things. I'm really best at cleaning up after him." Again they both laughed. "But seriously, I am learning a lot from him. Maybe someday I'll be able to take over."

Amanda smiled. "Maybe someday," she repeated.

"I ordered the pizza tonight and paid for it out of our joint checking account."

Amanda laughed again.

"Don't laugh. It's weird for me to have a joint checking account or even one that has more money in it than I can spend in a week. Well, maybe not that much. Anyway, he pays all the household bills, and I pay for the groceries and all of the expenses from my house still. It's weird being a landlady, but the situation seems to be working out so far."

"I'm glad to hear that's going well. Have you made a decision about what to do with the salon?"

"When Elizabeth's roommate graduates and gets her license, we've decided to have her work with me for a couple of months, and then she'll probably take over all my clients. I can already see how much more I'm needed here than I am as a hairdresser. If this girl is good, then I won't mind leaving my clients to her.

"Did you know she came to church last week with Elizabeth?"

"I did notice someone sitting with Elizabeth, but I never got a chance to meet her. Is she a Christian?"

"Elizabeth said she is. That makes me feel even better about turning the salon and my customers over to her.

"What's going on with Ronnie and Laurinda? I heard they set a date."

"They're trying to decide when would be the best time to leave my husband alone for a week so they can take a honeymoon. We told them it would be better to think more about when *they* could afford to miss the time and less about what Edwards Construction will do without them. I've done payroll before. I can do it again if need be.

"No one will be working Father's Day weekend because we're going to Janesville for my grandparents' fiftieth wedding anniversary, but that's only four weeks away. I think they want a bigger wedding than you had, but not as big as what Calvin and I had."

Bill stuck his head in the room. "Are you two staying in here all night or do you think you are woman enough to take us on in euchre?"

Judy smiled at her husband. "We're discussing wedding plans."

"It's a little late for that, isn't it? We're already married."

"Not our wedding," Judy said as she got up and walked over to him. "Ronnie and Laurinda's wedding. You know I'm perfectly happy with the wedding we've already had. "

"I do know that," Bill said as he kissed her on the forehead.

Amanda joined them by the door and they all returned to the kitchen eating area. Judy gently caught Amanda's arm and held her back for a second. "I want you to know I'm not having as much trouble in the bedroom as I am the kitchen, thankfully."

They laughed and then took their spots opposite each other so they could be partners for the first game. Since the women won the first game, the men decided it might be better to split them up, so each took his own wife to be his partner in the next game.

*   *   *

The next morning after breakfast, Calvin said, "If you don't mind, I'm going to go to Jackson today. We're getting close to being finished with the station. The guys really appreciated the free gas last time we finished ahead of schedule, and the cash bonus the owner gave us wasn't bad, either. I think that's where Ronnie got most of the money for Laurinda's engagement ring."

"I figured you were going. Is anyone else going?"

"Ronnie is 'watching' Jayson today and said they'd be stopping in for a while. I think they're both more interested in the extra money working on Saturday gets them than hanging out with me all day."

"Oh really," Amanda said. "Now if it were me, I'd be more interested in hanging out with you all day than the money."

"Then put your *money* where your mouth is and come with me."

"What would I do?"

"You still know which end of a hammer to hold, right?"

"I do, but I doubt you're still knocking things down. What would you *really* have me doing?"

"Hanging, taping, and mudding drywall. Interested?"

"I might be. How much *money* will I make?"

He tickled her. "I make all the money around here, except for the part that gets returned to the Family Christian Store," he teased. He tickled her some more, and then in one move pulled her shirt off over her head.

She squealed. "I thought you wanted me to go to work with you. This," she gestured toward her topless self, "doesn't look like you have work on your mind."

"Oh, but I *do* have work on my mind." He grinned at her.

She blushed.

He dangled her shirt in front of her. "You can't hang drywall in this. For that matter, I've half a mind to take your pants off, too."

"You're right about that half a mind thing," she teased him. "But I believe I'll take my own pants off. How long do I have before we leave?"

"Five minutes."

"That's all?"

"Honey, if I stay here looking at you half dressed much longer, we won't make it there at all."

Amanda grabbed her shirt. "I'll be ready," she said over her shoulder as she went to the closet to find grubby jeans and a work shirt. "Wait a minute, this means I'll have to ride in that yucky old truck, doesn't it?"

"It does." He smiled.

The couple arrived at the station a few minutes after nine. Ronnie and Jayson were already there.

"I hope you two haven't been waiting long," Calvin said as he walked around to open Amanda's door. "My helper had to change clothes before we could leave."

The younger men acknowledged Amanda, and then said they hadn't been waiting long.

Calvin unlocked the station door and let Amanda inside first. Ronnie and Jayson followed and Calvin locked the door behind himself. Amanda turned to look at him questioningly. "I don't want any of you to get away until we're done here."

Amanda squinted at him. "Do you really expect us to get all this hung today?"

"I figured the three of us could get it done, so with you here it'll go even faster."

"Boss, I don't mean no disrespect to Mrs. E., but you sure 'bout this?" Jayson asked.

"She helped me hang drywall when we converted her parents' attic playroom into our first home. She's a great helper. If we get this all hung, taped, and the first coat of mud on it, it will be dry by Monday. When we come in Monday, we'll start sanding at one end and get the second coat of mud on after that. If we paint by Thursday morning, we'll begin putting the flooring down on Friday. If we finish the floor by Saturday afternoon, we'll get the fixtures in the following Monday. It's possible we'll finish a week early."

"Why would we wanna finish early, boss?"

"I got this one, boss." Ronnie explained what had happened with the free gas and the cash bonus the last time they completed a job early for this owner, while Calvin and Amanda cut apart the first two pieces of drywall.

From then on the foursome worked together like they'd been doing it forever. As soon as one piece was cut, hung, and screwed into place, another one was ready for the next spot. Calvin and

Amanda worked in the bathroom together, while the other two continued with the main part of the building.

"I am glad you suggested I come with you today," Amanda said once they were alone in the bathroom.

"Why's that?"

"I didn't want to sit around the house today. Mom and Dad left this morning to stay with Maria, Don, and the kids. Doreen is joining them there tonight. I didn't have anything to do or anywhere to go."

"I'm happy to have you. If you ever feel like this through the week, you just let me know and I'll be equally happy to keep you busy then, too." He kissed her on the nose.

As soon as they finished in the bathroom, Calvin set Amanda up to mud everything she could reach in the room. Later, while she made the lunch run, he mudded what she'd been unable to reach. After lunch, she started mudding the main store as high as she could reach, while the men finished hanging the rest of the drywall. Calvin was right about how far they'd get if they worked together. Except for the short time Amanda left to get lunch, she stayed working right beside them.

Calvin locked the door behind them as the crew left for the night. Ronnie and Jayson declined the Edwardses' offer to join them for dinner at the Old County Buffet. They said their women were much less likely to join them in an all-day project like Amanda'd done, and they wanted to get back to them.

"Thanks for your help, guys. This was a productive day." The men shook hands, and the two younger ones were gone before Calvin opened the truck door for Amanda.

"I guess they're in a hurry," she said.

He leaned over and kissed her. "Not every man is as blessed as I am to have a woman as wonderful as you."

"You know Laurinda and Melissa are both wonderful women. They have lives and I don't right now."

He started the truck. "You have a life. It's just different than it was when the kids were with us," he said, trying to keep her tears away.

It was too late, she was already crying. "I know. I just miss them so much."

He reached over, taking her hand in his. He kissed her gently. "I know, honey. Me, too." He looked at her, tears streaming down her face. "Do you still want to get dinner down here or would you rather go home?"

She sniffled and wiped her eyes. "We better eat here. I don't have anything defrosted for dinner, and it would take me a long time to get anything ready."

"I don't mind waiting if you don't mind cooking."

"I mind waiting. You worked me hard today and lunch seems like it never really happened. I'm hungry," she rubbed her left shoulder with her right hand, "and sore and ugly."

"You've never been ugly a day in your life. I'd offer to let you go back inside and wash your face, but as you know, there's no running water at the moment."

"I'll go straight to the bathroom when we get to the restaurant."

He put the truck in reverse and said, "Okay. Did you want to drive?"

She shook her head and laughed. "No, I'm good."

* * *

"I don't want to go to church this morning," Amanda said, pulling the covers over her head.

"Why not?" Calvin asked.

"I want to stay in bed and not deal with this."

"What does your favorite verse say, Amanda Edwards?"

355

"Which one? I have lots."

"You know exactly which one I'm talking about."

"You know me too well." She pulled the sheet and blanket off her head. "Philippians 4:13," she started. "I can do all things through Christ who strengthens me. Just because I can, doesn't mean I want to," she said as she pulled the covers back over her head.

He pulled the covers off her. "I know, but I will be right beside you all the way."

"What if I have to go to the bathroom?" she protested.

"Then we'll go into the unisex bathroom and I'll still be with you."

"I don't have anything to wear."

"You can wear that beautiful white outfit you've wanted to wear but say you are saving for a special Sunday."

"You have an answer for everything, don't you?"

"I do. Just call me the objection answer man."

"I'd rather call you than have you here not letting me go back to sleep."

"If you really don't want to go, I'll understand. I don't want to leave you alone. That's not good for you. Going to church is."

"I know. What happens if I cry?"

"I'll hand you a clean hankie and you'll wipe your eyes."

"What if people stare at me?"

"How long have you gone to this church? Do you honestly think people would stare at you, especially today?"

Before she could answer, he went on. "You've gone here all your life and not one person who knows you would deny you crying today. If there are guests and they stare, let them. I'll have my arm tucked securely around you, no matter what."

Amanda couldn't think of any more objections, and even if she did, she knew he'd just shut them down. Knowing he was right enabled her to climb out of bed.

He'd pondered getting her a Mother's Day card, but decided against it. Instead, he got her a card telling her how grateful he was she's his wife, and reminded her how happy he was she loved him. She found the card on the table when she sat down to have breakfast.

She cried over breakfast, and then showered, dressed, and went to church with the only person on earth who she felt truly understood her pain, the children's earthly father.

*　　*　　*

At church, Amanda saw Judy on her way to the nursery with Emily. She thought she should have gotten Judy a first-time Mother's Day card from work. She could tell by the flower pinned to her dress that Bill hadn't forgotten it was her first Mother's Day. She smiled as she thought of how wonderful Bill was for her best friend.

Amanda waited for Judy to leave the nursery to tell her Happy Mother's Day. She didn't like the idea of going into the nursery where she herself left her daughters once they were too big to sleep through the service and too small to sit through it without misbehaving. Amanda thought of the last Sunday she had brought Katrina here. Jessi had been able to stay upstairs without trouble for several weeks so they kept her with them that Sunday as well.

Amanda was so deep in thought she didn't realize Judy'd left the nursery and was standing a few feet away talking to Beth Baxter. It wasn't until she heard them laughing that she realized she'd been so deep in thought. She wiped her eyes, but discovered no tears. Remembering didn't hurt as much anymore, she thought.

Calvin joined her in the hall, apologizing for taking so long to finish up in Sunday school. "You ready to go upstairs?"

"I wanted to tell Judy Happy Mother's Day, but she's busy. I'll wait until after church. We may as well get up there and get this over with," she said.

"Have I told you how beautiful you look today?"

"Only a dozen times already."

Amanda made it through the service with the aid of the man she loved close beside her. She told several of her female friends Happy Mother's Day, and accepted their kind words about her situation. Laurinda hugged her and promised to pray for her during the day. Judy invited them over for lunch. Amanda thanked her for the offer, but declined.

Once she and Calvin were alone, she asked, "May we go out for lunch? I'm really hungry." She was in no hurry to get back home to a childless house.

"Tell me where and I'll drive us there." He paused when he realized what he'd said. "Hey, I'm a poet."

She rolled her eyes at him. "You're a poet and don't know it, but your feet show it because they're Longfellow's."

It was his turn to roll his eyes at her. "And I thought I was bad." They both laughed. Something they needed right then.

Chapter 29

By the end of the week, Edwards Construction was on schedule for finishing the gas station ahead of time just as Calvin predicted. Jayson worked in town with some of the crew on another job they had going so he wouldn't have to lose time on the long drive. He showed daily progress reports from his teachers to someone on the crew, who wrote his initials on it to prove they'd seen it. On Friday night, Jayson gave them all to Calvin when he delivered their pizza to them. He'd gotten a real delivery job where Melissa worked.

On Saturday, Jayson was contacted by the guy who gave him the drugs and the directions to the drop, which changed every week. The police set up a global position system in his car trunk and followed him around from a safe distance in unmarked cars. Since there was more than one drop spot, they told him he had to keep going for more than one night. That meant they'd bust more people, but it also made it more dangerous for Jayson. If anyone ever suspected what he was doing, they wouldn't think twice about killing him.

He asked Calvin if everything could be done before he turned eighteen so he wouldn't have a record. Calvin discussed it with the officer in charge, who said they'd try.

The following Monday all of the Edwards Construction employees that worked on the project were scheduled to be at the gas station in Jackson first thing in the morning to finish the job. Jayson had permission to leave class as long as Calvin or Ronnie picked him up. The school staff was very understanding and helpful to his situation.

Ronnie picked Jayson up from the school when Jayson got there, signed in and out. By the time they arrived in Jackson, the crew was on their way to having all the fixtures in place. Ronnie and Jayson jumped right in and began helping.

The gas station owner showed up at noon and brought everyone subs. Then he made them an offer they couldn't refuse. He'd brought a truckload of supplies for the shelves they'd just installed. He offered each person an extra one hundred dollars cash to stay and stock the shelves. Not everyone took him up on the offer, but everyone accepted the free fill-up before calling it a short day. Calvin also declined the offer, leaving Ronnie, Jayson, and Joe. The owner offered each of them two hundred dollars apiece since they were the only three left and he'd been expecting to pay six hundred dollars anyway.

"This is a better way to make extra money, don't you think so, Jayson?" Ronnie asked him once the two of them were alone in the truck getting more supplies.

Jayson smiled. "You bet, and I can't get into trouble for it." He slapped his friend on the back. "Melissa said you asked Laurinda to marry you. That true?"

"Yup. I've been praying about it and getting plenty of godly counsel from Calvin."

"Whatta ya mean by godly counsel?" Jayson asked as he held the door for Ronnie to get inside with his boxes before he drove the dolly full of boxes into the store.

"When you have a decision to make, it's a good idea, no, it's a great idea, to get input from people who love and care about you. People who have your best interest at heart and a good relationship with God. That's why it's called godly counsel."

Ronnie cut a box open and the two men began stacking bags of chips on the shelves. "Take your *other* part-time job, for example.

If you'd asked me if it was a good idea, I'd have said no." Ronnie stopped working and looked directly at Jayson until he had his undivided attention. "I think it's time you knew something about me that I haven't told you yet."

"You ran drugs?"

"No, I never got into that, but I belonged to a gang while I lived at home with my mother and brother in Chicago. I would've turned out worse than I am now if I'd stayed there. Or I might be dead."

"I woulda never guessed you as a gangbanger. You're clean cut and nice and Christian and all that."

"Wannna hear something funny?"

They broke down the boxes they'd emptied and returned to the truck for more.

"I like a good joke."

"It's not a joke. It's the story of why I met you and Melissa." Ronnie handed him some boxes to put on the dolly. "It happened a few weeks before we met you. I was in Sunday school and mentioned I'd been in a gang. One of the guys suggested I consider signing up at the youth center to be a mentor. I said, 'After I've been telling you how bad I was, what makes you think I'd be a good mentor?' Know what he said to me?"

"No." Jayson held the door for Ronnie again.

"You're not in a gang any more, are you? I said no, because my boss would bust my chops if I was." They both laughed. "He said I had a story to tell about how God had worked in my life." Ronnie cut open the top box to figure out where its contents should go.

"Then he said I might help steer kids clear of ever joining a gang. I don't think there are a lot of gangs around here, but obviously there are other ways to get into trouble."

"Tell me 'bout it. I love Suzie, but I wish Melissa and me'd of waited 'til we got married before we had sex."

"Do you plan to marry her?"

"If she'll want me after all this trouble, I'm in."

"Maybe we can have two weddings the same day."

"Sounds good to me. Then I'd only have ta dress up once." Jayson and Ronnie both laughed.

They were still working when Calvin returned from talking to the gas station owner.

"Aren't you boys done yet?" he asked teasingly.

"No, sir," Jayson replied. "In case you didn't notice, Joe got his two bills and split an hour ago."

"I was with the owner when he paid him. Are you interested in some good news?"

"Who's the good news for?" Ronnie asked.

"Everybody in the company."

"Does this dude have another gas station?" Jayson asked.

"Or gives us free gas for a year?" Ronnie asked.

"Neither. But it certainly could help pay for gas for a year. How would you gentleman feel about building your first house for him?"

"Where and when do we start?" Ronnie asked.

"It's about halfway between here and his station in Lansing. He's tired of driving for an hour to get to Lansing to check on the station, so he wants a house in the middle."

"You don't usually build private homes, do you boss?" Ronnie asked.

"I have when the project and timing are right. Did Laurinda tell you she'd taken in several applications from very qualified young people since Jayson started with us?"

"She mentioned the apps but didn't say they were very qualified." Ronnie slapped Jayson on the back. "Why didn't you tell us you had talented friends?"

"None of my friends are talented. You know any of their names, boss?"

"No. But with this project now on the list and some of us leaving town in three weeks, maybe it's time I met them. I'd like you to look at the list of names tomorrow after school to see if you know any of them and what kind of recommendation you'd give them. I believe most of them are looking for summer work before going to college. One of them said he'd worked for a construction company last summer before his family moved up here."

"I do know that guy. Did he say anything about playing ball?" Laurinda didn't mention anything about him playing ball.

"I'll bring you my daily report to the office when I can get out of class tomorrow. That okay?"

"That'd be great. I'd appreciate the help."

"I don't have a daily report for today."

The three men laughed, and then everyone worked together to finish stocking the store with everything from the truck.

"Whatta ya doing with your extra cash?" Jayson asked Ronnie on the drive back to get his car from Melissa.

"Laurinda and I are going to see my mom on Father's Day weekend. She fell a while back, and when they X-rayed her to see if anything was broken, they found a spot on her lung. The doctors are monitoring it for growth. I want to go, but I shouldn't go so Laurinda and I don't start our marriage in debt. I owe $500 on my car and $500 on her engagement ring.

"I don't want her parents to pay for the whole wedding, and my mom can't afford to help, so I want to cover things that the groom's family usually covers, whatever that is. I'm hoping to show up after Laurinda and her mother work everything out and tell me where to stand."

"Amen, bro'. When I marry Melissa, we'll go to a justice of the peace."

"It was good enough for Laurinda's friend Judy and her husband Bill. But maybe Melissa will want a fancy wedding."

"We're poor. Both our mamas don't have much. Everybody hopes my scholarship with the university will help me get out of the poor side of town and become a rich and famous football player. I ain't even decided on a subject to study when I get there. The counselor said I'd need me some basic classes the first year so that's how I'll start."

"Have you considered construction as a major?"

Jayson shrugged. "I hadn't thoughta that."

"You're certainly physically fit enough to meet the demands. Tell you what. Let's take this house project as a fork in the road."

"What?"

"Work on the house 'til it's finished, and then see how you feel about construction as a career."

"Maybe I'll design houses and leave the building part up to you and the boss. I love to draw. I'll show ya some of my drawings the next time I see ya. Deal?" Jayson said as he stuck out his right hand to shake Ronnie's.

"Deal."

* * *

Calvin walked through the door to a wonderful mixture of smells. The kitchen was especially warm so he was certain Amanda had the oven on for quite some time. As he took another step in, he noticed the table piled high with cookies. He was sure he made out at least three different kinds. He sat down to take off his work boots as quietly as he could. He planned to help himself to some of those cookies, but he didn't want to alert the baker. Since she wasn't in the kitchen and he didn't hear her downstairs, he presumed she was in the bedroom and wouldn't hear him.

He was wrong. He had his hand just above the table trying to decide which kind to take first, when he heard her yell from the bedroom that he wasn't allowed to eat any of the cookies. Like a scolded child, he quickly pulled his hand back, turned on his heels, and made his way to the bedroom.

"Why can't I have any cookies?" he asked when he found her folding clothes on their bed.

"Because, my beloved cookie monster, I'm making them for the bake sale Wednesday night at church."

"Today is only Monday. You can make more between now and then." He looked at her with puppy dog eyes. "Can't I have just one?"

"I suppose you *could* have just one, but which kind will it be?"

"I could try one of each kind to be sure they are okay for sale."

"You're sooooo self sacrificing. I'll let you have one of each if you promise to help me finish baking the rest."

"Yes, ma'am," she said as he ran out of the bedroom toward the kitchen.

He returned in just a matter of minutes and asked, between bites, why there was going to be a bake sale at church.

She said the women's group was filling a dresser for a young mother in need.

"You ladies are gonna fill the dresser with money?"

"No, we're raising money to buy baby supplies to put into the dresser. I thought I'd use some of the stamps I've earned from work to purchase a woman's devotional Bible for the mother. The contents of the dresser don't have to be all about the baby's needs. One lady said she'd get lotion and pretty smelling soaps for the mother."

"You ladies sure are thoughtful. I'd have filled the dresser with money, or your cookies," he said as he popped the last bite of the last cookie into his mouth. "What's for dinner?" he asked with his mouth full.

She threw one of his T-shirts at him. "Don't talk with your mouth full. We're having hot pork sandwiches with mashed potatoes and gravy if that's okay with you."

"Last night's meal, new presentation."

She threw a sock at him. This time he ducked and it missed him. He stepped toward her with his hands poised to get her.

"I didn't mean it," she squealed.

"I'm going to tickle you anyway," he said as he wrapped his arms around her waist.

Suddenly, the timer on the night stand began to buzz. "My cookies!" she exclaimed.

"Saved by the bell," he said as he released her. "I'll finish up in here while you get dinner ready," he playfully growled.

Over dinner she filled him in on everything she'd learned at work. "I'll be working more hours next week. Michael's taking time off to spend with his grandchildren in Ohio and asked if I could help Aimie by being at the store more often. It's like she's taking his place and I'm taking hers."

"Will you get a pay raise? Oh wait, that'd just give you more money to spend there."

"I'll have you know, I've put my last two paychecks directly into our savings account. Now we have ten dollars in there."

The timer went off again. She dealt with the cookies before returning to the counter where they were eating.

"I have more news. I had a visitor at the store today."

"Someone famous again?"

"Not exactly. Laurinda came by to update me on the wedding. She and Ronnie spent last night at the Bowman's making plans. She'd gotten several dates that the church and pastor would be available. She also called around to see about a place for the reception. She presented everything to her parents and Ronnie. Ronnie asked her to make this as easy on him as possible. He likes to be told what he needs to pay for, where to go, and what time to be there. Typical male."

"Sounds good to me." Amanda rolled her eyes at him and took a bite of her sandwich.

"That's pretty much what you did for me, so why shouldn't Ronnie have the same thing done for him." Calvin thought for a moment, and then added, "I didn't pay for anything, did I? My parents took care of that."

"Traditionally, the groom's parents pay for the cakes and the rehearsal dinner the night before the wedding. Laurinda said Ronnie wants to pay for whatever his mother would usually have paid for." Amanda changed the cookie sheets in the oven again and came back to the counter with a big grin on her face.

"I know that look, Mrs. Edwards. You're up to something. What is it and how much is it going to cost us?"

"How about we let the Family Christian Store pay for it?" she smiled.

"Mike is forever telling you he doesn't have a budget for anything. What makes you think he'll pay for this idea?" He thought for a moment. "How'd we get from wedding plans to work?"

"We're still talking about the wedding, and Michael won't be paying for this directly. I'd be using my paycheck to do it."

"I'm beginning to understand. You want to pay for anything Ms. Colthorp or Ronnie might have to pay for, is that it?"

"Kind of."

"And I thought I was doing so well at beginning to understand."

"Well, you have it mostly right. However, I was thinking of asking someone else to cover the cakes. Actually, better than cover the cakes. I'd like her to bake and decorate them."

"I'm sure Judy would love to help out. I trust you haven't talked to her about it yet."

She put the last bite of her dinner in her mouth, picked up her plate, and headed to the dishwasher. She swallowed, and then asked him to keep an ear on the timer, replace the baked cookies with the next pan of unbaked cookies, and not to eat any more so she could call Judy. "I'll be right back, and I'll be listening for you while I'm gone." She poked him in the side as she went to the living room to call her friend.

"Yes, mother," he called after her.

Judy was helping Bill with dinner when Amanda called. She had a few minutes so she listened as Amanda explained what she'd like Judy to do, saying she'd pay for all the ingredients. She just needed an expert cake baker and decorator.

"I don't know about an expert, but I'll do it," Judy told her. "Do they have a date set yet?"

"She has two picked out and is making more calls tomorrow. We're sure it won't be until after Labor Day. The house Calvin is planning to build in Mason or Leslie should be done by then, and Ronnie will have no more debt."

"Okay, hold the phone a minute here. Did you say that your husband's going to take on a new build again?"

"Sounds like it. The owner of the two gas stations they've already done wants to live in between them. He's asked Calvin to build him a house. I don't know if he even has plans for the house yet. The guy didn't even ask for a bid, he just asked Cal to build it."

"From what I've seen of our house, I know the guy will be pleased with the outcome. What debt does Ronnie have? He's just a kid. Besides, shouldn't his parents pay for this stuff?"

"Laurinda said something about her engagement ring and his car. He hasn't seen his father in years, and his mother isn't able to help out. That's why Calvin and I want to help with the dinner, and I was hoping you'd help with the cake."

"Now things are making sense. I've got to get back to my KP for now, but I expect you to keep me posted on this wedding thing. Be sure to find out what kind of cakes they want."

"No problem. Thanks for your help. Tell Bill and the kids we said hello."

"Will do. Talk to you later."

Amanda returned to find her husband had not only done what she asked, he'd also removed the batch from the pan and was in the process of putting more dough onto the cooled pan.

"Thank you for your additional help, sweetheart. That was thoughtful."

He looked at her with a cute smile. "Does that mean I can have cooookie?"

Amanda laughed at her cookie monster husband and nodded her head.

*   *   *

"Who was that?" Bill asked after Judy said good-bye and returned to help with dinner.

"Amanda. Laurinda and Ronnie are working on a wedding date. She wants to know if I'll bake and decorate the cakes."

"You can do that?" he asked, surprised.

"I can't cook, but I can bake and decorate cakes. It's been a while, but I think I'll remember when the time comes." She thought for a moment, and then added, "Kind of like other things in my life."

"When's the wedding?" he asked with a grin.

"Sometime after Labor Day. Why do you ask?"

"Then you'll have plenty of time to practice your cake baking and decorating skills on us." He wrapped his arms around her and pulled her close to him. "Except for the cake that our friends brought over last weekend, I don't think we've had cake in this house yet." He patted his stomach as best he could with her pulled so tightly to him. "I'll gladly be your guinea pig for this project."

She pulled away from him so she could check on the kids in the playroom, and then set the table. "You're beginning to sound like Calvin. He's always willing to sacrifice his stomach for sampling Amanda's cookies."

She put a plate on the table and had an idea. "I just remembered that there's going to be a bake sale at church this Wednesday." She explained why. "I think I can find time between now and Wednesday to bake a cake and get it frosted."

He joined her at the table, bringing the main course with him. "I think that's a wonderful idea. But why will it take two days?"

"I'll explain over dinner. I'll pour drinks if you go get the kids."

After everyone was seated and the food had been blessed, Judy explained why it would take two days to do the cake. The boys became very excited about the idea of having cake, until Judy explained that she'd be taking it to the church for the bake sale and that someone else might buy it. Justin was very disappointed until his father suggested he could buy the cake since the money was going to a good cause.

"I can't wait 'til Wesday to have cake!" Justin exclaimed with lots of little-boy excitement. "Can't we have cake now?"

"It's pronounced Wed-nes-day," Bill explained to his son. After he heard himself say it, he told Justin, "Never mind." He leaned over to Judy and whispered in her ear, "Maybe we won't have too many cakes around here. They usually involve lots of sugar." He kissed her ear and they laughed.

Chapter 30

The Wednesday evening bake sale was a wonderful success. The Cummings family went home with the beautiful cake Judy'd taken. It cost Mr. Cummings more than he'd planned to pay. It was the item that had the most bids and highest price as well. Amanda and Judy volunteered to do the shopping for the items not yet donated for the dresser. This had been the big push to finish filling it, and with the nearly two hundred dollars raised, the ladies were sure they could finish filling it and have it ready for pick up by the following week. The ladies group decided to leave it in the sanctuary through Sunday so everyone in the congregation could see it before it was delivered to the home for unwed mothers.

The following week Amanda was grateful for the extra hours at work and the distraction. She was beginning to think more and more about Father's Day weekend and what she hoped would happen. Aimie tried to keep her busy, but sometimes she found Amanda staring out the front window with a dazed look on her face. Aimie and Amanda became even better friends now that they worked together, so Aimie understood when she found Amanda that way. She didn't say anything directly about the subject, but instead would gently direct Amanda's attention to something inside the store. Michael left them instructions about cleaning the store from top to bottom. When they weren't busy helping customers, the women's time was spent moving books, cleaning off shelves, and replacing the books.

Laurinda came in on Monday to tell Amanda that Judy had volunteered to bake their wedding cakes, as well as doing her hair for free. Amanda only smiled when Laurinda said Judy had volunteered to bake the cakes. Amanda and Aimie spent as much time as they could helping her pick out wedding invitations. They narrowed it down to three. Laurinda said she'd bring her mother back later in the week to help decide on the final one. Amanda offered to give her a twenty-five percent off discount coupon she had recently acquired after getting ten punches on her perks card. Ronnie already asked Calvin to be his best man so Amanda knew they'd be told where the rehearsal dinner would take place as soon as the bride knew.

By the end of the week the store looked and smelled brand new. Before she knew it, it was Friday night. Amanda was preparing for story hour on Saturday. Calvin had brought home dinner on Tuesday, they'd eaten at church on Wednesday night, they had clean out the refrigerator night on Thursday, and now they were settling in for their usual Friday night pizza. Amanda brought home four books to choose from for the reading the next day. Calvin sat and listened as she read the first book aloud to him between bites. When the pizza was gone and the four books all read, they discussed the story line and the advantages of each. They finally decided on a book by Max Lucado called *The Wemmicks* about a craftsman named Eli who made little wooden people, and they gave each other gray dots and gold stars based on how well or poorly they did things. The main characters were a boy who had nothing but dots and a girl who had neither. She told the boy the dots and stars didn't stick to her because what other people thought about her was less important to her than what Eli thought about her. The Edwardses decided the story would be good to share with children so they'd understand that what God thinks about them is more important than what others think of them.

Amanda was pleased to see Mrs. Cummings and her two recently adopted sons at the store on Saturday. Amanda was concerned when she saw how tired and pale her friend looked. Judy assured her it was nothing and promised to make a doctor's appointment if she didn't feel better soon.

Michael returned on Monday and was pleased with the way the store looked and smelled, so impressed he offered to let them attempt the same wonderful feat with the back room and the storage area in the upcoming weeks. Amanda and Aimie looked at each other and laughed.

"We'll do it," Aimie said, "but you have to give us some budget to work with."

"Define 'some,'" Michael said.

"We actually talked about doing the back room but ran out of time."

"And energy," Amanda added.

"We'd need to get a few storage containers, and I'd prefer plastic over cardboard. They'll last longer."

"We'll discuss it when you tell me *exactly* how much money you want."

"Agreed," the two women said simultaneously.

Amanda was grateful for more busywork this week, as well as the extra income it would provide for the "special project" as she and Calvin called it.

When Amanda arrived home, she found Calvin at the table with a set of blueprints spread out. He was so engrossed in them he didn't hear her come in the door.

"I see you're home early," she said as she took off her coat.

He stood up and stretched as if he'd been there a while. "I didn't hear you come in." He met her as she came into the kitchen and hugged her. "I've been here for a couple of hours, I think."

"What's that?"

"Blueprints for the house we'll be building this summer. The gas station owner found a piece of land that's perfect for this house."

"May I see?"

"You know I'd love to show it to you. This is going to be an incredible home. He has one child left at home, and his ailing mother-in-law will be moving in with them so he's adding an extra bedroom and bathroom just for her. She'll have a separate entrance onto the porch."

"I love the wraparound porch."

"Me, too," he said as he returned to his seat at the table. "It will work really well with the walkout basement he wants. I'm going to meet him tomorrow to look at the land he has picked out. I'm contracting the basement work. He wants a wood basement and I've never done one of those before."

"That never stopped you before."

"I know, but it'll work out, because if the property deal goes through as soon as he hopes it will, they'll break ground in two weeks just before we leave. I've already talked to a company I want to do it. The owner is meeting us there tomorrow. By the time we get back the following Monday they should be ready to pour the basement floor. On Tuesday our crew will start the first floor."

"Aren't you good?" She kissed him on the head and went to start dinner. "Will there be anything for me to do on Tuesday?"

"Darling, I can *always* find something for you to do on any job site. You're not only my best employee," he hugged her from behind, then turned her around to face him, "you're my favorite employee." He kissed her gently, then with a little more passion.

She returned his kiss and her cheeks grew hot. She pushed him away and drew a deep breath. "Do you want dinner or something?" she asked him, all flush.

"Don't be silly, of course I want dinner. I also wanted you to know how much I love and appreciate you. Do you know yet, or would you like me to continue?"

She waved her hand in front of her face, fanning herself. "I get the picture." She gathered her senses and returned her attention to the refrigerator. "Do you want to eat at the table or the counter?"

"I'll clean off the table when you tell me I have to. Do you need my help with anything besides cleaning off the table?"

"No," she said, waving her hand in front of her face again, "You've helped enough for now."

*   *   *

"Welcome home, honey." Amanda greeted Calvin at the door Thursday when he returned from work.

"Thank you, sweetheart." He eyed her suspiciously, curious about her greeting.

"How was your day?" she asked.

"Long and difficult without you there." He looked at her again. "Is there something you want to tell me, but are afraid to?" he asked, beginning to recognize her nervous behavior.

She looked at the floor, then back at him rather sheepishly. "I kind of did something today that you may think borders on insanity."

"Go on."

"I prefer to think of it as a leap of faith, a Hebrews 11:1 kind of thing. You know, hoping for something you want, and believing in what you can't see."

"I'm familiar with the verse. Please don't keep me in suspense any longer. I need to know if I should have you committed for an act of craziness or if I should applaud your faith."

"I went shopping."

"That's neither faith nor insanity, that's just plain scary. How much did you spend?" he asked.

"It wasn't about how much I spent as much as it was about *what* I bought."

He raised an eyebrow at her, and then widened both eyes. "What did you buy?"

"I went to the mall for some last minute things for the trip. While I was there I stopped in the little girls section." She paused and looked at the floor. "I bought an outfit for each of the girls. I had to guess their sizes, but I think I got pretty close."

"Is that all? I thought you'd bought a new vehicle or something like that."

"You're not mad?"

"No, and I don't think you are, either. I have been praying all week that we find them as soon as we pull into the gas station. I know it may not happen that way, so I'm willing to settle for however God wants to bring it all together. I think it's a great idea that you got them something to wear. I suspect for the anniversary party."

"You know me so well. They're the prettiest little matching dresses. I didn't get shoes because I had no idea what size to get, but I did get tights and little hats. They both love their Easter hats."

He hugged her to himself and kissed her on the head. "How 'bout you show me these beautiful dresses and hats so we can get on to dinner? I'm starving."

"Gladly," she said as she removed herself from his arms. "Afterward you can get a shower and then dinner will be ready."

After seeing the dresses, hats, and tights, then a shower, the couple sat down to what would be their last meal at home for several days. Amanda made small portions of everything so there'd be no leftovers. Since she'd worked all day, she hadn't been able to make cookies for the trip until she got home, so there was a little bit of a mess to clean up, and she still had laundry to do. After dinner she left

Calvin on kitchen duty and returned to the basement to work on the laundry.

A short time later the phone rang. Calvin was right beside it so he answered it. "Hello. Yes. She's working on the laundry while I'm cleaning the kitchen," Calvin told the caller. "Just a second, I'll tell her to pick up."

Calvin laid the phone on the counter and went to the top of the stairs. "Judy's on the phone. You better pick it up quick. She's talking a million miles an hour again so it must be exciting news."

They both knew Judy well enough to know that whenever she had good news, she rivaled the best auctioneer for talking fast. Calvin thought, every auctioneer I've ever heard, I was able to understand everything they said. That wasn't always the case with Judy.

Calvin waited until he heard Amanda say hello before he hung up the kitchen phone.

"I can't believe it," Judy repeated several times before Amanda was able to ask her what she couldn't believe. "You're not going to believe it, either," Judy said.

"I can't very well believe it if I don't know what *it* is," Amanda said.

"You know I haven't been feeling very good. I finally went to the doctor today."

"You told me you were feeling a little run down. But you also said you thought it was from trying to do too much."

"This isn't because I've been doing too much. It's a lot more serious than that." Judy paused, still trying to take in the information herself. "Manny," she used Amanda's childhood name more as a way to sooth herself, "I'm pregnant."

Amanda pulled the phone away from her head and let out a squeal that brought Calvin running downstairs. He arrived in time to hear Amanda tell Judy, "That's wonderful news. I'm excited for you."

I can't believe after all the months and hours of planning, we're finally on our way to Janesville," Amanda said to Calvin as she placed the personal items she'd need for the trip into her smallest suitcase.

He touched her hand gently, knowing her excitement included the idea of being in the same place Laurinda had seen the girls a few weeks before. They'd said little about it, but both knew stopping at the gas station was high on their list of things to do this trip.

Her parents left on Wednesday and had stopped there. They called to tell Calvin and Amanda that they stayed in the parking lot for an hour but they hadn't seen the girls.

Amanda clung to the hope of seeing her daughters at the gas station. Her nerves felt like hot wires running through her. She tried to eat breakfast, but everything stuck in her throat.

"Is that the last suitcase you're packing?" Calvin asked her as she closed the top and latched it.

"Yes." She smiled at him, the best she could. "Why?"

"I thought I saw an empty one downstairs that you missed," he teased her, trying to lighten her mood even though he was almost as tense.

"I'm only taking what I need."

"That's what I'm afraid of." He smiled and then kissed her on the cheek. "If you'll bring the makeup case, I'll get the rest."

"I'll bring this suitcase, but it's not a makeup bag. It's holding some of your toiletries, too, my good man. We can't have you stinking up the van on the way over."

He bowed at the waist, partly to her, partly to pick up the suitcases waiting by their bedroom door. Once the van was packed and the house door securely locked, they were on their way.

"I filled the van with gas last night so our next stop will be Gary, Indiana."

Amanda's heart skipped a beat. She took a deep breath and tried to concentrate on a book she borrowed from the store. She read a few minutes, then looked out the window, even though she knew they were nowhere near Indiana. She alternated between the two until finally Calvin said, "It's been about three and a half hours since breakfast. Would you like to get some lunch before we go to the gas station?"

"Not really. Besides, I just saw the sign that our exit's only five miles away."

"I'll just keep driving."

Amanda looked at him with a weak smile. As they got closer to the exit, they realized it was closed for repair.

Tears immediately sprang to Amanda's eyes. "It's okay, honey. We'll take the next exit and backtrack." He touched her left cheek to wipe away a tear.

"You're right. It's just that I…" She sniffled.

"I understand," he said lovingly as he reached for her hand.

Calvin maneuvered the van through traffic, going in the opposite direction their journey should have been taking them, until the gas station finally came into view. They stopped talking. Amanda was afraid she'd stop breathing, too.

I can do all things through Christ, who strengthens me, she said over and over in her head.

Calvin pulled into the small station and parked in front of a pump. He hadn't noticed the price of the gas, but decided it didn't really matter because this was the only place he was going to buy gas in *this* city.

"Are you going in," he asked her, "or do you want to wait for me?"

Amanda swallowed hard. With tears in her eyes she nodded weakly, brushed away the tears with the back of her hand, and pointed at the door. *I can do all things through Christ, who strengthens me,* she repeated under her breath as she reached for the door handle. *All things.* She opened the door. *Christ strengthens me.* She stepped out and her eyes focused on the door to the station.

Strengthen me. She wanted to run, but her feet barely moved. She was afraid she wouldn't see them. She was afraid she would see them but not recognize them. She was afraid, period. *Christ strengthens me.* She walked to the door, took another deep breath, and placed her hand on the door. She looked up just in time to see a man on the other side of the glass door. He appeared to be waiting to see what she was going to do before he moved. Time stood still for Amanda as she took a small step back to let him open the door for her on his way out.

He nodded his head at her and said, "Excuse me."

She smiled and said thank you. The station smelled of fresh popped popcorn. She looked to her left to see if the elephant display was still where Laurinda said it'd been the day she saw the girls. A display of stuff animals took its place. Amanda's heart sank a little. She looked around the small station and realized that if their daughters were there, she would have seen them already. She looked at the bathroom in the corner.

"It's for everybody," the woman behind the counter said. "It's unisex. It's clean cuz I just cleaned it fifteen minutes ago." She continued talking until Amanda heard her. "Lady, are you okay?"

"I'm sorry. Yes, I'm okay. Do you have a minute?"

"Sure, whatcha need?"

"I need to find my daughters."

"I haven't had any girls in here since I started my shift an hour ago. Did you send 'em up for something?"

"No. They were stolen from my husband and me almost a year ago. Four months ago two of our employees were here and one of them saw our daughters, but she didn't recognize them because they'd changed so much."

"I'm so sorry. I just had my first baby four months ago. I can't imagine having her stolen from me, even if she does still keep me up nights. Do you have pictures of them?" the clerk asked.

"I do, but they're old." Amanda retrieved them from her wallet to show the clerk.

"They are precious."

"You haven't ever seen them, have you?"

"No, ma'am, I'm afraid I haven't, but I was on maternity leave when your employees were here."

"That's my husband out there beside our van. When he finishes filling up and pays, is it all right if we stay in your parking lot, off to the side, of course, for a little while?"

"It's fine with me. As long as we don't get too busy and need the parking spot."

"Thank you very much, and thanks for listening."

"I'm a good listener. All my friends say so. I'm sorry I couldn't do more for you."

"That's okay." Amanda turned to leave.

"If you leave me a phone number, I'll call you if I ever see 'em."

Amanda gave her one of Calvin's business cards and wrote the number of the private investigator on the back, just in case.

"You try to have a good day," the clerk said.

Amanda smiled and waved good-bye as she walked out the door. When she returned to the van, Calvin was still on the other side dealing with the pump.

"Back so soon?"

"I'm afraid so. The building is as little on the inside as it looks from the outside. It was deserted."

Calvin wrapped his right arm around her and kissed her on the head. "I'm sorry, honey."

"Me, too. The clerk said we could stay in the parking lot until it got busy. She looked at the girls' pictures to see if she recognized them, but didn't. She said she'd call us if she ever did see them, so I gave her your business card and wrote the PI's number on the back."

After an hour Calvin said, "You realize it is kind of silly for us to just sit here."

"I know. I was just thinking the same thing. Even though we gain an hour, we still have a long way to go and I don't want to get there so late everyone's in bed. I'm ready whenever you are. We should get some lunch on our way back to the highway. Maybe a McDonald's hamburger to settle my stomach."

"Like they did when you were pregnant?" Calvin started the engine and pulled onto the road that led them back to Highway 80 West. "It should only be about four and a half more hours from here if we don't stop any more. Do you think you can make that?"

"Funny," she said as she tried to resume reading her book, but her eyes kept drifting from the pages to the cars on the streets around her. She wondered what they'd do if she thought she saw the girls in a car they were passing. Amanda closed her eyes and tried to imagine holding her daughters in her arms again. She breathed deeply as if trying to smell them.

Calvin took that as a sign she was relaxing, and began to do so himself. He'd wondered how they'd deal with disappointment if that's how the trip ended. He pushed the thoughts from him mind, willing himself to not think that way. *Negative is not good,* he thought to himself. *I have to stay strong and positive, not just for Amanda, but myself.* He found a McDonald's but he wasn't sure about stopping because it had a playland. He didn't want to upset Amanda.

"Here's one, or do you want to wait a little longer?" he asked as he pulled into the right lane just in case.

"This is fine. At this point I think I really could use that hamburger. I don't know if my stomach feels like this because I'm hungry or sad."

He reached over and squeezed her hand after putting the van into park. There were things he thought of saying to her, *we knew this might happen, there were no promises,* but he knew she wouldn't be comforted by them any more than he'd been when he thought them.

He brought her hand to his lips and kissed her gently before letting go, getting out, going around the front of the van, and opening her door. His concern about the playland was unfounded as she walked zombie-like through the door.

"Why don't you sit down and I'll bring the food over." She squeezed his hand that she was holding, and then released it to find a spot to sit.

Without thinking, she gravitated to the playland. It was open, not like the playlands at home where they were enclosed by glass. She walked to the side opposite where they'd entered the building. She mindlessly sat down at a table directly across from where children exited the slide.

Just then Calvin came over to ask if she wanted one burger or two. He looked at her, then followed her gaze. He saw a girl about Jessi's age and size coming out of the slide. He looked back at Amanda who'd obviously noticed the girl.

He reprimanded himself for not passing by this particular McDonald's.

In an instant, Amanda was standing up. "It's her."

"Honey, I saw her, too, but I don't think its Jessi."

"Calvin, I'd know my daughter if we'd been apart for ten years," she said. "Turn around and look again." But the girl was gone.

"Why don't you move away from the playland or come place an order with me. I needed to know if you wanted one burger or two."

"One is fine, but I'm not going anywhere. I suggest you get the manager, because that little girl is our Jessi, I just know it." Amanda prayed that a father knew his children, too.